Shakespeare
UNLEASHED

MONSTROUS
BOOKS

Shakespeare
UNLEASHED

EDITED BY
JAMES AQUILONE

SHAKESPEARE UNLEASHED

Editor: James Aquilone
Cover Illustration: J.K. Woodward
Cover Design: STK•Kreations
Interior Design Layout: Qamber Designs & Media W.L.L.
Interior Illustrations: J.K Woodward
Monstrous Books Logo: Darran Robinson
Proofreader: Kenneth W. Cain

Hardcover ISBN: 978-1-946346-18-6
Paperback ISBN: 978-1-946346-19-3

Worldwide Rights
1st Edition

Printed in China

Published by Monstrous Books
MonstrousBooks.com

For Shakespeare Lovers
and Horror Fiends Everywhere

O HORROR, HORROR, HORROR!
TONGUE NOR HEART CANNOT CONCEIVE NOR NAME THEE!
– *Macbeth*

BLOODY THOU ART; BLOODY WILL BE THY END.
– *Richard III*

HELL IS EMPTY, AND ALL THE DEVILS ARE HERE.
– *The Tempest*

THE PRINCE OF DARKNESS IS A GENTLEMAN.
– *King Lear*

WHY, THERE THEY ARE, BOTH BAKED IN THAT PIE,
WHEREOF THEIR MOTHER DAINTILY HATH FED,
EATING THE FLESH THAT SHE HERSELF HATH BRED.
– *Titus Andronicus*

BEWARE THE IDES OF MARCH.
– *Julius Caesar*

FIRST WITCH

WHEN SHALL WE THREE MEET AGAIN
IN THUNDER, LIGHTNING, OR IN RAIN?

SECOND WITCH

WHEN THE HURLY-BURLY'S DONE,
WHEN THE BATTLE'S LOST AND WON.
– Macbeth

MY THOUGHTS BE BLOODY OR BE NOTHING WORTH!
– Hamlet

THOU ART A BOIL,
A PLAGUE-SORE OR EMBOSSED CARBUNCLE
IN MY CORRUPTED BLOOD.
– King Lear

IS THIS A DAGGER WHICH I SEE BEFORE ME,
THE HANDLE TOWARD MY HAND? COME, LET ME CLUTCH
THEE!
– Macbeth

VENGEANCE IS IN MY HEART, DEATH IN MY HAND,
BLOOD AND REVENGE ARE HAMMERING IN MY HEAD.
– Titus Andronicus

BY THE PRICKING OF MY THUMBS,
SOMETHING WICKED THIS WAY COMES.
– Macbeth

Table of Contents

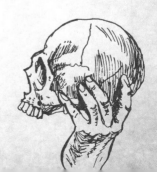

Foreword

O God, I could be bounded in a nutshell and count myself a king of infinite space, were it not that I have bad dreams. — Hamlet

I fell in love with Shakespeare in my final high school English class. We were assigned *Hamlet* on a Friday morning. I finished it that afternoon, which was unusual for me. Usually, I'd read only the back cover or watch the movie, and then wing it during the exam. Remarkably, that worked more often than not. Come that Monday, I learned we'd be reading *Hamlet* in class over the next two months. Instead of going over the text again, I read *Macbeth* and *The Tempest* at my desk like a true book nerd.

A few years later, I watched the movie *Rosencrantz & Guildenstern Are Dead* late one night on PBS. Seeing Tim Roth (Guildenstern) and Gary Oldman (Rosencrantz) wandering in and out of scenes from *Hamlet* blew my young mind. I didn't know a writer could do that. I ran out to the library and read Tom Stoppard's play, and since then, I've been intrigued by the idea of playing in the Shakespeare universe.

After the success of my first anthology, *Classic Monsters Unleashed*, the decision was made to do an *Unleashed* series. I immediately had the idea for the sequel's theme. Thus was born *Shakespeare Unleashed*, wherein some of the greatest writers in the business create horror stories and poems inspired by the Bard of Avon.

As with *Classic Monsters Unleashed*, we have an eclectic collection of stories and sonnets…a prequel to *Othello*, sequels to *A Midsummer Night's Dream*, *Twelfth Night*, and *The Merchant of Venice*, reimaginations of *Romeo and Juliet* and *Julius Caesar*, and meta-stories about *Rosencrantz & Guildenstern* and *Macbeth*…all with a bent to terrify and delight.

Now, on with the show…

James Aquilone
Staten Island, New York
March 2023

The Darkness of Shakespeare

An Introduction by Weston Ochse

Let's talk of graves, of worms, and epitaphs;
Make dust our paper, and with rainy eyes
Write sorrow on the bosom of the earth...
– Richard II

My journey to Shakespeare started at the Tivoli Theater in Chattanooga, Tennessee, in 1979. In a shattered world where Walter Cronkite still breathed fear into everyone's dinner with stories, a troupe of traveling performers tried to bring us back to a simpler time when the Globe Theater was the modern version of the television. Amid such current world events as the Iranian Hostage Crisis, Three Mile Island nuclear meltdown, and the Soviet Union's invasion of Afghanistan, Viola and her brother Sebastian are both shipwrecked. Each believes the other is dead, man becomes woman, woman becomes man, and the birth of the "romantic comedy" is solidified.

And Malvolio.

Pour misunderstood Malvolio.

But being fourteen years old, I barely understood this, so my father sat behind me and spent the entire play leaning forward and whispering into my ear the twists and turns of the plot as they transpired. I was instantly addicted.

For a long time, Shakespeare was seen as *littérature d'élite*. The words and cadence of iambic pentameter were considered beyond the ken of the commoner. Instead, we had other voices in literature to read—something more recognizable, more relatable.

Then came Mel Gibson's haunting retelling of *Hamlet* (1990), the farcical coin flipping in *Rosencrantz & Guildenstern Are Dead* (1990), Kenneth Branagh's memorable St. Crispin's Day speech in *Henry V* (1989), and of course the Denzel Washington-Keanu Reeves-Kenneth Branagh-Michael Keaton retelling of the original romantic comedy, *Much Ado About Nothing* (1993) (with *As You Like It* being the second of the three Shakespearean romantic comedies).

Suddenly, in the late 1980s and early 1990s, Shakespeare was for the proletariat. Television and film democratized that which had once been elite by transforming it into something the general rabble of society could embrace. This mirrors what Shakespeare did in his own time with the Globe Theater: a small but reputable place where all levels of English society could see Shakespeare in a small wooden open-air enclosure as men dressed as men and men dressed as women shouted their lines to be heard.

Although my father was able to guest-direct at the Globe Theater, I never was, nor have I ever seen a play performed there. But I did have Shakespeare in the Park in Los Angeles, where, with the dramatic backdrop of the angry Pacific waves crashing into the cliffs, Caliban thrashed upon stage as we consumed wine and cheese and merrily watched the monster rise and fall.

But there is a darkness in Shakespeare. He didn't invent the horror story. That was invented long, long ago when humans still scratched pictures on cave walls and whispered over their fires. No, he didn't invent it, but he did mature it. From the ghost of King Hamlet to the monstrous Caliban, the fairy Ariel, Sycorax (Caliban's mother), and the wizard Prospero from *The Tempest*, to the witches of *Macbeth*, Shakespeare has provided iconic imagery from which quotes are still given.

Why, one would think that Shakespeare and the devil were besties the way he seems to know him and the darkness that can invade a human heart.

"The devil can cite Scripture for his purpose. An evil soul producing

holy witness Is like a villain with a smiling cheek, A goodly apple rotten at the heart. O, what a goodly outside falsehood hath!" – Merchant of Venice

"The evil that men do lives after them; the good is oft interred with their bones." – Julius Caesar

"The Prince of Darkness is a gentleman." – King Lear

"Hell is empty, and all the devils are here." – The Tempest

And let's not forget Shylock, who could flay all of us with his words.

Let's spend a little more time examining Shakespeare's connection to horror. The ultimate question has always been is horror a feeling or a genre. Scholar and philosopher Noel Carroll states that "horror, like action-thrillers, comedy, and the tear-jerker, is one of those genres that takes its name from the emotional state it's designed to arouse. Consequently, the key to understanding the genre of horror is to grasp the nature of the emotion that it is intended to engender. This is how Aristotle proceeded in his analysis of tragedy, whose function he contended was to elicit pity and fear. But to consider the philosophy of horror, we should begin by asking: what emotion is a work of horror supposed to provoke?"

Our most famous and successful horror author, Stephen King, has said that "first you create characters you care about and then you put them in the cooker." This argues that horror is an emotion. Shakespeare was a master at creating characters one cares about. His cookers were many, but he often was visceral and embraced the techniques of horror to create the emotional resonance necessary to make his audiences fearful of a character's demise.

Shakespeare was ahead of his time in often eschewing the hero protagonist (except for his histories) and often creating characters that were unlikable or unlikely, dolling them up with charm and appeal, then putting them in Macbeth's witch's cauldron, which I would imagine was the cooker of his time.

Falstaff, Shylock, Titus Andronicus, Hamlet, and even Macbeth were characters who we probably wouldn't allow past our front stoop, but with the genius of characterization, Shakespeare was able to make us care about them and want them to survive their demons.

In this anthology, we have more than just a remembrance and a homage to the Great Bard. We have reinterpretations of his plays and sonnets by some of the brightest lights in literature. Many of these names you will know, but some you won't. The brilliance of such a work you are now reading is that this anthology will join the incredible library of Shakespearean liturgy and be read five hundred years hence, just as we are reading the Bard now.

Imagine if you will, a thousand years of influence by a man who not only wrote words that still live on our tongues, but invented words we use today. His influence can't and won't ever be mistaken. Just as the influence of these tales and poems shouldn't be soon forgotten. It has been a joy to read them before you, and I envy your discovery.

And if for some unenviable reason thou shan't approve of this offering, let me leave you with Puck, from Scene 5 of *A Midsummer Night's Dream*.

> *If we shadows have offended,*
> *Think but this, and all is mended,*
> *That you have but slumbered here*
> *While these visions did appear.*

Enjoy this offering of ours and, above all, read more Shakespeare.

Weston Ochse
Nevermore House

Ides

(inspired by Julius Caesar)

Gwendolyn Kiste

The knife in her back should have been the end of it.

This should have been over in a moment, all of us together with our sharp blades and our good intentions. After all, this was the only way to save ourselves. We knew that. Everyone knew that.

But I suspected from the start it wouldn't be that easy.

By the time we murdered Julia, there were only eight of us left. Her antics had already scared away the others. When the skies first went dark and the oceans started to boil, the men fled at once, their calloused hands no match for her calloused heart. But the rest of us stayed behind. We were the women Julia plucked from obscurity, from nothing little towns where we were destined for nothing little lives. That is, if she hadn't found us.

Her precious priestesses, she called us. The ones she trusted. She brought us to this strange compound, tucked back beyond a creaking gate, a thin fence limning a few acres of rural property. We didn't have much here. Just a row of shotgun houses and a small arena built of stone in the middle of a barren field. The same arena where she used to regale us with stories of the coming Armageddon.

"It'll be so bright and beautiful, the sky lit up like neon," she'd say, and somehow, she always made the apocalypse sound sweeter than a carnival.

Together, we would listen, the other women and me sitting cross-legged at her feet, our eyes set on her like she was a prophet. And maybe she was, because her proselytizing would go on through the evening, long past midnight, sometimes past dawn. She'd delight us with all the ways the world could end and how glorious it would be.

"Maybe we'll go out in flames," she'd say. "Or maybe we'll perish in ice and tar."

But no matter how the tales turned out, one thing was always the same. When she was finished, she'd turn toward me, her gaze blazing like wildfire, and she'd flash an impish grin. And every time, in spite of myself, I'd blush like a schoolgirl and smile back. It was so intoxicating, the way we got wrapped up in every word she murmured. That was how we ended up here in the first place. Her acolytes, her true believers.

The people in the nearby town, however, weren't so convinced.

"Nothing but a bunch of weirdos out there," they used to sneer. Their eyes peering over our makeshift fence, they never liked us, never trusted what we were up to. And it turns out they had every right to be worried. With our chanting at midnight and our spells cast in stone circles, we managed to do something that no one thought was possible.

We were a doomsday cult that conjured up a bonafide doomsday.

Only at the last minute, the other women and I got cold feet. We decided that maybe having a world was better than not having one.

Except nobody could quite convince Julia.

"It's already too late," she told us, her voice like an uncanny aria. "The world's already gone. You just don't realize it yet."

But for the first time, we refused to believe her. The eight of us gathered together in the back room of the last shotgun house, whispering to each other in the dark where we hoped Julia wouldn't discover us. Me and Cassy and the others, all of us unlikely conspirators in a plot we never wanted to forge.

"It's the only way," I said, a pewter dagger quivering in my hands. By then, we had all chosen our impromptu weapons, pilfered from drawers and cabinets around the compound.

A cleaver. A rusted switchblade. A boning knife. All that mattered was that we were ready.

This was for the best. That was what I told myself.

It was midnight in the middle of March, the threat of spring shuddering through the earth, when we knew we couldn't wait any longer. Overhead, the sky churned, eager as a jackrabbit. The end was edging closer—you could feel it haunting the air, potent as a promise, dangerous as a first kiss.

"Come on," I whispered, and together, we went roving across the compound.

We found Julia alone at the stone arena, the eight of us surrounding her in an instant.

"Hello," she said, her lips curling in dismay, the realization of what we'd planned sinking in a moment too late to matter.

The others went first, their nervous hands removing their hidden blades, all of it playing out in hideous flashes in the dark. The glint of metal, the flesh tearing, the bones shattering into dust.

Julia didn't scream. She barely fought back. With the last bit of life lingering in her, she did just one thing. She whirled around to face me, as though half-convinced she must still have one ally left. But with the dagger in my hand, I did my part, burying it softly and slowly in the flesh of her belly. I did it because I had to. Because it was the only way.

For a bottomless moment, Julia gaped back at me, a hint of heartache in her eyes.

"And you, too, Brystol?" she asked me, and I parted my lips to speak, to scream, to take it all back, but it was already too late.

Without another word, Julia wilted to the stone floor of the arena, her body like a broken mannequin, the betrayal still lingering in the lines on her face.

Now here we are, huddled together in the moonlight, all eight of us gazing down at the crumpled remains of our prophet.

Above us, the sky's gone gray and quiet, the end of the world ebbing away from us, our fearless leader resting among the fearsome dead.

"Let's get out of here," Cassy says, a sob lodged in her throat. Our heads down, we turn away from the body, stretched out on the stone like Julia's posed there, like this is all a game of make-believe.

At the gates of the compound, a crowd is gathering, their murmurs rising up like smoke rings into the night.

"Is she gone?" they ask us. "Is it over?"

My conspirators flash their tight smiles and tell them yes, greeting the townsfolk like we're politicians on the take, like we're their very best friends and always have been. Like we weren't responsible for nearly ending the world and only had a change of heart at the eleventh hour.

I stand back from the others, Julia's blood still wet on my hands.

"What if this isn't enough to stop her?" I whisper, but nobody listens.

The decay starts slowly, almost too slow to notice. The way the shingles on all the roofs start peeling up like old fingernails. The narrow cracks in the sidewalk, opening a little wider each morning, an ethereal darkness yawning within.

I try to tell someone, anyone who will listen, but the others don't want to be bothered. They're too busy rebuilding their lives, all of them basking in the precious glow of celebrity. We saved the world, after all. Now we're practically royalty in the eyes of the town.

That leaves me on my own, the only one who can see it happening. How the sky seems lower than before, the clouds as gray and oppressive as the past.

"You're just being paranoid," Cassy tells me over coffee at the diner on Main Street, the grill hissing and sputtering grease behind us. She's happy to be away from the abandoned compound, to have a second chance.

Cassy's like me, like all the others. We were misfits, the forgotten, the kind of women nobody could be bothered with. Nobody except for Julia. She saw us, the potential brimming in our wide eyes, and that's why she brought us here. To conjure up the vision of the future she wanted. Which, it turned out, was no future at all.

"Isn't it an odd thing to wish for the world to end?" I asked her once.

Julia only laughed. "Not at all," she said, as we curled together in her bed, her hand wrapped tightly around mine. "Not if you see every end as a new beginning."

I shivered. "But what kind of beginning could come from an apocalypse?"

"You always ask the wrong questions, Brystol," she whispered, resting her forehead against mine. I asked her what she meant, but she never bothered to tell me.

Everyone thinks that's over now. Everyone besides me.

I fold and unfold my hands on the chipped Formica table. "Julia wasn't like us," I say, dread settling in my guts. "What if she doesn't die like us either?"

Her lips pursed, Cassy stares off through the smudged window. "You don't have any proof of that."

What she doesn't know is that I do. At night, when nobody is around, I return to the compound, to the scene of our crime.

Julia's body is gone. Vanished into thin air, as if it's merged with the earth below us. There are no bones to speak of, no skin or hair or sweet scent like morning dew. But in a way, that doesn't matter.

"I'm sorry," I say, and I'm sure she can still hear me, the ghost of her leaking into every crevice of this place.

And I can still hear her, the way she'd whisper to me in the dark when we were alone.

"My beautiful girl," she'd say, her hands drifting softly through my long hair. I came to this compound because I wanted to, because every other avenue had closed off to me, my life like a series of slamming doors. Julia offered me something better, that new beginning she promised. And I offered her nothing but an end.

"Don't worry so much," she used to tell us. "It all comes back around, an infinite cycle."

It's not until the first anniversary of her death that we realize exactly what she meant.

"She's back."

The voice pierces the night like a blade. It's one of the townspeople, returning from the abandoned compound. They wander up there sometimes, just to check, just to be sure she's really dead.

And tonight, apparently she isn't.

"I saw her," the man says, breathless and red-faced. "Right where you left her. She's alive. Alive and dangerous."

We're together in an instant, the eight of us from before, headed on foot to see for ourselves, convinced it's a hoax. Convinced we did the job well enough the first time around.

But there's nothing we do well enough, certainly not when it comes to Julia. With that impish grin, she outfoxes us every time. Now here she is, resurrected from dust, her body returned like she never left at all. With her chin tipped up, she paces the stone arena, as if waiting for us.

"Hello," she says as we arrive, stumbling like fools over one another. My heart held tight in my chest, I want to greet her with open arms, to beg her forgiveness, to make up for what we've done.

But I already know I can't. Above her, the sky is churning faster, threatening to finish the job she started.

Nothing's changed. She's still ready for the end.

"Please," I whisper, but she gives me a quick shake of her head, as though to say there's no stopping this. The best we can do is stop her.

There's no chance for us to plan properly this round, no way we can make this civilized. Instead, we do it with our bare hands this time, pummeling her into nothing, our fists flying, her flesh tearing like thick canvas. In mere minutes, Julia's body is reduced to gristle and thick plasma and squelching membrane, everything about her less than the sum of her parts.

Once again, I tell myself this is the only way, but the whole time, I do my best to keep my eyes closed, pretending I don't remember the way her hand feels against my thigh or the melody of her laugh at midnight.

Or how she'd never do this to me.

"I love you," she'd whisper. "Even if the whole world burns away, nothing could change that."

But as her brittle bones snap apart in my hands, I can't help but wonder what she thinks of me now.

A demon goddess. That's what the townspeople call her.

"What will we do?" they ask us, and the others swear up and down that it's over now. That we finished the job right this time.

But I won't make promises I can't keep.

"We'll just kill her over and over again if we have to," I say, desperation seeping into me marrow-deep.

The month of March creeps in again, the ground barely thawed, the oak trees naked and hungry, and she returns to us, haunting the spot where we gathered together like gleeful pagans two years ago, spilling her blood as sweet and bright as the finest merlot.

"Won't you ever rest?" I ask her, and she only smiles.

"Won't you?"

This time, I don't wait for the others before I start, my dagger quicker than before, carving out her heart like a keepsake.

She's got no more than a moment, the blood sputtering up her throat, painting her mouth red. But that's enough time for her to utter her last words.

"See you soon," she whispers, and I choke up a scream because I know she's right.

It's a week before Christmas when all the waters run red.

It doesn't matter where it's coming from—the rivers or the oceans or the meager tower on Main Street. We listen to the staticky radio where we learn that it's happening all over.

"Nowhere is clean now," Cassy says with a shudder, as we hunch together on a street corner, eating condensed chicken noodle soup straight from the can. It's briny and rank, and it's also the best we can do.

We're almost to New Year's before we figure out the water is still more or less drinkable.

"It's better than nothing," everyone says, their mouths smeared red like hungry vampires. Like Julia's mouth before she died the last time. Her body is gone again, dissipating into the earth. She's patient—I'll give her that.

I'm patient, too. I wait until the middle of March when I can ask her about it. She's barely returned to life before the question buds on my lips.

"Are you poisoning us?" I say.

Grinning, she shakes her head. "You're poisoning yourselves."

Maybe she's lying. Or maybe she's right. I've never known what part of this is her fault and what part of it is ours. But we don't have time to worry about that now.

Knives in hand, the eight of us descend on her, doing our best, tearing her to pieces.

"It's the only way," somebody says after it's over, but we just shake our heads, because no one believes that anymore.

The months drag on, proffering us one natural disaster after another. The sea rises up, crashing over the cities. Then it dissipates altogether, the crimson saltwater vanishing into mist.

"Such funny tricks," Cassy says, her face gone gaunt and scared. All of us are going gaunt, our starved bodies as brittle as chipped porcelain.

It's a Sunday in September when the sky cracks open, and the rain comes down like colorless tar, sticking to the streets and the houses and the people, filling up our lungs with its viscous embrace.

Cassy and I hide out in a dank basement, shielding ourselves from the worst of it.

"Do you think this is still part of her plan?" Cassy asks me, as she cradles her head in her hands.

"Maybe," I say. "Maybe all we managed to do was to delay it a while when we killed her."

"Do you think what she wanted would have been better?"

I shrug. "I think it would have been quicker."

After the storm has passed, Cassy and I walk through the town, observing the aftermath. With the ground slick beneath our feet, we see them. Whole families splayed out in front yards and on front porches, their mouths plugged with goo, their eyes filmed over, forever staring up at the very sky that doomed them.

Unless of course someone else doomed them. Someone like us.

"Do you think we did the right thing?" Cassy asks me that night, the two of us sitting over a taper candle burned down almost to the wick.

"I don't know anymore," I say, as together, we wait for it. We're always waiting for it. The Ides of March. The middle of the month, the liminal space between seasons. Not quite spring, but not entirely winter either.

"We'll get her this time," the others say, even though there are fewer of us than before. One by one, the conspirators are vanishing. Most of them have done their best to flee this dying place, dragging their hopes behind them like a rusted wagon. Some have made it past the city limits, venturing into the wasteland of what remains of the world. A few haven't been so lucky. Cassy and I find their burnt bodies in the middle of Main Street, a warning to those of us who remain.

"You should have left Julia alone," the lingering townsfolk sneer as we pass by, my dagger always gripped knuckle-white in my hand to ward them off. They blame us for this, even though they wanted her gone, too. They still want her gone, and they hate us because we can't make that happen. Not for long, anyhow.

It isn't safe in town now, so Cassy and I hide out at what's left of the compound, wiring the gate closed, desperate to believe that will be enough to keep the world out. And to keep ourselves in, just the way Julia wanted.

"We belong together," she says to me when she returns, but I won't listen. It's just me and Cassy now, and these days, Cassy's too shaky to be of use to anyone. She collapses on the stone arena, sobbing to the sky, which means this time, it's all on me. With my eyes open, I bury my dagger in Julia's heart and watch as her body disintegrates into nothing in front of me.

Then I count the days until I have to do it again.

"You were always her favorite," Cassy says to me one afternoon while we're scrubbing our clothes in the tub, the bright red water seeping into every fiber of the fabric. All our chores seem pointless now. Everything we do only seems to make things worse.

I purse my lips. "I wasn't her favorite," I say, but Cassy scoffs.

"Sure you were. You were the one she looked to the most." A long moment passes. "You were the only one I thought might be able to convince her to stop."

Instantly, I bristle. "Don't put this on me," I seethe. "I never asked for this."

But Cassy won't let it go. With her jaw set, she slouches back in the corner, her knees pulled into her chest. "We betrayed her," she says at last. "Maybe this is what we deserve."

That night, as Cassy twists and turns through heavy dreams in the next room, I stay awake, creaking in an old rocking chair, the same questions spinning through my mind.

Is Julia a force of nature? Is she a cause or an effect? Who bears this burden, or are we all to blame?

I already know what she would say.

"You always ask the wrong questions, Brystol."

I only wish I knew the right ones.

At dawn, Cassy says she's venturing into town to see if there's any canned goods for sale at the general store. When she's not back by dusk, I go looking for her, only to find that there's no one left. The streets are bare and bleak as heartbreak, and even the bodies have vanished.

I call out for hours, searching every abandoned building, but there's no reply.

It's a long and lonely wait until spring.

I'm at the stone arena in March when Julia rises from the earth, like the goddess Athena emerging from Zeus's skull. I've grown older, but Julia never does. She stays the same, forever young, forever smiling.

Forever waiting for me to return.

"I've missed you," I say, as she paces circles around me.

"You've got a strange way of showing it."

I settle on the ground cross-legged, watching her above me, the same way I used to do. "I didn't want this," I say. "You didn't give us a choice. You would have destroyed us."

Her eyes flick over to me. "Like the way you destroyed me?"

She doesn't wait for me to answer. Instead, she nestles down next to me, the two of us side by side, our thighs touching. I sit all night with her, watching the clouds dance closer to us.

"What's it like out there?" she asks.

"The same." I lie. Then all at once, I ask something that I've wanted to know for years. "Can we still be saved?"

Julia lets out a laugh, sharp as glass. "You always ask the wrong questions, Brystol."

I stare back at her, my heart gone numb. "And what's the right question?"

"*Should* we be saved?"

I don't answer her. I already know the answer.

The world was decaying before we killed Julia, and it kept on decaying afterward. I don't know why we thought we could change that.

"This isn't my fault, you know." She gazes out at the horizon, as colorless as a blank slate. "This is where the world has always been headed. I just got us here faster."

"So we could have a new beginning?"

She smiles. "You're finally asking the right questions." A long, painful moment before she asks something herself. "Aren't you going to murder me again?"

I breathe deep, the dust and heartache of the past settling into me. "Maybe later," I say, even though I know that later won't come this time.

We wait all night for it to happen. The fires arrive first, burning away the clouds. Then the ice and tar descend just as she promised, chilling us to the bone, our bodies huddled and shivering together. And at last, the grand finale, so bright it's nearly blinding, what's left of the sky lighting up like the most glorious neon.

"It's beautiful," I whisper, and Julia gives me that impish grin, our hands wrapped together.

"The end isn't so bad, is it?" she asks, and as the world evaporates around us, the last thing I hear is the melody of her laugh, sweeter than a carnival, as unbreakable as infinity.

Casca's Lament

(inspired by Julius Caesar, Act 1, Scene 3)

Michael Nethercott

That night before our daggers drew his gore,
The slaying of proud Caesar was foretold
In methods such as found in monst'rous lore
Once whispered of in evil days of old.
True, Cassius and Brutus called me liar,
But I saw beasts and devils roaming wild,
And men whose hands turned into claws of fire,
A dancing corpse, a wraith, a faceless child…
More madness than my mind could hope contain,
And then, of course, the terror of our work.
We murdered Rome. Perhaps we went insane.
Yes, I am he who first did plunge his dirk
      Releasing demons gorged with wails and screams
      Who evermore shall savage my dark dreams.

A Soliloquy of Tongues

(inspired by Hamlet)

Hailey Piper

No one tells a king about his mouth noises. Royal men have no imperfections. Their people see them from upon bent knee, or from a crowd beneath a balcony, or from streetside beyond a palanquin. Firm layers divide the people from their sovereign.

If they could approach a king, they would notice his mortal imperfections. Sweat. Stink. The dull look in his eyes as he falls out of love with you.

And the mouth noises.

Imagine you're a blacksmith, and King Hamlet strolls into your shop on some business. You think, I am speaking to a man chosen by God to rule all of Denmark. Heaven's will incarnate. Above all others, he has the divine right to decide our paths through war and money and the bread on our tables.

But the grandeur fades when you notice his tongue sticks against his cheeks, and his teeth clack, and there's a wordless wet smack between his gums and the insides of his lips. The combined damp cacophony drowns out every other sound, from the subtle rumble of street conversation to the forge's roar and hiss, until your insides scream for silence.

At that moment, you would have to question the very existence of God.

No blacksmith stands close enough to the king to have these thoughts, but I do. There was a time when I loved King Hamlet, but nowadays, he is two things to me—the sire of my dear son and the hell of a slopping tongue.

I have to close that wet hole in his face. Forever.

Mouth noises are not hereditary. My husband passed his name to our son but not the way spit bubbles every time his lips part. Likewise, however the noises found our king, they have not found his brother.

Claudius won't like my suggestion, not for this reason. He's been close to his brother longer than I have and doesn't seem to notice, or doesn't care, or like me, he holds the scream inside him when King Hamlet speaks. I can't assume anything, but mouth noises won't move Claudius's hand.

Power makes a better motive.

There's only so long any wife can avoid her husband, even a queen. When a king beckons, you come.

He only wants a little company; I only want to spare him. Put as many walls between us as stand between him and his subjects, and we could be happily married for the rest of our natural lives.

I'm forced instead to sit beside him and attend court, where every murmur, whisper, rumor, and request sputters beneath his restless tongue and the muscly licking behind his teeth. My hands claw at armrests, the fingernails sealing his fate. Any doubts for what I've asked my brother-in-law to do die in King Hamlet's saliva.

Should Claudius's poison end the mouth noises, I will make him king.

In all the wisdom of prophets, and the promises of priests, and the ringing of church bells, you could never find such a blessed sound as this silence when the king is dead.

I hear it in the weeping. It crumbles in the soil around his casket. Silence bounds from the holy man's mouth as the king's brother honorably takes my hand in marriage. Relief untwists my nerves and unclenches my hands, and I'm so relaxed that I even enjoy this wedding night with my new husband. I let the screaming rush out of me, my body a glorious cathedral of heavenly silence.

Claudius is king—may his reign be a quiet one.

A tongue slops in the night.

I thrust up from bed, thinking the murder, the wedding, and last night were all a dream, except Claudius rests beside me. The only Hamlet among the living is my son, and mouth noises are not hereditary. I sit perched on my elbows as the night crawls by, listening for the slightest smack of lips or gush of spit through teeth.

Only my breath and heartbeat haunt my ears. Have I misheard? Was it a dream?

Another possibility shares my bed. I creep closer to my new husband and lean an ear over his bearded open mouth, listening hard for an exploratory tongue or popping jaw. He breathes in and out, his mouth's only noise a faint whistle between dry lips. Even if I hear worse, can I really blame Claudius for what he sounds like in his sleep? Who he sounds like?

I wait half the night, expecting the dead king's phantom to come gurgling out of the walls, but if there's a ghost to King Hamlet, he does not visit me.

The hellmouth has closed.

Every night, I wake up listening. Stay up listening, too. Claudius recommends a sleeping draught, some gentler variety of poison than his murderous potions, but what if the dead king visits in nightmares and I can't wake up? My screams have spent too long locked inside me; I can't be locked up with them.

Sleep isn't my solution. Distraction will do.

Like my son's play. He's thrown together entertainment for his mother and stepfather, and we're both delighted to see him busy for a change. His mood has been dour, and I'm unsure if Claudius's advisor, Polonius, is right that the boy's heartbroken over Ophelia, which should soon be mended, or whether Prince Hamlet still misses his father.

He wouldn't if he heard the disgusting truth, but since when has my son ever known his father to be less than perfect? They were and are royal men.

The players assemble at Hamlet's behest. His command is gentle but inescapable, and I know he'll make a fine king someday. Better than his father. He turns now to address the audience, and light, love, and pride join the silence inside at seeing my boy look to me and then to his uncle, new father, new king.

Time to introduce the play.

My son's mouth opens, and those gentle lips stretch wetly from his teeth. His narrow tongue traces pink gums, loud at every bump. A throat quivers as if sucking at the world.

No one reacts. Maybe they're like me, listening for kingly ghosts, holding themselves together while everything inside them screams.

Or maybe no one tells a prince about his mouth noises.

Has Hamlet uncovered why his father died? Or who's responsible? Has he been visited and possessed by the dead king's ghost?

Or does the mouthy wetness wriggle in his blood after all?

I'm left alone to question everything I know about my late husband and beautiful son while Claudius sends Polonius to spy. He worries about discovery; I worry about the noises. Little time passes before we learn the old man is dead, and my son has fled Denmark. Prince Hamlet is supposedly a murderer.

But I wonder, did Polonius hear mouth noises before his death? If so, did my son really drive steel through the old man's flesh, or did Polonius impale himself to escape the prince's inherited tongue? Even thinking about it dredges up that slopping nightmare, the death throes of a bog-drowned calf caught in my boy's mouth. To listen intently like Polonius? He must have taken his own life.

I won't walk that road. Can't. My son has run away, and that should allow for peace even as Ophelia mourns her father. Let them think he's been murdered. Let them bury him in God's sacred ground. All that matters is this precious emptiness.

My husband, my silence, and me.

Nighttime vigilance lingers unending. The dark plays tricks on the eyes—everyone knows that—but only I've figured out that it likewise plays tricks on the ears. Sleep-hungry minds, when at last sinking out of conscious thought, will jolt for the surface if they find mouthy mud beneath them, figments of what they see, or hear, or know.

The longer I listen inside the blackened bedchamber, the worse memory and immediacy blur together. Am I hearing the ghost of my dead husband? Or do I only remember him? Did his specter pour fluid noises between our son's lips? Or is it all a dream?

And if it isn't a dream, which mouth will suffer the dead king's wrath next?

I lower myself against the bed as a dry tongue scrapes wet lips, and my eyes fall on the dark silhouette of Claudius beside me.

Their bloodline is cursed.

My son Hamlet has returned to a Denmark of enemies and death. Ophelia is gone, drowned by accident or choice, and if he was heartbroken over her once, he's heartbroken again, but ask him to describe the pain. Ask him! He'll only burble and croak. He confronted King Claudius at the graveyard, and I wanted my new husband to do with the son as he'd done to the father. Steel, poison, anything, and I don't care if I'm an awful mother. Someone has to close the hellmouth.

But then Claudius parted his lips and waggled his tongue up and down. It stuck to the roof of his mouth and stretched loose like tearing cloth. Another mouthful of noises.

Brother to brother, father to son, uncle to nephew—it's all of them.

Even now, Claudius and the prince argue back and forth, murmuring nonsense and smacking their nothings while the dead pile around us. I can't help envying poor Ophelia in the cold earth, where she hears nothing but worms. Did she hear these tongues, too, before the end? Like father, like daughter, finding escape by their own hands.

No, I won't walk that road. This curse can't fester in Denmark's rot. Is rulership left only to kings with bubbling mouths? Of course not. I've already moved a crown from one troubled brow to another, and I'll do it again. A queen has responsibility, too.

I must have a sharp tongue and sharper measure.

Kings are vulnerable in their sleep. I learned this from Claudius when he murdered his brother. I show the power in the lesson when I wake in the night and drive Polonius-slaying steel through my second husband's chest.

His mouth makes noises again, but they're different from his haunting tongue. Blood bubbles thicker than saliva, and I don't mind the croak of a pierced lung. No one hears Claudius cry out, same as they never noticed his swampish maw.

New silence finds me in the night. I can sleep with this tiny heaven inside and trust the world to stay gentle until morning. At daybreak, I call out for my son.

You can hear him coming as he walks the stark streets, his mouth gushing like boots in mud at every step. My hands twitch to cover my ears, but I squeeze the scream inside while I lead Prince Hamlet toward my bedchamber in the castle's depths. I have a gift for him, and I aim our path toward it until his mournful eyes at last find dear Uncle Claudius. Look, son—I've avenged your murdered father. You can let go of his ghost. Be your own man, and then your own king.

I can't tell if he notices my blood-drenched arms and gown and crown, not when his eyes wander, so fatherly, and his cheeks sallow and puff with fluid. He might not even appreciate the sword jutting from his uncle's heart, and I pretend I've done it for him. For the dead king.

Hamlet licks at his lips and lets silvery strands unglue cheeks from teeth.

I can't stand it anymore—father and son will meet again. I jerk the sword from Claudius's chest in sticky fits until it slashes free, and then I drive the blade into my poor son's heart.

He won't gag on his own blood if I can help it. Mine is a sweet boy, and I don't want his own disgusting noises to fill his head when he dies. I cradle his body the way I did when he was a babe, and I sing to him as he slips away.

A mother's final lullaby ushers in precious silence, almost heaven sent. In this emptiness, I can again believe there is a God.

Until a tongue slops in my ears.

I twist around to accuse Claudius, who lies prone across the bed. My eyes fall on young Hamlet in my arms, but he is stiff and cooling, my princely boy with his bloodline's malady. Neither of my men will ever move again.

Where the hell is that noise coming from?

The wrongness soaks into my ears, a spittle-soaked coat of fresh poison. Rulership is not left only to kings, but neither are their flaws. When you wear a crown, does it not sit uneasy no matter the sex? The walls that divide a king from his people also keep his wife. Is it King Hamlet's ghost possessing my mouth?

Or does no one tell a queen about her mouth noises?

I can't stop it, can't stop hearing it, can't endure it. My hands shake the sword loose from my son's chest in a wrenching splatter, and I pause my slopping tongue long enough to sob, but soon my throat fills with renewed sticky clicks, and I can't let it go on.

The sword turns in my hands, aiming the blade at my face, and I begin the careful work of sawing every moist heresy along its steely point. Tooth by tooth. Tongue-layer by tongue-layer. Peace in meaty chunks.

It is not a self-made death like I've wondered for Polonius and Ophelia; I won't lock myself up with this nightmare. Each cut pours gore over the damp hellmouth in a thickening caul to help to seal it over. Every crimson finger down the blade is one more grasp for sweet relief.

I bleed out the screams, and the noises, and by hollowing steel, my body again becomes a glorious cathedral of heavenly silence.

Something Is Rotten

(inspired by Hamlet)

Jo Kaplan

After many hours' ramble through the Danish countryside, the carriage bearing Leonora Carmichael, famed spiritual medium, at last arrived in Elsinore. The sea's briny stench intensified as the carriage approached the castle, half-ruined from a fire two centuries before, against a uniform gray sky.

Two other carriages had arrived before hers: that of her benefactor, William Brooks, and another transporting the McLeods, husband and wife scientists who dabbled in debunking psychic phenomena. Leonora could not say she was glad for their presence.

"Madam Carmichael," greeted a tall, slim man just past his mid-thirties, with a prematurely balding pate. William Brooks had grown his fortune, so she heard, by investing a modest inheritance in railroads, and now he had the funds to bring this curious group all the way to Denmark to explore an abandoned and reportedly haunted castle, one might suppose to sate his curiosity. Leonora had scrabbled her way into comfort from destitute origins and had discovered how the whims of the wealthy so far often outweighed the needs of the poor. This was exactly why she catered to such whims, of course; it was a lucrative business.

"Allow me to introduce Dr. Graeme McLeod." William nodded

to the small, bespectacled man with thinning hair and a round face. "And Mrs. Opal McLeod." The woman wore a plain dress, hair knotted in braids, and her pronounced nose and sharp eyebrows imposed on her a severe appearance.

Leonora's driver began unloading her bags as William led them to the crumbling castle entrance. In its shadow, the air grew brisker. Leonora paused, laid a hand on the grimy stone, and closed her eyes. "Many have died here."

"As you well know," said Graeme. "The story is infamous. Murder. Betrayal. Revenge. These intense associations spark the imagination and inspire tales of spirits—psychological embodiments of violent history."

Inside the castle, shadows clung to a rundown front hall, and the temperature dropped. Leonora shivered. "What you are feeling, Dr. McLeod, are the trapped souls who linger here, stuck in their own misery like flies in a web."

"There are some chambers that remain inhabitable," said William, "if only just." He waved them onward.

To find these chambers, they had to pass through the kitchen, which lay black and ruined, and the great hall, which stood cavernous in the broken windows' gray light. The far chambers had once belonged to royalty but now reeked of corruption: dusty with cobwebs, moldering tapestries, rusting suits of armor. "The Hamlets lived here," Leonora said. "The king and queen. And the prince. Their horrible deaths have bound them to this place."

After a few hours' respite they gathered in the great hall for a simple meal of porridge and bread that William himself had apparently prepared, there being no one else in the castle. Leonora was surprised that a wealthy man would allow for such a meal, but William seemed unbothered. He produced a bottle of wine, and they toasted to this joint investigation to find definitive proof of the afterlife—or lack thereof.

Opal declined the drink. "One must work with a clear head"— she spoke like a teacher—"if one wishes to produce credible work."

Her husband mumbled his reluctant agreement.

"What do you plan to do once you have successfully disproven the spirit world? Write a paper, or a book, perhaps? And which of your names shall appear on the cover?" Amusement twisted Leonora's lips when she saw Opal's cheeks flush. "This is why I work alone. And never married."

"Do you have many suitors in your profession?" Graeme's question did not sound sincere, and Leonora did not answer it.

Soon the creep of dusk reached the light of their candles. William, setting down his wine without a sip, asked, "Do you know the story?"

Leonora smiled coyly. "Murder. Betrayal. Revenge."

"King Hamlet's brother Claudius poisoned him in his sleep, then married the queen. Her son concocted a plan to avenge his father, but they say he went mad doing so. He killed those who got in his way and drove his lady love to suicide. In the end, he poisoned the king and queen, and he was slain in a duel. Their corrupted reign of lies ended in bloodshed."

"And do you believe their souls remain trapped here?" Leonora asked.

William's smile did not reach his eyes. "I believe nothing."

"We plan to conduct an experiment using lights," Graeme said. "One theory is that ghost sightings are afterimages resulting from overstimulated optical nerves. Illusions of an unpredictable psyche."

"Illusions experienced by many?" Leonora furrowed her brow. "How would you explain such a phenomenon?" She took a long drink of wine, not expecting an answer. "Shall I propose something I can do right now?"

William nodded. "By all means."

"Splendid. Arrange the candles here on the table like this, and take hands." They all complied, in spite of Opal's obvious disdain and Graeme's patronizing amusement. They sat in silence while their breathing shivered the flames. After the quiet had fully settled, attuning them to every whistle through the shattered windows, Leonora threw back her head, eyes closed, and commanded, "King Hamlet! Queen Hamlet! Prince Hamlet! Come to us. We call you to us." She let her voice echo around the hall, then fall to quiet before she continued. "Knock once for yes, twice for no. King Hamlet. Are you with us?"

Two thunderous bangs made Opal let go of her husband's hand. "She knocked on the table."

Leonora looked at her, still clutching Graeme and William's hands in each of her own. Without responding to the accusation, she continued: "You're not the king, then. Prince Hamlet? Are you here with us?"

One knock.

"Her knee," said Opal. "This is ludicrous, expecting us to believe cheap parlor tricks."

"Now, now," said Graeme. "We can have a bit of fun."

Leonora closed her eyes and rolled her neck. "Prince Hamlet, is there anyone with you?"

One knock.

"Is it your mother?"

Two knocks.

"Is it…your lover?"

One knock. Wind flicked at the flames.

Opal stood quickly and knocked over one of the candles. "This is a waste of time."

As Graeme beat out the flame, Leonora said, "Don't be frightened. Most spirits cannot harm us, and those few with the power to influence our world, should they manifest, I will banish from here."

"Frightened?" Opal scoffed and sat down again. "You misread me, Madam Carmichael. Your tricks bore me, and I am an impatient woman. I do not attend to frivolities."

"It seems to me you're in need of a good frivolity." Leonora fetched from her reticule a pen and paper, which she placed on the table. "This may prove more tangible for you." She closed her eyes and set the pen on the paper.

"What are you doing?"

"It's called automatic writing," William explained. "Letting the spirit guide the pen."

Again Leonora's voice took on that commanding tone. "Prince Hamlet, if you are there… Ophelia, if you are there… Speak to me, and say what you will." Her breath quickened as her hand began to sweep back and forth across the page. Soon the looping movement took on shape and definition as messy words emerged. William leaned over to read aloud, haltingly, as she wrote.

"Quoth I before you tumbled me you promised me to wed he answers so would a done by yonder sun an thou hadst not come to my bed…"

Leonora continued to write, groaning and weeping now, her hand seeming to move of its own accord. More words spilled across the page.

"He is dead and gone lady he is dead and gone at his head a grass green turf at his heels a stone."

Leonora gasped and dropped the pen, which rolled across the table. She reached for her wine with a trembling hand and allowed William to refresh her glass. As he poured, he asked, "What does it mean?"

"I couldn't say." Leonora took a steadying sip. "Someone was speaking through me. A very strong presence. And terribly sad." She looked down at the paper and read the words. "Some sort of rhyme," she murmured as if just discovering what she had written. "Wedding, and bedding. And…dead-ing."

"I would call this a somewhat inexact science," Graeme said.

Leonora explained, "She says that he promised he would marry her before they did the deed, and *he* says he would have waited had she not come to his bed first. And now…someone is dead."

A gust of wind shrieked through the window, blustered into the hall—and blew their candles right out. Darkness spread with the smell of dissipating smoke. As William fumbled to relight the candles, the hall fell still, and they could hear the burbling of a nearby brook. William struck a match, but it didn't catch, and the darkness pressed in as another sound, high and musical, drifted from outside—a woman's voice.

"Hey non nonny, nonny, hey nonny…"

Someone gasped, though in the dark it was hard to tell who. The next match caught, springing flame to life in front of William's face before it guttered.

"Someone is out there," Graeme murmured.

William lit several lanterns and suggested they investigate. Each with their own paltry light, they followed him down another hall, past burnt portraits, and then outside, where clouds tugged at the moon. Just visible in the gloom was the churchyard and its weed-shrouded tombs.

The singing spilled out from the trees. "*They bore him barefaced on the bier… Hey non nonny, nonny, hey nonny…*"

"Hello?" Graeme called out, raising his lantern to make the light go further. It passed over several graves, throwing shadows behind their stones. "Who goes there?"

The voice faded and returned when the wind blew.

"*And will he not come again? And will he not come again? No, no he is dead.*"

They followed until they reached the edge of the brook. Moonlight shimmered on the surface. Leonora tugged up her skirts to crouch, drawing her fingers through the cold water.

"Hello?" Graeme called again. "There's no need to hide. We heard your singing."

There were no footsteps. No movement, save wind that stirred the ink-black night, which seemed both pregnant and empty.

Leonora looked down and for a moment saw another face looking up at her from just under the surface—a face other than her own. Bloated and pale, with mouth hanging open. She started, leaving angry ripples that distorted the face, and when the water smoothed again she saw only her own reflection. Sweat bristled at her temples. She tried not to back away too quickly lest they see how she'd been startled. But she could feel her heart banging. The bank smelled of rosemary and rot. "She died here, Ophelia," Leonora said. "She floats here."

William shook his head. "I believe I'm ready for a nightcap."

Sat at the fireside in the royal chambers, Leonora realized she was drunk. A hasty self-assessment concluded that she must have drank half the bottle. Of course, she had always been a bit of a lush, and she certainly couldn't pass up good wine. The seances she held for her wealthy clients often ended with strong drinks and good cheer. The delighted astonishment on their faces made her the center of their adoration, which she devoured like a woman starving.

When the McLeods retired to their bedchamber, the room felt somehow more intimate. "So tell me, Mr. Brooks. What would make such a wealthy and handsome man so interested in the afterlife?"

His words came out somber. "My father died suddenly, and after, my mother took her own life." He frowned. "I suppose I need to know…whether or not I shall ever see them again."

Feeling warm toward him, Leonora lay her hand atop his. "Have faith you will."

William looked at her with something like disgust, but the expression was fleeting, and he assumed a melancholy aspect. "I thought to follow her, my mother," he mused. "I did not, of course."

"Well, I'm glad for it."

William appraised her ruefully and said, "Are you?"

It seemed an age till dawn, whereupon Leonora found herself in thrall to a bout of morning fog, her head pounding and eyes bleary. A desperate dread, too, plagued her: for in all the séances she had held over the last twenty years, only one had yielded anything approaching a true ghost encounter, while the rest were, as Opal had called them, parlor tricks. But sometimes her intuition seemed so strong that she found she knew things without knowing why she knew them, and this made her a very talented psychic medium. After a séance at Inverness in Scotland, she'd seen the shadows of three witches lurking against the wall. They had followed her wherever she cast a light, and she'd smelled smoke even where there was no fire. Like Elsinore, that, too, had been a place of death.

They gathered to breakfast. William produced tea and bread with jam. Afterwards, Leonora returned to bed for a lie down while the others got on with their experiments. It was as if the castle's sickness had infected her: its dark blood spilling into her heart, saturated with the misery of all the lives lost within its walls. Even at midday, its corridors and chambers remained dim as dusk and blighted with a constant chill. The hollow whistle of wind against stone rose and fell in eerie symphony.

The carriages were set to return for them in six days.

Though she wasn't yet recovered, Leonora dressed to join the others for supper. From the subdued conversation, she took it the day's experiments had not yielded much for the McLeods. This gave her a small measure of satisfaction.

Yet it was her mysterious benefactor that most interested her. Leonora was good at reading people. Subtle cues in one's manner could divulge that which remained unspoken. He was attired elegantly, though not ostentatiously, signifying that he had not always been wealthy and perhaps disdained the extravagance of old money; he occasionally checked his pocket watch, a signal of impatience or simply a mindless habit, though his hand always lingered in the pocket as if checking for something else inside; he kept a handkerchief in his breast pocket embroidered with the initials "M.B." Yet he did not bear the strain of desperate hope in his eyes the way some of her other clients did, those who begged to speak with their dearly departed.

Leonora was curious about the man but kept that curiosity to herself. The persona she affected when in the company of clients acted as a privacy screen of sorts: unruffled and self-assured, captivating and dramatic. Nothing could hurt her beneath the persona. Yet it was one she had donned so often, she could never quite tell when she was acting.

She sipped her wine. "Tell me of your mother. What was her name?"

"Marian," William said. "Her name was Marian. My mother was a kind woman. A truly decent person—of the sort that seems so rare. She saw the good in everything. That she ended her life over a man who…" He choked himself off. Leonora saw furious tears in his eyes and could not help feeling sympathetic. "My father was not a kind man."

"How did he pass?"

William blinked and composed himself. "I'd rather not discuss it."

Laying her hand over his, Leonora told him, "I will prove to you that there is life after death. And then you will know that you shall see your mother again. Perhaps you can even speak with her."

"Such lofty promises," William murmured.

"Empty promises do seem to be part and parcel to the Spiritualist movement," Graeme said. "I certainly hope we can find some answers here. What sort of natural phenomenon generates the experience of spirits? Is it a malfunction of the brain, or a result of external stimuli?"

"A haunting is like a disease," Leonora suggested. "Like a poison. If a place has been poisoned, it will begin to rot, exposing the spirits trapped there. Do you find it curious how we humans are so drawn to misery? We feed on it, even after we are dead."

Opal turned to her husband. "Now that Madam Carmichael is feeling better, we might run the experiment on her."

"Experiment?"

They led her through a dizzying labyrinth of corridors and alcoves, and at last entered a room filled with old furniture and rotting books, pages stuck together and crusted with salt. They arranged their lanterns to give the room a pleasant glow and had Leonora sit alone on one end of the room while the others stood to the side. Graeme told her to describe her surroundings continuously—with no pause in speaking—while Opal would strike a series of tuning forks to produce various tones. "Do not describe the tones, but simply what you are seeing and feeling, or otherwise hearing, sensing."

"All right, then," she said. "We are in a room which appears to have been used formerly as a library, or a study. The old books smell of mildew. The air is chill." Opal struck a tuning fork as Leonora spoke. "The corners of the room lie in darkness, and the lanterns cast shadows against the stone." Opal struck a second fork, dissonant with the first, while Graeme wrote in a notebook and William looked on. "I almost sense the shadows moving just when I begin to look away." Leonora took a breath, and Opal struck a third fork. "I can feel my heartbeat quickening. There is a presence in this room. The shadows shift, and…" Her eyes locked on a hulking shape that rose before her, wearing a crown. Though she could make out no details, she felt unseen eyes boring into her soul. "It's him!" she cried out. "The murderous King Claudius!"

William chuckled. "Oh, the king, is it? I suppose it *is* his castle."

Leonora could no longer contain her shivering fear. But when she blinked, the king's shadow dissolved. "This place is more than haunted. It is evil," she whispered. "You must believe me—I have never seen anything of its like before."

"But my dear Madam Carmichael," said William, "are you suggesting you've never seen a ghost? You, the renowned medium?"

By now the tones had faded to quiet. Graeme finished his writing and set down the notebook with a smile. "Fear not, madam," he said. "I believe you've just given us some excellent evidence as to the sensory effect of specific frequencies. Your shadow king was merely a result of your brain interpreting the discomfort produced by tonal dissonance."

"Then one might use a specific set of frequencies to induce the sensation of a haunting," Opal added as she looked at her husband. "Perhaps there is a similar effect with light waves, and this results in the visual hallucinations which manifest in the luminiferous aether."

"Luminiferous aether?" Leonora asked.

"You've seen waves in the sea?" Graeme explained. "These waves do not exist without the medium through which they move: water. Light, too, moves like a wave and must therefore require a medium that exists all around us, the fundamental substance through which light is transmitted."

"Ah—a *medium*?" Leonora said. "It seems to me we come to the same point from two different directions. Different conduits for spirits."

Graeme took his wife's arm. "Well, we have much to discuss from today's work. Come, darling." Opal nodded. They said goodnight.

When they had gone, Leonora wiped her clammy forehead and reminded herself she was not alone, that William was here with her, solid and unflappable. Yet something in his manner seemed cold when he turned to her. "Are you a liar, Madam Carmichael?"

"I beg your pardon?"

"A moment ago you suggested you'd never seen a spirit." He stepped closer, satisfaction in the curve of his lips. "So I ask again: are you a liar?"

"My spiritual encounters are legendary," said Leonora. "How dare you." Yet her voice came thin, as if she could not quite catch her breath.

"How dare I?" His face twitched with suppressed rage. "Why don't you just admit it, and quit these games. Say that you are a liar and a fraud."

Leonora stood with outrage, but her knees buckled and sent her to the floor. "What are you…"

William's stare was bright, cold, sharp. "The name Marian Brooks means nothing to you?" Leonora shook her head, and he gave a soft, humorless laugh. "My mother, so distraught after the death of my father, sought out a psychic medium so she might come to peace over what had happened." He raised his eyebrow. "Is this beginning to sound familiar?"

Leonora froze with dawning recognition.

"She came to you, during one of your group sessions. She asked you to contact him. And *you*…" His chuckle disappeared into a frown. "You said that her dead husband was eager to see her again. You lied. And she killed herself."

Crouched by his feet, Leonora appeared pitiful, face pale with shock. "I cannot be held accountable for…what anyone may do with the truth…"

"The truth? You think this castle is haunted," he said with dry amusement. "But it is only the hallucinations, I'm afraid. As a result of the poison."

Leonora opened her mouth as if to speak, but instead she gagged as she broke out shivering. "You…"

"Not as perceptive as you claim, are you? I have been poisoning you from the moment you arrived," he told her in the dispassionate tone one might use when discussing the weather's turning. "I have been watching you die by degrees. I will make it appear as though you ingested a cocktail of drugs. Everyone will believe you an addict, and will know you for the fraud you are. The McLeods will corroborate my story with their own testimony as to your instability and deceit. Your reputation will be destroyed, and you will be able to do nothing to salvage it, for you will be dead." William stepped closer, looking down. "And the dead don't speak."

Fingers jammed into her throat, Leonora vomited over the floor, but William only laughed and produced a half-filled vial from his pocket. "Don't be stubborn, Leonora. I have more."

She dragged herself away from him as he laughed, but William did not let her get far. One or the other jostled a table, overturning the lantern. Its flame caught the old books in a cascade. With a burst of energy, Leonora snatched up the second lantern and ran from the room, into the forbidding entrails of the castle, where she could not hope to find her way. Even if she could, she wondered what would happen if she returned to the royal chambers—were the McLeods in league with William? She could hear him following as she ran, and then she came to a broad doorway. It seemed a place to hide, so she eased it open into darkness and descending stairs. After a moment's hesitation, she went down, and found herself in the dungeons. The air tasted of damp and rot.

At the bottom, where even the vaulted ceiling felt too close, Leonora heard William's discovery of the open door and the echo of his voice. "I suppose this is a fitting place as any to die."

The final words range out against the stone, *to die…to die…*and something in this resonance seemed to stir the waking dark, for soon another voice spoke as if from near and far away at once.

"For in that sleep of death, what dreams may come? Dreams? Nay, not dreams, but nightmares."

Her lantern did little to break the impenetrable dark. Leonora wondered if she had actually heard a voice or if it was only the poison consuming her brain.

Just ahead, at the edge of her light, appeared a pair of muddied feet—a man dressed in medieval garb, bloodied down his front and pale as ash. Black pits lived in his eyes, his face more like a skull than flesh. "The poison binds us here to these, our mold'ring forms." The prince clutched a dirt-crusted skull, worms crawling in its jaw. "The nothing that may be seems better suited to my nature than this endlessness." And then it seemed the skull he held was his own, even as he wore his upon his neck, and his own mouth filled with dirt, worms wriggling between his teeth—one dangled from his eye socket, probing the air.

Leonora told herself it was the poison. It was only sparks in her mind. She lurched past the ghastly prince, into a crumbling passage, broken rock scattering the floor. And at the end, an egress. Part of the wall had collapsed, leaving an opening at the top where moonlight winked. She reached up, found soft dirt, and pulled herself through the hole. Wind stirred the trees and made the brook shimmer.

Behind her, William followed. Leonora considered throwing herself into the brook. She thought how easy it would be, to sink. To let the poison take her. To die, to sleep. But then William was upon her, hands around her throat, and she gasped, tearing at his wrists with her fingernails.

"You're not a killer, William. You're a good man… A man who cares deeply for his mother. Please." Tears welled in her eyes and spilled over. "I'm sorry. I'm so sorry. I took advantage…I lied…to your mother. But I hope…they are together now."

His eyes met hers, but there was no sympathy in them. "I should hope not," said William. "My father was cruel to her. That's why I killed him."

Another resonance seemed to shiver the air. The water rose and split as a figure emerged, drenched with moonlight, speaking in sorrowful tones. "He is here with me, dead as I am…but a small thing, he cannot even cry…" The woman rose from the brook, clutching something small in her arms.

Leonora pulled in a ragged breath as William let go, eyes wide upon the woman, who spoke to herself, as if she did not know they were there.

"Hamlet, he loved me, then Hamlet, he spurned me, for he was not ready to become a father so soon after losing his own. Then he killed mine, and I tried to stifle his babe in the womb, but look—the rue did not work." Her voice became an anguished singsong. "So I killed us both…I killed us both…"

What she held became visible then: a dead fetus, umbilical cord still binding them together. She rocked the unformed babe in her arms, humming.

William whispered something so softly, the wind almost carried it away unheard. "Mother."

Reeling away from him, Leonora gasped and wheezed, gingerly touching the sore flesh of her throat. The wonder and terror of this moment humbled her, for she knew, with abrupt clarity, these ghosts were not induced by the poison.

William beseeched the woman, "Forgive me. I didn't mean for you…and the baby…"

Then Leonora shuddered as she understood the true, twisted depth of William's love for his mother. "Was she pregnant?" she said, voice a rasp. "When your mother killed herself?"

Tearing his gaze from Ophelia's ghost, William turned a rictus of fear to Leonora. His voice came out high and manic. "Don't you speak of her! She loved me, as I loved her."

"You killed her husband."

"She wasn't his!" William roared. "She was *mine!*"

"Yours?" Leonora scoffed. "She would rather die than have her own son's child. All this time, you've plotted your revenge against me— but it was *you* who killed her."

Shadows lurked and writhed and pantomimed, stirred by the trouble, the smell of death: a troupe of actors, the laughter of their audience rising in a wave, followed by a duel, by blood, and the shrieks of the bodiless dead consigned to Elsinore; and the prince emerged from his dungeon, skull crusted with dirt, his skeleton crumbling as he tried to chase Ophelia's ghost back into the brook, but she took the dangling umbilical cord and looped it around her throat, then sent it up to the branch of a tree, where she hung, still clutching the babe to her breast.

"This is a trick!" William cried, scrabbling across the dirt toward Leonora. "Banish them. You said you could—send them away!"

Leonora shook her head. Ophelia choked on the umbilical cord, and the others moaned so that William clapped his hands over his ears. When he could take it no longer, he pulled out the vial, unstoppered it, and poured the whole of its contents down his throat. At once, his body seized, and foam bubbled from his lips as his eyes locked onto the gently swinging, dripping Ophelia, who continued to sing to her dead fetus.

Leonora vomited again as William came screeching out of his own body, as the hungry shadows descended on him and began to tear him apart, thirsty for his poisoned blood.

Little recollection after that followed Leonora over the next few days, as she lay in a stupor purging the rest of the poison on a bed in the royal chambers, which the McLeods had carried her to. Opal proved a capable nurse. The McLeods, as it turned out, believed Leonora's tale, or at least the part that painted William a madman, and hoped to leave the wretched castle as soon as Leonora was recovered.

Sometimes, when she woke half-delirious, Leonora believed she heard Ophelia singing, "*Hey non nonny, nonny, hey nonny…*" out by the brook. And she shivered at the thought of all the dead, from all the years of misery and strife, trapped eternally in their own torment—William, trapped in his grief and his perverse love, for the child and brother that should never have been, and the mother who had borne enough sorrow and violence in her life. But then, what woman has not borne enough sorrow and violence for this world?

When the day came that their carriages returned, Opal and Graeme helped Leonora out to the castle's front gate where the sun rose bright, and she finally confessed that she neither knew nor understood the workings of the spirit world, only that death was a poison that stained certain places.

They heard the horses approaching, and saw the distant carriages drawing nearer. Nodding, Graeme said, "Whether it be haunted or not—whether the dead persist or that which haunts be only in the mind—there is something dark and rotted at the heart of this castle that is best left unmolested."

"On that, at least," said Leonora, "I think we can agree."

Ophelia After Her Distress

Mary Berman

My mouth is packed with earth. The slipp'ry worm
Undulates thickly through my throat and teeth.
White splinters split my flesh, and spiders squirm,
Spinning threads through the tendons underneath.
So 'tis that love unfurls, its sweetness soured.
My Hamlet, soft, spoke kindnesses to me,
'til cruelty or madness in him flowered.
The fool shrieked "Get thee to a nunnery"
As if it were not already too late.
"Take off my edge," he sneered. I swallowed rue
To scour my insides, to immolate
Myself for him. I could not love thereto.
      Only a black rage stayed; and it's still there.
      I rise from the black earth and taste the air.

The Beggars' Shadows

(inspired by Shakespeare's Hamlet, Tom Stoppard's play Rosencrantz and Guildenstern are Dead, and John Langan's short story "Technicolor.")

Tim Waggoner

In *Hamlet,* Shakespeare presents Rosencrantz and Guildenstern as former schoolmates of the prince, but in truth they are spies for Hamlet's uncle, Claudius. They're interchangeable ciphers, so much so that other characters have difficulty remembering which is which. When they die, it happens offstage, and it's announced with a famous—some might even say *infamous*—line of dialogue—a plain declarative sentence with absolutely no hint of poetry in it. *Rosencrantz and Guildenstern Are dead.* Arguably, their actions had no meaningful impact on the events of the play, and they could be removed entirely without anyone really noticing. Because of this, they've come to represent a specific philosophical concept. Anyone know what it is? No?

All right, I'll tell you: Existentialism. The idea that for all humanity's attempts to find meaning, to *create* it, we all die in the end, and our existence is revealed to be absolutely purposeless because there is no meaning. Meaning is a human construct, a fantasy that gives us a comforting illusion to insulate us from hopelessness and despair. Hmm? No, I'm not advocating this point of view. I'm merely discussing it in relationship to Shakespeare's play, or rather to these two minor characters who loom much larger in the modern mind than they ever did in Shakespeare's time. Tom Stoppard wrote a well-known absurdist play in the 1960s called—unsurprisingly—*Rosencrantz and Guildenstern Are Dead,* exploring the concept of existentialism as symbolized by the characters.

You two in the back. Yes, the ones in the funny clothes whispering to each other. Is there something I can help you with? Yes? Oh, still struggling to grasp the concept of existentialism, eh? Let me see if I can come up with an example that might help clarify it for you. Give me a moment...

All right, let's say you're sitting here in this class at this very moment listening—or rather, *pretending* to listen—to me talk about *Hamlet.* Your eyes are open and your face is pointed toward me in an attitude of feigned attention that everyone learns as a child. No need to feel guilty or defensive now. I may be a professor of English at a medium-level midwestern college teaching Introductory British Literature, but I was a student like all of you once. As I said, you're sitting here in class, bored out of your fucking mind. Perhaps you're thinking about assignments you're behind on in other classes—essays to write, tests to prepare for, presentations to create—or perhaps you're thinking about a date you have later tonight, about fingering your girlfriend or blowing your boyfriend. But before you and your significant other do what you like to do with each other, you have to go to work. Right after this class, in fact. You don't have time to drive home and change into your uniform, so you have it in your car, bunched-up and wrinkled, lying in the backseat. You haven't washed it for at least a week, maybe two, and it smells of grease and sweat. But you figure it doesn't matter. The so-called restaurant where you work always smells bad anyway, so no one will notice how much you stink. And why should you make an effort to go into work clean? They don't pay you enough.

The place sells bland, tasteless fare—soggy tacos with pet-food-grade meat, and little of it, or chicken that's been overcooked to the point it's as dry as desert sand, or hamburgers so rubbery it takes a herculean effort to tear off a piece, let alone chew and swallow it. The manager you hate the most is on duty this afternoon—goddamned *Todd*. And to add insult to injury, the coworker you hate the most—a fucking idiot named Destinee, spelled with two E's instead of a Y—is also scheduled. She's a complete mess, always getting orders wrong, charging customers too much or too little, making messes she doesn't clean up…problems *you* have to fix, because if you don't, Todd will blame you for them. You suspect Todd is fucking Destinee in the back during breaks, but so far no one's caught them. So with all this on your mind, is it any wonder that you don't give two shits about a couple minor characters in a dusty old Elizabethan play?

By some miracle, you managed to survive until the end of class, and I dismiss everyone—reminding you all about a homework assignment I know you won't do, which is okay, because I don't really want to read and grade it. You practically leap up from your desk and run to the door, trying to squeeze past anyone in your way. You don't look at me as you go. I no longer exist and won't until the next time you manage to drag your ass in for class.

You make it into the hallway, and for the first time in seventy-five minutes you feel as if you can breathe. Maybe you see some students who you know as you hurry down the hall, and you're tempted to stop and say hi to them. But if you do, you'll be late for work, and you've already been late twice in the last month. Todd has been hoping to catch you being tardy a third time because then he can write you up and send the report to the franchise's corporate office. If this happens, your hours might get cut, and worse, you might get fired. Not that you'd be sad to leave Tacos-Chicken-Burgers-R-Us, but you don't want to go through the hassle of looking for a new job. Better the devil you know, right?

You parked on the roof of the student garage this morning because you got a late start—don't you always?—and most of the spaces were already taken by the time you got to campus. The instant you step outside the building, you feel cold raindrops pelt your skin, and you let out a loud "Fuck!" You brought an umbrella today because the forecast called for rain, but it was still sunny when you got here, so you left it in your car like a fucking moron. There's no other way to reach the garage than by walking outside, and with the way this goddamned rain is falling, you know you'll be soaked to the skin before you can get halfway there. "Shit," you mutter, then start sprinting across the quad. As you feared, you're quickly drenched. You're surprised how cold the rain is for this time of year, and when you finally reach the garage, you're shivering so hard you can't stop and your teeth are chattering. The garage has an elevator, but it's only supposed to be used by students with mobility issues. You usually take the stairs—better for your health—but you're not feeling the stairs today. The universe has already pissed all over you. It owes you one.

You get in the elevator, and just as the door starts to close, you hear someone shout, "Hold the elevator, please!"

Through the narrowing space between the closing elevator door and the jamb, you catch a quick glimpse of someone in a wheelchair rolling toward you.

"Hold please!" they repeat, louder this time.

You reach toward the elevator's control panel, index finger stretched outward, intending to stab the HOLD button, but then you let your arm drop to your side. You watch the door slide closed the rest of the way, and the elevator shudders and starts to slowly rise. The person who you left behind pounds on the outer door of the elevator shaft and shouts that you're an ableist dickhead. And maybe you are, but right now you don't give a shit. The reason you didn't press the HOLD button wasn't because you're afraid of being late for work— not entirely, anyway. It was because you got a good look at the person's face before the elevator door slid shut, and you could swear that person was wearing your face.

Trick of the light, you think, and you believe it. Mostly.

When the elevator door slides open, you hear and see the rain once more. You pull your keys from your pants pocket, draw in a breath—wet air, cold and sharp—then you dash outside, leaving behind a large puddle of water on the elevator floor where you stood. The wind has kicked up since your cross-campus dash, and you feel it press against you as you run, as if it's deliberately trying to keep you from reaching your car. Although *car* is a generous descriptor for the piece-of-shit vehicle you drive, an old broken-down Ford with more rust than paint, bald tires, and windshield wipers badly in need of replacing. Your remote doesn't work, so you have to use the physical key, and by the time you finally get inside and slam the door shut behind you, you're so cold that you're numb from head to toe. Your hand shakes so much that it takes you three tries to get the key in the ignition and turn over the engine. You turn on the heater, which only blows lukewarm air no matter what setting you put it on, pull the seatbelt across your chest and click it in, flip on the only headlight that works, hit the wipers that do little more than smear water around on your windshield, and pull out of your spot.

The rain starts to come down even harder now, and when you pull out of the parking garage ground-floor exit, you can't see a damn thing. You hunch over the steering wheel, lean forward, and squint, as if somehow these things will allow you to magically see through the rain, and you drive twenty miles-per-hour all the way to Tacos-Chicken-Burgers-R-Us. You're supposed to park behind the building and leave the closer spaces for customers, but you're almost fifteen minutes late for your shift when you arrive, so you park in a customer spot closer to the front door.

Your phone *bloops*, indicating you have a text, and even though you're late, you grab your phone to see who it is. You're not surprised to discover it's your inamorata canceling your tryst for this evening. She works at an assisted-living facility, and she needs to take a night shift to fill in for one of her coworkers who got sick. Maybe that's true, maybe it's not, but one thing's for certain: you're not getting your bell rung tonight.

Sighing, you slide your phone into your pants pocket. You then grab your uniform—which is an ugly baby-shit brown—but since you don't have a plastic bag or anything to keep it dry, you wad it up as tightly as you can and stick it under your shirt. Then you get out, shut the door, and run for the entrance. Halfway there, you remember the umbrella in your car, and you feel like screaming, "Fuck my life!" but you don't in case someone inside hears you.

When you reach the lobby, you pull your uniform out from under your shirt. It's wet now, but not *too* wet, and that at least is something to be grateful for.

Todd, the asshole, comes out from behind the counter and scowls at you. You scowl right back because—like the person who tried to get on the elevator with you in the parking garage—he's wearing your face. You tell yourself you're seeing things, that you've been pushing yourself too hard, and you need to start getting more sleep.

Todd puts his hands on his hips to underscore how much of a bastard he intends to be about you coming in late. But it's still raining like a son of a bitch outside, and you look like a drowned rat, so all he does is sigh, shake his head, then say, "Get yourself together and get to work." The face he wears might be yours, but the voice is all Todd. He goes back behind the counter and you can't believe that something has finally gone right for you today. Sure, he'll probably ride your ass the rest of your shift, alert for even the tiniest mistake you might make, but at least he's not going to write you up for lateness.

Destinee's standing at one of the registers, and she gives you a smug look, as if to say *Smooth move, Ex-Lax*. Like Todd, she has your face, and you turn quickly away. You get enough shit on a daily basis as it is. You don't need any more from her.

You head to the restroom, and five minutes later you're wearing your mostly dry uniform, standing behind a register, hair a wet mess, a fake smile on your face. You look at the first customer in line, a man with a shaved head and a thick white beard who, like Todd and Destinee, possesses your features. You fight to keep your voice steady as you say, "May I help you?"

The man's eyes narrow as he looks at you, and his lips purse in disapproval. Is he reacting to your less-than-professional appearance? Or is he wondering why *you* have *his* face? He steps up to the counter, and without looking at the menu displayed on the wall behind you, he says, "I'll have a burger."

"Of course, sir. What kind would you like?"

There are a lot of options—single, double, deluxe, bacon, quarter-pound, third-pound, half-pound. And then there are the add-ons: catsup, cheese (three kinds), mustard, mayo, onions, jalapenos, chili, mushrooms…

"A *burger*," the man reiterates.

You look at him, trying to decide if this is some kind of joke, but his—*your*—expression is dead serious. Before you can decide on your next question, he speaks again.

"Burrrrrrrrr—"

He pauses, inhales.

"Grrrrrrrrrr."

You glance over your shoulder, hoping to see Todd standing close by, but he's not there. Neither is Destinee. They're probably in the back right now fucking, the one time you actually need the asshole.

You turn back to the customer. There are other people behind him in line—all wearing your face, of course—and they're becoming impatient, scowling at you, shifting their weight from one foot to the other, letting out theatrical sighs. Should you just get the guy a plain single burger? That's the closest thing you can think of that might qualify as a *Burrrrrrrrr-Grrrrrrrrrr*.

No, that's ridiculous. No one ever orders those.

"What *specific* burger would you like, sir?"

You add the *sir* in hopes the man won't feel disrespected by your question. You half turn and point to the menu on the wall behind you. Pictures accompany each burger that's available to order, and they all have numbers associated with them—#1, #2, #3, and so on. Surely the man can make a goddamned selection with all this information.

"How many times do I have to tell you? A. Bur. Ger."

Is the guy illiterate and embarrassed by it?

"Would you like me to tell you which burgers we have available? I'm happy to do so."

You're not happy. You're pissed off. This weird motherfucker is the rancid cherry on top of the shit sundae that has been your day. Any more of this bullshit and you're going to explode and go off on this asshole, really let him have it.

But the man doesn't react this time. Instead, he turns and walks toward the door. He moves at a normal pace, doesn't appear upset at all, and then he's outside and gone. You release a breath you didn't know you were holding and give the next customer in line an apologetic smile.

You've almost finished taking this person's order when the door opens and Burrrrrrrrr-Grrrrrrrrrr Man steps into the lobby. His hands are at his sides, and the right one is holding a gun. He went out to his car to retrieve his weapon, pulling it from the glovebox or maybe from beneath the front seat. The customer currently standing at the counter sees the man is armed and takes several steps back, as do the others in line, expressions of shock and disbelief on the faces they've stolen from you. The man's face—which is also your face—is blank, no more expressive than a mannequin's.

You speak in a quavering voice. "Burger?"

The man raises his gun and shoots you in the face, which also happens to be his face, and everyone else's in the restaurant. All of your faces explode and spray the air with crimson as the bullet ravages bone and flesh, and you all slump to the floor. You die almost instantly, but before the lights go off for good, you think that at least you don't have to deal with that fucked-up weirdo anymore. It's not much, but it's something.

And then you're gone.

And *that*, my friends, is existentialism. Any questions? No? Very well then, that's it for today. Make sure to come to class next time with topics for your research paper. Shoot me an email if you have any problems coming up with ideas, and I'll see what I can do to help.

(The students file out the door, eyelids drooping, feet shuffling. Zombies would demonstrate more life than they do. Each of them has the same face the professor has, but this doesn't surprise him. They always have his face, class after class, year after year. A pair of students—the ones who needed a more detailed explanation of existentialism, approach him. They each have the professor's face—or perhaps the professor has theirs. They both wear dark capes, vests over long-sleeved white shirts, dark blue pants, and black leather boots. Each carries a rapier at their side.)

STUDENT ONE
Actually, we *do* have a question, Professor.

STUDENT TWO
What, good sir, is your name?

STUDENT ONE
(smiling sheepishly)
Our apologies, but we seem to have forgotten it.

PROFESSOR
(opens mouth to reply, pauses, thinks for a moment, then answers in a voice filled with despair)
It appears I have, too.
(The three laugh uproariously as tears stream down their identical, anonymous faces.)

CURTAIN

The Votress's Daughter

(based on A Midsummer Night's Dream)

Seanan McGuire

❦❦ **I**f she'd had any idea the garden could be used against her, she would never have planted it. Of that you can be certain. But even the gods may be too shortsighted to realize the consequences of their actions—or perhaps especially the gods. They are, after all, above most natural consequences, too elevated to pay the price of their own folly. And yes, one can argue that the Queen of all Faerie is no god, is only a woman somewhat more than mortal, but if one did, I would counter that when something is that much more than mortal, it doesn't matter anymore. She certainly *thinks* of herself as a god, or as good as such, and in the end, that is what matters.

"Someone who believes themselves to be divine would never consider the necessity of precautions, would never take the time to protect themselves from the things they, themselves, are capable of doing. Such is Titania. The ever-living, the ever-blooming, the Summer Queen of the Fae. Oh, how she rejoices in her own arrogance, how she wallows in her hubris, how she amiably ignores the wreckage she leaves in her wake. My mother was a votress of her order, dutiful to the end of her life. My father was a mortal man. That much I know. The fairies who knew my mother in her life say that he was gentle; they say she went to him willingly; they say he lay with her in her lady's bower while the fair Titania was away.

"Perhaps that was his truly unforgivable transgression. That he tread on sacred blossoms, that he sipped at sacred springs, and that he lay on sacred bedding, all without consent of the Queen. Whatever his crimes, they do not speak of him now, any more than they speak of my mother. She has been excised from the tale, remembered only because her child—of necessity his child as well, for she knew no other in her living—became a pawn in a game that she had never asked to play.

"'*His* mother,' Titania said, when she did speak of me, 'was a votress of my order...'

"She had decided even then that mortal women could not be trusted, not after my mother's crime. Children were uncommon in the fairy lands even then, before the Courts were sundered. For a human to conceive and carry one when a Fae Queen could not...it was an unthinkable insult. And one that seemed likely to be repeated if she did not close her Court against them.

"There were many women then, or so the fairies say. Dark and light, merry and solemn, all types and kinds of women. My mother had been one of a sisterhood, and I envied her that every day of my childhood.

"What Titania did to them...

"The King and Queen are monsters, true, but even monsters are betimes loathe to do harm to children. The fairies of the Court told Titania that any magics aimed at me before I came of age would do more than she intended, and somehow convinced her such despite her wishing otherwise, and so they clothed me as they would clothe a boy, and taught me as they would teach a boy, and encouraged me in all ways to act as my father's son before I was my mother's daughter.

"Oberon cared less than she, when I was transferred to his keeping, but still the fairies recommended that I remain as I was, for it was at his beseeching some of the flowers in the Queen's garden had been planted, and it was to his ends their uses were directed. It was safer by far if he thought me a mortal man and not a mortal maid, especially with Titania's banning of all such from the Courts.

"So I grew in solitude and open secrecy, and when my majority approached, the fairies of the Court did tell me that there would be safety to be found in this township, and in the company of those who had been vexed by Titania's magic before."

And so the strange young woman concluded her tale, and turned her attention more properly to the bowl of stew and slice of bread that had been set before her after she stumbled out of the woods and into the company of the town players, who had been preparing for the next feast day in the town square. Seeing her disheveled and hearing her ravings, they had whisked her away to the inn, hoping that a bit of good meat and rest would see her fit for company, or at least for telling them her name.

If it gave the rest of them the opportunity for a break and a beer, well, where was the harm in that?

"Vexed by Titania," said the oldest among their number, striking his whiskers as he studied the girl. It was a nervous habit he had developed following their production of Pyramus and Thisbe, and one which he had been entirely unable to divest himself of since, even when his wife had complained that she woke in the night to find him stroking himself, or tugging at his ears as if he'd see them lengthen in his hand.

Neither could he eat meat, nor wear most shoes, for they were too large for his feet, the soles of which had grown callused until they could all but stamp through any cobbler's handiwork.

"You remember her, yes?" asked the woman, glancing up from her meal.

"Beautiful maiden of the woods who garlanded my brow with flowers and called me her darling dear until the moment that she took it all away? Oh, I remember her well, even if all among my company have laughed at me whenever I spoke of her."

The men weren't laughing now. Instead, they looked at the woman and then at Nicholas, brows drawn together and mouths drawn down.

"We thought you jested unwisely," said one.

"We thought what followed after was your punishment for speaking falsehoods," said another.

"We thought you had attracted the attention of the Fair Folk, when all know that such things are to be well avoided and prayers set against," said the third.

"No," said Nicholas. "I tell you now as I have told you so many times before, no. She came before me. She transformed me to make me her creature, and she lay with me for many hours, promising me such delights as mortal flesh was never meant to know. You asked why I did not mourn when my Bess left my bed to return to the company of her sisters. Now as then, I say it is because the touch of a mortal woman is the touch of rotting flesh when compared to the touch of the fae. You, girl!" He whirled on the woman, who was sopping up the juices of her stew with the heel of her bread, and looked at him in wary surprise, as if she had just been caught doing something entirely forbidden. "You tell me that my sweet lover of that long-gone summer's night was the Queen of all the Fairies?"

The woman swallowed her mouthful of stew, nodded, and said, "I thought you knew. All the fairies of her Court…we thought you knew."

"No." His expression turned wistful. "'Twas as a dream. A glorious dream, aye, but a dream all the same, and like all dreams, it faded into mist and memory upon the waking. I thought she had been a forest spirit, some Grecian nymph traveled over the sea to beguile me, some deep daughter of the wood risen to grace my senses for but a little while…"

The woman shook her head. "She is the Queen of the Fairies, and she is cruel as any wind of winter. She did not choose to do you harm—that was done to her, that she would do to you, for the Fair Folk care little when their games destroy the lives of mortals—but she harmed you all the same, and so we thought you might have sympathy for the plight of a votress's daughter."

"What would you ask of us?" asked a member of the company.

The woman took a deep breath. "Our Lady grows a garden. Fine and fair and ever-blooming is it, with no notice taken of the seasons. In it, she plants her rarest and most precious cuttings, the seeds that could destroy a kingdom, the fruits that could unweave a heart." Her gaze went to Nicholas. "It was one of these flowers that was used on her, sir, to make you think you her beloved. But as the fairies of her Court are sworn to secrecy where her Lord and master is concerned, and as the tincture was removed from her eyes when she woke, she knows not the cause of her brief and dreadful infatuation. You are her secret shame, and nothing more to her than that."

"Answer the question," he said, hand shaking as he raised his tankard. "What would you ask of us?"

"There are poisons in that garden that could destroy nations. A drop in the well would see England ended. Even the Queen of the Fairies cannot stand against them. She planted them thinking herself immune to the effects of her own creations. I intend to show her otherwise. I intend that you should aid me.

"None of mortal mien is meant to know the path to the Queen's garden, but I do, for I was taught by her own handmaids. They tire of tyranny as I do. Consider how terrible your own kings can be, and ask yourself what happens when those kings need never fear death nor succession. The fae are ready for a change."

Her smile was a terrible thing, the smile of a wild beast backed into a corner, prepared to bite and tear. "Will you help me?"

"We are terrible unwise to do this," grumbled one of the younger members of the company. He had told his wife to dress the babes in their nightclothes inside-out before he left to join the others, and now accompanied them ever deeper into the tangles of the wood.

They had already passed outside the limits of the wood he knew, for all that he had been born in this village, had spent his boyhood running through these trees. Yet now they walked in unfamiliar territory, the brambles more pointed, the chuckle of the running brook more cruel. They had wandered at some point, as they followed the yet-nameless woman, onto fairy ground.

The others looked at him, and he could tell by the anxiety in their eyes that they agreed, for all they would not voice it aloud. Their path was set, and had been so since the moment they left their mortal wood for the tangles of the Fairyland.

"Too late now," said Nicholas.

"Mind your step as we cross the stream ahead," said the woman. "It flows not with water, but with the blood men shed in mortal lands, and it will claim you if it can, for it remembers the veins of the living, and yearns for a return to them. You would burst like a tick."

The men grimaced.

"Dangerous indeed, this land of yours," said one of them.

"Not my land, for I was of woman born, but then, neither is yours, for I was nursed by a fairy with stars for eyes," said the woman, her tone as matter of fact as her words were not. "I am a child of both worlds, a countryman of neither, and I take no blame for the Lady's choices."

The stream she had mentioned appeared ahead of them, and the woman moved quickly to the banks, stepping lightly onto the first of a series of stones that would allow them to cross the fast-moving, bubbling tributary. As promised, it ran red with blood, rather than water, but it was narrow enough that a good jump would see a man to the other side.

Of the five in their company, three followed her across the stones. The two youngest stepped back, getting a running start, and leapt the brook, even as the woman made a sound of wordless protest.

The first landed confidently, continuing forward to join the others. The second landed, only to slip and fall backward, into the bloody stream.

For a moment, nothing happened, and it seemed her warnings might have been in vain. Then his body began to swell, rounding out like an inflatable bladder. He screamed, staring at his bulging arm with equally bulging eyes, before he rolled onto his stomach, reaching beseechingly for his fellows.

It was almost anticlimactic when he popped. There was no vast spray of blood and gore, no bath of livid red; only a sound like linen being torn and, for an instant, the shape of a man etched entirely in red hanging where their companion had been. Then it fell back into the stream and was gone, washed away in the flood.

"I warned you," said the woman. "The dangers of the fairy realms are not to be trifled with."

On she walked with the four men yet among the living, deeper and deeper into the tangled territory claimed by Titania's Court. As they approached a wall of thorns, she addressed them again.

"Take all care," she said, "for a single scratch of a single thorn will see you sleep a hundred years away, and as none among the fae are here to claim you, there would be no spell of youth or vitality cast upon your sleeping form. You would dream the remainder of your days away, and your defenseless form would be stolen away by the predators that haunt these woods. Never would you see them coming, nor have a chance to run away."

Nick scowled at her. "Every time you speak a danger into being, it seems we suffer for it. I thought we were but to raid a walled garden to have revenge upon a Court that's treated both of us quite shabbily."

"And that is what we seek to do, but the land has its hazards. Would you rather not be warned?" She tilted her head, looking at him evenly.

He swore and looked away, and they followed her onward, past the thorns, without a single scratch.

Beyond it was a low wall of unchiseled stones piled one atop the next with an artisan's eye, so that they stood strong and stable despite the lack of any joins between them. Moss coated their sides and tops, creating an uneven quilt of green and gray, as lovely and natural as any fragment of the wood. And beyond *that*...

It was a garden such as none of the men had ever seen, green and lush and bursting with fruits and flowers in a thousand colors, scenting the air in a riot of perfumes. The woman continued onward without pausing, hoisting herself up and over the wall, gesturing for the men to follow.

Three did. The fourth shook his head as he backed away, before finally turning and running back along the path they had followed to the garden wall. So consumed was he by the urge to flee that he didn't slow as he passed the thorns, and a single briar caught his arm, breaking the skin in a fine red line that had barely begun to bleed when he struck the ground, asleep beyond all waking.

The forest, and the night, was silent.

Beyond the wall, a woman and three village actors moved through a treasury of fairy flora, the men trying to match her footsteps with their own, treading only where she had already tread, touching only what she had already touched. The last among them paused to admire a bush of bright purple berries, and died with a lilac smile upon his lips, the taste of the one perfect fruit he had thought to steal away still sweet upon his tongue.

His companions didn't seem to notice. The now-trio moved on until they reached an herb garden and the woman bent, pulling a small glass bottle from inside her skirt and holding it in one trembling hand beneath the crimson bell of a flower that looked something like glovewort, if glovewort had ever been known to grow in vivid red, or to glow with a rich and bloody light. Nicholas and his last surviving friend watched in silence as clear liquid ran from the inside of the flower and down into the jar, drop after drop, until the woman pulled her hand back and stoppered the jar, holding it up to the light.

"The deed is done," she murmured. "The table set."

"What do you mean?" asked Nicholas.

She turned to him, a slight, almost regretful smile tugging at her lips. "Dear Nicholas," she said. "The fairies did speak well of you, and often. The donkey-headed man who had beguiled our Queen, all without knowing it. The man she spared. I knew you would come if I but called you, for none may sit once at a fairy's table and not yearn to do so again, even if they thought their dalliance a dream. I am sorry that it had to be you who would come with me."

"What—" he began, but had no time to finish as she tucked the bottle back into her clothing, threw her head back, and screamed.

Nick Bottom had been a village player for many years, and even as the realization that they had been betrayed and he would no doubt pay the consequences began to stir itself in his thoughts, he admired the strength and vigor of her scream. Why, she could convince an audience that she was being murdered, if she saw cause to claim it! She could rend a heart, with a scream like that.

She could call all the hosts of Fairy to her aid.

They swarmed out of the trees on wings like cobwebs stretched over branches, surrounding the two men, stabbing at them again and again and driving them to their knees. The woman moved closer, leaning down to murmur in Nicholas's ear:

"Everything I told you was the truth. My mother was as I have named her, and what you've helped me to gather is for the table of the queen. You shall be remembered long after the world you knew has fallen, for what you have done, for the aid that you have given to the least among Fairy's citizenry. And I shall see my parents avenged."

She straightened then, watching with cold eyes as the fairies continued to swirl and stab, as they cut the two men to the ground. She was walking away as Nicholas slumped, his eyes going unfocused, his vision going dim.

"Ah, my dream come again," he whispered, and in the garden of the Fairy Queen, long years after first they dallied, Nicholas Bottom left the stage at last.

The Woods Are Dark

(based on A Midsummer Night's Dream)

Vince A. Liaguno

I fear these woods where feral fairies lurk,
My fellow thespians swallowed by fog,
Lost in forests of miasma and murk,
Among the night creatures of the black bog:
Quagmire that threatens every step;
Tricky as the machinations of sprites,
Who hoodwink rude mechanicals in prep,
For wedding theatrics festooned with frights:
Comedy quickly turns toward the tragic;
As death comes to this oft-haunted marshland,
And woodland terrors turn sarcophagic,
Screams heard 'til grimaced mouths fill with quicksand:
     Is this a curtain call as it would seem,
     Or perchance a nightmare within a dream?

When I Waked I Cried to Dream Again

(A Story of The Tempest)

Jonathan Maberry

1

It moved through the shadows, making no sound, drawing no eye.

The storm above lashed the ship, pummeling it with fists of seawater and howls of bitter wind. The crew fought to trim the sails, and the sailing master and two mates wrestled the wheel, trying to keep the vessel's head toward the gale. It rose on the crest of massive rollers and plunged into troughs so deep that walls of water rose higher than the topsails.

The passengers huddled out of the way and prayed to a god who seemed indifferent or deaf to their pleas. Sailors swore and cursed and wept for their mothers as the ocean became a monster.

And in the shadows of that ship a truer monster watched with a hidden smile and naked hatred in its eyes. The ship moved through the maelstrom and not one living soul aboard believed they would ever see land again.

2

"I thought you said the seas would be calm and the weather fine," complained the boatswain.

The ship lifted heavily on a roller, poised high in the troubled air, and then plunged down the other side. All aboard clutched manropes with one hand and their crucifixes with the other. A few—Stefano notable among them—cried out in terror with each rise and fall, each burning spear of lightning, each howl of the wind. When the thunder tore open the sky, nearly all of the passengers cowered.

Nearly all.

Prospero did not.

He stood on the raised poop, a lifeline looped around his right forearm while with his left he made furious gestures at the storm, cursing it and commanding it to abate.

Which it did not do.

"Father," cried Miranda, his daughter of fifteen summers, as she clung to him. "Father, make it stop! Please, save us from the storm."

He ignored her, though he chanted long strings of spells in Italian and Greek, in ancient Hebrew and classical Greek. His passion was as intense as the storm itself; his will and that of the gale warred in the troubled air. When the lightning flashed, the glare etched deep stress lines in the sorcerer's face and washed nearly all color from his eyes. In those moments, Miranda thought her father looked like the death mask of some ancient king—grim and terrible and unyielding.

And yet there was also a shadow of doubt in his eyes, and that frightened Miranda all the more. Never once in all the years they had been alone on the island—except for mad Caliban and the spiteful sprite Ariel—had she ever seen her father look uncertain. Now, as he chanted his spells and the storm did not yield to those commands, she saw the vulnerability edge toward actual fear.

"I need my staff," he whispered between stanzas of the latest spell. "I should never have foresworn it and broken the thing."

That had been part of the strange ritual of departure. When King Alonso of Naples, his son, and key courtiers were shipwrecked, Miranda had first been filled with joy at seeing other human beings for the first time since she was three. She had met Prince Ferdinand and they had instantly fallen in love. There had been the conflict with the others, though—duplicity, attempted murder, and finally a reconciliation that had lifted Father's heart and in doing so, opened it. There he had foresworn his long-held dream of vengeance against his brother—the treacherous and ambitious Antonio—and the king who had exiled them, hoping the sea would kill them. It was a hard-won appeasement and a harder act of mingled contrition and forgiveness. It was then that her father promised to give up his pursuit of vengeance and of the magics he had used to shipwreck his enemies. He had tossed his spell books into the briny deep and broke his staff across a rock before stepping into the boat that carried them to the ship.

Now, she could *feel* his regret. The action, grandiose and even sentimental, was ill-considered when measured against the perils of a long sea voyage. She knew the crystal that topped the staff was how he focused his will, and that had fallen into the surf and was whisked away by the tide.

The storm, which had come out of nowhere, seemed to be a rebuke by the spirits of the air, she thought. Or maybe a punishment for a mortal who had wrestled magic to his use. And even Miranda, who dearly loved her father, knew that those uses were not always pure. His bullying of Caliban was obscene; and the lengths to which he compelled Ariel to do his will by dangling freedom always out of reach…that was cruel.

Now Caliban ruled his empty island, with his only company the memory of his witch mother, Sycorax, and the enigmatic and secretive Ariel. Miranda tried hard to hate Caliban because of his vile threats to rape her, but she did not believe the monster would ever have acted on those threats. He was, in many ways, an innocent despite his size and power. He had lived alone on the island for years after his mother's death, with no company and no one to teach him how people behaved. Then Father and she had been stranded there, and the process of civilizing him had been fraught with perils, misadventures, mistakes on both sides, and then the ongoing and comprehensive bullying and torture by Prospero. She had hated and feared Caliban, but now regretted her hard words.

That was all behind her—behind them all—and now the ship sailed into the teeth of the storm and nothing her father attempted eased the wind by a knot, slowed the rain by a drop, or pulled the teeth of the wind.

3

The thing was a shadow within shadows.

Even when someone turned toward it, they saw only darkness that roiled and moved as the ship was tossed about with all the fury of a sky gone mad. That made the thing smile, for chaos was its friend.

4

The scream was so loud it tore through the howl of the wind and the roar of the thrashing ocean.

It froze everyone who heard it because it was no normal scream. Not a shriek of unwelcome surprise, or the howl of a seaman falling from the shrouds to break a leg. This scream was sharp as a knife, and it rose and rose and rose until it filled every ear and turned the blood of even the most stalwart among them to ice.

And then it stopped.

Just like that. The scream was cut off in a wet and ugly gurgle and then nothing.

"Wither that cry?" demanded the boatswain, but the sailors all looked around, each certain of a different direction.

A hatch opened and King Alonso and his brother, Sebastian, rushed on deck, each with a naked dagger in his hands.

"What's amiss?" demanded the king. "Are we attacked? Are there pirates?"

The sailing master, who had lashed himself to the wheel lest the storm knock him down and the ship founder, shook his head. "The scream came from belowdecks." He then yelled for the boatswain to search below to see if the cargo broke loose and crushed someone. Half a dozen men hurried down the companion ladder.

A few moments passed and everyone on deck huddled in the hypothetical shelter of the canvas stretched over the wheel. One lad squeezed into the manger aft of the hawseholes, though this was no better, for the wind was ruthless and determined and it celebrated finding each man and dousing him with frigid saltwater.

Then the boatswain came blundering back on deck, his face pale as old milk, his mouth twisted into horror.

"God save our souls," he gasped.

"What is it, man?" demanded the king.

The boatswain touched his forelock though his hand trembled badly. "It's th-the ship's s-surgeon, Your Highness," he stammered

"What about him? The man's a drunkard. Has he accidentally stabbed himself with a lancet?"

"Weren't no accident what was done to him, Highness."

Every eye was upon him.

"Speak plain," said the king. "What has happened?"

"He's been done for," said the boatswain. "Done for bad. Done for evil as I've ever seen, and I've seen my share."

"Are you saying that it's murder?" cried Alonso.

"Sire," said the boatswain, "on my word as a Christian, I can call it nothing else."

"Send Prospero to see it," said the sailing master. "He's learned in such things."

But Prospero was not on deck and when his name was shouted man by man he did not appear. Miranda came on deck at the call, though.

"My father was feeling ill," she said. "He took a sleeping draught and retired to his bed. He sleeps deeply and will not wake for hours."

The king glanced at his brother, Sebastian. "Go see this thing and tell me the truth of it. Be my eyes."

Sebastian drew himself up and nodded, though it was clear to all that he had no heart for it. He nodded and followed the boatswain down the companion ladder. Four others went with him—two burly sailors, the wise Gonzalo, and Lord Francisco. They vanished below.

The king came and stood beside the master. "Have you anyone aboard who is known to be violent?"

"None that would murder, My Lord, no."

"Did the surgeon have any enemies?"

"Only the bottle, but it was a love and hate thing."

After five tense moments, Sebastian came up on deck. He accosted the king's butler, Stephano. "Your bottle."

"Bottle…but I have no—"

"Damn your eyes," growled Sebastian and patted the man

roughly until he found the hidden flask. He fair tore it from Stephano's inner pocket, uncorked it, and took a long draught. Then he thrust it back into the butler's hands and wheeled around as if already drunk. But it was clear to everyone that he was unsettled in body and mind by what he had witnessed.

"Brother," said the king gently, "tell me of what you've seen."

"Seen? God above, Alonso, I have glimpsed Hell." He waved a hand toward the hatch. "To say the doctor is dead is to call the ocean a puddle. Someone took a knife to him and cut him to pieces. And do not, I beg, think I am guilty of hyperbole. Pieces, I say, and pieces it is. Head and hands, feet and entrails cut from him and placed around his cabin as a child might arrange his toys. And blood? Dear heavens, the place was awash in it. You would not credit that so much of life's wine could fill ten men let alone one." He shook his head, then spun away, ran to the rail, and vomited into the churning sea.

King Alonso waited for his brother to return and placed a steadying hand on his shoulder. He kept it there while he looked around, his eyes fierce. "Who has *done* this?"

No one spoke.

"Damn your eyes, the lot of you," roared the king. "A man has been savagely murdered on a small ship. We are all struggling to survive a storm and now *this!* I want answers and I want them now."

The crew, all who were on deck—and by then it was everyone, including all the passengers save the sleeping Prospero—milled and stared. They looked frightened and no one dared meet anyone else's eyes.

Finally, a ship's boy—trembling with fear—took a tiny step forward. "Sir…?"

The sailing master cuffed him above the ear. "Damn your eyes, boy. You call him *Your Majesty* or *Your Royal Highness* or you damn well keep your gob shut."

But Alonso raised his hand. "Peace, my friend," he said to the master. "Let the child speak."

The boy, rubbing his head with one hand and pawing tears from his eyes with the other, looked sheepishly at the king.

"Excuse me your royal himself," said the boy, but no one corrected him. "I think I…I mean I'm sure I think I saw…"

"Saw what, lad?" asked the king gently. "Speak true and fear not."

"I saw a…a shadow in the companionway," said the boy. "Near the surgeon's cabin."

"When was this?"

"Just after six bells in the middle watch. When the thunder was booming so loud as fit to break my head."

The master said, "That is scant forty minutes ago, my liege."

"Surely," said Sebastian, "no man could…*do*…what was done and not be painted head to toe in blood."

"But we are all here," said the boatswain, looking around. "And no one is bloody or shows a drop on their face or clothes."

Ferdinand spoke for the first time. "My father," he said to the king, "I almost dare not say it, but there *is* one missing from our company."

Miranda caught his meaning, and her eyes went huge and round. "Say it not, my husband."

"I must, my love," said the young prince. "Your father is not here and with such a crime there is no one removed from suspicion until the truth exonerates him."

"But husband!" cried the girl, "he is my father. He is the one who saved us all from that island. He gave up everything to come away with us and blessed our marriage. How could you ever think so ill of him?"

Ferdinand took her hands in his and squeezed them. "I do not accuse him, my love. Never that. But in fairness everyone should be examined if only to prove their innocence beyond doubt."

"Yes," said the king, "we should. Master, see it done and if any of my soldiers may be of service, command them as I would. Adrian, Francisco, oversee the search."

The two senior courtiers bowed, and each drew a knife.

Before they began their search of the ship, the two courtiers and the boatswain made each of the crew stand with arms out in cruciform as their rain-sodden clothes and bodies were examined. It took a quarter of an hour, but the crew was declared free of incriminating stains.

"There must be a stowaway aboard," cried Miranda.

"Who could there be?" asked Adrian. "Everyone who was on this ship or with us on the island is right here, save your father, and you say that he has dosed himself to sleep."

Miranda stiffened. "Perhaps that scoundrel Caliban sneaked aboard."

"If so," said the king, "we will hunt him down and hang him from the highest spar on the ship."

The party broke apart. Adrian and Francisco consulted with the master and picked six men each. They went to opposite ends of the ship and, knives in hand, descended into the heart of the vessel.

Hunting.

5

It heard them coming, the groups of men with their bright blades and red hearts.

As the boots thundered down the tilting companion ladders it moved away from them, found an unlocked door, and vanished inside a cabin.

6

Miranda fled below with Ferdinand, though there was now some tension between them. It curdled the food in her stomach and set fire to her cheeks. They paused in the passage between the rows of tiny cabins. Theirs was on one side and Prospero's across from it, the door shut.

"You look so distressed," said Ferdinand, his voice soft with concern as he reached for the door to their cabin. "You should rest, my dear one."

"No!" she cried. "I need to check on Father."

Ferdinand touched her arm. "My love, leave him be. I do not for a moment think he is involved in this horror."

Adrian said, "Innocent he may be, my prince, but your wife is quite correct. We must needs look in upon Prospero."

But Miranda wheeled on him. "*Look* in, yes. Disturb him or accuse him, no. I will not allow that."

"My lady," said the older courtier, "it is the king's wish that we are thorough in this investigation. We must ask him some questions. If any are exempted, then the truth may elude us."

Miranda expected Ferdinand to side with Adrian, but he shifted to stand between his wife and the courtier. "Prospero is the author of our survival and he has labored for days fighting the storm."

"Fighting it or causing it?" asked Adrian. He was a kindly man, but these were not kindly times. His face had become stern during the endless hours of the storm, and now it was set in a scowl tainted by fear and suspicion.

"Dare you ask such a thing?" demanded Miranda.

"I dare anything in the service of my king, my lady. No slight is intended for this is not a matter of politics but of a response to a crisis. Surely you must understand."

Miranda and Ferdinand argued with him for several minutes, but Adrian was steadfast. He ended the debate by stating with certainty that his own life was forfeit for failing to obey the will of the king. Ferdinand sighed and nodded.

"He is right, my love," he said to Miranda.

"My father's men will sort this out, my love," he said. "Although he is my father, we are all subjects of the king. This we must do."

Miranda had tears of anger glistening in her eyes, but at length she nodded and stepped away from her father's door.

"Be gentle, I beg," she said.

That simple entreaty softened the stern look on Adrian's face and he nodded. "I will," he promised.

With that, he tapped lightly on the door. Once, and then again. When there was no answer, he opened the door and let the lantern light in the passage spill into the room. There, sprawled upon the bed as still as one dead, lay Prospero. He still wore the robes he had worn since boarding the ship.

"You see?" declared Miranda. "He sleeps in the grace of God. And look, his clothes are unstained and there is no drop of blood on his hands or any on the floor. Could a man who has done such villainy as was described be thus unmarked by it?"

Adrian called Prospero's name several times, but the sorcerer slept on and did not stir. Greatly relieved, the three of them withdrew and closed the door.

"Your pardon, my lady, my prince," said Adrian as he withdrew, taking his men with him.

7

Miranda and Ferdinand lay entangled in the swaying cot, which hung from the ceiling on four stout ropes. For all its movement, it was the most fixed point on the storm-tossed ship. Miranda had to keep her eyes closed, though, because the difference in motion of slung cot and ship made her stomach want to rebel. She closed her eyes and burrowed against her husband's chest.

Sleep was an impossibility, though. That's what she told him, but his answer was a soft, buzzing snore. It amazed her that he could sleep so easily.

She shook her husband to try and rouse him, but he groaned softly and turned his head to the wall.

"I am all alone," she murmured, wondering how deeply her meaning went. And yet…she loved this handsome young man. It hardly mattered that they had known each other for a handful of days, or even that he was the first person other than her father she had ever known. Love had been its own raging storm and it swept through her—and him—and shipwrecked them both on an island of passion.

So strange a thing that was.

They had yet to consummate their love, but a storm-tossed ship was hardly a fitting marriage bed for a prince and the daughter of the newly reinstated Duke of Milan. Soon, she thought, and then snuggled close and tried to imagine what that night would be like. Miranda understood what sex was, for the island was filled with animals and husbandry of that kind was how they raised their food. But rutting like pigs or hounds was unseemly. Surely between lovers it would be gentle, like the tender encounters spoken of in poetry.

She wished they were in a palace in faraway Naples. In a grand bed with satin sheets and brocade pillows and no storm howling outside the window.

That made her turn toward the small porthole as if she could see the sundrenched hills of Italy—a place she knew only from Father's stories. The porthole was small, but she could see the slanting rain whipping past.

Then suddenly that rain was obscured and for a moment she thought it was a dark cloud or the back of some seaman.

But only for a moment…

Then she saw what truly filled the tiny opening.

It was a face.

And her blood turned at once to ice in her veins. A scream rose in her throat, but it caught there, choking her, the trapped air in her lungs turning to poison.

The face.

Oh god, that hideous face.

Miranda's chest seized tight and she thought her heart would burst if she did not scream. She had to scream. She must scream or die.

And then it tore from her, ripping the lining of her throat as the scream burst out, louder than the storm. A rising, wailing shriek of total terror.

As, through the porthole, the grinning, leering, awful face of the monster glared dark joy and hatred at her.

8

Ferdinand sprang away with such force that it overbalanced the swaying bed and they both spilled out, turning Miranda's scream of horror to a sharper cry of pain as he landed atop her.

That moment their door burst open and two of the king's soldiers leapt inside, swords drawn and eyes wild. They saw Miranda in her shift and Prince Ferdinand naked to the waist, and they paused, uncertainty warring with their fear that some terrible harm had come.

Ferdinand saw them and snarled them back, his voice thick with fury. He shot to his feet and got up in their faces, fists balled, eyes wild.

"My wife is undressed," he roared, "and you fools barge in? Get out or I'll have you flogged."

They stumbled backward but crashed into the king himself and his courtiers. The small doorway became a tangle of arms and legs, of desperate apologies and regal threats. Adrian and Francisco waded in and pried the tangle apart, helping the king regain his balance and thrusting the two hapless soldiers out into the hall, where Gonzalo chased them down the passage with kicks and threats.

"My son," gasped Alonso, "what is amiss?"

But Ferdinand turned to Miranda. "My love…did you have a nightmare? I mean, how could you not after all that has—"

"No!" she cut in. "It was the monster. He was at the window."

They glanced at the porthole, which was empty of all except the steady rain outside.

"Monster…?" echoed Sebastian. "What do you mean? Did you see the face of the killer?"

"I did," she said, clinging to Ferdinand.

"Who was it?" demanded the king. "Tell us and we will hunt him down."

Miranda was so shaken that it took all her courage to even speak the name.

"He is here aboard this ship. I saw his face…that awful, grinning face."

"Name him," commanded Alonso.

"*Caliban!*"

9

The sailors and soldiers searched the ship. Every cabin and sail locker, the shot locker and powder room, and all through the hold.

"Nothing and no one," growled Sebastian. "This is madness."

A storm as fierce as the one above raged in the king's eyes. "Where is Duke Prospero?"

"I am here," called a voice and they all turned to see the sorcerer climbing up through the hatch. "The sound of shouting and the thump of boots everywhere tore me from sleep. What's amiss?"

Miranda flew to him and buried her face against the side of his throat. "Oh father, it's awful! That monster has pursued us."

"Monster?" asked Prospero, his eyes still cloudy with the draught he'd taken. "Speak plain, girl."

But it was Adrian who explained the situation, laying out the details quickly and concisely. Prospero's face drained of color even as his eyes sharpened to clarity. He looked about as if expecting to see Caliban leering from behind the wheelhouse.

"How came this to be?" he wondered. "He was not in our boat and surely even he could not swim out and board without being seen. Every man of this crew was at the rail when we came aboard because the king was in our company."

"We do not know that it was Caliban," said Alonso.

"It *was*," cried Miranda. "I saw him leer at me through my cabin window."

"And yet two of my men were stationed on that part of the deck," said the sailing master. "Beg pardon, good lady and esteemed sirs, but we have checked everything from stem to stern. Not a cockroach or a rat could have hidden from us."

"Then look again," snapped Miranda. "For I saw him. Do you say I lie?"

"Hush, hush," said Ferdinand. "My love, we had been sleeping and each troubled in our dreams after all that happened on the island and then here aboard. I know I dreamed of skulking fiends and no doubt you as well. It was that, a lingering phantom from a dream that filled your mind and told lies to your senses as you woke. Only that and nothing more."

"I saw him," she repeated, but now doubt had stolen the emphasis from her word.

"You have the truth of it," said Prospero. "Caliban's dearest wish was to be king of his island, and we have left it to him. He is there now and many leagues behind us. As is Ariel, who I have likewise freed from bondage and who shares that island with Caliban. You are safe from them both, my daughter."

"Safe? *Safe?*" she cried. "While you slept there has been a terrible murder. Who but Caliban could have done such a thing?"

Prospero turned to the king. "Who indeed, my liege?"

Alonso stood with feet braced wide on the slanting deck, his face lashed with rain. "We have searched and searched, and no culprit has been found. There is a madman among us, and he will be found out." He paused. "You speak also of Ariel, that demon who so confounded us on your orders. He is a creature of great and terrible magic. Could he have stolen aboard?"

"How, father?" asked Ferdinand. "And why? Prospero freed him, and surely his gratitude would encourage him to protect us were he here."

"Agreed," said Prospero. "Ariel was a good and trusted servant who loved me and my daughter. He did much in my service and I freed him with a glad heart."

"Was it so?" asked Miranda. "You dangled freedom before him like water to someone parched and dying of thirst. Time and again you said you would release him from bond and then asked more of him. More and more. It was only when you had gotten all you wanted and knew that your dukedom was restored and the king welcoming you back into his confidence that you freed the sprite. You believed his smiles and his gratitude, but he was ever a trickster and I trusted him not."

"Those are hard words," said Ferdinand. "Peace, my love, for we are free of him and he is free on that island."

"That is the point, my son," said Alonso. "How sure are you that Ariel did not swim out and climb aboard? Sprites, as we all have learned, are powerful and clever."

"Sprites cannot cross running water," said Prospero. "This is known about creatures such as he. Else Ariel would have fled that island ages before. And God save anyone should he find a way to leave the island, for he—in his wrath—would be a plague in Europe." He shook his head. "No, this is neither Caliban the monster nor Ariel the sprite. If murder has been done, then we need look for a human hand, even if it means that one among us is that fiend."

"Father," said Ferdinand, "I have to agree with Prospero. Would a sprite need so common a thing as a knife? He is a trickster, as my wife says, and would have a thousand ways to do evil. So, we must look to each other for the culprit, and be wary and vigilant."

The king considered, then turned to Prospero. "My friend,"

he said, "even with your staff broken and your powers reduced, can you with your magic help us discern the identity of the killer aboard?"

Prospero felt the weight of every gaze upon him and he turned and staggered toward the rail, leaning on it as the ship rose and fell on the stormy rollers. He brooded on the waves for a long moment.

"I am weary," he said. "Fighting the storm these past days has drained me and I am empty of strength." He turned. "Let me take another draught and sleep through a whole day. Once I am restored, I will summon what powers I have and help you find the killer. This I swear to you, my king. This I swear, my daughter, for your life is my life, and I have promised long ago to keep you safe. Let me sleep and become powerful again and then we will hunt this fiend and put him down like the dog he is. So say I."

King Alonso went over, slipping on the sea-washed deck but regaining his balance. He laid his hand on Prospero's shoulder.

"Then sleep and when you wake you shall save us all."

Ferdinand wrapped Miranda in his arms, leaned close, and murmured to her. "All will be well, my love. For we have mighty Prospero to protect us. Now, let us return to our cabin. Soldiers will be posted in the passage and sailors outside on the deck. We will be safe together."

10

Miranda and Ferdinand did retire, and despite—or perhaps because of—the fear and stress and uncertainty, they clung together in passionate embrace. Their sweet kisses, slow and almost shy at first, caught fire and soon kisses bred touches, and touches became a desperate fumbling at ties and fastenings.

In the swaying cot, as the storm raged without, Ferdinand undressed his bride and they made love for hours upon hours. She was so shy, so innocent even with her knowledge of the mating of birds and deer and hounds and all. This was different. There was pain—a little. And blood. But there was intensity and heat, there were cries and moans and gasps. And there was pleasure. So much and in ways that were unlike anything Miranda had ever imagined. Ferdinand, despite his youth, seemed wise in the ways of flesh and he awakened within her a sensual response that grew into a passion that exceeded the intensity of the storm. When their lovemaking drove her up to the crest of her own towering wave, she grabbed a pillow and jammed it against her mouth, biting it, screaming into it lest the guards and sailors hear her.

She came like that again and again and again until she was spent and sodden and breathless. Ferdinand, still inside of her, kissed her flushed face and whispered sweet love words to her.

"You are mine forever," he murmured. "We will make love every day and every night and passion will be our kingdom to rule. Even now my seed takes hold within your womb and the child you bear will one day sit upon the throne of Naples. This I promise, my love."

She looked up at him, seeing him through tears of joy and passion. "I love you now and will love you forever."

"Yes," whispered Ferdinand. "You will."

11

The thing moved down the passage, silent as a ghost.

The soldiers did not see him at all.

And woe to all aboard that this was the truth.

12

The cry went up like a shriek.

"*Murder! Red murder!*"

At once there was a response as the bare feet of sailors and the leather boots of soldiers came pounding down the companion ladders. Mixed among them were the softer shoes of court nobles. They clustered together at one end of the passageway.

Adrian stood there, his face gone death pale and his eyes filled with horror and pain. He could not speak, but merely pointed.

Antonio, brother to Prospero, the honest old councilor Gonzalo, and Lord Adrian, Lord Francisco and the jester Trinculo, and even the drunken butler Stephano. All were there and all cried out in grief and horror and despair. They fought to get into the room to see what was amiss for that cabin had been the sailing master's but had been turned over to King Alonso.

The king's cabin it had been, but now it was an abattoir.

It was awash in blood. The walls and even the ceiling was splashed with crimson, and it ran down in crooked lines to pool on the floor around the *thing* that lay there. Not a body, but a ruin. Not a whole form, but islands of bloody meat scattered from wall to wall; and few parts recognizable as having come from a man. It was only the head that seemed untouched and whole, and even free of blood. That head hung by its hair, which was tied to a beam. As the ship swayed, the head of King Alonso swayed in counterpoint, glassy eyes filled with a never-ending shock. Those eyes seemed to look at one person and then another, and at no one at all.

Trinculo fell to his knees and beat his hands upon the floor.

Sebastian tore out his knife and made as if to cut his brother's head down, but grief and horror stalled him in place, and after a moment his fingers twitched and the dagger fell to clatter wetly on the gory decking.

There were fresh steps in the hall and after a moment Ferdinand entered, dressed only in a nightshirt.

"What has happened?" he cried. "Wait…that is my father's cabin and…and…"

When he saw what was inside, the prince collapsed onto his knees and sent up a howl that shook every timber on the ship.

"*Father!*"

Adrian knelt beside him, his arm around the young man's shoulders. Together they wept.

Then Trinculo, of all of them, turned and looked at the blood and frowned. He raised a trembling finger.

"Look and tell me if I see what I see," said the jester. "For in truth that is not the footprint of my fallen master."

They all turned to follow his finger and saw there, near the doorway and half obscured by the shoes of the courtiers, a trail of footprints. They led to the cabin door. The men stepped quickly back so the full trail could be seen, and though the blood faded greatly from one step to the next, the direction was clear.

"The killer went that way," said Trinculo. "For who else would have been here? Oh, god, let us find the monster who did this! All jest and humor, all love lies slain and we must have blood for blood!"

"The fool speaks truth," growled Ferdinand, springing to his feet. His face was dark with rage. "Find me this killer and let us avenge my father and our king!"

The gathered men became a mob with drawn blades, hard eyes, and murder in their hearts. They rushed into the passage, bumping and elbowing each other as they fought to be first to find the villain.

The footprints faded out but not before they reached the very end of the hall and the last print—only a faint shadow of red that had been overlooked in the darkness—was revealed now to lantern light and desperate eyes. They could see only the ghost of the heel for a closed door cut off the rest.

They stopped there as both the answer and the enormity of the truth reared up before them.

"No," said Ferdinand, aghast. "It cannot be. It *must not be.*"

Trinculo looked confused. "God save my soul…has the villain slain Prospero, too?"

Sebastian pushed past them both, but paused and half-turned to Adrian and the soldiers, who looked wild and heartbroken that their master had died and they had been unable to do a thing.

"If I am right, and I pray to heaven I am not," he said quietly, "then stand ready for we may need to stand against more than a killer's steel."

Adrian looked stricken, but he nodded his understanding. "What must be done will be done and may the angels in heaven protect us all."

"We are ready, my lord," said the captain of the soldiers. He had drawn his sword and its edge gleamed with silver fire.

Sebastian crossed himself—and then everyone in the passage did the same—and he turned the handle of the door. It swung open on silent hinges and Sebastian crept into the tiny room with the others following.

Prospero lay upon the bed, his chest rising and falling with deep sleep.

There were faint red footprints on the floor, but here and there were drops of scarlet on the decking. And more of that unholy color was smeared from fingernails to the elbow of his right hand. Still more was spackled across the sorcerer's broad chest, and two drops burned as bright as rubies on his cheek.

They all stared at the blood.

But their eyes were drawn inevitably and completely to the thing that was clutched in the sleeping man's hand.

A knife.

Sharp and wicked and covered from point to pommel in bright blood.

For a long time, nearly a full minute, they stood in a cluster, stilled to silence by shock and horror and ultimately by understanding.

Only one word was spoken. Ferdinand whispered it.

"No…"

But they all knew the answer was yes.

And, like a pack of wolves, they fell on Prospero.

13

It was a long and terrible night.

The winds howled like demons and the sea went mad in its rage. The body of Prospero hung from a yardarm, his slashed and beaten corpse swaying as the ship rolled in the tempest.

No one spoke, but the wail of Miranda's grief rose like a banshee and its force seemed to tear the storm apart. The rain, having washed the murderer's body of blood, slackened to a drizzle and then to nothing. The winds recoiled from the girl's screams and fled, leaving the ship wallowing in seas that gradually lost their fury. Even the waves smoothed out and let the ship float, restless and weary, in calmer waters.

Ferdinand stood with his father's courtiers.

"Look," he said, "the storm has died with the murderer. Proof that it was his creation to deceive us and distract us from his crimes."

"Aye," said Antonio. "Although he was my brother, I have long suspected that his heart was black. We were so caught up with gratitude for his rescuing us from that accursed island that we too easily forgave his having shipwrecked us there. This—all of this—was his plan to get revenge on King Alonso."

"Without doubt you would have been his next victim," said Ferdinand. "For Miranda has told me how he hated you and was consumed by thoughts of revenge."

Adrian said, "I had been willing to forgive him, too, for I thought his exile had been punishment enough, and believed—as we all did—in his repentance. More fool me for having that faith."

Another of Miranda's wails spiraled up from below and the men looked in that direction, their hearts heavy.

"It will be hard for her," said Antonio, "and for a long time. Ferdinand…you will be king now, and she your queen. I know you will give her the love and care that she needs, for she is quite the innocent here. I, for one, will never tax her for her father's crimes."

"Nor I," said the prince. "She is my love, and I will go below and offer what comfort is mine to give. It is possible she is with child now, and I will make sure she has every comfort, every easement, every distraction to soothe her broken heart. And if love can heal, as the poets say, she will have enough and more."

The men all shook his hand and bowed to him and wished the young prince and his heartbroken wife—soon to be king and queen of Naples—god's mercy.

Ferdinand, heavy of heart, took his leave and went below.

He knocked once, very lightly, and then entered the cabin. Miranda was huddled in the swaying bed. She had torn her nightdress and even handfuls of her hair. There were bruises on her face and shoulders where—in the throes of grief—she had beaten herself.

"My love," said the prince, rushing to her. "Oh, my sweet love. I am here. Weep upon me. Drown me with your tears if you must, for I love you and will never leave you."

He climbed onto the cot and she flew into his arms, clutching at him, pulling herself into the shelter of his embrace. Her words were a confused tumble of apologies and denials, of pleading and prayers.

WHEN I WAKED I CRIED TO DREAM AGAIN

Every now and then a scream would tear itself from her. Twice he had to hold her arms to keep her from doing herself more harm.

"Shhhh," he soothed. "Shhh, my lady, my princess, my queen. Be at peace, be at ease. Sleep and I will watch over you."

"Sleep? *Sleep?* How can I ever sleep again for my life is hell and the world itself is broken. I will never sleep again. I will never know peace again."

"No, my love," soothed the prince, "you will sleep, and in that sleep your heart will find its peace. And then we will sail home to Naples, where I will be crowned king and you will be by my side forever. We will have many beautiful children and they will grow up strong and powerful and the world will be ours."

"I don't care about any of that," she wept, "I want—"

"Shhhh," he said and as he murmured he passed his hand over her face. Immediately, all of the tension went out of Miranda, and she settled back against him, her body totally slack. He laid her down on the mattress and smiled at her.

It was a strange little smile. Not at all like Ferdinand's.

As he smiled that face fell away and another took its place. Eyes, vastly old and strange, watched the girl sleep. He touched her stomach and felt the new life there. Strange life. Strange, like his own.

"Sleep, my dear," said Ariel in a soft voice. "Sleep, my queen."

She slept and he held her, and the ship sailed on, pushed now by a steady breeze toward Naples. All the while, Ariel never stopped smiling.

All Hallowed Tides Break Upon These Shores

(after *The Tempest*)

Marisca Pichette

In my salt-stained house I keep shadows as pets. My moonlight siblings wear gowns of midnight, their whispers filling the cracks between creaking floorboards. I have chandeliers dripping dark spots that never touch me—but they may touch you. Add freckles to your goosebumps, memories to your scars. Remind you what lingers on the underside of your fragile skin.

This tidal house was built inside a cave that never sees starlight. Each board was wrapped in vellum, each nail soaked in pitch. Iron comes from more than mountains. You taste it on this tempest-night, the night where your deepest wish may be granted—if you live till morning.

I invite you in, beckoning with my clean, clean hands. Iron on the air, pitch in your lungs. Sweet and sharp, crystalline—but not brittle. Nothing under this roof is vulnerable to breaking. Except you, of course.

Shipwrecked, nerve-wracked. You sailed to my island knowing the risks, tasting the gains. How wet and cold you look, shivering before me. Sailor or passenger, it doesn't matter. I treat all visitors equally.

Now you're here, let me give you a tour. It begins with your scalp.

Shards of moonlight pierce the air around us. I see you flinch, but you don't run—though the door is just behind. You know this is your chance, our blessing.

76

Stand still. With the distant chime of darkness, let the test begin.

My moonlit siblings take your hair, pluck it strand by strand from your tender head. They ask you questions with each pluck, pluck, pluck. You hear them in the space between your eyes.

A bracelet or a necklace?

A basket or a brace?

Sweaters for rats or socks for spiders?

Collars for cats, for horses—bridles?

I dance to their asking. When all your hair is gone, all the choices given, you must pick the fate of your locks.

I ask, "What do you choose: adornment or usefulness?" This is just the first step, one of many. In that way, what you decide is of little importance.

But your first step will tell us where all the others are bound. And considering what you seek…be meticulous.

"Basket," you choose. My siblings intertwine your strands, weaving your choice into being. Two hours have passed now. You are tired, frozen. It takes a long time, losing your hair.

The basket takes minutes. When my siblings have finished, they place it in your shaking, calloused hands.

You cannot alter things now.

I see in your eyes that you comfort yourself, bald and bleeding, with the notion that your hair will return, in time. You do not know what else you stand to lose, here beneath my ageless roof, on the cusp of November's chill.

We have time. You do not.

Now you are ready to proceed. My siblings leave us, and we are almost alone. But in this house, there is no solitude.

The walls have eyes, you know. I see you glancing, blinking, waiting for them to blink back. They will not return your gaze. They are dead.

The eyes are not mine. They belong to the house, to him who cast away his staff and grew into beams and foundations on this rocky coast. He lives still, spreading to surround us, swallowing us whole.

Do you feel him breathing? Do you feel his charms? He never left. He never granted the freedom he promised.

Even houses need to collect things.

I collect things as well. They used to be shells. They used to be sailors. No longer.

But you are tired, and cold. Let us not linger here. First, let me show you my favorite room.

Through double doors that smell of sticky iron, carved in serpent shapes, I bring us into the dining room. The table is set for infinity, but you see just twelve chairs. Their leather is imperfect, hairy. I pull out one at the head of the table and sit. You are obliged to follow, setting your new basket on the table.

We sit in silence for some time. Your scalp clots. Your hands shake less. I sense you longing for sleep—but we don't sleep here.

Here, we dine.

A shadow enters through the doors on the end of an intestinal lead. You don't look at it, but watch me. You learned something, then, before coming here.

When my pet reaches my chair, I remove my shoes and drop them into its mouth. It comes to you. You repeat the motion, removing your shoes and placing them into its darkness. It leaves, intestines dragging behind.

My second pet enters in a swirl of black. It comes to me, and I feed it my gown. You remove your clothes after me, dropping them into darkness. It leaves.

My third pet drags a lead of poison ivy. I feed it my jewelry. You do the same.

We are both naked, now.

I rise, drops raining from the chandeliers above us. They hit your skin and leave tracks like open wounds. They miss me, always.

I will show you the rest of the house, but stay a moment.

Do you feel it: the hunger? But no. You are just a living thing. Your senses limit your perception.

In exchange for the sky, I took this house. Bartering for my freedom, I sold off my family.

When I finally lead us away from this room, the eyes on the walls watch.

Your steps are quieter now that you have no shoes. The house likes this. It secretes liquid from its boards, wetting your soles. The puddles are warm, like saliva. I notice how you try to avoid them, before realizing that they are everywhere. You watch me closely now, mimicking where I place my feet. You are smart. You have much to give.

Perhaps it will earn you what you seek, if you are strong enough.

I show you the library next, its door covered by a curtain of ivory beads. You think they are ivory. You are watching me too closely to see the truth.

In the library, I house the collections of my siblings.

Boxes fill shelves, stained dark by their contents. You are uneasy in here, even more than the last room. I feel your fear, but I feel also your determination. You believe you will make it through all the rooms, emerge on the other side of my house, and ask me a question I can't refuse. I see you watching me, hoping.

Watch all you like. I can't tell you what will remain of you when we are finished. When the house has claimed its piece, when he has had his fill.

I pull an empty box from the shelves. It is small; this makes you less afraid.

"Your hair," I say.

You hold up the basket.

"No. The rest."

I hand you tweezers. I sit.

You begin with the hairs on your arms. Now, your legs. Your groin. Where you can't reach, I help. Pluck. Pluck.

Your back, your armpits, your face.

Pluck. Pluck.

We fill the box. When we've finished, you're red all over—no trace of your true color remaining. The house likes you this way. I feel its pleasure as clearly as I feel your pain.

I place the box back on the shelf. It will add to my siblings' collections.

You are lucky they didn't ask for something else.

I lead you limping from the library through a soaking hallway. Shadow pets cross our path, neither touching nor being touched. Do you wonder which has your clothes? Do you wonder which was once like you, or me? I know some of them, but so many are beyond recognition.

Sycorax's children, island-born. Island-slain. None of us looked the same, after he became the house.

I bring you to the kitchen. The tiles are abyssal green. "You are hungry," I tell you. Many hours have passed now. Soon, you will need sleep. Perhaps you already do. Perhaps you long for it, like you long for your hair.

We sit, you opposite me, your basket in between. Moonlight hands deliver platters of dust. There are no spoons, no water glasses. I scoop my dust into my tasteless mouth. You copy my actions, though you choke for want of water. Still, you eat until your plate is clear.

Not all who come here have passed this test. Some who refused to eat ended their journey in this room.

You know, looking at me, that it is not so easy as a single course. More platters arrive in the hands of my siblings. These hold sand. We eat.

Your mouth bleeds. I admire you. What question burns in your bloody throat? I almost hope you have a chance to ask it, on the other side. Maybe you are dying. Maybe a lover. Maybe a parent, child.

Or have they already passed, and what you long for is resurrection? That, too, can be arranged. But first you must pass the tests.

When you've finished all courses, grit in your teeth, I stand and lead you from the kitchen down a hallway ankle-deep in hungry liquid. You stumble in my wake, basket clutched to your naked chest.

Upstairs, to the bedrooms. You have performed well. I offer you a choice between a bed of nails, or embers. You choose the embers. Do you long to impress me? You've already made it further than most.

I lie on the nails, lulled by the scent of your smoking skin.

When one hour has passed, I rouse you. Blood has dried your mouth shut.

"We have one more room to visit."

In the dripping hallway, you drop to your knees. You drink the house's liquid, wash yourself in viscosity, charred skin floating away. I admit, this surprises me. I didn't expect you to risk this—to deviate from my actions so dramatically.

I watch you, small and shaking. I feel the pleasure of the house around us. He loves so much to touch you, to be touched in return. More liquid seeps from the boards, washing across your burned back, caressing. The house wants you to stay, face submerged. He wants you to sleep.

You rise as suddenly as you fell, gasping. *Close.* You almost failed. My disappointment drizzles away. Another pass.

"One room more."

I feel your desperation keenly now. You don't know what you drank, whether it will stop you from leaving. You're wondering perhaps if others have done as you have. I can say that, yes, a few have folded to that temptation.

What does it mean for you? That I cannot answer, until after the last room.

I bring you into a hall of broken glass. You hesitate only a moment before stepping in, blood flowing gladly from your feet. I walk atop the shards without incident; I do not cut. I do not bleed.

In the center of the last room, I turn to you, wet and torn, tears marshaling in your eyes. "Scream."

You stare at me. Maybe you don't believe me. Maybe you're afraid that, after coming so far, I would seek to trick you by ordering you into wrong.

Know you not that I cannot lie in this house? Know you not that each ceiling has ears, harvested from visitors like you?

Know you not that my fate is as bound to his will as yours?

"Scream," I tell you again. "Scream until you can't."

You do as I say. Opening your scabbed mouth wide, you wail. Your scream fills the hall, and I close my eyes. We each have our collections, here in the house that doesn't age.

Mine lives here, in this room. I want your voice.

You scream, and scream, and scream. Mirrors crack, shatter to the floor, adding their angles to the confusion under our feet.

Your screams hold no words. Just keening, shrill and exhausted and full of fear. I love it. I know it.

I love you.

It takes a long time to exorcize your voice. When all the mirrors have shattered, and your breath has run out, you wheeze at last into silence. I open my eyes and turn away, heading to the last door.

You follow me on bleeding feet.

We step out into the night. Sand absorbs your blood. In the dark, you turn to look at me once more.

I see your disbelief. You didn't expect to make it through, arriving with this much of your body intact on the other side. Below us, the sea throws itself against the rocks, breaking again and again, yet always remaining whole.

Starlight glitters in your eyes. I ask you now for the question you came with, weighing so heavy it demanded your hair, your skin, your blood.

"If there is anything you wish for, state it now."

You open your mouth, but no words come. I have taken your voice. I see the hideous realization in your eyes, the way you look frantically back at the door. Your jaw works, and you know that I have you: here between the house and the sea.

"If you have no request, you have a final choice." I spread my arms. "Stay with us, or join the waves."

You look from one to the other. In anguish, you hold up your basket of hair. *Did it mean anything?* you ask with your eyes.

I know that look. I saw it in Caliban first, and all those since. I wore it once, on my own fair face.

"It means he was always in control. The house had you, from the moment you stepped inside." I know the fears running through your mind, the impossible choice before you. Will you stay, or jump?

Outside, the house's ears can't hear us. The house's eyes can't see us. I lean close to you, my ageless lips brushing your ear.

"Jump."

You look at me, tears on your cheeks: saltwater reaching for the sea.

Most choose to jump. It's the easy choice. But staying—that

takes courage. It's painful, but you can rise from a pet to a sibling, and maybe, one day...

You could be like me.

I close my eyes. When I open them, you are gone, waves crashing over more than rocks. I pick up your basket. I will add it to the library, and remember you.

You meant more than the others. The house liked you. Looking into your eyes, I saw the sky I'd almost forgotten. I heard my own pain in your voice. I may have loved you, or I may have loved the world you lost in the storm. It doesn't matter now.

If you'd chosen differently, you would have done well. You may have even one day replaced me. And despite all my love, I can't let anyone threaten my position within these ageless walls. I've sacrificed too much.

I walk back inside alone, my master's door locking behind me.

(based on the character of Caliban from The Tempest)

Steve Rasnic Tem

Edna heard the shuffling and the giggling on her front porch with dismay. She suspected it was those young hoodlums again, the neighborhood terrorists. Her Shih Tzu Tingling began barking. She hugged him to comfort them both.

They'd harassed her before, simply because she was an old woman living alone, who refused to put up with their foolishness. More than once they'd roughhoused on her lawn, trampling her carefully curated flowerbeds. Of course, she called the police, and of course, the police did nothing.

She waited until they left—a confrontation might be dangerous. Then she opened her door. She almost had a heart attack. They'd spray-painted an enormous yellow X across her beautiful, polished front door. Were they cancelling her? She'd heard about cancelling people—was this what they meant?

She felt a pain in her stomach. The young hoodlums had given her an ulcer. She supposed it was a small pain, a discomfort, but it had persisted for weeks.

It was the worst timing. Her new renter would be arriving soon, an injured man requiring a quiet place to recuperate. What would he think of the neighborhood? What would he think of her?

She surveyed the street looking for the perpetrators. The schools had let out and there were students in the street and on the sidewalk, headed for the old library. Many of them carried backpacks of sufficient size to hold numerous cans of spray paint. Many were laughing and chasing each other. She didn't see anything funny about destroying property.

"I can clean that for you." The voice was low and muffled. "Expunge it completely. I have the necessary skills."

Edna glanced around. At first she didn't see him, then spied him standing in the shadows just beyond the left edge of the porch. He wore a long charcoal-colored coat and matching scarf, a floppy hat pulled low in front. What little of his face she could see was wrapped in bandages, leaving only small holes for the mouth and one eye. "Mr. Caliban? Is that you?" When he'd told her over the phone he was damaged, she'd imagined nothing like this.

Before she knew it, he was up on her porch, inches away. He was short—an inch or two shorter than her—and he stood with a pronounced twist, one shoulder lower than the other. He smelled vaguely of spicy fish. She reached out to touch him but stopped herself in time. What was she thinking?

"At your service," he said. "I saw the ones responsible running away. Perhaps next time I can catch them for you, brain them, batter their skulls."

Caliban did not have a short person's voice, but that was a silly thought. Edna admonished herself, saying a silent prayer asking for forgiveness. He did have an accent, but she couldn't place it. Italian maybe. One of those hot countries. But as much as she liked the sentiment of *brain them and batter their skulls*, it frightened her to hear him say it aloud.

Tingling came rushing out, stopped, and stared at the man, then began barking furiously.

"I'm so sorry. He barks at—" She stopped herself, about to say *trouble*. "Hush, Tingling! Your luggage," she said, "is it coming later?"

He stepped aside to show her the wheeled suitcase with an attached book tote he'd been dragging behind him. "I travel light. A change of clothes and some medical supplies, and of course my books. Do you enjoy reading, Missus Gerber?"

"It's miss, and of course I read." She'd just lied to him. She'd never had the patience for reading, but he didn't need to know that.

Tingling sniffed the suitcase, the edge of Mr. Caliban's coat, his shoes. He reached down and petted her. The dog allowed it. It would be nice having a man in the house, especially one who spoke so politely. It had been years.

Edna noticed the crazy lady across the street staring at them from her front door. She'd drawn a red oval around her mouth as if she'd forgotten where her lips were. Edna stared back defiantly. Edna wasn't sure where the woman was from, but she certainly wasn't American.

The rental included one meal per day, dinner with her at the kitchen table. Edna could hear Caliban moving about—upstairs, on the steps, in her living room, outside—while she cooked. It made her nervous. He was everywhere at once. When dinner was ready, she went looking for him. She found him on the porch, gazing at her now-pristine door.

"How did you do that?" She could find no traces of paint, and if anything, the door looked nicer than before the vandalism.

"I have a knack," he said. He raised a gloved hand. It occurred to her then he'd been wearing gloves this entire time. "I believe I've inherited it from my mother." He'd removed his outer garb and now wore a loose-fitting shirt and sweatpants. His head was completely wrapped in bandages, like that old movie; what was it? *The Invisible Man*, yes. Claude Rains.

He continued to wear the gloves at dinner, which seemed outlandish to her. Was this the way they behaved where he was from? She'd made a nice stew, but she never anticipated she'd be so repulsed watching him eat. He stained his bandages getting the food through that little hole. It looked as if he'd been eating blood, or mud, or worse. A dull gray eye peered at her through the other, smaller hole, like that of a dead fish.

"Can you tell me what your ailment is? Will it get better?" It embarrassed her to ask, but she had a right to know. What if he carried one of those Asian viruses?

"It's a disfigurement. A birthmark of sorts. It hasn't gotten much better, but it's unlikely to get much worse."

"But I thought you wanted your room for recuperation."

"I do. I expect my recovery to take the remainder of my days."

She was angry. He'd tried to fool her. What else hadn't he told her? "Pardon me for asking, but exactly what nationality are you?"

He tilted his head, as if to pour something out of it. "I am between nationalities now I'm afraid. I once owned an island, but a powerful man took advantage of me and caused me much suffering. Then rich developers moved in. I'm sure you can imagine what followed."

"The rich have their own rules. They're not like the rest of us."

"Quite true."

"You were royalty then?"

He laughed a laugh so hideous she wondered if he might be faking. Then he began to choke, and more reddish-brown spots spread through the lower quarter of his bandages. It was a terrible thing to see, and Edna got up immediately and pounded his back. But what she felt beneath his shirt was far from normal: a mass of ridges, bubbles, and bones where no bones should be. She jerked her hand away in disgust.

He jumped up. "Terribly sorry. I must change." He moved hurriedly but awkwardly toward the stairs. Tingling tried to follow, but Edna pulled her back. Edna couldn't imagine allowing this man to live in her house for long. She didn't know what to think about someone whose face she could not see.

A pain ran through Edna's torso, extending from her private area to right beneath her heart. It was an agonizing moment, but so quick the pain was gone the moment it registered. Tingling barked at her. She hoped it wasn't cancer. So many she knew had died of cancer. She should have her new doctor check it out, she supposed, but she didn't really trust him. She wasn't a racist or anything, but she figured he got his diploma from some Caribbean medical school.

She sat down. Tingling crouched before her, growling and snapping at…what? Edna's female bits?

Later that evening she brought up some towels. The door to Caliban's room was open a couple of inches. He was lying on the bed, reading. Several books were stacked on the bedside table. *Robinson Crusoe, Treasure Island*—at least she'd heard of those, but *Nightmare Alley? The Geek?* They sounded horrid. He did have fresh bandages on, thank God.

"I have fresh towels," she said through the narrow opening. She supposed she could open it farther. She had the right; it was her house. But it was a man's bedroom. This was safer.

"Oh, thank you. You can bring them in."

"No, these go in the bathroom. What…what are you reading?" She could see that gray eye again, the dull gleam of it. Wouldn't it give you a terrible headache to read with one eye? Did he have another?

He didn't say anything for a moment. Then he held up the book. "This? It's *Grendel* by John Gardner. It's based on the creature from *Beowulf,* that ancient poem? He's a monster, 'a creature of darkness, exiled from happiness and accursed of God, the destroyer and devourer of our humankind.'"

Was he playing with her? "I don't like…monsters," she said. Something stirred in her belly. She was afraid she was going to be sick.

"You and the rest of world," he mumbled, but she was obviously meant to hear. She hated when people did that. He sat up and put the book down. Within that narrow two-inch gap, she felt targeted. "I came to reading late in life. As a youth I didn't really talk. I gabbled. The first words I learned to say were curses. They called me *moon-calf*, as you would name a pet or livestock. They were my gods. I was a slave; there are still slaves, did you know? People like you, you cultivate ignorance of certain facts. But I learned how to read. Then when I was left alone I kept reading. When I was forced from my island and spent all that time on ships, I didn't do anything but read. Whenever I finished a book, I tossed it into the ocean, thinking I'd teach my cousins, the fish, to read."

He was joking. Why was he joking? "And you like to read about monsters?"

"I like reading about myself!" He laughed. Why was he laughing? Edna could feel the pain begin in her abdomen again. "We're all monstrous to somebody, haven't you heard? But I've never found myself in any of these books, just a few poor souls no one cares about with similar tales of woe, of toads, beetles, and bats, and suffering from being pinched more stinging than bees. But I have learned many new words besides the ones for the bigger light and the less—words like *exile*, and *expulsion*, *monster* and *beast*, and *xenophobe*. I love the Xs, both letter and symbol in one."

"Well…well." Mr. Caliban was crazy. She had no idea what to say. "You have yourself a good night." She pulled on the doorknob until that terrible wrapped face disappeared.

Edna had made a terrible mistake letting this stranger into her home. Clearly he was dangerous. No one safe ever talked that way.

She thought about calling the police, but she had no idea what to tell them. They never took her seriously. She couldn't lie. She'd tried it before with an annoying neighbor, reporting what awful things he was doing, when she was just describing what she imagined he wanted. She didn't see much difference, but they did.

She dreaded her meals with Caliban, afraid he'd do something disgusting with his mouth inside that hole, afraid of that dull eye, afraid of his jokes, which she never understood, but most of all afraid the bandages might slip. They were old, and he'd been reusing them, and once or twice she'd seen some bit of twisted skin or blistered callus. Every dinner felt like a catastrophe in the making.

"I intend to become a citizen of your great country," he announced one evening. "You have such a great library system. America for Americans, as you people say."

"What people?"

"Why people like you, Edna, of course. Wasn't that what you told your Japanese families during World War Two?"

"I never—"

"Oh, I suppose you're too young. But wouldn't it have been grand to live during those times?"

Edna's stomach roiled. She had to run from the table.

She was in pain again, doubtless from the aggravation of Caliban's foolish, insufferable behavior. She could not stand the way her clothing scraped against her skin, like a rabble of hungry insects with their barbs and claws. She wanted to wear as little clothing as possible, but she couldn't risk it with such a male living in her home.

She went out onto the porch in search of a cool, soothing breeze. But he was already there, sitting on the edge of the porch, reading. She felt betrayed. He rarely went outside. The outside, at least, had been hers.

"I thought you were in your room."

He looked up from his book. "Noises, sounds and sweet airs that gave delight and hurt not, a thousand twangling instruments, and sometimes voices so terrible they brought tears to my eyes."

"I beg your pardon?"

"I've been dreaming about home, the island. But so often those dreams turn into nightmares. I came out here for a momentary escape. I've been studying up on your biology."

"*My* biology?"

"That of human beings, a sorely self-inflicted race, best avoided."

"But *you're* human." But it felt like a lie in her mouth.

He gazed at her, or his bandaged head was pointed in her direction. It was disconcerting, staring at that expressionless bust. "Of course. We are all the same here. Did you know there are microscopic creatures which live on your face? Skin mites. Demodex. They eat your oils. But they do not have an anus. Imagine that! They eat until they explode and die."

She needed to get away from this vile creature, whatever he was. But a sharp pain was playing with her lower belly, teasing her with intimations of how terrible it might become. Then she felt a slight itchiness within her panties which was almost pleasurable, then a scratchiness on her leg, tracing down inside her pants, then spilling out onto her porch.

It was a kind of insect, or not. A rusty red thing with claws and many segments, a hard shell, eyes on stalks moving this way and that, but one of the stalks was broken, so she wondered if it was half-blind. More like a baby crab, and yet not a crab. And she could feel another on its way.

"Oh my. Is that yours?" Caliban asked.

It hurt when she exhaled, as if something were broken in her lungs. She was terrified of vomiting, of what might come out she would be forced to see. She stripped naked; they'd already reduced her clothing to rags. Those creatures emerged from her all afternoon, until they were a red tide covering her kitchen floor. Sometimes they pinched and clawed and bit her in their hurry to get out, making her an island amidst a rusty sea of carapace and claw and clickety clackety taps, a tempest of sound, motion, and color. Tingling barked and snarled and hid beneath whatever shelter was available.

Caliban had retreated upstairs some time ago. The sight of her must have disgusted him. But he was the one who brought all this into her home. He was the one who had infected her life. She'd had enough. She stomped her way out of the kitchen. She could feel them snapping and struggling under her bare feet. She kicked several out of the way as she ascended the staircase. There were none on the steps themselves, or on the landing above.

Caliban was on his way out of the shower, naked and dripping wet. They met in the hall outside his room.

She stared at his hideous form, worse than she imagined. Not merely non-human, it resembled something extraterrestrial. One eye had been closed by rigid folds of flesh, the other, the one Edna was familiar with, gray and in constant motion. The lips appeared misplaced, as did the teeth. The neck was several stacks of muscle, and those muscles continued down like roots or stalks ending in a bubbled field of blisters across the belly, and what hung between his legs…some sort of giant, twisted root?

She realized then she was holding a knife, and she quickly used the knife to cover her sex. She could feel more of those vermin dropping out of her, seeking fresh territory on the upstairs floor.

He laughed. "Don't worry, madam. There are no females of the Caliban species. Even if there were, I lack the desire."

"You, you brought these!" she cried, running forward. Before the horrid jokester could reply she slashed an X deep across his belly, making four triangular flaps. He sank to his knees as his insides began to spill. He smelled of fish, but held no secrets inside, no parasites, no vermin of any kind.

He coughed a laugh up again, burbling off his lips. "All...*yours. Your* legacy...madam," was the last thing he said, as he fell across her teeming red offspring.

Vile Jelly

(inspired by King Lear, Act III, Scene VII)

Dan Coxon

When we were children, our parents warned us to stay off the heath after sundown. We didn't know what went on there, or why our fathers might so often be seen breaking their own rule; we only knew we would be punished if we transgressed. Ten lashes across the knees with a gorse branch, an hour mucking out the pigs with our bare hands. The heath was forbidden land.

None of this stopped us from trying, of course. We would dare each other to run down the heath path as the sun dipped, swap stories of our own brave trespasses. The heath squatted on the land and laughed at us, flat and sandy, its tufts of grass and heather sprouting like the hair in our pubescent armpits. Mocking us with its open spaces: there is nothing to fear here, is there? Maybe our parents knew we would like it more there than in our squalid cottages. Maybe they worried we wouldn't come home.

Looking back, they were right. The heath was no place for children; no place for any man, if we're honest, although a good few ply their trade there, under cover of darkness. Because that's when the heath wakens, truly. When the sun sleeps and the light bleeds out of the world—then, it comes alive.

We should have listened to our parents.

I find it as we tidy, Barnaby and I. Barnaby had missed the hurly-burly, our duke laid low—in his own castle, no less. He had duties in the stables, and when he returned he looked about the room with horror writ on his face. Blood sprayed up the walls, piss on the floor. He settled on Gloucester himself, our lord and master, a makeshift poultice of egg whites pressed to the weeping holes where his eyes should have been. He couldn't restrain a cry then, in fear more than sympathy. I knew where his thoughts resided: if this might happen to Gloucester, where would our futures lie?

"Stop your fretting," I told him, doing my best to take charge of the mess we were left in. "Get this place clean. We can worry about the rest later."

"But who…" He gestured with his hand, unable to speak the words.

"Regan—so let's speak no·more of this. The duke needs us more than ever, and blame will help no one. Nothing is right here. Do your work and all might still turn out for the best."

Barnaby cries as he cleans. I see the tears crawl wet like snail-slime down his cheeks. He's shocked, and scared, and I shouldn't have spoken so harshly.

"Here." I take the mop from him, ease it from his grip as others lead the duke away to rest. "I'll finish this. See if they need a hand in the kitchens, or on the walls. I doubt tonight's mischief is done yet."

But still he stays, struck dumb by the violence that has visited our house. He watches as I push the mop into the corner, across the hearth, under the chairs. The piss is getting old already and the entire room stinks like soured wine. It reeks like another man's fear.

It's as I push the mop beneath the last chair that it rolls out, dusty and smeared with our lord's blood. Barnaby vomits where he stands, his stomach finally relinquishing. *I shall have to mop that up, too*, I think.

"Is that what I think it is?" he whispers, his bile-wet fingers half covering his mouth.

"Never mind that," I say. "Why aren't you at the kitchens already? Clean yourself up while you're at it, won't you. We still have standards."

As he leaves, I pick up the eyeball between thumb and finger, and slide it carefully into my pocket. I know exactly where to take it.

It wasn't on the heath that I first met Cleeve. At least, I don't believe it was. In the dark of night it's sometimes hard to know exactly who you meet there, or whether they even exist in the daylight world. But the first time I know of—the time I remember—he was sat on a wall outside the village, a sackcloth hood pulled up so far that I couldn't see his face. I would learn later that he rarely showed himself in daylight; when he did, he always hid his face from sight. I can't say I blame him, knowing what I do. People are quick to judge around here, even at the best of times; and these times are far from good.

As I passed, he lifted his hand, and I thought I saw a lizard slither from his sleeve into a crevice in the rocks.

"Wait," he said, his voice wet and broken, like water running over pebbles. "I need directions. Do you know a John Bayley around these parts?"

Naturally, I knew old Brownbeard Bayley; we all did. I said as such.

"Can you point me there? I can make my own way, but the directions I have are vague. A yellow door? A discarded wagon wheel?"

I nodded. "You won't miss it. Take a left here, then follow the street 'round. Brownbeard is there, behind the yellow door, as you said. Expecting you, is he?"

The hood moved, in what might have been a nod. "He has something to sell me."

It was a couple of days later I was told of Brownbeard's daughter's passing, and I figured I must have misunderstood. Surely this stranger was there to sell him a coffin, or a burial plot—for what could Bayley have been selling on the day his child died? Still, I knew what I had heard. I recalled watching the strange figure limp away down the road.

That was Cleeve. I'd come to know him better than I liked.

Night has already fallen by the time I leave the castle. There is so much to do, with the master laid low and the country in turmoil. The king cast out by his daughters; every dark thing slinking from its corner as Nature turns her back. The gates are bolted and I have to call in a favour to be let out at all. They tell me to hurry and I do not wish otherwise.

It doesn't take long to reach the edge of the heath. From the hinterland I can hear occasional rustles and yelps in the blackness. Stumbling, I push past the gorse, its slender needles scratching at me unseen. Something moves beneath a bush and scuttles away into the night.

The prize is wrapped in bandages now, cleaned as best I could manage, teasing out the specks of grit with the tip of my little finger. Even divorced from its socket, Gloucester's eyeball is deserving of our respect. The cord still dangles from the back, thick like plaited string, where Regan ripped it from his face. The pupil has glazed over with a milky film. It smells a little like day-old fish, or soured vomit. When the breeze blows the wrong way, the stench makes me gag.

I know where I'm going. Cleeve has his patch, the same as they all do. If he were elsewhere, then none of his clients would find him; nobody would dare try to oust him, for fear of the war that would follow. As wild as it looks out here, far from the light of the castle, there is an equilibrium to be maintained. Upset that balance and what comes after may be even worse.

I do my best to ignore the noises as I follow the sandy path between mounds of grass and sun-bleached heather. I do not turn my head when somebody shouts nearby, a guttural word that I don't recognise but which turns my skin into gooseflesh. I do not question whether the scream I hear soon after is one of pleasure or pain. Instead, I stay true to my path, knowing I am safest within Cleeve's domain—for whatever he is, he is a businessman, and what I bring is too precious for him to allow any intervention. This thing I have found is more valuable than gold, in the right hands. This orb is worth a kingdom.

He's there as I push forward through more gorse, its thorns snagging my sleeves. He's under his tree, its trunk bent like a wizened giant, branches spread, leafless and ancient. I can see the shapeless hood, hear him shuffling to stand. He is taller than I remember, although that may be a trick of the dark.

"You have something for me," he says. His hand thrusts out from beneath his cloak. "Let me see."

My mother died on Samhain, two years to the day since my father passed. She lived with me still; I found her when I returned from work at the castle that night. Bent double as if someone had kicked her in the gut, her body already stiffening. I wish I could say she looked at peace, but the opposite was true. Her eyes were wide and the fear had crystalized within them, the knowledge that this was it, the end of everything. I don't know what she saw in those final moments, but it had filled her with terror.

Cleeve's note was slipped under the door that same night. There were precise instructions, written in ink the colour of rust: what he wanted, where to bring it. A price he would pay if I did as he asked. None of us are wealthy, so I could not say no. If my mother's death meant I could eat for the next month, then it had not been for nothing.

We met under the same tree that first time. I could barely breathe for fear of whatever lurked in the dark, and I wondered if my time had come, too. Maybe Mother's warnings about the heath had been justified, and I would be the poor soul who dies at the end of a morality tale, too stupid and mean to heed the advice he'd been given. An example for all the children who might come here in the future.

Cleeve took care of me, though. I passed him the package, tied up in cloth I had torn from her dress, and he unwrapped it slowly and patiently while I waited. Weighing them in one hand, he held her eyes up to the moonlight. I'd had no implement to extract them, had made do with a blunt spoon; one was red from the trauma, its insides filled with blood.

"I can take these," he told me, that unnatural voice of his hard to understand above the wind. "The price is as I stated. You will speak to no one of our transaction, or I shall come and retrieve my payment any way I choose. Is this acceptable?"

What else could I say? There was no returning my mother's eyes to whence they came. I had no use for them.

His hood shifted, and his hand reached inside his cloak for a purse. "Our business is done."

Cleeve doesn't need me to unwrap the bandages for him. News travels fast on the heath, doubly so in troubled times. He knows of Regan's treachery, and the price Gloucester has paid. He knows what I bring.

This time the purse he retrieves from his cloak is four, maybe five times the size of the one I received before. I don't count it in front of him but snatch it greedily; almost as greedily as he snatches the package from me. There's a waft of that sour stench again, although I'm unsure whether it comes from the eyeball or Cleeve. He cradles it in his palm like a pearl.

"This is good," he says, something like pleasure in his voice. "You'll find the payment is fair. Leave me now. Speak of this to no one."

A choking noise comes from within the hood, and I think he may be laughing. As I turn to go, I see him lift the sacking from his head and unveil the ruined mess of his face: his jawbone broken and fixed half open, the cheeks seared with burns like melted candle wax. Nobody knows how he got them, but there are rumors that he was driven from his last home, set upon by those who did not appreciate his trade. That he barely escaped with his life, and maybe not even that.

I turn away in disgust, but not before I see his hand lift to his mouth and that slimy pearl slide between rotten teeth, destined only to see darkness for ever more. I cannot return to the castle quick enough.

There is no ending to this story. We are not in a morality tale, you and I. There is no lesson to learn, no comfort in the sorting of right from wrong, no divine justice holding the scales. All is chaos here as the land weeps. We are all living on the heath now.

I have not heard from Cleeve since that night. Some say he has vanished from our land; others that his bones are worm food beneath its sandy soil. A few say he obtained something which lifted him beyond us mere mortals, and that he sits on a throne now, looking down on us as we scurry like termites. I tend to believe these people most of all.

One day, I know, there will be another note pushed beneath my door, with a time and a place written in rust. And then I shall reach my finish.

Usurping Monster

(a found sonnet carved from the words of King John)

Stephanie Ellis

The moon does ascend, awakes the serpent,
ungodly creature, born of devil spite,
with breath of malice and bitter intent,
to destroy hateful man and murder night.
Usurping monster, sin stained, bastard son
of death, shakes heaven with a plague of lies,
spits distempered fury to imprison
dreams of the wanton soul whom God denies.
This prince of the dead walks murderous streets
with warlike spirit to lay claim the damned,
in whose bosom the heart of evil beats,
to burn his vile canker upon the land.
  Follow this butcher and be lost, forsworn
  and rue the doleful day that you were born.

To Keep a Corner in the Thing I Love

Geneve Flynn

he is not dead.

The taper's flame flickered, as if something else breathed in the crypt below the church of San Zaccaria. The ceiling arches pressed close and the statue of the Doge Pietro Tradònico seemed to lean in to hear who it might be.

Atrea closed her eyes against her tears, her thoughts a constant, looping prayer: *She is not dead.*

Yet a week had passed since her daughter's murder. Her body had been bathed in water and berry leaves, then camphor, and wrapped in linen. When the ship had arrived from Cyprus, Atrea had not been able to bring herself to look upon her face. Surely, it would still have borne the marks of violence.

But seven days was too long—and yet still too soon—for a mother to leave her child alone in the bitter, echoing, dark.

Atrea drew a quavering breath and stepped toward the catafalque. The light from her candle fell upon her jewel, her beloved, and she gasped.

Her daughter lay as serene and unblemished as the day she had set sail to join the cursed general. A faint blush still coloured her cheeks, and her lips were gently parted, as if ready to curve into a smile and spring her jest.

With trembling fingers, Atrea reached out and caressed her daughter's face. Fresh grief pierced her, sharp as a knife; Desdemona's flesh, though yielding to the touch, was like ice.

Atrea stood at the door to the parlour, the words to speak of what she had seen fading on her lips.

Her husband, Brabantio, hunched in front of the fire, staring into his wine. He refused to eat; he barely spoke. He slept fitfully, if at all, and any talk of Desdemona's burial sent him into hiding. He seemed more kin to death than she who had gone to death's embrace. Small wonder the wag-tongues say he had died upon hearing of Othello's foul deed.

To have her husband beyond the walls of their bedroom was a little triumph; she would not jeopardise it, not with Tantalo's visit within the hour. The senator was Brabantio's oldest and dearest friend, and she hoped news of the senate would break him from his lethargy.

"...Leandro is opposed to any changes to the citizenship laws, as is his way. Honestly, the man would argue if you proposed that the sun should set in the west." Tantalo forced a laugh and took a sip of his wine as the conversation petered into yet another difficult silence.

Atrea held tight to the smile on her face as Brabantio continued to stare at his plate of uneaten food. Gods. Another hour of this was beyond endurance.

Tantalo set down his cup and pushed to standing. "Thank you for your hospitality, old friend." Brabantio made no reply, nor did he look up. Tantalo nodded to Atrea, his expression one of sympathy. "My compliments on your table, Atrea. As always, you create alchemy in your cucina."

"You flatter me too much, Tantalo." She joined him at the doorway. "Allow me to see you out."

As they walked toward the portico, he took her hand and gave it a gentle squeeze. The kindness almost broke her control and she pressed her fingers to her trembling lips.

"Dear Atrea," Tantalo murmured, "my heart aches for your sorrow, and for the lonely grief you suffer now. Would that my thick-headed friend could surface from his mire to see that a mother's agony is the hardest to bear."

Atrea closed her eyes, searching for something, anything, that would help her pass this moment with dignity. Desdemona's face, perfect and peaceful, floated up to her. "I saw her. This afternoon. For the first time, since…"

"Did Brabantio accompany you?"

She shook her head. "He is not ready. But all was not sorrow. My daughter, though a week in her grave, lies unspoiled and as beautiful as ever." She smiled. "Tantalo, she is pure."

He stared at her. "Desdemona is incorrupt?"

"What say you?" Brabantio asked, and they startled at his sudden presence.

"'Tis a miracle, good Brabantio," Tantalo said, looking to Atrea for confirmation. She nodded, and he continued, "Desdemona is immaculate."

Brabantio stepped forth and gripped her arm. "Is it true? Did you see it with your own eyes?"

Atrea nodded again. "In death, as in life, she is without flaw."

"What-ho!" Brabantio swept her into a crushing embrace and brayed laughter. Atrea's head spun at the sudden change in him. "It is proof! Proof that my Desdemona is innocent, and that—that black-hearted devil bewitched her!" He released Atrea as suddenly as he had seized her, and his gaze turned inward. "I had the right of it." He grimaced. "And the wrong of it. Alas, words are as water: once they are spilled, there is no recall."

Tantalo laid a hand on his shoulder. "Perhaps it is time for forgiveness. Go. Look upon your daughter and see this miracle for yourself. Perhaps then you may recover a measure of Brabantio as I knew him."

Panic skittered across Brabantio's face. "No. No, I cannot bear it." He firmed his mouth then broke into a tremulous smile. "But you speak true, my friend. I must reclaim the title of Brabantio, senator of Venice. I have neglected my duties. But no more."

Atrea bowed her head. "I am glad to see my husband so renewed."

Brabantio pressed a kiss to her palm. "Forgive me, my treasure. I have been a poor husband, and a poorer father. I will not let our daughter's death be without meaning. Tonight, I will draft a motion to bring before the senate. I mean to revoke the citizenship of all Moorish hounds. Has their greatest general not proven that they are naught but savage appetite and temper?" He clasped Tantalo's hands in both of his. "I must away. I burn with purpose." He hurried off, muttering to himself.

Tears fell as Atrea finally allowed herself to admit the depth of her loneliness. "Thank you, Tantalo. You have returned my husband to me."

"I fear his is not a complete homecoming," Tantalo said with a frown. "Tend to him, Atrea. He may seem revived, but it would take only a slight injury to strike him down again."

"I will. We will lend each other strength as we begin to properly mourn."

"You are a good, forgiving woman." Tantalo opened the door and crossed the threshold, then hesitated. "He suffers so for his final words to Desdemona in the Sagittary."

Atrea's pulse quickened. "What words?"

"Did he never tell you?"

"No, the memory pained him too greatly."

"As it would any father." Tantalo sighed. "After she professed loyalty to her husband, Brabantio spoke: 'Look to her, Moor, if thou hast eyes to see. She has deceived her father, and may thee.' I pressed upon him that it was a small thing, a thing said in passion, but he laments planting the seed of doubt in Othello's brute mind, and unleashing the jealousy that led to Desdemona's destruction." He sighed again and gave her hand a final squeeze. "Do not judge him too harshly. He is simply a father who loved too fiercely."

Atrea stood, unseeing, as Tantalo climbed into his carriage and departed. Winter crept into her chest, spreading fingers of burning cold, and she did nothing to stop it.

Late that night, the ceiling arches and the Doge Pietro Tradònico did not lean in to listen. Atrea thought that even things of stone would crack and cleave from the pain that swelled and swelled inside her. There was nowhere for her hate and grief and fury to go. Othello was dead, by his own cowardly hand; the villain Iago was dead, tortured and executed; Roderigo, Emilia, all dead. All who had a hand in her daughter's death had been punished.

All but one.

Yet she had sworn her loyalty to him, and he was the only one who shared the vast, tearing wound in her heart.

With great effort, she swallowed the scream in her throat and looked down at her daughter. How cruel that she should seem only to sleep. Would it be so terrible to climb into the casket with her child and hold her one last time? What blessed relief it would be to close her eyes and drift away.

Atrea bent down to Desdemona's face. No bruise nor line marked her cheeks. Her lips were still sweetly parted.

"I am lost," Atrea whispered with a sob. "Please, my jewel, tell me what to do." She closed her eyes and inhaled, aching for the soft milky smell of her daughter when she had been a baby. If only she could return to that moment.

Atrea's eyes snapped open. She frowned, then leaned in closer to Desdemona's lips and inhaled hungrily.

Rosemary and fennel flowers. Almonds.

The veal breast was almost ready. Atrea had cut across the ribs so they accordioned open as they roasted. She stripped the rosemary and fennel flowers from the stalks and dropped them into the mortar. With a pinch of salt and a splash of verjuice, she ground the boiled egg into a sauce. Anise and camphor, wood and tart grapes. The scents brought back Desdemona's quiet laughter at the table, her insistence that others were served first, her grace as she helped Atrea to clean afterwards.

Atrea paused for a moment, staring at the pestle. Whose hands were these that would do this monstrous, poisonous thing? Should she take up her knife and smite them from her body?

There was still time to turn from this dread path, time to put an end to this headlong tumble into tragedy. *To mourn a mischief that is past and gone, is the next way to draw new mischief on.*

Then the fragrance of rosemary and fennel flowers bloomed in the air, heady and strong. Atrea sucked in a deep breath and resumed her work.

She took the roast meat from the oven and placed it on a board. It was perfectly cooked: golden and tender with just a hint of char. Her stomach clenched; the smell was almost too much to bear. She gave the sauce a final stir and drizzled it across the dish, sprinkled the slivered almonds, then took it out to her husband.

"Where is Pelopia? And Thyestia?" he asked, seeing that their cook and maid were absent. "Why do you serve me yourself? You are the wife of a senator, Atrea."

Atrea carved a slice for his plate. "I sent them away. And Demetrio. I need the solitude. Besides, it helps keep me busy."

"Ah, in that case, that is good." Brabantio stabbed the meat with his fork then closed his eyes as he chewed. "Even the gods do not dine like this," he said with a groan. Green sauce dribbled down his chin.

The next few minutes were filled with sighs and moans as he continued to gorge, first using his knife and fork to eat, then taking the ribs in hand and tearing the meat from the bone with his teeth.

When they had been picked clean, he sat back and belched. "Atrea, my love, you have restored me. For the first time since…in many days, I feel alive." He noticed only a little cheese, bread, and fruit was on her plate. "Do you not share in this meal with me?"

Atrea picked up a crust and nibbled delicately. "I am content with what I have. You deserve to feast."

He took her hand. Although it was still smeared with lard, she did not withdraw. "Thank you. For a moment, you returned our daughter to this house." He blinked away tears and gestured to the empty chair that Desdemona customarily took. "To serve Desdemona's favourite dish, it was like she was here, do you not think so?"

Just before midnight, Brabantio began to stir. After several minutes of tossing and huffing, he sat up. "I am hollowed with hunger!" He lit the lamp beside the bed and gave his head and chest a mighty scratching. "It must be my returning strength. Atrea, bring me more of the roast."

She rose and wrapped a drape around her shoulders. "There is none, but I will fetch you something from the kitchen."

He scowled then nodded.

Atrea returned with a bowl of leek soup. Brabantio took a mouthful and pushed it aside. "It tastes like ash. Take it away." He rubbed his stomach forlornly. "Are you certain there is no more of the veal? I can think of nothing else."

"Rest easy, husband. I will cook something that will fill your belly, and your soul, tomorrow night."

With a few more unhappy exhalations and turns from one side to the other, Brabantio finally fell back to sleep. His snores grated the air as Atrea lay beside him, motionless and awake.

The next day, Atrea had the villa to herself. Brabantio had departed, after a hurried and disgruntled breakfast, to present his proposal to the senate. Twice, he had returned, having forgotten some vital piece of writing, or some other essential trinket, before finally leaving the house silent and empty.

Atrea spent the afternoon churning butter and harvesting the parsley and onions necessary for the dish she had planned. As the dinner hour neared, she added salt and pepper to the liver, but did not taste the food. Years of preparing meals had refined her instincts and she knew exactly how Brabantio preferred his seasonings.

With a slam of the front door and a curse, her husband returned. "Atrea!" he bellowed, clattering through the house. By the sounds, he was divesting himself of the trappings of his position and casting aside every item he had deemed indispensable and fortuitous that morning. Atrea allowed herself a cold smile.

"Atrea!" He bulled through the kitchen door and slapped his hands on the stone counter, nostrils flared, face florid. His white hair was a wild nest. "Calamity! I fear I have made a pretty farce today in the senate." He clenched his hands and cursed. "I have lost the practice of speech. Instead of the roar of a lion, I grunted and snorted like a boar! I could scarce string two words onto twine. My thoughts were caught in the base needs of this belly." He slapped his large stomach and growled. "I could think only of the roast: of the flavour of it bursting across my tongue, of the sweet deceit that my jewel still supped with us."

Brabantio sagged. "How can I press my case for the vote when my brains are no better than those of a baconer snuffling in his trough for scraps?"

Atrea wiped her hands on a cloth and laid her palm against his fevered brow. "Peace, good Brabantio. See what I have made for you."

He raised his head and sniffed the air. "Fegato alla Veneziana?" He snatched up the ladle, shovelling a spoonful of liver and onions into his mouth. His eyes drifted shut. "My god, Atrea. This tastes of home, of family." His face twisted into a snarl as he wolfed down another mouthful then another and another, faster and faster, hunched over the pan covetously, barely pausing to chew before swallowing.

Atrea watched to see if he would choke.

When the pan was scraped clean, he blinked and stepped back, dropping the spoon on the counter. The mad light in his eyes faded. "I-I did not mean to eat it all. I could not stop myself. Forgive me."

Atrea took the pan then steered him from the room. "There is no blame. I intended the fegato only for you. I am heartened to see it brought you respite from your trials, if only for a moment."

Brabantio resisted her guidance and stopped in the hall. "My trials. Unhappily, a meal does not erase my mortification. How will I reclaim my standing in the senate?"

"Can you not speak to the duke? You've served him well these past years. Surely he will lend his support."

Brabantio's expression cleared. "The duke! Yes!" He captured her head in his hands and planted a kiss on her mouth. The stink of butter and onion and liver filled her nostrils. She flinched, pressing her lips tight; she dared not swallow even the smallest amount. "I will invite the duke to sup with us tomorrow night," he announced. "With an audience of only one, I will regain my lion's roar and press forth my proposal. You will cook another meal, this one exactly, from the same calf. Buy the whole thing from the butcher if you have to. One taste, and the duke will surely be won."

Atrea's breath caught and the room contracted around her. To bring the duke into this noxious sacrament would surely condemn her to Hell. "But, husband, I cannot—"

Thunder gathered over Brabantio's brow. He clutched her shoulders and gave her a hard shake. "You would deny me this? In my time of greatest need?"

She stared at him, the grip of winter tightening around her heart.

Very well. Let the duke share your fortune.

She would continue to play the part of the doting wife and let the fates decide the outcome. "I only meant that I cannot make the same dish. There is no more liver to be had from the calf."

The storm darkened.

"But I will make a feast to surpass even this," she said. "It will leave you both in a delirium. This, I promise."

Brabantio's brow smoothed and the vise around her shoulders loosened. He lovingly brushed the hair that had fallen from her braid from her face and beamed. "This vote is important for our family name, for both of us—you must see that. We must ensure that no other daughters suffer the fate of our darling Desdemona. The Moors cannot be allowed to remain among the noble society of Venice." He pressed a kiss on each cheek. "Be a good wife, Atrea, and we will see all plans come to fruition."

Atrea rose at dawn to gather what she needed for the dinner. The senate was called today to discuss laws other than citizenship, and Brabantio had deemed it safe for him to attend.

In the quiet warmth of her kitchen, Atrea rolled flanks and prepared to cook them with white wine and garlic. She made ciabatta for sopping up the juices. Osso bucco simmered on the stove and a tray of fave dei morti cooled on the counter. Although the aromas were rich and hearty, and she had grown thin and sallow in recent days, she did not taste a single morsel. At midday, she ate a slice of biscotti and a fig.

In the afternoon, she made bone broth and tomato passata, picked the red pepper, onion, and bay leaves, and, finally, cut the heart into pieces.

"Your table is a marvel, Brabantio!" the duke said as Atrea presented the soufritte, completing the display of her culinary efforts.

Brabantio beamed and toasted him with his cup of wine. "It is all the hand of my darling Atrea. Heed me, your grace, once you taste of this ambrosia, you will be transformed."

The duke leaned in his chair so Atrea could serve him. "I can scarcely hold myself back. The smell is enough to drive a man to madness."

Atrea fumbled and the shank slipped from the end of her fork. She swallowed and forced her hands steady as she continued to fill his platter. What she was about to unleash was Brabantio's doing, as much as hers. She finished serving both men then sat.

"Is that all for you?" the duke asked, nodding at the meagre platter of bread and olives in front of her. "Why, I shall become green with envy and steal it from under your pretty nose."

"You have me, your grace," Atrea said. "I must confess to being too liberal with my tasting spoon this afternoon. Brabantio impressed upon me the great import of this meeting, and I wanted to ensure all was perfect." Brabantio took her hand and gave it a loving squeeze. "Alas, I am now much too full to join you in dinner."

The duke stabbed a piece of heart from the soufritte with his fork and held it up to her. Sauce dripped onto the table, red and thick. "Not even a small mouthful?"

"Don't worry for me, your grace." Atrea gave him a mischievous smile. "I have kept back a mouthful—or two—in case I manage to find room for a midnight bite."

The duke burst into laughter. "In that case, I shall hold my-self back no more." He popped the meat into his mouth, chewed, and swallowed with a mighty sigh. "By heaven, Brabantio, you speak the truth. It reminds me of…summer, and olives from Cyprus, and…what do they call those delectable little pickled songbirds?"

"Ambelopoulia," Atrea murmured. How fitting. Her jewel once sang as sweetly as a wild bird.

Sing, willow, willow, willow.

But the men were thick into their feasting and discussion, and she had disappeared to them.

As the night wore on, the duke and Brabantio grew barbarous, eschewing cutlery to rip and tear the bones free, sucking on the mar-row, scooping great handfuls of stew into their mouths. The bread and sweets lay untouched.

Dark shadows flickered over Brabantio's face as they ate, his eyes narrowing and his lip curling like a starved dog whenever the duke reached for another serving. The savagery surfaced and sank like a bob-bing lure; neither man aware. Atrea's pulse thudded in her throat. All was set in motion and there was no turning back now.

Finally, the men pushed back from the table, faces smeared with sauce and grease, bellies distended. "By the gods, Brabantio," the duke groaned, "I have been transfigured. You have my full support in the senate."

Brabantio bowed his head. "My law is just and right. You will not regret it."

"My only regret is my indulgence tonight. Strange. I am a tem-perate man, but from the first bite, I was overcome with a demon's hunger." The duke struggled to his feet and clapped Brabantio on the shoulder and laughed. "Alas, now I pay. My homeward journey is long and I am sorely tempted to lay my head down on this table."

"Then put your regret to bed," Brabantio said. "Sleep, here un-der my humble roof, and when you wake in the morning, you will be refreshed. The senate is not far from my door."

The duke stifled a huge yawn. "A kind offer, and one I will gladly accept. Again, you prove yourself to be a gentleman."

It took an hour of scrubbing and washing to return the dining room and kitchen to cleanliness. After she had wiped everything down, Atrea took the pot containing the last of the soufritte and set it squarely in the centre of the marble counter, where it could not be missed.

Atrea listened as Brabantio's snores were replaced by rumblings from his stomach. Dawn was still an hour or two distant, and although she had not slept, she felt no fatigue, only a sick, thrumming anticipation.

She lay, drawing the slow, steady breaths of sleep, watching through her lashes as he pushed upright with a muttered curse. His belly gave another empty gurgle and he groaned softly. With a stealthy backwards glance, Brabantio crept out of bed, wrapped his robe about himself, and disappeared into the hall. Atrea tugged her drape around her shoulders and followed on silent cat's feet.

Unerringly, Brabantio headed toward the kitchen. He shuffled down the hall, nose lifted and snuffling like a swine.

He stopped suddenly, trembling before an open door.

The duke's room.

Brabantio's form hunched into itself, as if he were transforming into a beast. The air throbbed with his fury, and Atrea almost took a step backwards. She pinched her breath and forced herself to remain motionless in the shadows.

Brabantio stormed towards the kitchen, unheeding of any further need for stealth. He snorted and wheezed, hands clenching and unclenching at his sides. "Oh, thou foul thief!" he hissed.

He slammed the door open, and there, in the centre of the kitchen, stood the duke, face lit below from a single taper, smeared with sauce as dark as blood, hand thrust into the pot, eyes, lunatic black. The duke snarled and crammed pieces of heart into his chomping maw, jaws working furiously.

"THIEF!" Brabantio lunged.

The duke screeched an inhuman sound and danced away, shielding the pot with his body. He shovelled frenzied handfuls of meat into his mouth. With a shout of triumph, he flourished the pot. It was empty.

Brabantio roared and snatched it from him. He whipped it across the duke's face, sending the older man staggering. "THIEF! THIEF! THIEF!" Atrea stared, hands clamped over her mouth. With each bellow, Brabantio brought the heavy iron pot down on the duke, shattering his eye socket, cracking his jaw, driving him down, down, down, as if he would pound him through the terrazzo floor.

Cries sounded from outside the villa.

"What devilry passes?"

"Thief? Who has been robbed?"

"Summon the watch!"

"Alarm! Alarm!"

Brabantio was deaf to all but his own hell. Even when the watchmen rushed in and dragged him from the pulped body, he continued to cry, "THIEF!" It was only when the pot slipped from his fingers—slick as it was with sauce, grease, and blood—clanging across the kitchen, did he finally stop.

The sentencing was swift and without mercy. In seven days, Brabantio, senator of Venice, would be tortured, then hanged to death. As he languished in the city watch house, the wag-tongues said that he had gone mad, and that no guards would enter his cell.

Atrea suffered her own confinement. Although no one blamed her for failing to visit her husband, rumours swirled like swarms of midges. Whispers spoke of a curse on the family, of Othello's witchcraft reaching from beyond death, of possession—of poison. The last sent a shiver through her. Still, no guards came to arrest her.

She was left alone.

On the sixth day, Tantalo came to her.

"Dear Atrea." He once again took her hand. "I can only imagine your torment."

Atrea remained silent. All words had been stolen from her tongue.

"I beg of you—see Brabantio, one last time." He shook his head. "If only I had known the depths of his grief, his insanity…"

She tried to shape her face into an appropriate expression but she seemed to have forgotten how.

"He will take no food," Tantalo continued. "I have never seen anything the like. In only a matter of days, he has wasted to half of his former self—a quarter. It is as if something is eating him from the inside out. He is a creature crept up from its sepulchre. Will you not at least say farewell?"

Atrea raised her eyes and nodded.

He sagged in relief and squeezed her fingers. "Perhaps bring him something to eat? A man should have one final moment of comfort, one taste of home and family, before he meets his fate, no matter how deserved."

Atrea smelled Brabantio's cell before she found it. A guard, wide-eyed and young enough to be her son, stood back several feet, refusing to come any closer. In the first few days, Brabantio had attacked any who came near the bars, and they had given up trying to provide him food and water.

Bowls of stew and bread lay scattered about the chamber's stone floor, blown with flies and cockroaches. The insects seemed to be the only things moving within the shadowed space. If her husband was here, he had crawled into the very darkest corner.

"Brabantio?"

"Desdemona?" a hoarse voice replied. "Is that you, my daughter? Have you come to forgive me?"

Atrea's lip curled and her hands shook as she gripped the pot. A handkerchief, embroidered with strawberries and draped over the lid, trembled. He deserved no such mercy.

"It is Atrea. I have brought you your last meal."

"Atrea?" Brabantio's voice cracked. A soft sniffle. "Thank you. Thank you."

Atrea turned to the guard. "Open the door."

"Signora, it is not safe," the guard stammered. "Madness hides within this cell."

She raised her chin. "Open it. I have nothing to fear from my husband."

The guard reluctantly nodded and, with fumbling fingers, hurriedly opened the door. Atrea thanked him and stepped inside. The door clanged shut behind her, and with another jangle of keys, was locked. The guard's footsteps hurried away.

"Atrea, my love," Brabantio whispered, "what kindness have you brought me?"

Atrea took the handkerchief from the lid and held it out. A filthy, skeletal hand reached from the darkness and plucked it from her fingers.

A crackling sob. "This is Desdemona's. My jewel."

Atrea placed the pot on the ground. "It is not the only thing of hers I have brought for you."

A long, greedy sniff echoed from the back of the cell. "My god." A scuffling noise and Brabantio's face swam out of the shadows, his eyes two vivid black gems in gaunt sockets. He seemed to be on his hands and knees, the bottoms of his legs unseen. Saliva dribbled from the corners of his mouth, leaving clean tracks down his blackened chin. "It smells like heaven." He lifted the lid.

With a cry, he slapped the pot away.

A pair of delicate hands and feet, charred to remove any hair and nails, simmered in salted water and marinated in garlic, parsley, oil, and vinegar, spilled out onto the ground.

"Peis de boi a scabecciu," Atrea murmured. "Calves' feet. Your favourite."

Brabantio curled into himself, clutching his head, rocking and wailing. "Why? Why would you bring me this?"

All of Atrea's grief and rage boiled up, filling her until she could not see. "You had rather be a toad," she snarled, "and live upon the vapor of a dungeon, than keep a corner in the thing you love, for others' uses." She straightened and stepped back. "So here is the last of what you love," she spat. "Take it, and be done."

Brabantio's wails petered out. A high, wild chuckling rose, growing and growing until it shook against the walls of the cell. He gasped to a stop, his breath still hitching in his chest. "Oh, my darling Atrea," he said, shuffling toward the light. "My heart is ice and my stomach hollow, but I'll partake no more of my jewel." He grinned, all trace of sanity gone from his face. "Why, look! I am become the monster that doth mock the meat I feed on." He giggled and swung his legs around.

Atrea stumbled back.

His shins ended in two bloody stumps, mangled and oozing, the ankle bones gleaming white and gnawed with teeth marks. The glee fell from his face, leaving him blank as a slate. Without another word, Brabantio crawled back into his dark corner and fell silent.

Atrea swayed on her feet, the world spiralling away from her.

Villain. Oh, wretched villain.

She had defiled that which was most precious to her, and for what? Why was her heart still so bitter and raw? All who shared in the blame for her daughter's murder had been punished. Was there no respite for her? No end to this agony? She moaned, rough in her throat, then slowly collapsed to her knees.

This close to the pot, she smelled the meat. Brabantio, and the duke, they had both experienced rapture: the taste memory of home, of joy, of love. Why not her? She picked up a piece and inhaled. Soft milky sweetness. Tears burned down her cheeks as she placed it into her mouth. Gentle laughter, a tender embrace, the gold of her child's hair, tumbling in curls about her face. Atrea chewed and swallowed, eyes closed, weeping at the oblivion that swept through her. She took up another piece, and another, crunching and gulping until there was nothing left.

She opened her eyes, and together, she and Brabantio stared at each other in the prison they shared. The hunger was already growing inside.

(I always thought there was one person in Othello who escaped fitting punishment for Desdemona's murder. Inspired by the Greek myth of Tantalus and his descendants — Atreus and Thyestes — and drawing on the legend of the wendigo, I made sure he got his just desserts. – Geneve)

No Rest Nor Relief For You With Me Dead

(based on Sonnet 71,
"No Longer Mourn for Me When I Am Dead")

Rebecca Cuthbert

No rest nor relief for you with me dead,
than I shall thrice ring the gravedigger's bell—
give fair warning to you, my dear, who shed
my blood without tears, and laughed as it fell.
Nay, if you can sense me, remember not
your adoring wife; for I loathe you so,
that I in your nightmares won't be forgot—
even in sleep will your dread of me grow.
O, if (I scream) you do feel my sworn curse,
From 'neath (where you put me) six feet of clay,
do not the grieving husband act rehearse,
for soon, alongside me, will *you* decay.

      Lest our friends believe your broken-heart con,
      I'll come for you, darling—I'm dead, not gone.

A Pound of Flesh

(based on *The Merchant of Venice*)

John Palisano

The air feels damp and smells of the sea. Everything I touch feels sodden. It's amazing Venice hasn't decayed and crumbled into the canals. The sea spreads like a disease, its reach ever advancing, reclaiming the city and everything within.

The Rialto Bridge looms near, its shape and form forever etched into my memory. A silhouette of two strolls across and I can only assume it's a couple. Who else would venture out at such an hour other than me—Shylock, the notorious? It is a time when few look at me. For those who do, there's a chance they might recognize me. Even seven years after Portia and Antonio and Bassanio tricked and humiliated me in the queen's court, Venetians still point and jest. The duke did nothing to assist. Useless and cruel. It's been enough trouble I've taken to operating at off hours, living like a creature of the night instead of a proper Venetian. So be it for now.

The Grand Canal smells of salt and sea, the tide high with a late Autumn surge. Tied to their docks, gondolas float on the waves. The water shimmers peculiarly. It's as though there are lights underneath and creatures have gathered for an otherworldly party. How Divine. It's a wonder.

Something scurries from the water. Dark and insectoid, it scales the canal wall, over a small porch, and up and onto the side of the bridge's fence. I can't see it once it's on the other side, but I feel its glare from the shadows.

What did I just see? Was it real? Maybe it was just a rat. From far away, light played tricks.

Gazing down at the water, I wait for other creatures to emerge. Of course, rats can swim. It takes a lot to drown them, and for certain, our Venetian breeds are used to water life. Ripples reflect across the canal, but no more signs of life emerge. Just my imagination projecting something supernatural onto a normal old rat.

I imagine boarding a trading ship bound for Cypress, everything I own within a small bag. Sometimes, I wish to escape this haunted city, but it is home. The court took half of everything, ruling in favor of Antonio, forfeiting all my Jewish possessions, even my family's Torah. I had to adapt. I live in a small room at St. Peter's. I surround myself with others wishing to live an austere life in their Christian God's eyes. Mine now by official Venetian order. I won't dare speak otherwise or risk their wrath. They stopped the barbaric hangings and public torturing, but I'm unsure such remedies don't still exist out of sight. I will pray to their God, but people have many layers. They can only know what's inside my head as much as I will say. I'll need to keep the charade going until the day I can…

No. Do not think of revenge. It's a path leading nowhere. Look where it's gotten me. Alone and ostracized. Scuttling along the night streets like a starved mouse.

"Vermin." That's what the boys called me, too, during the trial, even after I gave them a loan. "Scum dweller."

No sooner do I realize the sound comes from a real person than a blow lands to the back of my head.

The gang's upon me.

"Shylock! Shylock! A pound of flesh! How about we pound your flesh, you flea-bitten dog!"

Their kicks and punches hit hard and I'm on my back when I peer into their grinning faces. One punches me in the face. I try to block it, but I'm too slow. I hear a crack. My nose fractures. Another blow hits my right eye socket, making a horrific, breaking sound.

Pain explodes. My shaking hands cover my face, but the damage is done.

"You are dirt. Unfit to be a Venetian." They spit. I'm spared it landing on my face. My hands block the humiliation.

I want to fight back, but I'm no longer a young man. I'm weak.

"Stop!" A man's loud voice. "Leave him be!"

They utter more insults. It's as though I've sunk inside my body and my senses are muffled.

"Shylock." Someone close lifts me from under my arms. I recognize the voice. I sink into nothingness. The painful world fades away.

"How are you feeling?" Sebastian asks, his hands folded before him. The monk from St. Peter's.

"More monster than human." Fluid runs down my throat, making me cough, hurting my eyes, nose, and right ear.

"It's enough," he says. "Don't speak if it's too much."

"No. I want to speak. Please." I steady my cough. "The boys who did this?"

"If I find them…" Sebastian shakes his head. "I may break my vows for a quarter-hour."

I wave my hand. "Don't. God sees all."

"Yes. True." He looks away, nods. "You are safe here. You have a home with us. I'm sorry this happened," Sebastian says. "I hope you'll think twice about going out during the night alone."

I sigh. "It's the only time I can go outside without people noticing. My reputation…"

"All that matters is what God thinks. God loves you. We'll take care of your means. Don't burden yourself."

Peering down, I see my wrapped legs; I won't have a choice, at least not soon. My bandaged right eye closes and the intense pain forces the left to squint.

"Time for some more wine, my friend."

"Yes," I say. "Quickly."

I wake covered in sweat, yet my room is cold and damp. My left hand feels slick with slimy moisture. My room reeks of the sea.

Has the city flooded? Maybe I've passed out and missed it. Mold. Water. Everything is moist. Eyes upon me. Foreign gazes. A creature's eyes housed inside a human-like form.

I must be dreaming. A fever explains such strange visions.

The being steps toward me, graceful and sure, similar to a squid pushing and pulling its legs to motion through the canal.

I blink, expecting my eyes to refresh and wipe away my visitor. Instead, the being gets closer. Staring. Sizing me up. Its stare does not falter. What does it want? I try to reason that it's another unmentionable like me that the church has given shelter to. Another monster, under their care, locked away from the taunts and humiliations of everyday Venetians.

A second set of eyes opens above the first. They're silver with large dark pupils. Reflective in the same way as a fish. A third set blinks from near the top of the being's head, though much smaller than the first two sets.

The impossible creature leans down. My body goes cold. What horrific hallucination am I experiencing? The blows from the gang must have damaged my perception.

It puts out a hand, its fingers webbed, its ends pointed. In its palm, a rough, silty white substance. Nodding for me to take it, I put out my own hands. The being places its hand over mine, turns it so the material falls onto my trembling palms.

With the transaction complete, the creature nods and backs away. It's to the window, then out before there's time for me to register.

I look at my hand. It tingles. Whatever the stuff is, it's acting like a numbing agent. I put my hand to my side table and turn it slowly so the material can fall off, reminding me of sand or salt. Dark specs run throughout the material. My palm feels completely numb.

Instinctively, I rub what's left on my right chest and side—areas where I've had heavy bruising. Maybe it will help take the pain away.

Perhaps the being tried explaining it to me. Why? How did it know? It made no sense.

Regardless, within moments of the salt touching the affected areas, the pain subsides. I gasp. Relief. A miracle!

Water rises, filling Venice like a bathtub. Yells of surprise and screams crack as the seawater seeps in. Under pressure, foundations snap. I'm up high, so I'm not in immediate danger, but the building might collapse.

I get up and off my bed and step toward the window.

Below, the streets are submerged. The water crests higher than the plaza's second stories. It's never been this high.

We don't have a protocol for such an event. Can Venice survive such a tragedy?

Clouds cover every meter, turning the sky gray. A light and steady rain falls.

Whoosh.

Water surges.

What causes such momentum?

The waterline rises more, nearly to the third story. It consumes the bridge with only its highest poles still visible. The water creeps only twenty stone from my feet. Any more and I will wash out, too.

Debris flows in the water. Broken pieces of wood. Pieces of smashed gondolas. Hats. Shoes. I don't see any people, though. *They've already washed away, gone before they even had a fighting chance.* How do I even know such a thing?

I see lights inside the water, as if candles burn underneath. It should not be possible, but it's as real to me as the stone making up my home. The lights move and swim. They swarm and emerge from the flowing water. Their source? The bodies of beings, brothers and sisters of the one who delivered salt to me. They scale the walls like lizards as easily as you and I walk the streets.

The salt.

My side burns. When I look down, I see it glows, too. The areas where I'd rubbed it onto my body have become inflamed. Bulbous growths bloom and glow. I go to touch one, but as soon as my hand gets close, the blooms hurt worse. It's as if the blooms know I'm coming.

As I peer down at the blooms growing from my side, I see water trickling at my feet. Oh, no. The trickle quickly becomes a stream. I rush to my door but find the water is already covering my feet. Heading back into the monastery would be a death trap. Turning back to the window, I struggle to make way. The water rushes inside with such force! It's nearly to my knees.

It takes all I can to push through the current to the window. I must get out! I think of the monks…of Samuel…and hope he's gotten out somehow. I force myself up and onto the windowsill. As I do, I'm shocked to see the sea is only a foot below. Venice is nearly underwater. I'll have no choice but to swim.

I jump in the water and am shocked at the current's strength. There's no one else visible swimming, either. *Is this my end?* I flail around, but all my actions do is keep me reasonably afloat. I spit out saltwater; the waves batter me and threaten to pull me under.

Where am I going to go? How long am I going to keep up with this?

Please, deliver me somewhere dry. A rooftop. A ship. Something where I can wait this out.

I can no longer see any signs of Venice. Just water.

Am I being pulled out to sea?

Oh, please be a ship with someone to scoop me up and out. I'm an old man and I can't swim forever. Don't let me drown like a rat. Please.

Everything lifts. I'm on a wave going up and up. Many stories high. My heart races. I'm sure I will die as soon as the wave passes and I'm brought down low. The wave on the opposite side…as massive as imaginable…approaches. Its top curls.

There is no way I can fight such a force.

Maybe if I curl myself into a ball and hold my breath, I might go underneath it and come out the other side.

No. This is how you drown. This is how you die.

I shut my eyes for a moment. If I stay put, I may be lucky and ride the wave. I may be lucky and find myself in just the right spot to do so. If not? I'll get pushed under deep enough I won't be able to recover. Even if I do, there are more waves to battle. Endless waves.

Something grabs me from behind. Slips under my arms and lifts. Another person. Another swimmer. A ship! Something arrives to save me.

I can't see who it is. The fingers and hands don't feel normal. They're thinner. Stronger. It's one of those glowing creatures, I'm sure. Like the one who gave me the salt. They must have seen me washed away.

We go high on the vast wave. I'm shivering. I've never been so high in my life. The sea's scope is impossible to imagine. *If I make it through this, I'm moving far inland. As far away from water as I can find.*

From behind the opposite wave, a large shape rises.

Formless and absent of light, this thing is larger than any wave. It opens itself. What at first look like flippers stretches into massive arms. Eyes open near its top. Many sets of eyes. Gaping holes that may be mouths or may be something else.

Its dark form gives way to countless orbs lighting up.

There is light behind me. The being connects to the larger one. It makes a high-pitched singing sound that hurts my ears. The larger creature makes a harmonizing sound. I look around and wonder how we are still on top of the wave, which should have passed long ago. We are not. Instead, when I look down, I cry out as I see a long tentacle-like arm, its length twice as high as even the highest steeples in Venice, extends and holds us up.

The sound…the music…intensifies.

There are others like us. Other beings hold the nearly drowned. The colossal beast looks on, its many eyes sizing up the countless offerings.

That's what we are. Offerings to this larger beast.

It cries out. A sound like thunder, only a hundredfold louder. I scream as we drop. The arm pulls us down. So fast. And we're going to be devoured by this thing. Assimilated and taken, vanished into its belly as it dives back into the unknown depths of the Adriatic. This would be my last moment. I wish I'd just drowned.

When we hit the bottom and crash into the water, I see blue, then dark blue, then bubbles everywhere. From the seemingly endless and bottomless dark, I see something light and gray come before me. At first, I think it is a unique species of sea creature. A dolphin or whale? A cephalopod? No. It's something else, with long ornamental fins on its several long arms. A figure unravels from one end.

Leah.

My first wife.

This happened to her? She drowned, and this being found and protected her. Impossible, I know.

She opens her eyes and stretches out her hands. She isn't scared or upset. She smiles and nods. A picture arrives in my mind. Venice floods. Covered completely with water. Citizens float on fizzy water amidst concentrated debris. So many dead. Everyone dead. Our city is lost forever. On the horizon, a tall and shadowed figure surveys the scene. Three glowing lights hover near. The water deities flank and float like glowing beetles. They are hungry. Starving.

For what? My mind asks, sending the idea to Leah.

She nods, and her gaze drops to my middle. I follow her eyeline down and see not one but five or more large bumps growing on me. They pulse and grow and ache. I am their farm. I am their host. They will feed when the growths mature and separate from me. A pound of flesh as penance. Payment for my past life and atrocious deeds.

"Why me? Out of several thousand Venetians."

"Because I need you." Her voice as I always remembered it.

"Me?" I ask.

She nods yes.

"Am I not here?"

Leah loses her smile. "Not like this. Piece by piece, so you can acclimate."

"Acclimate?"

"To the sea. Your form won't live here as it is. You need to be remade."

The being wraps her again. She is controlling the beast. She is not its victim or captive. It is hers. She fades and descends so quickly into the void. The strength of the water pulls me. I am just a leaf in its wind, unable to fight. I'm sucked down. Then dark, and there is just the pulling, pulling, pulling. Or is it falling? I lose consciousness. I know I've drowned and have died and feel at peace with the fact.

Once more, I am covered in water. It is not seawater as in my dream, but my sweat. Again with this, I think. Another awful dream. My fever is producing horrible hallucinations; they feel authentic enough to stop my heart.

Grasping my blankets and pulling the material into fists, I shut my eyes. Please. Let it all stop. I just want to feel better and get back to my life.

When I ease my grip, I brush against something on my side. I may have had a bad dream, but the things growing off my body…the blooms…are very real.

Scanning the room, I'm grateful to find it has not flooded. I sit up on my elbows and peer out the window. There is no water cresting just under the window line. The flood ruined the city only in my dream. I lie back down. Put a hand over my face. What have I done? What evil has happened to me? Why do I deserve such a fate? Was I that bad a man?

The door opens. "You're up." It's Samuel.

"I…am." My voice is weaker than I expect.

"Are you hungry?" Samuel asks. "I've brought you bread and wine."

"No," I say. "My stomach is in knots."

"This may settle it," he says, placing a small tray on the table beside me. "When you're ready."

Samuel sits on the edge of my bed. Looks at the blooms. "Do they feel any better?"

"Worse."

"I'm sorry." He nods.

"I'm having very vivid and frightening dreams," I proclaim. Maybe doing so will exorcise them from my head.

"Fever will bring such things on," he says. "It's to be expected."

"True." I reach out. "Thank you for caring for such an uncaring man."

He shakes his head. "You are not uncaring. You are reborn through Him. You are not the man you were before. Remember as much."

"I'm trying to. It's difficult." I look over at the table. "The smell of the bread is irresistible." He's made me feel better about myself.

"Good. Eat."

"I shall." I squeeze his hand once again and let go. Taking the bread, I pull a piece off. "Would you like some?"

He laughs and stands. "I've had more than my fill of bread for a lifetime," he says.

The crust is hard. The inside, soft and warm. "Delicious."

I look to make more conversation, but Samuel's already at the door. "I'm happy to hear so. I'll check on you later, my friend."

"Gratitude, Samuel," I say. "Deepest."

In no time, I devour the bread and finish the decanter of wine. Feeling stronger than I have as of late, I sit on the edge of the bed. I know I'll soon need the bedpan, so I gather myself and stand. My head spins with the first few steps, but I soon find balance. It's the wine, I protest. Not my state.

I want and need to look out the window, the dream still frightening me. When I peer out, the walkway below is in its normal dry state. The canal waters remain mostly still. The sky is blue with only a few small clouds. No sign of a storm. I squint to look beyond, out at the first parts of the sea visible from my perch. There are no towering water gods or city-sized waves to see.

Something pierces my side, like a needle or tip of a short sword. I put my hand to the area and look down. Nothing is sticking out of me, of course. No hidden assassin has bettered me.

The bloom.

It hurts. It makes me cry out in pain. I touch it gently and sense it is not totally stuck to me. There is a minor break to one half-finger-sized ridge. It's like the edge of a scab. Even the slightest touch makes it sting.

Do I have any water to put on it? Something to ease the ache? Can I call for Samuel? Maybe he's still close enough to hear me.

I spy a small amount of what looks like sand on the floor. Had

Samuel tracked it in? More sand appears sprinkled on the cabinets near the far side of the room and window. I recall my dream of a being visiting me and giving me a similar substance, of which I rubbed on the blooms and made the pain go away.

It's not sand, I'm sure. It's the same magic powder the being gave me…the stuff it'd scraped off the walls of the canal. I dip my finger into the substance on the cabinets. It is not coarse like normal sand. It's a soft powder. Within a moment, my fingers tingle. Taking more, I sprinkle some over the bloom, breaking away from me. It stings for a moment before going numb. With more, it feels good. Unusually and impossibly good.

I spent my next hour gathering what I'm able of the powder. Using two pieces of wax paper as shovels, pushing them together to trap the powder where I find it, I empty it into a small decorative ring box, which I've lined with another bit of wax paper. There is a good amount by the time I'm done.

Thinking back to the night I was first given the powder, I realize how I greedily applied the substance, using it all in a single application. I will be frugal with what I have in the future.

Spent from the work, I make my way back to my bed, box in hand. I place it under my second pillow and out of view of Samuel or anyone else who may wander in. No questions, no answers. My head spins from the exertion. I'm tired, but the bloom does not hurt. Eyeing it once I'm on my back, I find it's separated even more from my body. Within the slit—fresh, pink flesh. *I will heal from these. I will heal from this. I will be better soon.*

I don't want to sleep again; I've spent so much of my time blacked out. I'm in no hurry to revisit any nightmare worlds. My body has other plans, though. Blessedly, my slumber is undisturbed and my mind still.

"Why does it not rot?"

Waking minutes, perhaps hours, later, I notice the bloom has detached. On my side, an oval patch of fresh baby skin, reddened and raw. The blob-like bloom rests at my side. I lift the warm, soft bloom and study it. The flesh looks eerily like my own; not young, as I would expect.

Bulbous and dough-like, I feel hard, bone-like pieces inside. I picture them jutting out like hornet stingers. I put the thing inside the wax-paper-lined box on my bedside table, not wanting it in my hands a second more.

I check my side. The area stings like a scab pulled off too soon. Do I use the powder? Not a good idea.

I don't want to look. Maybe it'll go away if I do.

When evening falls, I feel better and I feel worse. My body heals. At several spots, my skin warms and tingles. The powder must work its magic.

Making my way into the main eating room, I see my caretaker but can't recall his name. I wave. "You're up and around," he says, the delight in his voice genuine.

"Y-yes," I say. He gestures for me to sit.

"Are you hungry?" he asks.

I look down at the shapes on his plate. I know the food, but its name escapes me. How? I've seen and eaten it nearly every day of my life.

"I know it's just bread and porridge, but it's not too bad, judging from the look on your face." He and the others laugh.

Bread. That's its name.

I enjoy the evening, even strolling into the back courtyard with some of the other monks. I look up at the stars and think of numbers. Infinite mathematics. There must be a reason for where they are all placed. They must set things a certain way. My obsession with order since childhood. If they keep the universe in order, we need to do our part to keep the balance by doing so in our everyday transactions. What goes out must come back in. Even if it seems irrelevant to the universe to many, such as my daughter and her husband, these things cannot be upset. Doing so risks a reaction rippling to the stars. Doing so calls attention. Doing so can bring unwanted things forth. What was taken must be given back. A pound of flesh for borrowed ducats or the dark ones will come to take it themselves.

Blink and I see my estranged daughter Jessica with Lorenzo, retired and laughing, enjoying my stolen ducats and ring. Then there is Leah. Deceased long ago, but impossibly alive once more. Is she one with them? Picturing her at the root of it all, her soul deep in the Adriatic. She wants to remake me as a being of the sea. That's why she needs my mind and sent the creature to collect me. Taking me bit by bit so what she is building can acclimate and change. If she does not get me back, the Venetians will suffer for their cruelty and hate against me…their very mindset wiped from existence. If she gets me—this remade version of me—she will call off the water deities. Her voice in his dreams. "Wait until time prevails and generations break and soften their hate for us. We will wait for them to grow past this as I wait for your mind to return to me, piece by piece."

Blink and a conversation remembered. Telling Leah numbers are the secret universal language. How they are love. They are the cipher to know God and to see the workings of life itself.

She says, "Your amazing, beautiful mind. So misunderstood, my Shylock."

Leah knows when the numbers are not in order, they move worlds to return order. "Vacuums disintegrate worlds. Time is broken. Laws we know as true cease. Balance must be maintained. Or it could have effects far-reaching," I say. "This is why I am so obsessed with ducats."

I think back to why I'd chosen a pound of flesh to be taken from Antonio. It came as a vision when I was submerged, but the details are lost. When had it been planted inside me? When I swam as a boy? Was it during routine washing? Somehow, the deities had planted it inside me and waited.

"Shylock?" says the monk. Oh, what is his name? How can I not remember? I knew it just yesterday, I'm sure. He is over me. How did I blink and end up moving from the courtyard to my bed? There are others nearby. "You were talking in tongues. You're still warm with fever. You blacked out, but we caught you." Another leans in from behind him, I recognize him as Rod Cressy, leering like one of those awful

Venetians who voted to banish me at the trial. Why must we remember those who are most cruel to us so clearly?

"You spoke of numbers and creatures and called for your wife," Rod says.

I make to speak and feel my lips and mouth move, but only soft sounds escape.

"Easy," the first monk…my friend whose name is still out of reach…says as he puts a hand on my shoulder. He turns and they whisper. What are they saying? Finally, when they turn, they address me. "We need you to rest, Shylock. Please don't get out of bed without help again. We are afraid you suffered an incident."

An incident? I want to say. Again, no sound.

"A stroke," he says. Why can't I recall his name but know the other's? Is it true? I've had a stroke? I feel burning pain throughout my body as though they have burned me multiple times. I try to speak to let them know, but cannot. I try to move to show them, but nothing cooperates.

"We will be back to check on you regularly, Shylock," he says. "God loves you and you are in His hands."

"God loves you," Rod says. I can't raise my head to see.

It feels like a lifetime after they leave. Tears run down my cheeks, but I don't recall crying. I blink and see the blanket moving. Something is underneath me. Several things. The blooms crawl out from under the fabric and trot on top of me, coming up to my face. These are more advanced. The bones I felt inside the first have broken free. Stalk-like appendages carry them. They have three sets of eyes. It lives in the small box on my bed table, curling into wax paper like a blanket.

I wish I could get the powder to rub on the sores. My fingers twitch, but I can't so much as turn my hand.

What else will I be able to do to survive this? How could it have all happened so fast? One minute, I was fine. The next? Bedridden and unable to move or speak. Is this how strokes go? Will I have another one? Will I be forever bound? Is there a chance to recover? To heal.

Come to me.
I hear her voice.
Leah.
It's time.
This is the call.
Come.
To.
Me.

My God. Her voice is so clear. So real. It cannot be. I am just hallucinating. An effect of my condition is the only explanation.

Come.
To.
Me.
Shylock.

I look around the room. The strange, gray blooms have climbed onto the walls like spiders. There are so many of them. How had I farmed so many without even knowing?

They're not taking my flesh. They're taking my intellect. Why? What could they want with it? Why do they need it? Is it just a game? How is taking me preventing them from smashing Venice.

They hear me. Hear my voice inside. And in response, the ones on me pull back the covers. My body is emaciated and covered in red sores where they've grown and peeled from me.

It.
Is.
Time.

I'm so weak. I'm so tired. Everything hurts.

I try to speak. I can't. I can't. I can't. Move.

A bloom trots onto my left hand and nudges it just as a dog would if it wants a pet. My fingers do move and can curl. Blood rushes into them. Yes. Life enough.

But what is to be?

A flash. So bright. A sound like a million buildings falling. How much time passes? Seconds? Hours? Days? I don't know.

One of my eyes doesn't seem to work. The remaining one is cloudy. Another stroke. Pain is immeasurable. Every pore pulses.

The blooms watch.

Come.

There is nothing left. Your body has served its purpose. Join me underneath.

Yes. I am ready. But how?

Something scuttles into my left hand. I recognize its form. I've used it almost every day of my life. Long. Hard. Sharp. Can't find its name in my head.

A pinch at my wrist. I look down and see a bloom, a proboscis sticking into me like a needle. The fluid it injects burns before feeling good. Then great. Energy enough, I realize. I won't have time to hesitate. I must do what I must do.

My hand makes a fist, and my eyes shut. One last rally of strength. One last, quick gesture. One last exhale as I feel the pressure invade my left ear, so fast, so hard. This last farming is enough. My pound of flesh has been given.

The bloom takes on a life of its own. It pulses and moves. I cannot form a single word; I'm locked inside. A bright pain fills my ears. So loud. Everything is so bright. I hear only water and I can't breathe, but my limbs are free. I'm falling. Drowning. Sinking.

Leah looks up at me. She stands on the ocean floor, arms outstretched. The blooms swim around her. They climb onto one another like crabs in a fishing ship's hold. They form a shape. The familiar figure looks like me. Its eyes open. When our eyes lock, there's a flash and I am seeing through their eyes.

I look back at the emaciated man floating. His body stiffens. His

eyes shut. I feel fire and heat inside my new form. I raise a hand and
see it is new, the skin gray, soft, and smooth. I feel Leah's hand take
my other and we watch my old husk float away, deep into the sea. My
thoughts are my own. My body does my bidding. I take in a breath,
and it feels like I've done so near the sides and top of my neck instead
of my mouth and nose. I can breathe underwater. I am alive once more,
remade into something the same and remade into something altogether new. United once upon a time in life. Reunited in death to share a
life everlasting.

Samuel knocks on the wooden door, just as he's done a thousand times.
The old man doesn't answer. Not even a grunt. He inches it open and
peers inside. Sees Shylock on the bed. His eyes wide, his mouth open.
It's as if he's in shock. His left hand is up near the side of his head.
Samuel believes he's reclining but has never seen Shylock make such
a pose. He's barely able to move his limbs far enough to get a drink.

Stepping close to the bed, his stomach knots. He knows something is wrong. At the foot of the bed, he notices something in Shylock's ear. Something sticking out. A handle? He gasps as he realizes
it's the ice pick, stuck to its hilt, his hand still grasping the device.

Samuel stares a moment more, covers his mouth, then turns away.
The stench hits him. Buzzing. The flies have all gathered on the ceiling.
Hundreds. Thousands. He thinks it's impossible for there to be so many.

Rushing toward the window, he opens it. They swarm outside,
forming a dark cloud. They disperse as if they were never there. Beyond, Samuel sees the bay. The water is higher than he's ever seen. He
realizes it's rising quickly, strongly.

Beyond the canals, the sea rises. A dark figure the size of an island breaks the surface. Samuel doesn't wait to see what it is, but turns
and runs into the halls, shouting for everyone to wake and get out and
up. No one seems to hear. Near the end of the hall and stairs, his feet
splashing in the invading water, he eyes the old man's door a last time,
sees it open, sees water pouring out, hears a loud, deep bellow unlike
anything imaginable.

He's up the stairs and onto the roof where the sky remains blue. Says God's name repeatedly. Snippets of prayers. *Look up at the sky. To heaven*, he implores himself.

The screams below multiply for what feels like an eternity. Until they drown. He shuts his eyes and kneels. Water laps against the building; impossibly close, as if he's on a ship.

Water rises over his knees. Samuel stands until it covers the top of the building, until there's nothing to do but swim and hope he can float until the waters recede, until the nightmare ends. If ever it might. "God has made us pay," he says. "Every single one of us."

I Demand the City of Flesh

(inspired by John Palisano's "A Pound of Flesh")

Maxwell I. Gold

My mind tortured by songs unspoken,
Ne'er enough, until cursed Venice, lost to death and sea,
The price paid with flesh, sorrow, a life unbroken
Piece by piece, gods and monsters, take me
Deeper into the sea, away from dark days.
Illusions of love, the one who-used-to-be;
I demand the city; the flesh be paid!
Drowned in wrath and joy, I am free!
A voice too familiar, songs unspoken,
Pulled me closer by webbed hands towards the foam;
Through the waves, the blood of Venice spilled,
Bone and gold, repaid to the god's own,
    With great dread and wrath, but tribute unpaid,
    I demand the city, your flesh, they said.

Scourge of Rome

Amanda Dier

You thought I could not communicate after my hands and tongue were removed. You were wrong.

I would apologize for the buzz—does it bother your ears? It should—but since you took a knife to my mouth and then robbed me of the ability to write, it is the only way I can get my point across.

Ah, yes, speaking of points. Did that hurt? I am glad of it. The pain of a thousand stingers in your flesh is nothing to what you and your brother did to me. You left me bleeding in the forest, alone, deflowered, and dying. Is it any wonder that the gods themselves came to my aid? Is it any shock that, upon seeing me covered in ants and beetles and the horrors of the woods, they granted me intimacy with them? The gods have a sense of irony, but this is better than death. I appreciate your horror. You have no idea how long it took me to learn to talk using the drone of wings, the click of pincers and the rustle of a million tiny legs.

The gods are cruel, but they have granted me life to regain my pound of flesh from you.

How much do you suppose two hands and a tongue weigh?

Are they valuable to you? My honor was, as was my beauty. They were worth much to my father, Rome's triumphant general against the Goths. I will not say that was the sole reason for your crimes; my beauty was well-acknowledged and my temperament fair, but this was to be a blow more against him than me. Access to me was just a bonus.

To my father, Titus Andronicus, I was a dutiful daughter. I served where he willed, betrothed where he willed it, and did not raise my voice when Saturninus sought to take me for his own. I was proud to see the people choose my father as emperor and prouder still when he stepped aside to allow someone younger and fitter to rule.

Saturninus had always had his eye on me, and when my father declared that he was to be emperor, I could not speak against him. Bassianus refused to surrender me to his brother and I loved him for it, even as my father cursed us both.

If you think Saturninus then chose your mother for her come-liness or nobility, rest assured, he did not. He saw in your treacherous mother what he valued in himself: a desire for vengeance, for insults large and small, and a willingness to do anything to get there.

My father *made* him emperor when Saturninus would have torn heaven asunder to gain the role, and that was still not enough for him. When Saturninus could not marry me, he picked your mother. She could have been happy with this. Empress of Rome would have been her title; there was no higher honor! And yet she swore vengeance for the death of her son even as her two sons declared their love for me, though you scarcely knew me. You could have pursued me honor-ably, though it would have caused quarrel with your brother, who also wanted me, and quarrel with your mother, who wanted her enemies to suffer. You were free citizens of Rome, thanks to Saturninus. It should have been enough.

Does that sting? It should. Your violation of me stung more. Did it hurt to know that though you could share me with your brother Chiron, I would never truly be yours? Yes, I know. The insects have brought me the whispers of the conversation you had with the Moor. The bees write their eavesdropping in wax and pollen. He told you that you could have me and insult my father at the same time.

What, you thought it would remain secret? How you flinch! Though you took the slave's advice and thought to slake your lusts in me, I can still hear your plans as though you speak them now. I hear everything. Every whisper, every secret conversation you had. Every lie, even now. I can feel the shiver of your skin underneath my gnat's feet, smell your heavy expirations with a mosquito's nose. Would that I had been able to smell your approach after catching your mother with her lover.

He told you that the pair of you should have me, and instead of remaining honorable and behaving as citizens of Rome, you returned to your barbarous, animal roots. You Goths are churlish, and though my father treated your brother Alarbus as an honorable sacrifice, you refused to do the same to me. You ruined my honor and that of my family. You dragged me into the woods and rutted in my treasury like animals. You sought to have me in whatever small way you could, blaming my beauty for your crimes. Hush now, a-hush your screaming or I'll muffle your throat with flies.

There. That is a small thing. Your ego, worn down along with the skin of your face. Now it is nothing more than a leprous beggar's mask. When you were done with your horrible deeds, you cut away parts of me and then asked who I could tell, who I could name as my assailant with no tongue. Speak my name now, Demetrius! Chiron has no hands to write with, no fingers now to even draw in the dirt. You could not hear him screaming over the chittering of the spiders in your ears, the cloud of wasps around your head as my new hands of vermin ate his own away.

See? You aren't alone here. I was lucky to catch the pair of you together, scheming still more in the palace gardens. None shall approach us here; my insects keep them away, and the longer we linger here, the more insects I call to me. Rome is rich with vermin. I never knew how much until now.

The first time I awoke to feel the insects crawling on my skin, I shrieked with the horror of it. Bees fell in my mouth, and to feel their tiny legs tickling the bottom of my mouth as they floundered in the blood pooled there was more than I could bear.

But they kept me warm. Do you know what it's like, to use thousands of living insects to keep the cold at bay? The buzzing of their wings generated heat and it kept me from dying from the shock of your insult to me. Pincers closed off the gushing veins in my wrists; wax stuffed in my wounds kept them from reopening, and though I hated the gentle scratch of vermin in my mouth, the sweet honey and wax and resin they brought to soothe the pain was a balm. Do you know the agony that awakens every time you try to swallow with no tongue? You will soon.

There was no note to tell me which god sought to bless and punish me; no bath of moonlight to show Diana's favor or a feeling of vitality to signal Juno's attentions. No sunlight could pierce the darkness of those woods, so it mustn't be Apollo. Whichever god I roused, I can only be thankful to them.

You sought to punish me because of who my family was, and the fact that your family led the Goths as mine led the Roman army. Allow me to do the same. Do you hear the screaming? No? Is the buzzing too loud?

There. The gnats in your ears have stopped for now. *That* noise is not your brother. It is the Empress of Rome. I believe her highness does not like how the stag beetles are treating her. I found her at the edge of the palace walls mourning the absence of her baby and seeking sight of the Moor.

Can you see now? I had to turn your head for you; the number of beewolves I had to sting you with was quite large, and you are regrettably swollen. Do try to keep breathing. I would hate for you to choke with how tumescent your neck is.

Queen of Goths, Empress of Rome, her majesty Tamora. Mother of Chiron, Alarbus, and yourself. I called her a gentle queen and begged for death's respite after you stabbed Bassianus, but she denied me. Can you speak? No?

Watch as these insects do to her what she ordered done to me. Your actions ate me from the inside out; now they do the same. See how her stomach swells with maggots? She misses her baby who the Moor fled with; here is her replacement. This will take days, Demetrius. As I learned in the forest, maggots take a terribly long time to grow, but they are hungry little things. They don't normally eat living flesh, but under my direction, they will eat anything. Her children were the greatest value to her; now she will be mother to millions, harboring them all within her living flesh.

All of you have weaknesses, flaws, and strengths. These have become your undoing.

When I find the Moor Aaron—and I will. I have eyes everywhere. You cannot hide from insects; his plotting brain will become food for my swarm. You carried out his orders, but would you have had the courage without him telling you what to do? Would your mother have dared conspire against the sons of the Andronici without his honeyed words in her ear?

Their heads now rest in my father's lap and I fear he is not long for this world, for as I lost my hands to you and your brother, he lost one of his to the ax of your mother's bastard lover, the Moor, in an attempt to ransom my brothers. Alas! He will pay when I catch up to him. Even my father does not recognize my tender touch now; my new hands feed upon my brothers' broken flesh and all my father does is stare at their empty eyes. I am there with you, Father! I am everywhere.

And yet I do wonder if I should let my new hands eat your hands and Chiron's tongue, too. After all, they are hungry, and wherever Saturninus's cuckold is, they will need the energy to find him. Your mother, thin quim that she is, can only provide so much.

I think I shall, but first, I need to first take my original pound of flesh from you.

Open your mouth, Demetrius, son of Tamora, Queen of the Goths, and mother of corpses. Open wide so I can show you what happens when you wound a woman of Rome.

(inspired by Titus Andronicus… Aaron was right. Why should wrath be mute and fury dumb?)

Unrepentant

(based on Titus Andronicus)

Cindy O'Quinn

Look around me, people are struggling.
Your droplets contaminate all the air.
Everything, everywhere! Titus, you
inconsiderate fuck. Why share now when you
refused before, when it mattered the most?
You don't care who you kill or who you spare
for another day. Plucking us off one
at a time. Leaving no hope, nothing more,
except one last thing—*the world is dying.*
I am Queen of the Goths, set on revenge.
Rape and murder, your answers to madness.
Hands and heads roll, bake, and burn forever.
    No one's safe around you, never again.
    The final act plays—*the world is dying.*

Uneasy lies the head that wears a crown

—Henry IV, Part 2

The Hollow Crown

(based on Henry IV Pts. 1 and 2)

Gemma Files

astcheap. The smells, the sounds. John Falstaff—*Sir* John, still, thank ye—wakes from nightmare battle all at once, still clenched against the pikeman's charge, eyes bleared beyond sight and knotted in a nest of drunk-sweat soaked sheets; it's cold in this room, the one he sometimes shares with young Prince Hal, whenever the latter deigns to do so. Even the bile a-roiling in his mouth is cold.

I'm told you're a witch, that familiar voice says from somewhere to the left, words drawling alike with aristocracy and its owner's own cup-dregs. *In your other moments, mind…those in between when I, or others, pay to have our pleasure of you.*

And who might you've heard that rumour from, exactly, your Highness? Just so's I can thank them kindly, I mean.

Don't use—

—that title you pretend ain't yours, no matter how far you sink? Oh ay, I remember.

John of Gaunt's grandson sits the floor here, John thinks, *cross-legged, like a Saracen. Sits my floor; chew on that, Bolingbroke, who slew my true king and made a sottish thief of me. You, whose son rejects the very dynastic lineage you thus murdered to confirm, in favour of committing old sins fresh new ways, alongside th' exact same outlaw company I'm forced to keep.*

Good Christ's own wounds, if that bastard only knew the things they've gotten up to, him and Hal. Would be enough to make his own dead war-horse cackle.

Doll Tearsheet a witch, though, after every other strange thing John's lived through, these last few years? Well, why not. Even whores have their secrets.

Scry my future for me, then, Doll, my sweet. Before I slip yet farther down into the mire.

With a glad heart, milord, so long's you pay me. Since payment's th'one thing trumps all, here as elsewhere.

A shudder, time slipping past in one long, slow blink, and John breaks surface once again, rolling up. Beside the bed, Doll peers into a bowl of water as a candle flickers on the planks nearby; Hal seems to watch her closely, head at almost the same angle, bare new-moon back bent and white, dark mop of hair hung down far enough to render eyes indistinguishable from brows. For all they're both topless, John finds it hard to find the prospect of Doll's small, high-slung breasts anything but sad—though should he fear her now, knowing what else she's capable of, besides the usual? Too hard a riddle by far for a fat old fool like him to ponder, 'specially without a fresh tankard of ale to help his wits along that particular narrow, crooked path.

You see wrong, Hal says, at last. *You must.*

Never, milord, she replies, without glancing up. *Against the witches' creed, that is.* Then shoots him a sly wink, a gap-toothed grin thrown in on top, for good measure. *Assuming you believe there's such a thing, that is.*

I do not.

Nor should you. Yet I see true, as ever.

Hal looks up, too, at that. *You must,* he tells her, voice softer than John's heard it since the night they met—tells himself, perhaps? *It cannot be. My father…he would never choose me now, not with all I've done to sully myself in his eyes, or the world's. All my hard work.*

Ah, should I pity you, milord? Must've been some strain, to wench and drink one end of Eastcheap to t'other, in John Falstaff's wake. Or was it him, in yours?

Hal's quick to take bait more oft than not, but this morn's different, apparently; he thinks instead, takes pause for one long breath, the sketch of one more. Then asks, his gaze holding Doll's: *I'd pay well for your teacher's word on this same subject, you took it as no insult.*

Insulted by more coin, me? I thought we knew each other well by now, milord.

Hal smiles at that, face immediately more like his own. *Thank you, Doll,* he says.

Ay, well. Might be you'll think better on that, after.

Mistress Quickley's has a stout oak door that bangs open to the front and a leather-hinged one behind, for far less public deliveries. This latter is the one lets in Doll's hag, a braw Scots woman almost John's own height with cataracts on both eyes and rusty grey braids hung to her waist, their ends tucked back inside her belt like pannier-ropes; Quick Nell herself steps aside when she catches the first glimpse of her, wetting the beldame's shadow with spit to turn ill-wishes, but the witch pays her no mind.

You'd be the prince, then, she says to Hal, without an introduction, sniffing hard 'til her head turns, as if she's traded sight for smell. *He who'd no' be king, if that's a fate can be avoided.*

And can it? Hal asks, sliding the table out so she can seat herself by his side, even while John's hand goes to his hip without thinking. The witch gives him a ghost of a laugh and Hal a strange, stately dip, half nod, half curtsey; she's light on her feet for one of such size, that's for sure. Then comes sliding in like a girl to plant one leathery palm astride Hal's knee, pointing her other forefinger at John's knife and wagging it sharply, in silent order: Put that back where it most often hangs, my bonny lad, before I'm forced to do more—which John can all but hear behind the eyes, and does.

Most things can, once you know their price, she says to Hal; meanwhile, out loud, *for all that price be high. So would ye be told yours, or are ye content to stand fast, given the risks?*

Don't speak to me of risk, madam; the thing's impossible, plain and simple. Name your payment, therefore, and let me take my chances. God only knows my purse runs deep, even in disgrace, as Sir John here can tell you.

The witch laughs outright at his vehemence, making Hal blink, obviously uncertain whether or not to take offence; John leans in to head him off before he can, voice pitched low, advising him: *Best to think on't further, young Hal, perhaps, before you slap your last coins down on the word of a woman you've only just met with. Many might say destiny's not so easily eluded, by craft or otherwise...as the Classics state, she's a goddess, not some servant to be pensioned off at will, whenever the fever takes you—*

Another chuckle cuts off John's argument here, almost affectionately. *Oh aye*, she agrees, *the God yuir churchmen prate of does know much indeed, true enow...and He whom I serve yet more besides, if He be questioned nicely. For instance, 'twas not sae long past I counted as three for many a year by the Black Man's grace—three always, a coven together in single company, myself by self, self and self. Wi' all of us full able to walk destiny's path in different directions at once 'til we met again, were that only what we cared to.*

Yet now you sit here alone once more, Hal notes. *How comes* that, *I wonder, if the Devil be so mighty?*

Because my others were ta'en and murdered both most foully, by cunning rather than force, the witch replies, *as 'twas always possibility. Same as ye—even were ye to split yersel' in two, dooming one to wear the crown, while t'other escapes it—might still end up the same, or even worse.*

There, then; John opens his mouth to warn Hal, only to spot that most dangerous of glints already lighting up his royal bloody eyes—same one which tells him no drink's ever too large, no woman's ever too taken. Same one will make him believe he can challenge five soldiers and a bear, or at least believe he can tongue-lash John into challenging them *for* him.

(Which he will, damn his own eyes, without faintest hope of slight reward, let alone proper compensation. Has already, and on more than one occasion.)

You forbid me the spell, then, Hal says, meeting her smile with his own.

She shakes her head. *Grammarye canna be withheld, not when 'tis asked for; how else may new witches be made, after all? I only warn, young master. Only that.*

Ah. Yet I'm incapable of taking such things into fullest account, or so I've been told.

By him here, who yearns to save ye from whatever filth I might whisper in yuir ear, were ye only bent tae let him? Ay, I see.

And she leans in close, then closer, even closer still—enough so's to press her corpse-lips past Hal's lobe, reciting the receipt (for all John can tell) full on against that tiny hole where meat gives way to skull. Stab a man there deep enough, you'll kill more than his hearing. John raises his dram and watches Hal nod, draining it hard, trying not to choke. Praying the witch will take her leave long before he grows far too drunk to keep himself from blurting out, in one sloshed rush:

Two of you, then…one good, one bad, like mystery play angels? Or both the same, but each…less?

Than what? Hal considers, well in his cups himself by now, as John shrugs. *Uh…the former, I'd surmise; not much point to the latter, if I hope to have my way. Though divided more according to my best and worst qualities, a well-made and ill-made Hal by moral standards…identical from skin out, yet disparate beneath.*

Poor England, John thinks, but doesn't say—left with only half a king, and not the better half. By his own admittance.

Will you do it soon? He makes himself ask, instead.

Later, perhaps. Perhaps never. Adding, as John opens his mouth to interject: And *only if I must, that's the point of it…Doll may yet have read my fate a-wrong, much though I'd hesitate to suggest the idea to her face once more, without never tempting her to bed again; what I learned tonight will keep 'til then, either way. You know me.*

'Tis certain, John replies, as the tavern dims around them; no longer quite sure what he's agreeing with, or why it matters. *I do* know *you, good my liege—in sickness and in health, prosperity and…lack of such. Sworn bullies together, blood of my blood, my…Hal. I do.*

As I do you, Hal assures him, with equal-besotted emphasis. *Now put thy head down, old man, and sleep.*

John does, gratefully: Sleeps, dreams, even in the midst of riot, the tavern's snug and stinking din. Forgets, or tries to.

Until—

The Tabard's rat-pit, Southwark, where John is oft not welcome due to funds' lack or debts let slide, or both. Tonight, however, he's flush with coin after a thievery arranged with Beale, who slouches by his side where Hal was once wont to. Then again, Hal's king now, as he never wanted; said so, any road. Bolingbroke's true heir at last, that pretty bitch.

John has glimpsed him from afar, crowd-caught, upright and grave, lank mop of hair bowl-cut to fit beneath a helm. Killed Hotspur Harry Percy himself, or so John hears, then walked the barefoot path to his coronation. John wants to approach him soonish, remind him of his many unpaid-for kindnesses, and yet—can it be he fears to? Can it?

At his elbow, Beale's become somehow ensnarled by fellow thieves, rivals all, pushing through to trade blows and insults while the blood sprays, dogs' and rats' alike. *We know the king, you cunts!* John hears him cry, as if that solves anything. *Harry's our Hal that was, the skinny fucker wi' no head for ale! John, Sir John, come aid me—*

So he does, of course. Then finds himself slipping fast away through mud and ordure, brown to the waist, holding Beale up with one arm, his own wounds closed with t'other. Through an alley, 'round and about, bruising his shoulders blue by pushing through the crack where two wattle-and-daub shacks collapse far enough to hold each other up. Slams hard against a man's back and curses it for some bloody stupid bastard's, only to have it turn upon him, disclosing Hal's face re-cut as Henry V of England's signet: A sovereign profile, nose sneer-set, eyes like cold blue chips under those slant black brows. The very image of his vanished companion, and yet.

And yet.

Hal, boy, John calls him, unable not to. *Where've thee been, lad? 'Tis not how we treat friends, this way...*

Hal—Harry—looks down on him, unamused. Was he always so tall? Did John simply deceive himself otherwise?

I know thee not, fat fool, the king replies. *Fall to thy prayers.*

And more, much more, following John as he scuttles away pulling Beale in his shocked and sorrowed wake, back into murk, into mire. Back into the scum where he belongs, exiled alone forever.

This is what comes of loving your enemy's kin, he thinks, hours later, shaking in fever's grip, a prey to quick-blackening infection: My just desserts, my justice, as traitor to my king, and his. For surely I am all he says, and more.

(The proud young new-made monarch's voice ringing still, in either ear: *How ill white hairs become a fool and jester! I have long dreamt of such a kind of man, so surfeit-swell'd, so old, and so profane; but being awak'd, I do despise my dream.*)

Presume not that I am the thing I was, for God doth know, so shall the world perceive, that I have turn'd away my former self; so will I those that kept me company.

Oh, the hurt of it. Were Hal still here, he'd heat a tool to sizzling and burn this disgrace from John's flesh, if not his soul. *Sir John has injured himself,* Beale would tell him, with no matter a never-a-mind to how, and even were the lollard still not sober enough to walk, he'd spring to the challenge. Anything to lord his learning over John, to reconfirm the distance between them—that same distance which shrank to naught whenever they shared their sins, overindulging alike in quim and brawling, in liquor, theft and blasphemy...

(*When thou dost hear I am as I have been, approach me, and thou shalt be as thou wast, the tutor and the feeder of my riots. Till then I banish thee, on pain of death, as I have done the rest of my misleaders, not to come near our person by ten miles.*)

Pain. Blind, idiot pain. Worse than he's felt since St. Malo. Bad as any he's ever felt, and he's felt plenty.

Oh god, oh please. Oh leave me here to lie abed and burn, then shit myself and die.

But: *Sit up, Falstaff,* a voice—one he thought he'd never hear again, given—orders him. *Open your mouth, drink this; yes, I know it tastes awful. Doll, help me cut his shirt away—Beale, take these, and burn them. Mistress Nell, a kettle—boiling water, hot enough to cook puddings. If cloth sticks to the wounds, we'll have to wet it before we pull it away.*

Bring that salve I mixed, milord, shall I?

Do you want him to live? Then ay, do so.

Burning and freezing together, shivering hoarse with thirst, his throat iron ball-stoppered; John sinks and sinks, not looking to rise again. The sun does rise once more, however, for all he feels like sealing wax used over, melted down and impressed so many times it barely holds its shape. Comes to with a jump between Doll's slack form and the wall, with Beale curled at his feet like a stinking dog and Hal—*true* Hal, John can see, even with his mane cropped and his clothes new-bought—propped up on a chair nearby.

Hal raises a brow. John coughs the taste of almost dying from his throat, draws fresh breath, then coughs again.

You did it, he observes, to which Hal shrugs, spreading his long-fingered hands in silent comment: Well, obviously. *Before or after you first sat the throne, you high-born brat?*

After, Hal allows. *Just last night, in fact.*

Oh, ay. In time to turn that other self of yours on me and laugh over the result, I wager.

I didn't laugh, John—never that—but yes. Adding, slyly, as John snorts his disbelief: *Though I did lay bets before, and collect, after.*

Hope the odds paid well, for all that. Better than usual, any road.

Hal smiles. *Much*, he says. *But then, I've never been much of a gambler.*

True enough, John agrees, feeling his heart squeeze tight inside his bruised ribs' cage.

Half a man's better nature and half his worse, John thinks. But as to which is which, can he ever claim to know? Can Hal?

They strut the streets of Eastcheap in dance-step, nothing left to keep them separate—plunge head-first into a well of strong delights, roister 'til early and sleep 'til late, spend freely 'til their pockets empty, after which an hour or so of red work's practice soon fills them up again. Still, the honeymoon runs brief; Hal's mouth grows cruel, his manners saturnine. He charms the lesser knaves 'til they tell him secrets, then uses those to goad them into picking fights with each other and sits in the corner, watching—true plays and mummery are as nothing to such dramas, from all that John can tell, given the way they serve to stretch Hal's smile sidelong.

And whenever John dare call him upon his malice, Hal simply turns aside to take his pleasures elsewhere…leaps bed to bed without a plan or pause, deliberately indiscriminate, not returning 'til John begs him to. He sows his seed and spreads disease, then slips away like quicksilver, untouched. His shadow, halved or no, darkens fast as rot.

He'll get you killed, Fat John, Doll whispers to him one night in Quickley's under her breath, one eye trained fast on Hal as he dozes nearby, like she wants to make sure he's not listening. *Same way's he did with Beale, and Poins. Same way he stood under Bardolph as he swung and grinned at how he danced, wi' never a stitch of sentiment in't.*

Ah, Hal'd never do that, lass—not to me. Besides, there's worse ways to die than for a friend, ain't there?

Ay, so the story goes. Yet who's to say which of 'em it was who truly called you friend, if either?

The paths diverge. England's Harry declares war on France over some tennis balls, or perhaps his grandmother's claim. When Hal of Eastcheap hears the news he hurls his drink against the wall, then hurls himself straightway into the fight that erupts, throwing fists 'til his hands and face are equal-bright with injury. Sinks his teeth deep in one man's face and shakes him by the wound, bites half another's ear off and chews it up, then spits it out once more upon the rushes; to save them both from murder or the gallows, John's forced to haul Hal bodily away, slung 'cross his shoulder like a kicking grain-bag as he punches them free. Not that any of that does much to soothe Hal's temper, which soon whips to levels of frenzy John's never assumed him capable of.

Idiot, madman, Hal raves into the night, cursing his double's bones, his eyes, his soul. *He's made himself our father—made us both him, damned and doomed, two Bolingbrokes reborn! Men will die like flies for this thing I've set the crown upon, his vanity, his pride. A minute's victory followed by a hundred years of war, that'll be his legacy...*

But you can't know that, Hal.

Can I not? Witchcraft, fool: I see it behind my eyes, awake, asleep— what he's apt to do wearing my name, and how he might not've, had he only been me as well. These awful things we're capable of, he and I! And I cannot dream other unless I drink to do so, drink 'til I'm like to soil myself...

You drink to sleep, John says, nodding. *Ay, well; me too, as you've seen before, and since. That's the price paid for freedom such as ours, who live wi'out penance, or salvation.*

We happy few, Hal replies, after a long moment. *Here in this garden of earthly delights, where naught's forbid, so long as it be done without regret—and god knows, since that night, I regret nothing. Which means you must bear guilt enough for both of us, from now on, I suppose....*

Silence again here, and longer, this time—the fire flickers, rimming them both in red. The bed is warm, Hal's sleepy weight against John's stomach slack, his breath's dim bellows almost comforting. And:

I can, is all John can think to say. *I will, always. You know that, Hal.*

I do, Hal agrees, eyes closing.

Yet none of it means anything, in the end.

King Henry V dies early, leaving both Lancaster and Plantagenet factions bereft; Hal Bolingbroke—Hal Commoner, he calls himself, when asked—feels it happen. *My heart stopped in my chest just now,* he says, *then found its beat again, but slower. So slow, now. And oh, I feel so cold...*

John sees it in his face, this change. Before, with half of him yet walking the world protected by knights-at-arms and royal title alike, working its will far beyond anywhere his enemies might think to reach, Hal must have felt himself inviolate. Now he knows better.

Even if the qualities left to Hal be more bad than good, how-ever, they still maintain him; this cannot be denied. Yet how long can a man live, John wonders, with half of all that makes him pared away? And to what end?

Only to endlessly thief and drink, by evidence of John's own eyes—to fuck and rout and rout and fuck, then move on, and on, and on. To love none and be loved by none, except…for one.

(One fool, old and fat and grown exceeding sad, inside himself. Who spends his days and nights in grief over whatever man his friend might once have grown to be while trapped beneath the crown, had he not so ably made his escape from it.)

Here, then, is how it ends: One night, they roister home to find Quickley's full of royal guards, a woman waiting in their midst. When Hal halts, combing back his hair, she gasps out loud; her hood slips down, disclosing the Valois nose and a simple coronet. Her hands, once folded patient at her waist, suddenly tighten 'round her gravid belly.

So it is *true,* she says, voice French-coloured, the words shot through with anger and disgust. *Dear god, what he could have been and done, but for you—what he accomplished nonetheless, even thus bereft! And you, just look; coward, heretic. You vile and selfish thing.*

John's back-hairs rise, but Hal just laughs, drinking up her rage like wine.

Oh yes, he answers. *Just think what further massacres might've arisen—how many more reduced to battlefield rags, their stinking corpses drowned in mud! And you, madame, who fear yourself impregnate by an incubo, yet clutch your swollen belly tight…a madman's daughter wed to a usurper's son, whose troth dooms war a century to come.*

Strange poetry in that last part, for all dead Harry's foreign drab seems immune to it.

Creature, she calls him, at last. *What right have you to live, when all my world is dead?*

John hears her voice break, and winces. Hal cuts a bow, mean-while, so deep it sweeps the floor, suffused with blackly mocking courtesy.

What right indeed, he agrees. *And so—Fat John, this rout be done; I take my leave of thee.*

Wait, John longs to cry…but late, too late by far. Hal palms the dagger from his sleeve and strikes, slitting his own throat wide, before any of the rest have time to try.

I understand, now, Queen Catherine says, once the guards have carried what's left of Hal away.

Why he faded so fast and seemed so hollow, my Henri; how he could talk me into loving him even in my family's defeat, but never love me in return. And should I kill you now, Sir Falstaff, for beguiling him so? Since 'twas to stay here, with you, he worked this evil spell, or so I hear.

If it please you, my grace.

It does not. Nothing will, from now on, I think.

She might as well have plucked the words from John's own head.

And indeed nothing does, 'til death finally takes him—the long path down, offence in every part of it, without even hope (no matter how faint) of seeing Hal once more, wherever it might lead.

The Witch Stained Red

Stephanie M. Wytovich

Beware the witch who hangs half split in trees,
a soft soliloquy of snakes, her eyes.
She birthed The Fates, raised strong women to be—
Present, Past, Future, she sees through man's lies.
That night, such delight, brought pain to her mark,
a horde of ghosts followed him into bed.
She scratched his initials into the bark,
her laugh rendered guilty, her hands stained red.
She slipped the noose off, fell down to the earth,
with bitter daggers, bit clean through her tongue.
His body shook broken, soulless in hearth,
A death she did summon, stale air, crushed lung.
     This reaper sulks angry, searching each night.
     Their sins a lit candle, always in sight.

(inspired by Macbeth)

A World of Kisses for His Pain

James Chambers

"Ah, Raffiano! Speak your witness."

"Iago, witness do I bring. Compelling circumstances didst Othello unknowing convey."

Iago flipped a jingling leather pouch to the alley cobbles. It landed by Raffiano's feet, a lump of shadow in the gloom. The spy's eyes broadened with avarice.

"For you, coins late of Roderigo's purse should your words satisfy my need."

"They shall, I swear, for I have heard most rapt and privy counsel twixt Othello and the daughter of Brabantio and heard the spells he cast about her wits, tales spun of far, exotic lands and beings, wild beyond imaginings of Christian men. To words, she swoons, as bodily she hews to him in manner fit to bring a blush to watching moon. Such witness might your wants fulfill?"

"Indeed, and handsomely, so onward speak."

"The Moor at rest in his high chamber Desdemona didst regale, and she enthralled, entranced, in every manner by his tale and touch, didst him entwine in her embrace, the lunar glow against dark night.

Of market stalls in the Maghreb, and journeys hither-thither, fierce on battlefields, and lands of conquest, even to his princely rise, he spoke. One episode above the others stood to meet such witchcraft ripe to seize to his dominion, heart and soul, Brabantio's dear daughter as you supposed. In youth, Othello trod those places where the cannibals of each other eat, the Anthropophagi, and where dwell the men whose heads grow beneath their shoulders. His accounts of barbarism, fear, and monstrosity thrilled Desdemona, who 'pon him showered pity for his sufferings."

"Hie, speak like this no more to me, who hates the Moor with heart confirmed, lest thine self infatuated seem. To me now deliver goods for payment rendered."

"Aye, good Iago, perched upon the window ledge, didst I this tale perceive while two reclined in satisfaction, their desires sated."

Othello stroked his calloused fingers over Desdemona's silken back and twirled them through her golden hair. She sighed, contentment in every atom of her breath. They laid together, embraced on an ornate and gilded daybed, its pillows and sheets askew from their exertions. A single oil lamp limned the shadows bronze.

"Speak more of thy life," Desdemona said, and in her voice whispered affection and admiration.

"Of my life, you know all worth telling," Othello said.

Desdemona rose on her elbows, her gown's loosened folds spilling around her. "No, some you have only hinted at in broad accounts that tease my imaginings. These you have withheld in full, bereaving me of knowledge I would have of the man to whom I pledge my being against the counsel of my father. What benefits us to have secrets? To you, my life is illuminated, yet you retain parts of yours in shadow."

"There are in this world things and places so dark and dreadful, I would spare you knowing them. I refrain from relating these histories to stop you a darkening of your soul."

"Have they darkened yours? I think not. For in you, for me, all is light, all life. Speak! Spare me nothing. My body and heart belong to you. I would have you share the same with me entire."

Othello slid loose from Desdemona's warm touch, left the bed, and pulled his clothes sloppily around him against a soft breeze that tickled at the sweat lingering on his skin. He peered through the window, as Desdemona rustled cloth to restore her modesty. The sweetness of her natural perfume drifted to him. He considered himself blessed to possess the heart of one so heavenly in aspect, so magnificent in being. A thousand men he would fight with but a club and dagger to serve her. For her, he risked his hard-won position of authority in Venice, his reputation as a general and trusted outsider, Arabian ally to the merchants. All for her, for fair Desdemona. Everything his life made of him, all the choices and chances that led him to Venice and his lauded status, he seconded to the affection and desire she awoke in him, and he in her.

Day after day, week after week, she had come to hear him speak his history. Their bond grew, impossible to deny, unbreakable, permanent. They had shared nearly all a man and woman could. What harm would come from giving a full account of himself? He bore no shame for his past but wished only to keep its terrors removed from his present. Yet he could deny this woman nothing. He pulled a chair by the window and sat upon it. Outside, stars glittered in the indigo night, outshone only by the moon—and by the light in fair Desdemona's eyes.

"Vaguely in the region of Ethiopia," he said, "there exists a land where strange beings practice stranger customs and devotions that to us seem cruel and inhuman, where small purse may buy the lives of many men. Into this land I once ventured in search of four soldiers under my banner, who vanished one night from our camp 'pon the shore of the Red Sea. There, my ship held anchor, awaiting rendezvous with an ally I learned later fell prey to Barbary pirates. My missing soldiers were abducted, their theft witnessed by a watchman, who survived mortal wounds long enough to yield good guidance for us to give chase." Othello removed a leathern volume stained by time and the elements from a nearby shelf. "The events that followed I recorded in this journal, one of many of my travels. I shall read aloud in your familiar tongue what I wrote here in Arabic."

On day two of our pursuit, a sea of dunes and sand surrendered to rocky shelfs, whiskered with scrub growth. On the horizon, stone ledges mounted themselves to the foothills of a jagged ridge that scratched wantonly at the cloudless sky. We camped in the lowlands, where nothing hindered us from observing at a safe distance any who might approach, and stood a night's watch. At sunrise we resumed our solemn undertaking, climbing increasingly rough terrain until we happened upon a gorge in which fixed stones offered easy ascent.

Whether aligned like rising steps by nature or man's intervention, I could not guess, but nearer the peak, we perceived faded images of odd creatures painted on the rock walls. Horned beasts with six legs, others sporting two heads, and still more in impossible combinations: winged panthers, scorpion-tailed lions, even great apes with the heads and faces of men. Would that I had heeded this as warning of the nature of the land we entered. But bloodstains dappled the way too, some old and dry, others sticky to the touch, fueling my concern for my lost soldiers and my hopes of rescuing them.

The path concluded in a clearing ringed by rose-colored stones protruding like giant's teeth from the earth. They surrounded a cave mouth, from which muted voices clamored. We advanced, cautious, our swords unsheathed. In the clearing lay scattered clothing and gear, which I recognized as that of my missing soldiers. I bid three from our party to investigate the cave, while we others remained on guard.

The voices continued muffled, indistinguishable between those of men and those of animals rooting in the darkness—when from the gloom came a great blood-chilling cry. Signal we had indeed found our lost fellows, but its tone announced them discovered not whole and well. I led the way to the cave, where one from the advance group guided me with a fresh torch into the darkness, while the others waited outside.

Oh, what a horrible, merciless, inhuman sight met my eyes!

I have seen much of pain and torture. Men murdered by villains. Warriors gashed, severed, and dismembered on the plains of battle. Poor souls mutilated by accident and happenstance. Yet never had I seen such gruesome devastation to a man's form as awaited in that forsaken cave.

My lost warriors, stripped to their loin cloths, lay side by side on the gravel. Each struggled to speak, hindered by having lost their tongues to a villain's knife, a favored tactic of abductors who wished to silence their prisoners. They struggled to breathe through blood clotted in their mouths. From thigh to shin, every part of their legs and knees lay smashed to bloody pulp and pulverized bone. Crimson streaks mottled with chunks of flesh led from the last man to a massive boulder that, I surmised, had been rolled across them all, leaving it smeared with gore. Their hands protruded from their wrists, broken into unrecognizable, fleshy mitts in pools of blood as if mashed with a mighty hammer. The stench of dread and viscera assaulted our senses. My men chattered in horror, questioning what purpose such brutality served. Even as the logic of it formed in my mind, shouts from without the cave confirmed my fear.

We had entered a trap.

"Hie!" I called, directing my soldiers to attend their brothers-in-arms outside the cave.

I lingered only to run my merciful blade across the throats of my ravaged warriors for I knew none could recover. Steeling my nerves, I dashed to meet the fray.

The rose-stones that surrounded the cave mouth had come alive, blocking our passage to the foothills. Two-thirds of my party writhed and bled at the end of spears thrust into their vitals. The scene spoke of madness, chaos, and treachery. Had the stones themselves come to life? No, not so, only the men—nay, not men, but *creatures*—beneath them. Concealed in cunning shells of hollowed rock, they emerged with spears and battle rage in their eyes, all the more terrible for the location of those eyes: one peering from each shoulder. Their mouths, located where a man's belly forms his center mass, bared cracked and yellowed teeth and emitted shrieks and growls of rage. Their nostrils flared from noses protruding where a man might thump his chest. They moved with swift agility on nimble bony legs and overran us in seconds. Five did we slay, three by my own blade, as more poured from the cliffs and other concealments until half my party lay as corpses, the other half wounded, at the mercy of our attackers, who bound them with rope.

I refused to surrender. I raised my sword at one who charged me with a barbed spear. I sliced the pole in half with my blade, an act that fair saved my life, then struck the beast a blow with the pommel of my weapon and flattened it to the ground. Attackers leapt around me, poking at me with their spears. With a cry of rage, I charged the nearest, only to suffer a stunning strike to the back of my head from an unseen foe. I reeled, senseless, and almost welcomed the oblivion that robbed me of the sight of those hideous demons whose faces glared and shrieked from beneath their shoulders.

The Blemmy took prisoner all of us who lived.

For that was who had trapped us: the men whose heads grow beneath their shoulders.

Bugbears on many a map of regions unknown except through harried reports of the very few civilized men who ventured into them and survived the return. Stuff of legend. Known by some for their hunched manner of combat, by others for their hypnotic dancing around great bonfires. Never had I heard of their use of such camouflage, dressing themselves like stones.

Unable to defeat our full party, they had devised a trap to abduct a few of us, thus luring a larger group into their domain for capture without great loss to their own. I deduced this while balancing on the tips of my toes as my body dangled by the wrists from coarse ropes, the other ends of which creaked overhead as they twisted around a wooden shaft in the cage in which the Blemmy confined us. The cage itself stood mounted atop a wooden cart with massive stone wheels. A dozen marching Blemmy, who bore its wooden yoke 'pon their powerful shoulders, drew it onward. Their monstrous eyes squinted at the effort. Did they mean to enslave or ransom us? I saw no other method in their action, but I would soon discover an even fouler purpose.

Around me, my soldiers wept, four to either side of me, all bound in like fashion.

In the steadiest voice I could muster, I spoke words of encouragement. These soothed some, who expressed relief that I yet lived, while others mourned harder, repenting their failure to spare me our capture. My men, my brave, loyal soldiers; the urge to weep for them and lament my own lapse as a general for leading them into a brazen trap stirred within me, but I suppressed it for a general may not reveal such weakness to his warriors.

The cart rambled and rolled, jolting over uneven, stony terrain. Each unexpected shift or bounce lanced pain through every part of me. Shocks threatened to wrest my arms from their sockets. Breathing hurt. My head did swoon. Some of my warriors passed into unconsciousness. I envied the surcease they found in senselessness but fought every effort of my body to shut down, for if I were to give up, there would be no escape from the Blemmy for any of us.

The headless men prattled. Their rough, hollow voices emanated from their guts as they yammered in animalistic sounds from fierce whispers to harsh grunts. I understood none of it. Each one bore a stubby stone knife at his waist. Those not pulling the cart carried their spears. They stood perhaps four to five feet tall, the height of a headless man, and their skin possessed the tone of pink sandstone. Their arms, as thin and knobby as their legs, waved and flailed when they walked. I studied them as I worked my wrists ceaselessly to find slack to my bonds. My sole purpose became to free myself and my soldiers and slay our captors to the last.

This, I am dismayed to confess, I did not achieve.

Though I forced looseness into the ropes round my wrists, we reached our destination too soon. The path widened into a broad clearing. At the western edge stood a white tent, outside of which watched two men armed with swords and garbed in leathery fabric of an odd hue and texture. Several mules waited, hitched to the trunk of a lonely fig tree. The Blemmy rolled our prison cart opposite the tent entrance then dropped their posts. The cart tilted forward, igniting bursts of pain in my bone and muscle as my body dangled. Screams of agony attested that my soldiers experienced the same.

The Blemmy's prattling reached a fever pitch. They thumped their spears on the earth.

My men pled with me: *What is this place? Who abides within the tent? What do they intend for us? Where have these beasts brought us?* I offered what reassurance I could and promised to free us if humanly possible. I bid them courage. *Mask your fear in the face of our captors and unknown enemies*, I urged. *Meet whatever fate awaits us as warriors.*

This calmed them even as it seemed to agitate our captors.

One of the Blemmy regarded me with cold and alien hatred, projecting from its weirdly placed eyes, the size of lemons. Its gaze felt like that of a demon out of hell set upon feasting on my soul. It whipped the shaft of its spear against my legs, wrecking my balance and costing me a painful yank on my arms. Then it thrust the tip at the bottom of my throat, its message clear: *silence*. I complied. What point to inviting unnecessary injury?

The tent flaps rustled as the two watchmen tied them back. Three men emerged, in garb similar to the watchmen, but finer and with more ornate swords at their belts, suggesting a higher rank. They spread across the clearing. Two others followed, appearing of even higher status, and dragging with them a woman stripped naked and matted in filth. They led her on long poles that controlled loops of rope encircled around her neck. Last, a lone man in the finest dress yet exited the tent. He bore no sword, only a knife with a golden hilt. His face lurked behind a mask, the monstrous countenance of which explained to me the unfamiliar fabric his people wore. The face of another man covered his, a façade of skin, a stolen face, ragged and wet round the edges, where a blade had severed it from a skull. These men wore human skin, tanned and tailored like that of any animal.

He spoke the Blemmy language, meaningless to me, but the headless ones ignited in titters of glee and excitement at his speech. The men escorting the female prisoner brought her to the heart of the clearing. She screamed and clawed at the ropes round her throat, at the poles restricting her movement—and then the men handed the poles to the waiting Blemmy. Half a dozen Blemmy rushed the woman, touching her, scraping the filth from her skin, pulling at her hair, yanking down her lips to reveal her teeth, and prodding their fingers in her most intimate places.

Enraged but helpless, I prayed for freedom and a sword with which to teach these monsters the proper way to treat a human woman. Alas, I remained a prisoner even as the mob of them rushed her out of sight back the way we'd come. For a time their dreadful screeches and the woman's cries lingered in the air, but soon these too faded from the reach of my senses.

The lowest ranking men among our captors set about tackling their mules to the shafts of our prison cart. The accompanying rocking sent waves of pain through us all. Overcoming my discomfort, I hollered at the one I took for chief. I offered to reward him if he released us and threatened dire consequences if he did not when the rest of my army found us. He ignored me at first but then diverted his return to the tent.

"You are the leader, the captain?" he said, in stilted Arabic.

"Yes." The word croaked from my ravaged throat.

"I am leader here. Welcome to my domain, man of the sea," he said. "You and your men belong to me now." He laughed.

I took advantage to act. With the cart stilled for so long, I had widened the knots of my bonds sufficient to slip my sore hands free. I leapt to the ground, seized the chief, and wrapped one arm across his throat, choking off his laughter. I drew the golden knife from his waist and placed the tip at his heart. The cold wetness of the man's macabre mask brushed my flesh and sent shivers through me. If his people did not understand my shouted threats to slay him, my actions spoke clearly enough. So did theirs. Rather than challenge me, three leapt into the cart, drew swords, and intimated by their posture that they would execute all my warriors.

I relented to spare my men's lives and released the chief. He laughed again, as he rubbed his throat. Then, unexpectedly, he invited me into his tent.

I joined him within, amidst an array of pillows and blankets, silks and linens. Incense burned in a censer hung from the tentpole. I eased my sore body onto the welcome softness of pillows and cloth. An oil lamp between us spit out a pungent smoke. His servers brought me water, which I drank greedily. I begged some for my men, and he assented. He regarded me, eyes peering through his skin mask. When he spoke, the lips moved in mimicry of his own.

He was called Chief Gobanki. And I, he claimed, resembled the man from whom he'd stolen the face he now wore, the man he had succeeded as leader of his people. I noticed the resemblance enough until the impression of looking at my own corpse, reanimated, and speaking through a trick of necromancy, caused a cold sickness in the pit of my being. Tradition, the chief said, required him to wear his predecessor's face for a ritual period to prove proper assimilation of his spirit and wisdom, the unbroken line of tribal knowledge.

"Such are our ways, sailor," he said. "Perhaps they seem cruel, but what do you know of our lands and beliefs? Would you like to hear how I came to wear this face?"

I did not, but he spoke anyway. I have set here, to my best recollection, the tale he told.

I was once wed to the woman you watched us trade to the Blemmy for you and your soldiers. The first of my wives. Ah, I see horror in your eyes. Is it for the trafficking of human life, the selling of slaves? This state, I surmise, is familiar to you, though you've enjoyed your freedom. Or is it repulsive that such a low price—one callow woman—secured the lives of you and your eight fine soldiers? To the Blemmy, we offered a bargain, for all their women perished generations ago. They require human females to reproduce. Ho, your eyes widen further in disgust! You are like a child peering for the first time into a brothel or a slaughterhouse and learning you are far less worldly than you believed, eh? You wonder, what could a woman do to deserve such a fate? What more fitting gift to give one who succumbed to lust and desire without heed to loyalty or promise? In this way, let her learn the true measure of her wantonness. She is fertile and strong and shall bear our monstrous neighbors many young. Spending the wealth of her flesh, I have completed the ritual of my ascension by securing food to last our village for many weeks. Aha! Forgive my amusement, but you now discern the intent of our barter and your soldiers' ultimate fate. This is the way of my people. I served my chief well, showered him with loyalty, performed his every bidding, thrust knives at the hearts of his enemies, and how did he reward my dedication? He seduced she in whom I placed all hope, affection, and endearment. She betrayed me to one I trusted most, one who now oversees the slaughter, where—at my delegation—he acts as the eyes of the one who rules over us all, the great god of teeth and mouth and throat, whose name we dare not speak except in whispers in the night. He who hungers. He who feasts. He who devours. We are his vitality. We take our sustenance in his manner to honor and enliven him as he protects and guides us. When I discovered their deceit, I waited for a night when they lay together in his hut then sprang upon them in the act, struck my woman senseless and thrust a knife into my chief-turned-enemy—but I did not pierce his heart; no, rather the place here at the lower back, where the wound rendered him immobile, but alive. Then I slivered this face from his head, dressed it upon my own, and declared myself the new chief. In this manner do our people govern. Are you shocked, appalled? I have heard the ways of the greater world from many who entered our village but never left, of their timid rights of succession or murder in secret to obtain seats of power. They say it is a grave sin to live the way we do, but what difference between our peoples except that we act in the open while yours conceal their evils. People of your world say human life is sacred, yet you enslave and you slaughter on a scale unattainable by us. By deceit you devour those around you, never tasting their flesh, wasting it. But we are all merely a type of beast, no? How foolish. You amuse me. I enjoy your resemblance to my former chief. I will spare you so you may serve me. In time you will understand, for all those who live among us come to acquire our tastes.

Upon completing his tale, Chief Gobanki dismissed me. For three days, we journeyed, and he pressed me into servitude, relieving all the duties of his attendants, heaping them upon me to exhaust me. The terrain roughened, a barren land of rocks, broken by patches of lush greenery sustained by the wellsprings of underground waters. Sheer cliffs dropped interminable distances toward vast pools of fantastically clear water that seemed as lifeless as the stone walls around it. Hawks rode wind currents, spying for meager prey that scurried in the brush of the oases.

By day the sun seared our brows, raised sweat from our skin, and dried us like beached fish. At night the air draped icy blankets around our bodies and set us all shivering. Two of my men succumbed to exposure and deprivation. Their deaths assaulted my conscience for I had failed to detect the trap laid for us, failed to win our freedom, but deceit has never been my manner. I speak my mind directly and value such behavior in others. I rally my forces for open conflict on the field and never send assassins in the night. I accept the word of those worthy to give it. This stung and pained me more than any physical wound.

At last our meandering trail terminated at the entrance of a hidden village.

Massive doors twelve feet high, carved from pale hardwood, filled a gap in rock walls overgrown with vines. Chief Gobanki's lieutenants hollered our arrival. The doors creaked open until our party and its prison wagon rolled inside then crept closed behind us. Villagers gathered to gawk, but none dared approach.

As their chief took his place at the head of our group, they awaited a woman, leading an entourage through the crowd. She wore a dress sewn of human skin and carried a staff, like a shepherd's crook. From its top dangled a trio of human skulls on a rope of dried viscera. Like Chief Gobanki, she too hid her face behind a stolen one, a woman's. She raised her staff and rattled the dry skulls above the chief's head while chanting in the tribe's peculiar language. Gobanki accepted the staff as she offered it to him, and a raucous cheer rose from the crowd.

Our group resumed its crossing of the village to a structure of wood and dried leaves. When we reached it, the full measure of abomination surrounding us afflicted me. My men screamed in terror and disgust. The villagers laughed at our dismay. They mocked our horror, miming my warrior's renewed struggles against their ropes even as the mules rolled them out of the sun, into darkness. The scene lives seared into my memory, but no words can capture the true sense of it.

An abattoir! A slaughterhouse! A butcher's workshop!

Not for birds, goats, lamb, or oxen, but for men. Corpses hung from hooks. Bodies lay on butcher blocks while butchers swung their blades, cleaved limbs apart, and opened torsos. They flayed the living skin from some. As I watched, a group of assistants lifted my warriors by the pole from which they hung to a sturdy rack to await their own vivisection. More horrible yet, at one side of the vast shed sat a man and a woman, bound to thrones adorned with skulls and bones. Flensed to muscle and tendon, their faces leered like ravenous demons, unable to look away with their eyelids removed. With a third of their bodies likewise mutilated, they writhed in agony, soaked in slicks of their own blood, incapable of screaming even as the butchers flayed off more of their skin and bits of their muscle because their larynxes had been removed. Here sat Chief Gobanki's predecessor and his wife.

Horrified and weak, I trod along behind the chief and did as I was bid, seeking at every moment an opportunity to act, but finding none, until that night brought a feast.

A troop of men delivered three palanquins to the village heart, where they set them upon rocks raised and smoothed for the purpose. Piled high on them were vegetables and loaves of bread, delicacies mounded around the corpses of three of my men, one per palanquin, their bodies split open, sliced, and roasted. Their dead faces stared unseeing into the night.

Chief Gobanki laughed uproariously at me. I looked to him, saw my own face, warped, distorted, ruined, laughing back at me. The sight of it so distressed all my senses, maddened my thoughts, and enraged my heart that of what happened next I record here only that a red haze welled up from the depths of my soul, so fiery and powerful it undid the tortures of the past days, banished all my frailty, and renewed my strength.

I seized the nearest guard's sword, disgust nauseating me as I withdrew it from its sheath of human skin—that much I recall—and I slit the man's throat. Before the moment of shock could pass, I thrust the blade deep into Chief Gobanki's chest, then plucked once again his golden dagger and used it to slice the neck of his new wife. I rounded to confront any challengers.

All stood too stunned by the loss of their freshly appointed leader. I waited not for them to recover their wits but ran across the horrible village, reached the wall, where guards did challenge me only to die at the tip of Gobanki's golden blade, a contest that lives in memory only as flashing metal breaking a red mist.

I scaled the rock wall, crested it to freedom.

Screams from the village haunted me. I vanished into the rough, mysterious terrain. It took five days to find my way back to the shore. Twice, cannibal search parties nearly discovered me. Once, I happened upon a group of Blemmy dancing around a bonfire, their bodies twisting and whirling in unholy gyrations, but I hid myself well. At the beach, the loyalty of my warriors proved true. My ship awaited as ordered. My crew dispatched a rowboat before I even reached the open beach.

Silence fell in Othello's quarters. The lamp burned low.

Desdemona looked upon Othello with wide-eyed awe.

"This you say is true?" she said.

"Have I ever spoke untruth to you?"

"Nay, for your soul is good and honest. I believe every word you've spoken, though I wish I could choose not to."

"I didst thou warn. I didst thou seek to protect from such horrors."

Desdemona rushed from the bed, fell to her knees before Othello, and laid her head in his lap. "These memories I would chase from your mind," she said. "You have suffered enough—nay, too much! You have won much acclaim by it, but you are only a man, and a man needs joy and light to balance these dark recollections. I am your joy and light. I promise always, like your loyal ship, to await you at the shore with comfort and escape."

"My love, my love," Othello said. "This I ask of you, your constancy and light, no more."

"I pledge it. I pledge myself to thee."

"Ah, what say you, Iago?" Raffiano bent and plucked the full purse from the ground. He hefted it in his cupped hand. "Have I this coin now earned in your esteem?"

"More well and fair than I could ever have demanded. Go. Speak not what you have shared to any other's ears. For in this tale, I see the barbarism hid within the Moor and mechanism sure to waken it and seal his fate. Begone now, Raffiano! Voices do I hear. Now Roderigo comes and I would speak with him in private. Begone, begone!"

Raffiano tucked the purse into his clothing then fled into the shadows.

Iago emerged from the alley to the narrow street. "Ho, Roderigo! You keep well, our 'pointed time, and glad am I for optimism found its way to me for you to one day hold fair Desdemona's hand in yours if only you a few more coins release to me."

(Since I first read Othello, I wondered about his life before Venice, which Shakespeare hinted at having an almost mythological scope, and so I chose to explore a possible episode from that time. – James)

Watch

(inspired by Othello)

L. Marie Wood

I conjure you though sweat comes and mouth's parched.
Watch as wildflowers bloom and fields consume.
Clear a path for bodies to lay, backs arched.
Lies root when darkness descends, pitch 'cept Moon.
Demon, your plight be heard; cold words hold sway.
They blight the beauty and spotlight the pain,
Cause nerves to fray even now, my last day.
No future, you deemed; no tether to strain.
And I will acquiesce; I'll take her down.
Words malicious to the soul soft uttered,
Torturing, desecrating hallowed ground.
Silence, beast; bitter pill down when muttered.
But know, what tongue you still nigh shan't abate.
'Twill stand to greet you at Hell's blood-slicked gate.

The Body, The Blood, The Woods, The Stage

Lisa Morton

Lavinia's bare feet sink into the blood-sodden dirt of the forest. She wanders among the trees, stripped of leaves and packed so tightly that light never penetrates. She doesn't know how long she's been here, but she knows that her unhealing wounds are why this ground is crimson now.

She's never stopped bleeding, from the stumps of her wrists and her tongueless mouth and what's torn between her legs. Her white dress, already tattered from what Chiron and Demetrius did to her, is permanently stained red.

Red is all Lavinia can see now. She doesn't think; it was easier to give that up long ago. She only moves, always moving. She sometimes hears distant sounds and staggers toward them, like an animal drawn to a shiny object. There might be words buried in the sounds, spoken by voices that sound as hers once did, but the words retreat as she nears. She remains alone, forever alone.

The words fire off flashes in her brain—are these memories? A husband, murdered; her father, murdering, his hands—no, *hand*—around her throat…

Is she then dead? But she bleeds, and not some milky ethereal substance but thick, visceral crimson, the stuff of the living, not the dead.

Her mind is not capable of solving such puzzles. Instead, she walks, always walking.

Ahead, from behind the black boles…words.
Lavinia follows.

"I'm sorry," Chiron says to Lavinia.

Or rather, the actor playing Chiron—Matt—says to Samantha. She blinks at him, uncertain. "For what?"

He steps up to her away from his brother Demetrius (a burly actor named Jacob), speaking softly. "Well, you know…what I have to…what *we* have to…"

Samantha is unsure how to respond. Should she say, "It's all right; it's not a *real* rape, after all"? Or perhaps a warning is called for: "Just be careful, please." Instead, she opts for, "It's not comfortable for any of us."

Matt grins, relieved. "Yes. Right."

It's the second week of rehearsals on Angel City Rep's production of *Titus Andronicus*; Samantha knows they glided over Act II, Scene 3 last week, just beginning to lay out the blocking, but now the real work begins, in a rehearsal hall as they await completion of the sets. Last night, Zach, the director, took her out to dinner to discuss the scene. Seated in a back booth at a trendy Hollywood diner, Zach told her, over martinis (as he occasionally waved at friends), that the rape is the reason he took a break from movies to direct *Titus*. "This is Lavinia's story," he said, "the story of one woman's tragedy that is also *all* women's tragedy. Yes, her attack is an assault on the whole Andronicus family, and even on the body politic of Rome, but it's first and foremost *her* body, isn't it?"

Samantha thought he probably got the "body politic of Rome" phrase from something he read, but she nodded, told him that she was excited to be part of the production. And that part is true; she may have been nominated for an Emmy last year for her performance as Chloe in the hit Netflix series *The Twenties,* but she hasn't tackled Shakespeare since her college days. She might have preferred another play, but this production has already generated buzz. The theater is the best space in L.A., with a modern stage and rehearsal space; the show has an ample budget; the cast and crew are talented and experienced;

and there are even banners advertising it around town. "Yes," Samantha said, "that's *so* right. Lavinia has been kept in the shadows for too long."

Zach's expression abruptly shifted, and he leaned in closer, speaking in low tones. "Look, the reason I wanted us to talk tonight—just the two of us—is that tomorrow we're going to start blocking Scene 3, and…well…things are going to get a little, uh—rough."

"I get that," Samantha said.

"There are going to be two versions of me in that theater tomorrow: Zach Mitchell the director, and Zach Mitchell the man. The first one might ask you to do terrible things, but the second wants you to know that you can call 'stop' at any time. I will be dedicated to *your* safety. In fact, Sammy, I want you to think of me as your ally."

Zach's smile and tone were sincere, but when he put his hand on Samantha's arm, she restrained an urge to yank it away. And she hates being called "Sammy."

Now, the day after that, Mindy the costume designer is showing Matt and Jacob how Samantha's white dress is built with strips of Velcro; it'll pull apart easily when they tear at it.

With his first attempt at following Zach's blocking, Matt pulls at the dress with one hand, yanking Samantha so hard that she stumbles, nearly falls. Mindy shouts in concern, leaps forward, shows him (again) that he must use *both* hands to part the dress. As he nods, Samantha glances beyond him to see Jacob leaning against a wood-paneled wall, smirking.

Matt and Jacob shout and mock as they strip Samantha; meanwhile, the actress playing Tamora stands nearby, watching coldly. The actress, Charlotte, is regal, a well-known performer in the local theater circuit with a handful of movie credits. Zach has chosen to begin the rape and let it proceed in part under Tamora's watchful eye before the victim is removed, screaming, half-undressed, from the stage.

At one point, as Jacob/Chiron brutally shoves Samantha/Lavinia into Matt/Demetrius's arms, Samantha staggers before stopping the action. "What's wrong?" Zach calls out.

"There's a better way to do this," Samantha says, demonstrating.

"But that was working fine," Zach answers.

Samantha responds, "We can't do it that way every night."

"Why not?"

"Because it's…" She was going to say "not safe," but instead substitutes "…it's awkward."

Samantha sees the scowl flicker across the director's face and knows what he's thinking: *This is how I've done it on the sets of movies that broke box-office records.* But he says only, "So how do we fix it?"

Samantha suggests a move. Jacob laughs. "Where'd you pick that up? During a girl fight on *The Twenties*?"

"No—I learned that in my Stage Combat class at Yale."

Jacob shuts up. They practice the move. It works. Zach is satisfied.

Later, as Samantha nurses the bruises she expects to sustain throughout this production, she changes in the dressing room beside Charlotte. The older woman sees the skin already bluing on Samantha's arms and shoulders. "You were right to change that blocking," she says.

Samantha shrugs. "Zach comes from action movies. He doesn't quite realize this is *theater*."

Charlotte fixes a hard stare on Samantha, and says, "Or he doesn't care. Can I offer some advice?"

"Of course."

"Don't let him, or Matt and Jacob, or any of them walk all over you. Don't buy any of their bullshit about how they're concerned for *you*, because they're not."

Samantha turns to the older woman, drops her voice. "You've been at this for a lot longer than I have, so…how do you deal with it? With the *men*, I mean?"

The weariness crossing Charlotte's face deepens the lines already there. "You get used to it."

Samantha tries to push down the growing sense of unease curdling inside her.

Tearing ripping held down pain PAIN—

The memories come unbidden into Lavinia's mind. She groans, the sound burbling up through the blood pooled in her mouth. *Why?*

She regains just enough rational thought to wonder what's drawn the vicious recollections to the surface again.

There: a voice nearby, closer than usual.

She follows it, catches fragments of sentences she can parse:

"No grace? no womanhood? Ah, beastly creature!"

The gore chokes Lavinia as she sputters in shock. Did she say that? Once, long ago, in those last moments when she was whole, imploring the woman who sealed her doom?

No, not just that woman, but also…her father. It was her own father who…

What—slew her? Then…what is *this*? This eternal stagger, on dirt made soft with her blood?

"…let my spleenful sons this trull deflow'r."

More words draw her attention.

She follows.

"Ahh, the blood suit has arrived."

Samantha looks up from the left side of the rehearsal hall, where Matt and Jacob have dragged her, to see Mindy and two men entering, grinning, wielding something *very* red.

She and the other two actors stand, gaping. Zach leaps forward, admiring the horrifying thing before him: it's a version of the same white dress Lavinia has worn thus far in the play, but now completely bloodstained, barely an inch of white left. The sleeves end in stumps; as they watch, Zach whispers something to the men holding the suit, they shift position, lay out a plastic tarp, and squeeze hidden objects. Scarlet streams pour from the stumps.

Zach claps in delight. The special effects men smile proudly. Matt stares in disbelief. Jacob murmurs, "Fuck me."

Samantha's dread grows.

She walks forward, numb. Zach sees her and gestures grandly. "Your gown, m'lady."

"I'll be wearing this?"

"Oh yes. We'll have Mindy waiting backstage with it. You'll have the rest of Scene 3 to change into it. The lights will be down when you re-enter. Mike and Willem"—he indicates the two men holding the costume—"will be offstage with the blood and the pumps. We'll figure out the blocking to hide the tubes, and it'll be *insane.*"

Jacob saunters forward. "So will there be plastic sheeting on the stage?"

Zach nods. "Easy cleanup—we just put in a new one every night."

"But…" Matt looks around uncomfortably "…won't we be walking through blood for the rest of the play?"

Laughing, Zach says, "It's hardly *real* blood, Matt. And it's only this scene; the stumps will be clotted after this." But Mike and Willem aren't laughing; they're looking at each other.

Samantha realizes: they're special effects technicians who've likely worked with Zach on some of the movies he's directed, and probably have no stage experience. They plainly haven't stopped to consider that actors will be performing for at least another hour after Lavinia has spilled her blood.

"We can thin it out some," Mike mutters.

Later, Samantha pulls Zach aside, expressing concern over the costume. "What if someone slips on the blood?"

"Trust me, Sammy," Zach says, stepping closer, "it's going to work. I want the audiences to experience the true horror of what La-vinia is going through, and this is one of the things that's going to drive that home."

Samantha doesn't say what she's really thinking: *Maybe you, Mr. Whizkid Director, just want to see it because you like it. Maybe it even turns you on a little, and maybe you want it to turn on all the other men in the audience.*

When she remains silent, he puts a hand on her shoulder. "It'll be great." Then he leans in, kisses her forehead, and walks away.

As she stands there, conflicted, Matt approaches. "I'm with you," he whispers. "This blood thing is nuts."

But Samantha can only see how he brayed laughter into her face as he pulled her dress apart.

For the first time (she thinks…or maybe it's not) Lavinia can see light beyond the massed trees. The words spring from the light that shines like swords around the black trunks. She moves forward, hearing words now that she doesn't entirely comprehend, except for one:

"…*blood*…"

Oh yes, Lavinia knows that word.

She follows it.

Samantha misses the cue when Dylan, the actor playing Marcus Andronicus, tries to pass her his staff so she can write the names of her destroyers in the sand.

Zach calls out, "Sammy?"

She shivers, startled. "Sorry, I…" She's plainly lost track, distracted by something.

Zach calls for a break. Matt asks her if everything is all right. "Yes, but I…" Her shoulders shake again as she blurts out, "Do you think this theater is haunted?"

Matt takes the question seriously, but Jacob rolls his eyes and stifles a laugh. "Wrong play, darling," Jacob calls before walking away.

Matt asks, "Do you?"

Samantha looks around uncertainly, clutches herself. "I've always known when a place…wasn't *right*. This place feels that way."

"You've *always* known?"

"Yeah, although it wasn't always just a feeling. When I was a kid we lived in an old house in Echo Park, and I used to see an elderly woman in the corner of my room, watching me."

Matt says, "That's creepy."

"It wasn't, though. She didn't do anything, and I never felt scared in that house." She shivers again and looks around. "But *here*…there's something old and angry, but it's either hiding or still coming…"

"Hey," Matt says, edging up closer, edging up *too* close, "if you ever need to talk about this stuff, I'm here for you. We can always go get dinner, or…"

Samantha involuntarily steps back, but smiles at him. "Thanks, Matt."

Zach approaches then, shoots Matt a fierce look before asking, "What's going on, Sammy?"

"Sorry. Nothing."

Jacob interjects, "She says she saw a ghost." He chuckles.

"No," Samantha says, "that is *not* what I said…"

But she still feels it.

Lavinia is looking at herself.

The light became a shape, a spirit in the woods. Dressed as she is, but not…

Not her. Like her, but not her.

But this woman has also been mutilated. She also bears bloody stumps, although hers have stopped flowing. The front of her gown is stained with blood, yet she speaks.

Lavinia's mind, as damaged as her body, can't make sense of any of this, so she watches.

Dylan/Marcus passes the tall, thick staff to Samantha. She feels its weight, grasped clumsily between her bound hands, sees the knobbed top (that was just in Dylan's mouth), begins to move it toward her own face…and hesitates.

"Why are we stopping?" Zach asks from where he sits at the edge of the rehearsal hall.

"It doesn't make sense to put this in my mouth." She moves the staff about, mimicking writing.

From somewhere behind her, Samantha hears a murmured, "Somebody's seen the Julie Taymor movie."

Zach throws up his hands. "Sammy, honey, it also doesn't make sense that anyone could survive alone in a forest after having their hands cut off and tongue torn out, does it?"

"No, but…" Samantha opens her mouth as wide as she can before saying, "I'm not even sure I can get this thing into my mouth."

Behind her, a male whisper: "Oh, I'll bet she can."

Samantha pushes down the anger rising in her gut to focus on Zach. "This woman's had her tongue torn out. Now, if it's more important to you to make it look like I'm giving a big blow job to a stick than the amount of pain holding this in her mouth would cause, then…" She trails off, her breath coming heavy.

The director considers; for a moment she sees his temper rising, but—to his credit—he tamps it down. "Okay. Let's see the scene without it."

Dylan asks, "Uh, Zach—do I need to put it in *my* mouth, then? Because it really *isn't*—you know, sanitary."

"Fine. Just do it with your hands or stumps or whatever."

After the rehearsal, Zach pulls Samantha aside, waits until all the others have left to say, "I love what you're doing so far, but you need to stop fighting me."

Samantha can't restrain herself from blurting out, "Fighting you? How am I—?"

"And another thing: you're holding back."

That hits Samantha hard, because she knows it's true. She looks away, shuffles her feet. "It's still only rehearsal…"

Zach leans in close enough that parts of him are pressing against parts of her. "I know you trained at Yale, that you've got more experience on stage than all the rest of us put together, but I also know when an actor isn't fully committing themselves. I need a hundred percent from you."

She forces herself to look up, right into his eyes. "And you'll have it." With that she steps away from him. He lets her. He smiles.

"Good." He starts to walk away then turns back. "Remember what we talked about—that we're going to make this production Lavinia's story."

Samantha nods, waits until he's left to sag. She's both relieved that he's gone and guilty over his accusation. She *hasn't* been giving her all to this performance, and she knows why: she's afraid. She's afraid of the pain, but mainly she fears the rage. It would be easy to get lost in that.

Samantha shivers, abruptly realizes the temperature has dropped in the rehearsal studio. The others have gone, but she's not alone; she feels that pressure she's felt since she was a child, just before she saw something that wasn't really there. She tenses, her heart pounding, eyes scanning the room…but there's nothing. After a few seconds the sensation fades, the temperature rises again.

But Samantha knows that whatever just came into the room isn't done with her yet.

Lavinia pulls back the arm that she's reached out, trying to touch the *other*. She felt *something* on the skin of her severed wrist, but it was insubstantial, like running through smoke.

This woman, though, draws her; she feels a connection between them, although she can't identify what it is. The other woman vanishes, the light surrounding her dissolving, but Lavinia knows she'll return.

She'll wait.

Act V is rehearsed on the stage, the sets now finished; for this act, the set is a stylized banquet hall, dramatically lit in vivid reds and pale blues. As Lavinia's father Titus offers the infamous pie to Tamora—the one with her two sons baked into it—Samantha stands at the side, wearing her bloody gown and prosthetic stumps, waiting for her father to kill her.

There is something in the theater. Samantha feels it more strongly here, on the stage, than she did in the rehearsal space. It presses on her, wrapping her in an energy that clings like a shroud. She struggles to focus on the action.

The actor playing Titus is Day Martin, a respected denizen of the Los Angeles theater scene. They've reached the part now where he stands, dressed as a chef, missing the hand he has chopped off in a failed sacrifice to save his doomed sons, and asks Saturninus, Rome's Emperor, his opinion of another father who slew his raped daughter.

"Because," Saturninus answers, "the girl should not survive her shame, and by her presence still renew his sorrows."

Titus agrees and turns to approach Lavinia.

Something rears up in Samantha, something she can't account for. Yes, she's thinking of Zach's urging, her commitment, her fear… and then she's *not* thinking. As Titus nears her, pulling a knife from his belt, wielding it with his last hand, her mind is blank…or, rather, it's no longer hers. She gives herself over to whatever has settled in.

"Die, die, Lavinia, and thy shame with thee," Titus says, spinning her around roughly, holding her in place with his maimed left arm as his right brings the knife to her throat—

She screams. It's a scream of fury at how she has been used to further men's lust and ambition and need for vengeance, it's outrage at how her final betrayer is her own father, who slits her throat because of *his* shame, not hers. The scream causes Day/Titus to step away in real shock. She plays the scene through, her throat stained by the false blood released by the prop knife; she finishes the scream as she falls, hits the floor, finally dies.

Silence follows. After a few seconds, a single pair of hands applauds. They belong to the director, who stands just below the stage. "Oh my *fucking* God," Zach shouts, "now *that* is what I'm talking about!"

A few other timid clappings sound from around the theater, now that the others understand the director approves. As Samantha stands, she sees first Day Martin staring at her in disbelief. "Jesus Christ," he says, "I wish you'd warned me in advance."

"I didn't exactly know I'd do that in advance," Samantha says, as she wipes at the sticky fluid on her neck.

In the blood-flooded woods, Lavinia feels something she hasn't felt in centuries: a small measure of release, a hint of satisfaction.

She wants more.

Opening night has come.

Samantha stands backstage as the play begins. She listens as the men onstage describe her as "Rome's rich ornament" in between mourning their dead sons.

The presence in the theater has never felt as strong as tonight. The pressure is so great that Samantha actually struggles to breathe, to hang onto her consciousness. She works to focus, but she also has a deep desire to just relinquish, to give herself over completely to what presses down on her with such force.

Lavinia's entrance arrives.

Samantha retains enough awareness to walk onto the stage, to say her lines, go through her motions. Lavinia's role in Act I is servile decoration, requiring little real acting. The act ends, the actors gather in a hubbub backstage, chattering about who's in the sold-out opening-night audience (Samantha's manager is there, as are three friends) and how the first act went. Samantha doesn't participate, though; she's already thinking about Act II, about the costume change when…

She tries to push the thought aside, but it rears up, threatening to overwhelm her.

When she's raped and mutilated.

When I'm raped and mutilated.

Another has settled in beside Samantha; the rage surrounding this other is like a fire limning her. But Samantha has given up fighting. She shares the fire's heat, lets it light her.

She hears the men onstage plotting her rape. She burns. She waits.

Scene I ends. Towering black trees canted in strange directions roll forward; the lighting is gloomy, emerald-hued, mocking Titus's description of a bright morn and green woods.

Lavinia steps onto the stage, moving mechanically. She delivers her single line in the scene without enthusiasm, but it's an unenthusiastic line, after all.

Scene III arrives. Lavinia watches, mute (although she still has a tongue) as her new husband, Bassianus, is murdered before her.

But the fire spreads.

She parlays with Tamora, pleading to escape her assault at the hands of the Celtic Queen's sons, Chiron and Demetrius, but Tamora is implacable. "No," she says, joining her offspring in a sneer, "let them satisfy thy lust on thee."

Lavinia watches as the body of Bassianus is pushed through a trapdoor into the pit, then Chiron and Demetrius turn to her, leering, licking their lips.

She turns and leaves the stage.

Ignoring the hissed whispers around her, she finds Marcus and takes the staff from him before he can react. She strides back onto the stage then, reveling in the confusion she sees in the eyes of Chiron and Demetrius, which changes to fear as she advances. They stand paralyzed as she hefts the staff, moving forward. Tamora watches from the side, as coolly regal as ever.

The heavy oak branch hits Chiron first, its swing ending in his neck which breaks instantly with a satisfying snap. Demetrius, eyes wide, tries to run, but she's there first, bringing the staff down in a great arc. Blood gushes from a wound in his head. He drops to his knees, but he's not done yet; he tries to stagger to his feet. She shifts her hold on the staff, pushes him hard with her foot so he's sprawled on his back, and then she drives the staff down into his mouth, widening it permanently. His last expression is one of agony mixed with surprise.

She doesn't pay attention to the screams surrounding her, barely feels it when the staff is torn from her grasp.

For the first time in centuries, Lavinia feels at peace.

Samantha's bare feet sink into the blood-sodden dirt of the forest. She wanders among the trees, stripped of leaves and packed so tightly that light never penetrates. She hasn't been here long, but somehow she senses this is her eternity, alone in these primordial woods, and she finds she can accept it.

At least she's whole.

(because after more than 400 years of suffering, Lavinia deserves justice — Lisa)

Lavinia's Revenge

(inspired by Titus Andronicus)

Megan Kiekel Anderson

My tongue, my hands, my pure honesty filched.
Embracing pole to breast, I scrape these words
In sandy plot, your names cement your guilt;
Vengeance upon my foes will be incurred.
Mine husband murdered, self ravished, enmesh'd
Vengeance escalating: sink another!
Not revenge enough to encrust your flesh
In bubbling pies set before your mother.
She dines on you; my father takes my life—
Charitable murder, an end to shame,
In other's eyes; in death I'll wield the knife,
My tributary tears for those defamed.
    Gentle Lavinia exists no more,
    A hunting haunt, I come. Even the score.

Thirteenth Night, or What You Kill

Ian Doescher

ACT V.
SCENE 2.
A grove, in the country of Illyria.
Enter FABIAN.

Fabian Joy reigns throughout th'estate entire today,
As weddings twofold we have solemniz'd:
Sebastian and Olivia the one,
Orsino and Cesario the next—
Nay, nay, the lady's Viola, sans doubt,
Methinks we must unlearn her former self
In celebrating who she hath become.
Cesario no longer, by my troth:
Her name is Viola forevermore.
A double wedding for a set of twins,
Event most jubilant and bless'd by fate.
Lo, Toby, spake a speech for lovers four,
Feste made much merriment as couples wed,

Red-facèd Andrew cried throughout the rites,
E'en sly Maria shed a tear or two.
Delightful was the scene in ev'ry aspect.
Divisions are there none—all are as one—
Yea, ending happier could none invent.

Enter MALVOLIO behind, unseen. He carries a shovel and a small barrel, and he sets them down.

Malvolio   *[aside:]* If murder be the food of hate, slay on.
Give me excess of it, that, suffering,
Mine enemies may sicken and so die.
Much preparation have I underta'en—
The traps all laid, my work begins anon.

Fabian   Maria bid me, through a messenger,
To meet her in this coppice presently.
She mention'd only 'twas of great import,
Though what the matter is I cannot tell.

Malvolio   *[aside:]* Behold the first: the noble Fabian he,
Who plotted with the others to make me
A mockery for all the world to see.
He, hidden, witness'd me as I did shame
Myself afore the lass Olivia.
Thus, hidden, shall I fall upon him now,
And take his trait'rous, wretchèd life from him.

[He approaches Fabian, throwing a rope around Fabian's neck.

Fabian   Alas, I'm undone—help, ho! Murder! Murder!

Malvolio   *[strangling him:]* Once, I declar'd to thee and thy
companions,
You should go hang yourselves, and off I fled.
No notice took ye, then, of my command,
Thus have I come to do the deed myself.

[Malvolio throws the end of the rope over a tree branch and hoists Fabian aloft, hanging him.

Fabian   *[choking:]* Malvolio, is't thee? Some mercy, pray!

Malvolio   What mercy was it, prompting thee to ply
Humiliation on an innocent,
A gentleman who never wounded thee?
This rope is thine inheritance most just—
'Tis thou who must untangle this, not I.
It is too hard a knot for me t'untie.

[Fabian stops struggling and dies.

[Sings:] The course of his sad life is run,
The fall of Fabian maketh one.
[Speaking:] I'll swiftly move, cut down the
newfound corse,
And place him in this empty, shrouded well.
Break, rope, and render me his lifeless frame—
Still warm, with yet no touch of stiffening.

[He cuts the rope and Fabian's body falls.

Aside, ye sticks that cover o'er the well
That yesternight I carefully conceal'd.
This well no more brings water, source of life;
Now it holds death—the final resting place
Of this foul Fabian. Nevermore shall he
Abuse the trust of hapless, blameless souls,
For his soul resteth, even now, in hell.

[He drops Fabian's body into the well.

Toby   *[offstage:]* Holla, Maria. Toby doth arrive!

Malvolio   The next one comes, like song in perfect time—
Prepare to meet my melody of death.

Enter SIR TOBY BELCH.

Toby   Malvolio! An unexpected sight—
              Thine absence at the nuptial feast was felt,
              For all proclaim'd they wish'd thee no great harm,
              And hop'd our merry pranks were all forgot.

Malvolio   No harm, no harm, all is forgot, my friend.
              O yea, a friend, a friend thou surely art.

Toby   Methought to meet Maria in the grove,
              For hither she hath lately summon'd me.

Malvolio   Good friend, kind friend, no harm, none, all's
                     forgot.

Toby   So didst thou say.

Malvolio   —'Tis fortunate thou com'st.
              I was a-walking through this pleasant grove,
              When I heard noises coming from this well,
              Which is, for years, unus'd and overgrown.
              A woman's voice, friend Toby, and upon
              The instant that I heard it, thou arriv'dst.
              Is't possible Maria's fallen in?

Toby   Alas, could't be? Hast thou inspected it?

Malvolio   The well is deep and dark; I cannot see.

Toby   I shall inspect its depths. Maria? Friend?
              Art haply drawn into this stony pit?

[Toby leans near the well, peering in. Malvolio pushes him over the edge.

              O, treachery! Fly, Toby, fly, fly, fly!

Malvolio   Would that thou couldst learn lessons from the
                     birds,
              Make of thyself a wingèd thing, and soar.

Toby	*[from the well:]* My landing broken by another's form—
	What hast thou done, thou mad Malvolio?
Malvolio	'Tis Fabian, who is thy companion, sirrah,
	Although thou shalt find him a grave man. Ha!
Toby	Yet wherefore hast thou plied this villainy?
Malvolio	Dare thou not speak to me of villainy,
	Unless it is thine own thou wouldst confess.
	Thou and this Fabian threw me in a cell,
	Kept me in darkness, separated from
	The light and warmth of any other soul.
	Was ever human in this humor us'd?
	Was ever human in this humor shunn'd?
	Beyond the limit of humanity
	Was that foul cruelty ye undertook.
	Days had I to bethink me of revenge,
	What I would do to those assailants who
	So callously my freedom did restrain.
	Now art thou in the darkness, as I was.
	The justice of it pleases.
Toby	—Free me, sir!
	Whate'er thou dost desire, thus shalt thou have.
	My faults I shall confess before the world—
	Is it my full dishonor and disgrace
	Thou crav'st? Dost thou expect that I should talk?
Malvolio	Nay, Toby. I expect thee but to die.
Toby	O leave me not without a single hope!
	Forsooth, the darkness is unbearable.
Malvolio	I say there is no darkness but ignorance.

Toby	Insensate beast! Thou folly-fallen scut!

Malvolio   Hold thou thy tongue, and I shall set thee free.
Thou hast been punish'd well enow, in sooth.

Toby   I'll be as silent as a candle's flame,
An thou wilt reason see and let me out.

Malvolio   Yea, in a moment. Patience first—and silence.
[Aside:] I shall return to thee, I'll not forget,
And soon shalt thou have further company.

Enter SIR ANDREW AGUECHEEK.

Andrew   A pleasant grove, in which shall be reveal'd
The subject of Maria's urgent call
That I should meet her suddenly herein.

Malvolio   Sir Andrew, by the heavens.

Andrew   —Good day, sir.
Hast seen Maria wand'ring in the wood?

Malvolio   Sir Andrew, nay, not I. Doth she expect thee?

Andrew   'Tis possible she comes in her own time,
Much like the daybreak or the dawn of spring.

Malvolio   E'en as thou sayest.

Andrew   —Kind Malvolio,
I hope we are not met as enemies.
Our jests at thine expense were all unmeant,
No insult to thine honor but a laugh.

Malvolio   A laugh, indeed. How did I laugh when ye
Conspir'd to make me wear those yellow
stockings
Within the presence of Olivia,
Whose adoration I had e'er pursued.

Andrew	A-ha! The yellow stockings were a ruse Too wonderful, too perfect a device.

[Malvolio produces two yellow stockings.

Malvolio	'Twas these same stockings!
Andrew	—These? The very ones?
Malvolio	The cloth containeth still the very sweat Which I put forth in speaking with the lady.
Andrew	How must they, like a shoreline, have endur'd Such vast amounts of salt and moisture both. Ho ho! And are they now become a keepsake?
Malvolio	Nay, nay, they serve a far more vital use.
Andrew	Pray, what?
Malvolio	—They are turn'd instruments of vengeance.

[Malvolio rushes at Andrew, stuffing the stockings into Andrew's mouth.

Andrew	*[stifled:]* What wilt thou do? Thou wilt not murder me?
Malvolio	With gladness in my heart, peace in my soul, I watch thee feast on my humiliation. Thou brigand, on these yellow stockings choke— With desolation and with fertile tears, With groans that thunder woe, with sighs of fire.

[Andrew dies.

[Sings:] Another knave doth earn his due,
Add Andrew and the sum is two.
[Speaking:] Sir Toby, canst thou hear my voice,
thou lout?

Toby	*[from the well:]* What sounds were these? Was that Sir Andrew come?

Malvolio	Fain would he visit thee where thou dost dwell.

[Malvolio drops Andrew's body into the well.

Toby	Alack! I am assail'd by falling corse! O butchery most savage and unkind.
Malvolio	Call me not butcher, thou who wrong'd me first. This is the recompense thou hast deserv'd.
Toby	In nature there's no blemish but the mind. None can be called deform'd but the unkind. Thou shalt an answer make, Malvolio!
Malvolio	When I am call'd upon at judgment day, I'll answer to whate'er divinity Doth call me forward. But, until such time, My soul is spotless as a newborn babe. Be not afeard, good Toby, for thy friends Shall follow by and by. Look, Feste doth come To join our fest and feast of punishment!

Enter FESTE, the FOOL.

Fool	*[sings:]* Journeys end in death's embrace, Every wise man's son doth know.
Malvolio	Well met, fool. What hath brought thee hitherward?
Toby	*[from the well:]* Nay, get thee gone, Feste, or thou meet'st thine end!
Fool	*[aside:]* Two voices from one mouth? A pleasing ruse, Which I shall study that I, too, may do't. *[To Malvolio:]* Dost thou possess a hidden vocal talent?
Malvolio	What talent meanest thou?

Fool	—One by the which Thy voice is hidden hither, yon, and back?
Toby	He is not what he seemeth!
Fool	—Ha, a lark! 'Tis wonderful, Malvolio, how thou Dost pass thy voice into another place, An 'twere another's voice.
Toby	—Nay, nay, thou fool!
Fool	Yea, wondrous is the trick, thou clever man. Not only dost thou speak sans moving lips, Yet thou dost imitate Sir Toby Belch. I would suspect the man himself were near, And aideth thee in this duplicity, Except I know there is, betwixt you two, An enmity that shall no friendship brook.
Malvolio	My many thanks, long have I practic'd it.
Toby	He lieth, fool, and is no friend to thee!
Fool	A deep impression hast thou made on me, Malvolio, and I must make amends: Methought thou wert a peevish simpleton, Whose sanctimonies far outweigh'd his wit, Whose anger soar'd above the bounds of reason, Whose foppery surpass'd the highest fop. Yet, now I wholly reconsider thee.
Toby	Thou art a dead man, Feste. He means thee harm!
Fool	Ha! Saucy answer—I expect no less.
Malvolio	Glad am I thine opinion is so chang'd, For long have I approval sought of thee. Good Feste, my newfound friend, I have a barrel

Of wine that I can scarcely drink alone—
Wouldst thou enjoy a sip of red delight?
'Tis smoother and of deeper hue than blood.

Fool I was to meet Maria in this grove,
But, as she hath not arriv'd, let us, as friends,
Drink to her health until she doth appear.
Where is the wine, sir?

Toby —He hath poison'd it!

Fool More of thy quips, Malvolio, thou rascal!

Malvolio I do confess my well runs full with mirth.

[Malvolio shows Feste the small barrel and opens the top of it.

Fool Hast thou a goblet or a flagon, friend?

Malvolio Alas, nay. Thou must sip, if thou wilt drink,
Like those few men of Gideon who lapp'd
Upon their knees like dogs, and were judg'd brave.

Fool Ne'er was it said I was above a dog!

[Feste gets on his knees and laps from the barrel.

Delicious vintage! Where didst thou acquire't?

Malvolio 'Twas taken from the stores of that same church
Near where thou livest. 'Tis as close as thou
Shalt come to knocking at the gate of heav'n.

Fool What dost thou—fie!—

[Malvolio seizes Feste by the neck and holds his head in the barrel of wine.

Malvolio —When I was lock'd within
The chamber dark, forsaken utterly,
Thou camest unto me as clergyman
And call'd thyself Sir Topas, he a curate,
And nam'd me lunatic Malvolio,

Dishonest Satan, and left me sans hope.
For that, thou drown'st in sacramental wine,
Ere thou dost taste of everlasting torment.

Feste   Sun, hide thy beams! The fool hath done his
                    reign.

[Feste dies. Malvolio carries his body to the well.

Malvolio   *[Sings:]* His foolish pranks did not please me,
And thus the number's up to three.
                    [He throws Feste into the well.
[Speaking:] Better a fool in pit, than pity a fool.

Toby   *[from the well:]* O horrid storm that conjureth
                    such rain—
Poor fool, I tried to warn thee urgently.

Malvolio   Yea, so thou didst, and were he not a fool,
Belike thy prating may have giv'n him warning.
Sir Toby, thou hast far too strong a voice
To risk my final quest upon thy quiet.
The time hath come for me to silence thee—
Thou must quietus make, and that anon.

Toby   What meanest thou? Speak plainly, man of filth?

[Malvolio picks up the shovel, heaping piles of dirt into the well.

Malvolio   I'll wager 'tis thyself who shall prove filthy.

Toby   Nay, thou wouldst not. Thou couldst not. Mercy,
                    pray!
Malvolio, you are the better man.
With formal tongue, I beg your sympathy—
We did conspire to do you wrong, I grant,
But never meant such injury to you.
Ah, dirt, more dirt, I have too much of dirt!

I am engulf'd in dirt, my living grave!
Mount, mount, my soul! Thy seat is up on high;
Whilst my gross flesh sinks downward, here to die.

[Toby dies. Malvolio continues to shovel dirt into the well.

Malvolio   *[Sings:]* Pray open wide the devil's door,
There's one who'd enter—he is four.
[Speaking:] Who calls me villain, when I bring
                     such peace—
The peace that passeth understanding, truly—
Unto this honor'd, gallant gentleman?
Peace sought is good, but giv'n unsought is better,
Thus I commit no wrong, but act aright—
He is not near my conscience, verily.
Yet now there is one more, and this the last—
The wickèd author of my degradation.

Enter MARIA.

Maria   Malvolio, why art thou in the grove
Where I should meet Sir Toby?

Malvolio   —He is here.

Maria   Where is he, rogue?

Malvolio   —At supper.

Maria   —Supper? Where?

Malvolio   Not where he eats, but where he is eaten.

Maria   Thine answer, sir, is enigmatical.

Malvolio   He's in this well.

Maria   —Thou liest. He is none.

Malvolio   I tell thee truly.

Maria   *[calling:]* —Toby, art thou there?

Malvolio   He shall not answer thee, for he is dead.

Maria   Dead?

Malvolio   —Buried, living, underneath the sod.

Maria   I'll not believe it.

Malvolio   —See, then, for thyself.

Maria   Nay, thou shalt have not th'opportunity.
                 I see how, like a pipe, thou wouldst play me.
                 If I should look, thou shalt push me therein.

Malvolio   Nay, on mine honor, I shall not do so.

Maria   There is no honor in thee. Yet I'll look,
                 For fear that what thou spakest is the truth.

                                  [She peers into the well.

                 Naught see I but a mound of fresh-mov'd dirt,
                 Which fills the well and stops it utterly.
                 Yet, what is that, which groweth from the earth?
                 A hand stretch'd forth and frozen in death's
                          clutch—
                 The band upon it is Sir Toby's ring!
                 Base monster, what hast done to him—alack!

                 [Malvolio produces a garter and strangles her with it.

Malvolio   Thou, final girl, shall not survive the end.
                 Cross-garter'd art thou, for thou has cross'd me.
                 Out of my shame have I a weapon fashion'd,
                 And out of fashion is thy little life.

Maria   O, I am slain! If thou be merciful,
                 Open the tomb, lay me with Toby Belch.

Malvolio   Maria, be thou not afraid of death:

Some are born dead, and some achieve their death,
And others have death thrust upon them. Ha!

[Maria dies.

[Sings:] O, never felt I more alive,
Maria makes the total five.
[Speaking:] The trick these ruffians play'd on me
        was vile—
Arraying me in clothes ridiculous,
Convincing me to smile and smile and smile
Before a woman whom I much admir'd,
And then compounding jests with cruelty,
Imprisoning me in the dark complete,
Persuading me that I was fully mad.
Such callousness I never did deserve.
When my humiliation and disgrace
Came to the light and all had witness'd it,
The lady sweet and kind—Olivia—
Said, "When we know the grounds and authors
        of it,
Thou shalt be both the plaintiff and the judge
Of thine own cause." Then were the wrongdoers
Made known most publicly, wherein I said:
"I'll be reveng'd on the whole pack of you!"
Olivia did speak the sentence just,
Which I confirm'd and have, this day, fulfill'd.
Who, then, can blame me for these righteous
        deeds,
Done in the light of day for all to see?
'Tis not the way, though, of the world unjust:
They'll call these crimes, name me a murderer,
Say jests and quips and even vicious tricks
Have never justified ends ultimate—

They'll say death is no recompense for pranks.
My stars shine darkly over me, I fear,
Yet I shall seize the thread of mine own fate
From those strange sisters who control the
        spool—
I shall not leave myself to human wisdom,
Nor be defendant in Illyria's court,
But fly from this, the country of my birth,
To seek my fortunes in a gentler place.
I shall, across the sea, to Italy,
E'en Venice, where I'll change my sullied name,
And join the ranks of military men.
No more shall I be nam'd Malvolio—
Henceforth, all folk shall call me Iago.

                            [Exit.

(inspired by Malvolio's amazing line near the end of Twelfth Night: "I'll be revenged on the whole pack of you." What if he DID?!)

Not From My Heart Do I Your Judgement Pluck

(inspired by Sonnet 14,
"Not From the Stars Do I My Judgement Pluck")

Linda D. Addison

Not from my heart do I your judgement pluck;
And yet methinks I have Telepathy,
But not to read others' thoughts run amuck,
Just your fading love as antipathy;
Nor can you run away, as your thoughts tell,
Pointing to another, younger beauty,
Removed arms, legs prevent cheating as well
Love was heaven 'til your mind whispered truth:
Then wine I served you bought sleep for a while,
To allow your mouth sewn shut, lies held in
Tongue cooked, a dog's meal, deceit reconciled,
Now your thoughts scream fear, finally honest;
     The flesh left of thee I prognosticate:
     Thy end in my arms and our minds peaceful.

The Hungry Wives of Windsor

Zachary Rosenberg

Sir John Falstaff knew it was better to be three hours too soon than a minute too late, especially when seducing a widow or murdering a king.

The old knight rapped his knuckles upon Mistress Page's door, dressed in the tattered finery that yet remained to him since his dismissal from King Henry's company and service. Just the thought of "Prince Hal" with his austere glare could arouse a fury in Falstaff the likes of which he had never imagined he might feel. Four years had passed since Hotspur's rebellion, the pivotal event that had seen the layabout Prince Hal become King Henry V.

But what of good Falstaff, who had mentored Hal throughout all walks of life, whose sword had bit into the flesh of the wicked rebellion leader, Hotspur? Hal had outgrown his teacher, he had made that clear. Falstaff could still picture Hal's eyes in his mind, staring at him as though he lacked worth and value. *I know thee not, old man.*

Falstaff knew he would simply need to kill Hal. The throne of England deserved better, and even if he had to shed enough blood to fill the Thames, Falstaff meant to provide it. There was just one minor problem: rebellions were expensive.

That had brought him to Windsor, just days before the king would be traveling through the city. The special knife he was saving for Hal's black heart was concealed in a sheathe at his side, the ornate leather hilt warm against his palm. Windsor had many things Falstaff needed: the perfect spot for an ambush, his supporters placed all throughout the town. At a word from Falstaff, his right-hand, Fenton, would lead their forces outward.

But first, he had to see to a pair of wealthy, lonely wives. He had begun writing letters to Ladies Page and Ford nearly a year ago, still in possession of the charms of his youth when he dared say he was known as Sir Falstaff the Dashing. He knew how to fill a love letter with poetry until it burst at the seams with the flowers of desire. He had been so proud of them that he had simply sent identical letters to both wives.

Their husbands were known to be often away, as was the custom of wealthy merchants. The wives had access to the funds he needed with it being well known Mistresses Ford and Page managed their household affairs. Falstaff had chosen well. All he needed to do was seal the deal, take his pleasure of each of the lovely wives of Windsor, and secure the money their lust-ridden brains would be unable to deny him.

Everything was going according to plan. Falstaff was even early to the occasion. He stood before the elaborate house with the rich red roof at the edge of town. This was a noble estate, the likes of which good Falstaff had not seen in years.

The door opened, Falstaff straightening immediately with the most gallant of poses. His hat left his head and he bent down in a low and sweeping bow, a gesture that had been so much simpler when Falstaff was a younger man. In the doorway was a handsome woman of middle years, her rich black hair tumbling free down her shoulders in a display of immodesty for which Falstaff felt himself enflamed with a burst of lust.

"Mistress Page." He breathed out her name like a benediction, his old heart quickening in his chest. "I sent my servants ahead to announce myself. My good Pistol and Nym. I hope my arrival does not come as a shock on this fine day."

Her smile grew deeper, intoxicating as a river of dark wine. "Sir John!" she said in a dulcet voice, rich with delight. "I beg of you, come inside my humble home. My husband is not present. I hope you will not mind such a breach of propriety."

Falstaff was well acquainted with women and their games. He hid his amorous smile behind his hat, smoothing out the few hairs on his balding head. Falstaff had seduced thousands examples of the fairer sex. His life was one of proud rakishness, the delights of which he had sought to teach Hal once upon a time. The prince had been an apt pupil in Falstaff's tutelage of debauchery until responsibility had warped him.

"Madam, but you do teach the torches how to burn bright! Of course I shan't mind if such a merry wife receives good John Falstaff on this fine day!"

"Sir John, I must hereby announce it would be my privilege to receive you," she said in a honeyed purr. "Wives are merry, but they are honest, too. Please, come in." The door swung open and Falstaff took a step forth, entering the Page household. He had written volumes of letters. Each was ferried by his good servants Pistol and Nym to the good wife here, as well as to Mistress Ford. Their responses had varied so little that he had found the game of seduction simple.

Mistress Page shut the door behind Falstaff. He took in her home, with its wide and welcoming hall. A lush red carpet greeted him, arrayed under wooden walls the same curious shade. Upon them were portraits, beautifully colored images of Mistress Page in noble garb with a beaming smile upon her face. Falstaff squinted at it, looking closely. Perhaps it was the dim light, but something caught his eye about the portrait. Her teeth almost looked—

"Might we interest you in some wine, good Sir Falstaff?" another voice pulled his attention from the portrait over to the doorway to the parlor. There stood another woman, tall and as beautiful as Mistress Page. Her hair was a collection of sunlit ringlets, pure as the smile on her face. "Surely you know me as well?"

Falstaff's mouth worked without breath, surprise overtaking him. "Mistress Ford?" he asked. He'd seen her and Mistress Page's images from a distance when he'd first instructed Pistol and Nym to ferry his letters to each separate residence. "I mean—" He caught himself with an internal curse, trying to think of an explanation.

"Oh, good Falstaff!" Mistress Ford exclaimed, her eyes sparkling with innocent joy. "You do not think we were unaware, do you? Mistress Page is ever so dear to me. Our husbands are never good for conversation, so she and I have found a great deal of comfort in one another. It did not take us long to discuss your gallant letters."

"And we were hardly averse to sharing your attentions," added Mistress Page, who walked to the other woman's side, so delicately that Falstaff did not even hear the sounds of her feet upon the floor. She slipped a hand upon Mistress Ford's shoulder, squeezed it gently. "We spoke about that a great deal. The noble Sir John Falstaff interested in those such as us? The tales of your bravery spread far and wide across the field of battle."

"And off of it," added Mistress Ford, giggling softly. "They say you are the Mars of malcontents."

Falstaff rumbled a laugh at that, hardly able to believe his luck. Something about them was too familiar. Perhaps he had encountered them before their marriages in his endless travels across the fields of England, through the countless houses of ill repute he had introduced Hal to. "I see my great reputation precedes me then." He dipped into a low bow, sweeping his hat out. "I apologize for my deception, my dear ladies. I am but your humble servant."

He was nothing of the sort, but as he viewed it now, it felt the entire world was an oyster he would open with his sword. One sword or the other, he thought with a salacious chuckle. "I hope your husbands shall not be back anytime soon."

"We shan't be interrupted," Mistress Ford and Mistress Page said as one, their hands running together again. "It is just the three of us."

So perfectly synchronized, they must have practiced it. "The three of us, indeed. I hope good luck lies in odd numbers." Falstaff stepped toward the parlor. To his surprise, upon the wall was another portrait. This time it was one of Mistress Ford. They must have been wonderful friends indeed to have the image of one in the other's house.

In fact, Falstaff could not even see any portraits of men on the walls. There was only Mistress Page and Mistress Ford. The candlelight flickered again and Falstaff looked closer at Mistress Ford's face. His eyesight was failing him in his old age, he decided. Mistress Ford's eyes appeared to be—

"In fact, Mistress Ford came over promptly when you were arriving here!" Mistress Page chirped as she seized Falstaff's hand. Her own limb was warm, soft as a handkerchief. "The moment I heard your knock. She lives ever so close and we do have secret entrances for such an occasion."

Falstaff's lecherous old heart quickened within his hoary old breast. "I would love to see more of such a home, my ladies. Particularly the chambers of the good Mistress Page." He let the offer dangle in the air, a squirming worm on a hook dangling ready for the fish to bite.

"Why, Sir Falstaff! To even ask such a question." Mistress Page's face was the image of offended innocence. The spark in her eyes told a different story. Falstaff read hunger there, a delicious longing to match his own.

Mistress Ford walked to a cupboard and opened it. There was a bottle of wine, brought out with a delicate flourish. "We get many visitors. More men than you might know when our husbands are indisposed. We know how to keep them happy." She smiled, catching the light of the candles on her white teeth.

She poured Falstaff a goblet of wine. He did not drink so much as quaff it, his mouth dry for the stuff as he swallowed greedy gulps. Wine was his passion almost as much as women. Wine had led him through so many battlefields and pillagings.

"I admit my delight to see such fine ladies as you here," Falstaff said after several cups. His words were slightly slurred from the good wine. "I hope Pistol and Nym arrived safe, conveyed everything I had hoped."

"They have been so forthright and honest with us!" Mistress Page said, leaning over a seat to display her pleasant figure to Falstaff. Her smile grew, just a touch too wide for her face. Her teeth were just as white as Mistress Ford's. "We sent them on their way, you see. In fact, a friend of yours arrived recently, too."

"To talk to our husbands about something very special," Mistress Ford added, taking up Mistress Page's words. When Falstaff considered it, their voices were oddly similar. Mistress Ford continued Mistress Page's sentence in such a way that it was like the former had never stopped speaking. He was still lucid enough to realize the pitch and cadence to their voices was wholly identical. Even the inflections were the same.

"A Sir Fenton, I believe," Mistress Page said, running a finger along her own arm, her eyes gleaming at Falstaff. "Our husbands are very rich, and the king is arriving very soon. Sir Fenton wished for some assurances."

The old knight lifted himself up, staggering across the kitchen to set the goblet down. Hal would be arriving; that was true. Which meant Falstaff had to kill him then. But he needed money for that, to buy off anyone in Windsor and to fund the rebellion after. Damn his eyes, he'd never been good with details!

That was what Hal had been good for, as well as Fenton. At least Fenton had foresight. "Ah, of course. Please, miladies, don't trouble yourselves about it. I promise to see to all your needs!" He chuckled. "For it is not only food and water that humans need, but love as well."

Falstaff lingered on his own words as he looked about the little parlor. There seemed to be no food. No scent of spice, nor of cooking meat, no aromas of freshly baked bread permeated the air. There was only a strangely metallic smell, which the fragrance of the candles and wine had briefly masked.

"Love," echoed Mistresses Page and Ford as one. They giggled softly again.

"Speak low if you speak love, dear Sir Falstaff!" Mistress Page tickled beneath his short beard, drawing a wide smile from the knight. He knew she was beautiful, and was therefore to be wooed. They were women, and thus would be won by him.

"Your servants were such fine men!" Mistress Ford rose and walked to a door at the side of the parlor. She opened it with a loud creak. "They told us so much of everything, before your friend Sir Fenton arrived. Our chambers lie this way, good Falstaff."

Falstaff was so quick to dart toward the doorway that he barely had time to note the strange wording she used. Our chambers? Did Mistress Ford not live apart from Mistress Page? But then again, they were dear friends. Who was to say they did not spend time alone when their husbands were away?

"We sent them on their way, knowing you would come to us soon." Mistress Page urged Falstaff on. "Our husbands were indisposed."

"But we did learn so much about you, dear Falstaff." Mistress Page took up the words as her hand joined Mistress Page's on Falstaff's broad back. "Was it true you slew the rogue Hotspur years ago?"

Falstaff was walking quickly, never one to miss a chance to regale women with stories of his nobility. "Plunged my blade into him on the battlefield myself! And urged the good Prince Hal—that's King Henry, I mean—to show no mercy to his malcontents!"

"Stabbed him, did you?" Mistress Ford pushed him forward to the door at the end of the small hallway. "On the battlefield?"

"Do you echo me, milady?" Falstaff wrinkled his nose at the encroaching tang of metal. His hand closed on the handle. "I say, is something wrong? This room seems ill perfumed."

"No less than the reek of the battlefield where you plunged your sword into Hotspur's corpse to steal the glory," Mistress Page purred, her voice low and husky now.

"No less than the fields where you saw countless men and women slain with your own blade, nor the cowardly pillaging you inspired others to," Mistress Ford hissed.

Falstaff's hand was already moving. He opened the door, even as he began to protest. The sound died in his throat as he beheld their bedchamber. The first thing he saw was the portrait on the wall: a combined image of Mistresses Ford and Page. And side by side, he could now see they were indeed identical save only for the color of their hair. In the portrait, their eyes were red pits of old blood, the pupils those of serpents.

But it was the smiles that drew his gaze. They wore twin grins with sharp teeth stained red. The painter had been good enough to capture little ruby flecks all over their dresses. The painting overlooked a room with a red carpet and floor.

Body parts lay strewn upon the floor, bones and white limbs. Corpses with flesh still upon them were missing chunks, as if they had been torn free by sharp teeth. Bodies hung from the walls, manacled there, red smiles carved across swollen throats.

Upon the mantle rested a man's head. The eyes were gone, but his mouth was open in an endless scream. Falstaff knew that face. "Fenton?" He breathed in shock, hearing the laughter behind him. He stumbled into the room, turning slowly while his hand closed around the hilt of his knife. "Back! Back!"

"Did you not want our hands upon you?" They teased as one. There, in the shadows of the hall, Falstaff saw their eyes burn so much redder than in the portrait. Their smiles were sharp, full of tiny little daggers. Their tongues emerged, long and black, to snake across their lips identically.

"Brave Falstaff," Mistress Ford teased.

"Despoiler of so many lives," Mistress Page hissed.

"Faithless to foes, treacherous to friends."

"Murderer. Ravager."

"Pistol and Nym told us everything," Mistress Ford said with an advancing step. She kept her eyes on Falstaff's, his heart furious in his old chest. "Your plan to seduce us. We were going to enjoy them for a while, but we found them just honest enough to release."

"We let them go," Mistress Page agreed. "And assured them their master would cease to be a problem. No such mercy was afforded Sir Fenton. He was sweet."

"Delicious," Mistress Ford added, lifting a hand to her mouth. She picked at her teeth with a nail more like the talon of a hunting bird. "But we're still hungry and we assured the king we would be quick."

"He's wiser than his father. He understands the necessities in such dealings. Perhaps we have you to thank for that, good Sir Falstaff." Mistress Page lunged for him, hands outstretched.

Falstaff screamed and plunged his knife into her chest. It sank to the hilt, and she staggered back against the wall.

"The only response men like you have," Mistress Page said, with a placid expression.

"Never expecting women will bite back." Mistress Ford remained in place, head cocked with her smile lingering.

Mistress Page placed a hand to the hilt of the knife, and she began to pull. The blade came free, bloodless and pristine. She advanced and took Falstaff's arm, lifting it and placing the hilt of the knife back into his palm, closing his nerveless fingers about it. "This belongs to you, I believe."

Falstaff shrieked, slashing at the air, wild and without precision. He screamed as loud as he could, both women stepping back to watch, unblinking, before Falstaff bolted for the door. Their laughter followed him as he fled down the hall, gibbering like a madman.

This couldn't be real. Falstaff was somewhere with Hal, lying facedown on a tavern table. It was the wine giving him a horrific dream. Hal had to know of it. He would laugh when Falstaff told him of this silly nightmare.

He ran down the hall, past portraits of women with sharp teeth and red eyes. He saw a figure in the hall, recognizing him from portraits he had seen weeks ago. It was Sir Page, standing rigid at attention. Falstaff ran for the man, dimly aware of slithering, shifting noises behind him drawing closer.

He grabbed the nobleman by the shoulders and shook desperately. "You have to help me! Your wife is…" he trailed off, Sir Page looking back at him with empty eyes, milky and vacant.

"Mistress is hungry," he said. He repeated it over and over again.

Falstaff heard the footsteps now, slow and deliberate. As if they wanted to be heard. He could not die. He was Falstaff and the Devil would not dare risk him damned, lest the oil in him set hell afire. So he ran for the door, trying the handle and finding it unlocked. Howling in triumph, he fled out into the day, stumbling down to trip over his own feet. He could hear voices, the sounds of footsteps and horses approaching.

"The king!" someone shouted. "Make way for the king."

Hal. Hal was here early. Oh, luck was on his side. He pulled himself up, running. Something bit into his back, nails digging into his skin, accompanied by the silken laughter. Falstaff ran from their house and their laughter, as blood ran free from his torn flesh. The cheers grew louder, and he screamed a name.

"Hal!" he howled. "Hal, please! Please!" He held his knife, once intended for Hal, but now he could think only of salvation. He fell into the road, dropping the blade before a procession of men and horses. Falstaff stumbled to the ground before the royal parade.

There stood Hal, Falstaff's prince. He wore the royal attire of the House of Lancaster, his handsome looks marred by the arrow scar on his cheek. He stared down at his former mentor, murmurs rippling through the crowd.

"Hal," Falstaff moaned. "Hal, it's me. It's John. It's your Falstaff. Forgive me, forgive me, please! Save me, Hal. Don't let them—"

"Good ladies," Henry said. The crowds of Windsor's people watched, silent as the grave. As one, they stared with vacant, curious looks on their faces. Something was behind Falstaff, a chill whisper of wind. Hands closed on his shoulders, breath reeking of twin abattoirs falling upon his face. "Is he yours?"

"He is," they said as one. Falstaff did not dare turn, could not bear to see those teeth. "One to be punished by the hands of women. With your leave, your Grace."

"Hal!" Falstaff screamed. He saw it then, in Henry's eyes. There was recognition, a moment of princely hesitation.

It was gone in an instant, replaced by kingly determination. "Fall to thy prayers. How ill white hairs become a fool and jester. I know thee not, old man." Henry turned away without another look.

Falstaff tried to scream, to protest. He tried to pray, to repent, but the hands bore him backwards.

Toward the house of the hungry wives of Windsor.

(Unlike "The Merry Wives of Windsor" following his first appearance in "Henry IV," it is unlikely that Good Sir John Falstaff will return. – Zachary)

Juliet

(inspired by Sonnet 113,
"Since I Left You, Mine Eye Is in My Mind")

Alessandro Manzetti

Since I killed you, mine eye is in my mind,
And that which governs me to go about
Doth part his function, and it's partly in the hunt,
Seems seeing, but again grants you life.
For it in each form delivers your face
To old and young ladies, to imaginary shapes;
Of those magic mirrors hath the mind special part,
And his own vision holds what it doth catch;
For if it see an odalisque or a beggar,
The most sweet thighs or deformèd'st creature,
Sees a pale shyness, hears the courtesan's sudden laugh,
The day or naked night, it shapes them to your feature.
  Incapable to stand, always thirsty for another you,
  My most true mind thus makes mine victims untrue.

these *VIOLENT* Delights

have VIOLENT ENDS

—Romeo & Juliet

Nothing Like the Sun: Rosaline's Satisfaction

Donna J. W. Munro

In Fair Verona, we lay our scene.

The heat of the morning promised an oppressive afternoon. The *cicale* sang loud love songs to summer, and the bright traitorous sun burned away courtesy and kindness in our kingdom.

I paced in my room assessing the problems facing Verona.

Two rival families fouling our city's streets, a weakling prince, declining trade from our neighbors—it won't be long until little Cesare Borgia and his papal-supplied army would smell Verona's weakness and come to pillage, rape, and conquer in the name of God and Pope Alexander. If only I'd been born a man, a legitimate boy to replace father's knock-kneed, drooling little prince, my brother Escalus, why...I'd have put the Montagues and the Capulets in the city's defensive ranks to serve me and Verona, rather than tear us apart. I'd march out and liberate all of Tuscany from the bastard papal prince and make Verona the great state it should be. Only I'm not a boy. I'm the illegitimate daughter of a dead king. A pawn awaiting my brother prince's play. A politically advantageous marriage? A lady in waiting to a future princess? A paid-for-prioress of a nunnery tasked with praying our father out of purgatory? How few choices a woman has, only—I wasn't just any woman.

"Sweet Rosaline, look on me with love this night." Romeo's love-sick warble sounded outside my balcony window for the fifth night in a row, distracting me from my ruminations.

I leaned out my window to gently shoo him away. No need to burn bridges as I plotted my path to freedom. "Forget me, sweet Romeo. I will never love you as you love me. I am bound for a nunnery if my princely brother will allow it. My body will never know the touch of a lover. Be satisfied and away with you."

Playing an unsullied maid for his ego was a thin role. The poor boy had to know about my dalliances. As careful as a lady can be, word gets out when one has appetites like mine. Unlike my thick-as-burnt-pudding half-brother prince who'd been born without the fire below, I'd made my way through the clergy, the footmen, and the ladies in waiting by the age of sixteen. And why not?

My mistress' eyes are nothing like the sun;
Coral is far more red than her lips' red;
If snow be white, why then her breasts are dun..."

Clumsy, artless boy.

"Ah, Romeo. Why not call me the silvered moon? Or the ocean tides that draw your heart's blood to shore? Away with you, child. I have more passion for the scriptures than you have in your soul for me."

As amusing as playing with him was, it was a distraction I could ill-afford. It was his father, Lord Montague, in my sights. He and the damned patriarch of the Capulet mob. The two old families battled in the streets of Verona destroying our infrastructure and ill-using our soldiers in their blood feud. Such a waste when the Borgia army crept ever closer to our city walls.

From outside my window, a final plaintive call welled out of the darkness:

"My mistress, when she walks, treads on the ground:
And yet, by heaven, I think my love as rare
As any she belied with false compare."

The boy was getting better. Even so, I closed my shutters against him.

A knock with secret rhythm at my door announced that one of my spies waited for me in the peristyle, just as I'd arranged. Some news of the Capulet household, I hoped. I veiled my face so I'd be mistaken for a courtier's wife and hurried down a secret staircase to the inner garden where my loyal emissary waited.

"My lady." He bowed with a depth that revealed his need to please me. He was new money, a household manservant, and a social climber. So useful a tool to old money like mine.

"Call me Rosaline, my love," I said with my breathiest voice. I gathered him up in a passionate kiss, then pushed him away with false modesty. "My dear, I must withdraw. You bring out such feelings in me…" I made to go and he threw himself at my feet, kissing the hem of my skirt.

"Please, Lady Rosaline, I know my place. Just to be in your presence…the radiance of your love…"

Maybe I'd kissed him too well.

"Sir, I know you haven't come just to fill my heart with vain longing…"

Get to it, man.

"No, my lady. I bring you an invitation to the party the Capulet family is hosting."

He handed me a gilt-edged invitation to the masked ball the family threw every year to celebrate its supposed dominance of the society of Verona. "This year my lord promises the event will be particularly important to our family." The manservant smiled and reached out a familiar hand to brush my cheek.

How I wished I could break those fingers for their uninvited familiarity, but they were useful to me, so I simpered under his touch. "The prince has agreed to marry your cousin Paris to their daughter Juliet. Imagine, the Capulet family finally raised to courtiers. Then, you and I…"

I tugged the invitation out of his hand and left him stammering there with his impossible fantasy. How dare they? I fumed as I turned this news over in my mind. Paris and the Capulet's young daughter? Paris should be mine to marry. As dull as a marriage to my cousin would be, I would finally be made legitimate. How could they do this to me? I'd waited so long!

I would bend the prince's ear for this. Perhaps it wasn't too late to stop them.

I rushed up the steps into the throne room where my idiot brother Escalus held court like King Solomon, pretending to solve the problems of the commoners with wisdom he didn't possess. His advisors allowed it since it pacified him. They paid each commoner a pile of coppers and sent them on their way after their audience—the money always enough to solve their problems even if the prince's wisdom didn't.

"…Montague boys dueling with the Capulets outside my leather shop. One of them stabbed my…"

I only heard part of the commoner's complaint as I threaded through the gathered courtiers in the throne room.

The prince intoned, "I will fine the families for your losses, and they will send skins enough to replace…"

I was distracted by an overly familiar hand in the small of my back.

"My lady." I knew this man's voice. The shiver it evoked was like silk shimmering across my bare thighs, an expensive thrill since I knew him to be a Capulet.

"Ah, Tybalt. How you purr." He'd been my lover for over a year, but I'd not tired of him and his heat yet. "In court? How now?"

He grinned with all his teeth and I nearly swooned, but I had no time for such nonsense. "I come to deliver the contract for Paris's marriage, the dowry terms, and the declaration of Paris's inheritance as the only male heir to the throne."

Inside, his words set me to boiling. Through Paris, the Capulets would inherit the throne. I'd waited all this time for my idiot brother to be killed or to pass so that I could assume the throne. I'd rise like that whore's daughter in England. I'd be their loving virgin queen if

I could just negotiate a path. But this betrothal set a mountain in the way of my hopes.

Next to Prince Escalus, Paris leaned against the throne's ornate shoulder and smiled as Tybalt strode up the dais as if he belonged there. That hot-headed ne'er-do-well and my beautiful, empty-headed cousin happily exchanged a contract for my throne, and my brother nodded and smiled, giving it all away without a thought of me. All so satisfied with their manly machinations.

I'd show them.

I drew the pentacle on my dressing room floor in blood that I'd cut from the meat of my palm, then spoke the secret words my mother, Queen Mab, had taught me. She'd been midwife to Hell, drawing many imps and demons from eggs and birthing patches in her day. She served her own mother, Lilith the Queen of Hell, pulling incubi and succubi from the first woman's distended womb. All my unearthly cousins owed her their lives, and by extension, they owed me. I just needed to remind them what I was owed.

I opened the gory passage to Hell so they could flow forth, all dreamy and beautiful but full of teeth and claws. My pentacle held them as I forced them to bow. I whispered what I needed them for.

A drop of blood and a promise, and they were all mine.

I went to the Capulet party dressed as the fairy queen bathed in the silvery light of the moon. Pearl white and delicate as fairy breath, I dressed like the queen I ought to be. The company parted for me with even my dull brother nodding at my dreamy visage. So many promises of love and dance requests found me, but I'd have none. I only flirted with Paris. My hand and words touched him in ways that should have won him over, but his eyes were full of the little girl Capulet.

Hair as brown as wet mink. Eyes bright and full of wonder. Her body barely awake to womanhood, but how she shone. Innocence is as bright as the sun on a summer afternoon.

I'd never been an innocent and so my stomach churned with a jealous rage.

Old Lord Capulet didn't see young Romeo there, watching his girl.

Something in me panged as I watched Romeo's heart soften when Juliet's longing gaze fell on him. Losing an admirer was nothing to me, but…the glow of his golden cheeks. His precious, desperate sigh I heard right through the announcement of Paris and Juliet's betrothal and the applause that followed. The cracking of the wall I'd built around his young heart stung.

But even so, watching him and the girl cutting eyes at one another, while my fool cousin Paris preened under the attention of the Capulet family, sharpened my path. I finally had a plan.

The party broke up with Old Capulet leading Paris away to discuss what family meant. They'd drink spirits and toast their relations in the paterfamilial tradition, but I'd send my family of spirits to torment them with sticky nightmares about each other's arms later. Let them try to explain that to the friar in confession.

It was Romeo I followed.

He snuck out into the courtyard and stood groaning under Juliet's balcony.

"*…It is the East, and Juliet is the sun.*
Arise, fair sun, and kill the envious moon
Who is already sick and pale with grief
That thou, her maid, art far more fair than she."

I'd told that cad to call me his moon and here he was poetically plotting my demise with this lovestruck little girl.

The spirits I'd raised swirled around me, excited by my fury. "Inflame them all," I ordered. "Sneak into their dreams and make their passions break the wall of their will. Hate amplified, foolish love magnified, filial devotion intensified to a rage."

And off they went.

That night I visited my brother and whispered to him of the Montague family's treachery.

He didn't believe me.

He didn't believe, but dawn would come and he'd see.

I went to the friar the next day, a humble penitent. A nun to be.

I confessed lies to him so innocent he chortled as he gave me a round of Hail Marys to recite. When we were done, I brewed us tea to sip in the shade of the churchyard's oak, where we could look out over the town's winding streets and see the peace that comes from a great distance.

"Father, I've heard whispers that the two great houses might be joined."

He'd always been a gossip, though he tutted with a false haughtiness. "You and I both know of the betrothal, Lady Rosaline."

I heard the rattle of a horse riding hard up the chapel hill cobbles. My invisible creatures whispered to me that Romeo was coming with plans of his own and I fought back a smile. How wonderful it was to control dreams.

"I hear of a love so pure and true; my little Romeo finally found another, more appropriate love. A Capulet, Father. Think now on this. You might be the man to end the war in the street. If you joined the two great families instead of letting the Capulets gain the upper hand in Verona through this ill-advised marriage, you'll end this infernal feud fairly. Mother of God help us, Father, and you might bring peace."

His brow furrowed as the main chapel door banged open and Romeo called for him with desperation plain in his voice.

The friar set down his tea and hurried to help Romeo while I made my way through the line of graves in the churchyard toward my coach waiting in the streets below. As I passed under an open window of the chapel, I heard them and smiled at my own cleverness.

The friar said, *"Holy Saint Francis, what a change is here!*
Is Rosaline, whom thou didst love so dear,
So soon forsaken? Young men's love then lies
Not truly in their hearts, but in their eyes."

I left my invisible friends to hear their plans, checking that the imps' whispers and the visits of passionate demon lovers enacting dramas inside their misty dreams through the night led them to the inevitable results.

Romeo and Juliet: a secret wedding.

Paris: a quick wedding to seal his standing and wealth.

Tybalt: a rage at the insult of Montagues at the Capulet homestead during the betrothal party.

And the prince?

He was too dull to push.

I let him dream of his own wisdom, strength, and prowess.

Leave a fool to his fictions.

The deed was done. The children were wed. I knew because the friar came for some camphor I'd blended, and he bragged as if the joining were his idea.

"Imagine, peace in our time, Lady Rosaline. Peace as the good Lord intended."

I smiled and gave him the ampoule as I had so many times before. We shared this sin of natural healing that was so against the teachings of the church. Had it not been for his vows and my standing in Verona, we might have been made to suffer for our makings. But with a little persuasion, he saw my craft as his science and was satisfied.

"See this plant, Friar?" I pointed to the nodding purple blooms of my belladonna. "Take a leaf and a bloom for study—Carefully, sir! In small amounts, this plant creates a sleeping potion so like death it might save someone from bleeding out from a mortal wound by slowing the breath and heart. Just this much causes a day of sleep so still even a doctor wouldn't know life lay in the dreamer's still breast, but any more than this and the sleep will last forever!"

His eyes lit up when I told him of its magic and planted a seed for later.

So short-sighted, our friar.

In this game, he was only aware of the chess pieces he held in his hand.

I had the run of the board.

"Good luck and Godspeed, good Friar," I said, bowed, and led him away from my roof garden with a light discussion of scripture and my intentions to take vows.

He left full of himself and his supposed goodness.

And I followed the trail my creatures had laid to my fiery Tybalt.

I arrived at the center piazza too late, though the effects of my workings still decorated the square.

Mercutio bled red rivers on the cobblestones, life running out between his clenched fingers.

My succubi echoed Tybalt's words…

"Romeo, the hate I bear thee can afford
No better term than this—thou art a villain"

…like a song in my ear.

Ay, me. The loss of Mercutio, the greatest wit, perhaps the only mind equal to my own, stung, but such delights bring violent ends.

Romeo cradled his man in his blood-soaked arms as Tybalt, shock plain on his features and stained blade dragging the ground, stared down at his accidental victim. Mercutio's gaze found me, hardened as he saw me as if he knew what I'd done.

"A plague on both your houses."

Romeo and Tybalt cried out and begged Mercutio's pardon from the curse, but his eyes were on me.

A plague on my houses?

I smiled.

The daughter of Mab had nothing to fear from Cousin Plague or any of the other horsemen of Hell. They were of my mother's house. I flicked my fingers and those that served me carried Mercutio's soul off to the place where he'd be punished.

Punishment awaits us all in the end.

Romeo screamed as his friend's body stopped its struggle. He turned his hate on Tybalt, forgetting his great love for Juliet with only a bit of a push from my creatures. Before either of my admirers saw me, I rushed back to my carriage and bade my driver hurry to the palazzo. I wanted to be by my brother's side when he heard the news of all the bloodshed.

Paris sat on Prince Escalus's right hand and I on his left. Dinner was all talk of wedding invitations and citywide celebrations until the court page broke through the joyful planning with his announcement.

"Mercutio is slain by Tybalt. Tybalt is murdered by Romeo. So much blood in the streets of our sweet Verona."

Lady Capulet and her lord came soon after demanding Romeo's head for the death of her favorite nephew.

By all rights of betrothal between Paris and Juliet, Tybalt was our nephew, too.

Paris rushed to comfort his would-be in-laws, leaving me the prince's ear.

"Brother, this blood feud will only get worse with the nuptials. You cannot take a side since you already are promoting the Capulets to courtiers. Any moves against the Montagues will rile up their people. There will be so much blood on the streets that Verona will be calling for your head."

He hissed as he imagined it.

The Montagues were a bloodthirsty bunch.

"What should I do, sister?" He turned to me with such earnestness, I almost felt bad for what I had to do.

"Banish Romeo instead of execution. Push forward the wedding. It will satisfy them all."

He stood and made the decree.

I went to my room to summon my army.

The demons swirled around my head as I gathered them to me, calling them from every corner of this world and the next. Doubt had to be sown. False solutions. It was a subtle dance I set in motion.

That night and the next day I didn't sleep, but I gave myself over to the workings of my demonic army. Together, we drew sigils in the guts of creatures we called forth from the dark. I made my promises in cuts across my pale skin and written in blood that the imps lapped off my breasts and arms. I let the incubi use me and the succubi invade me as they needed or wanted. Even Lilith took a pound of my flesh to serve up to her lord on the roasted back of an unbaptized child.

In the end, it was finally enough.

They left satisfied.

The friar's stolen letter to Romeo sat unopened in my hand and the sun had set on Juliet the night before her wedding. In the morning, she was a marble angel—breathless and beatific in her virgin bed. Paris wept and tore his wedding clothes and Verona decked itself in mourning weeds from every balcony and window.

Juliet was dead in the chapel waiting to be rescued.

How sad.

I stifled my giggles in my handkerchief when the friar gave the solemn benediction at her funeral. His words chided the two houses for their hate and hinted at a future where both houses would join.

He was the star of his own holy monologue.

And Juliet's fingers twitched.

Hurry up, you old fool.

When the chapel opened the next morning for the burial of the virgin bride, the mourners found unexpected horrors in that holy place. Juliet and Romeo embraced in a rictus pantomime of young love on the altar with valiant Paris stabbed, bled out, and facedown on the marble steps.

A comedy of errors.

A tragedy of heroes lost and love gone cold.

The friar told his story.

The nurse and Benvolio backed his tale.

I cried prettily at the prince's side as he pronounced the words we'd planned and practiced on the ride to the chapel.

"A glooming peace this morning with it brings;
The sun, for sorrow, will not show his head:
Go hence, to have more talk of these sad things;
Some shall be pardon'd, and some punished:
For never was a story of more woe
Than this of Juliet and her Romeo."

And as they all went away to weep, the pretend prince, formerly my brother, adjusted his skin suit with a gentle tug, then led me back to our coach. "This body suits us, don't you think?"

"As long as you remember who holds the strings," I said to my loyal army pressed inside his skin and bones. Inside the coach, they worshipped me with the body they'd taken as a reward for their works. Soon, they'd lose their grip on that flesh and our contract would end. They'd leave the throne to me and I…

I would finally be satisfied.

(Of all of Shakespeare's works, Romeo and Juliet is my least favorite. When I read it for my own good in ninth grade and a few times since, I wondered how Rosaline felt to be put aside so easily in favor of Juliet. Maybe she felt relief. Maybe it was the best thing that ever happened to her. – Donna)

Sonnet Fifty-Fleur

Lindy Ryan

beauty

looks fair, but

blooms

thorns,

When

unrespected

Die

sweet deaths

(based on Sonnet 54, "O, How Much More Doth Beauty Beauteous Seem")

The Montague Look

Epiphany Ferrell

I wake in darkness. I should not be in darkness. Something has gone wrong. I lie on my back, having no strength to move as much as a finger. I focus all my effort on a blink. There is no change in the darkness, eyes shut or open. But my eyes are not glued shut. Of that I am certain.

I am roused enough to know I am not in soil. There are no worms burrowing into my cavities, no beetles crawling across my face, my fingers. I can feel pressure on my midsection, as if my pants are too tight. Bloat. Autolysis. Four days dead, then.

I don't know how I know this. Not in my shriveled brain. In my consciousness.

It never should have gone this far.

I lay in the filth of my own bile. Though I can't smell, I know I stink. The bloat is uncomfortable. Microbes move in my organs, wiggling and consuming. I sense the ammonia and the hydrogen sulfide they produce, feel the gases swell against my putrid skin, pushing my stomach against the top of the box, ballooning my legs, my arms, my neck.

Or maybe I don't feel all that. Maybe I only think I do. Consciousness is my only existence. How much is physical and how much is what I know?

I can't be sure how much time has passed between now and my last thought. My stomach is deflated. My skin is waxy. If I could see myself now, I would be yellowy-green, my flesh stained by my own rotting insides. I don't want to see myself.

I wonder if I'll see the white light again. And if I do, is it too late to choose that path? It is. The owl that swooped over the beam of light took it with him as he soared through the shadows. It wasn't for me.

But I knew that.

I don't know why I am in a coffin. But surely that's what this is. The material beneath me is damp. The fluid is my own deteriorating cells. Not embalmed, then.

My eyes leak fluid beneath my closed lids. I try again to open them. There is nothing to see.

I have spent precious moments of consciousness in sleep. I waken to a pounding in my ears, a thumping that stereos across my moistening brain. My arms and legs itch, each nerve stinging. My face crawls and prickles. It is my stilled heart coming again to its purpose.

And what I feel in it is a stab. I feel, I feel.

I want to breathe; I remember now what that is.

Ants. There must be fire ants. Inside my skin.

No, it's blood. My blood. Inching from where it has pooled in my feet, my buttocks and back, the backs of my legs, my arms. Creeping like slow fire as my heart bumps in the clay of my chest. I count between beats: I count to ninety, to seventy, to sixty.

Panic. I cannot breathe, and I must. I must breathe! My fingers move, clutching uselessly at stained satin.

My jaw drops open. My mouth is not sewn shut. I heave, gulping like an unseeing fish dying on the bank, trying to force air into my dusty lungs. Breathe!

As soon as the breath comes, sensation comes with it. And another flood of panic.

I try to sit up. I cannot. The box is holding me in, and God, I think, how cruel—to go out this way, to defeat the worm and maggot only to be stopped by a dead tree.

I push my palms against the top, bucking my body, clumsily, my brain starting to work again. My muscles cramp and strain. The lid clatters off. I grasp the sides of the box, too weak to pull myself up, but my fingers feel cool air and I grasp at it, as if it were tangible.

The room is dark.

But not as dark as death. Not that dark. No.

I am alone. My eyes leak fluid, thin, like saltwater.

I crawl from the coffin, spilling out onto the floor next to it. It is little more than plywood, made with no hinges, the lid fitted down on top. The satin inside is white, clean. Except for the dingy, still-wet stain of my failed organs.

I must find her. My beloved.

I smell mold, old earth. The air is chill. I shiver, delighting in the sensation of hairs raising on my arms. My clothes are filthy. I can't abide them. I can't stand the fabric, moist and stiffening with grave secretions. Frantic, I claw at a button, at a zipper. My fine-motor skills have not returned. I tear at the shirt, feel the cool air on my skin. The clothes reek, but they cover my nakedness, are some protection against the chill of this place.

My hands were once unshakeable, surgeon-steady. Now they are liver-spotted, knobby knuckled. And yet, I am fascinated by the movement of my fingers, the curl and the clench, the miracle I have become, able to move and walk and breathe again after rotting in the grave.

I wait for my beloved. She will come to me, and hold me in her arms, and we will go home and love the grave away.

It has been a day and a night. Shall I wait three, like Jesus? Will she, like Mary Magdalene, mistake me for a gardener?

I will go forth at night. My eyes are adjusted to the dark. The daylight burns them where it slants in through the doorway.

I hold out my hand to look at it. It has become a strong hand now, a surgeon's hand. I stand straight. How long has it been since I was not stoop-shouldered, bent with age and care?

I am afraid to leave this place, but the hunger in me tells me I must.

I am in the cemetery, an alteration of our plan. I don't know what it means, but I laugh to think how I would frighten someone now, lurching on legs unused to walking, emerging from a garden shed into the rows of tombstones.

There is a ten-dollar bill in my pants pocket. Nothing else. No identification, no keys. I see lights ahead of me. It's a quiet part of town, but the corner diner is open. I order dry toast. When it stays down, when my stomach remembers to digest food and not itself, I order scrambled eggs, bacon, sausage, more toast. The bill is more than ten dollars. The waitress feels sorry for me, accepts the ten. She gives me coffee in a to-go cup.

I go.

I stagger down a street, my feet taking me without thought. I stop at a shop window and stare at my reflection, looking into my own eyes and I know what I see there. Something not sane. The Montague Look, they called it—those who hated my family. The same expression I remember on my grandfather's face at his execution. The same look in my mad brother's eyes when they locked him away.

Early frost gleams on the grass. I have no coat. It is a long walk home, though it is only a block.

The door is locked. The key is not under the mat.

Am I not welcome?

I go around to the back. It's a near-silent night. The house is dark but for a subdued light visible as a crack through heavy curtains.

I smell the grave on myself.

I enter the house through the cellar. And there I have a bad moment. That smell—the stale earth—reminds me of my dying. The slowing of my heart, the blood growing sluggish in my veins. How I needed air! Oh, the choking and the gasping!

And that was nothing compared to the coming back, to the knowledge of my own decay, the sensation of my own rot.

She was so afraid, my wife. She had no faith in the magic or the science. She pleaded with me. "Just let me die," she'd said.

I cringe, there in the cellar, remembering how I'd pried open her clamped-shut jaws, forced the spoon between her teeth.

Cancer will not win. I will not let it.

I drank the rest, the liquid numbing my throat. Our daughter, holding her mother's head, looking at me earnestly. She had been my assistant in the lab. She knew.

That look on her face. I shudder. The Montague Look.

I know now I took too much. I overdosed. That's why I went so far, was dead so long, why I began the process of returning to earth. The backup plan, to hide the dead among the dead.

But surely the rest has gone right. I was careful with my wife's dose. She'll awake, my Juliet.

The cellar stairs are steep. My knees ache when I reach the top. My hand on the doorknob is not strong. The un-aging has stopped, has reversed itself. I don't yet know what that means.

The house is arrayed for a vigil. The mirror in the hall is shrouded. I see a woman in a chair by the fire. My beloved.

She rises to meet me, and, oh, my young love returned to me. I long to hold her in my aging arms.

It is not my wife, her youth returned. It is my daughter. She looks so like her mother, so very like. She steps aside, rejecting my embrace.

"She is gone," my daughter says. "Beyond your reach."

Her face is her mother's, but the expression is pure Montague. I know that look.

My shoulders stoop with renewed age.

It was a wild experiment. Unholy. But it worked on mice. There wasn't time for more elaborate clinical trials. The research was sound, if incomplete. My daughter can vouch for that. She left university when her mother became ill. She was at my side through all of it.

My plan was for us, my bride and I, to die in body but not consciousness. The killing elixir would reverse itself, would replenish our bodies.

We would have more time. That's all I wanted, more time. Not eternity.

"She returned as your potion forced her to do," my daughter says. There is no joy in her voice. "Death is better than what you forced her to become."

"How?" It's all I can say. In that single word, the need to know what happened, what she said, how she died her final death without me there to hold her. And why. Why?

"This way," my daughter says, and offers me a cup of tea. I feel my heart breaking. Surely I will follow my dear wife soon. The poison in the tea—I want to be sure. I drink it all. It numbs my throat. My daughter smiles her Montague smile.

My darling lies in her coffin, one she selected herself when she received the diagnosis. It is now my marriage bed.

My Juliet's limbs are puffy and unyielding. Her parchment eyelids slit and beneath them is gel. I see my daughter has sewn her mother's mouth shut.

"You failed," my daughter says.

She helps me into the coffin, where I may embrace my dead wife. Where I may lie with her in death, as we walked together in life.

"Over and over," my daughter says. There is venom in her eyes.

She gestures at the cages where our resurrection mice hurl

themselves against the glass. As I watch, they die, stiffen, awake. "Over and over and over," my daughter says. "Until you remove the heart."

There is a hollowness in my wife's chest where her heart should be.

My own heart slows. I count between beats. Eighty. Ninety. I am gape-mouthed, instinctively gasping at air my lungs will not receive.

I feel the cycle begin again.

My daughter peers at me over the edge of the coffin, smiles a mad Montague smile.

"This time," she says, "I'll nail it shut. The time after that, you'll feel the worm. And the time after that…"

The pounding of nails covers her voice.

My eyes leak fluid. The microbes stir.

(Inspired by the many times my plans have gone awry. And by Romeo and Juliet. – Epiphany)

A Timeless Tragedy

JG Faherty

Lights flashed. Bells rang. Sirens wailed. Demons scampered to and fro, urging people to sell their souls for a chance to see something magical.

Hank Romanov smiled.

Tonight's the night, and damned if it's not. The past will finally be put to rest.

The Halloween carnival spread out before him. People hurried by, eager to play games, see shows, and try the rides. He breathed in pure nostalgia: the sweet, crisp scent of candied apples and cinnamon cider donuts, the mouthwatering smell of greasy fries and funnel cakes, the sharp tang of popcorn smothered in fake butter. It almost made him forget the pain in his lungs.

If he closed his eyes, he could imagine himself at seventeen, standing in a carnival very much like this one. He'd been nervous that night, too.

Someone bumped into him and kept walking without so much as an *I'm sorry*. Back in the day, that'd be more than reason enough to teach the person a lesson.

Like I should've done to Matty that night.

He'd been stupid that night, thinking he'd impress Juliana by not fighting. Prove he was different. Mature. Better.

Yeah, look how that turned out.

Funny how one action taken or avoided could have such an effect on someone's life.

Ah, who knows. Maybe I'd still be standing right here, alone, drowning in what-ifs.

None of it mattered anymore. There was only now, and not much of that left, either.

At eighty-two, Hank had reached the end of the line. Lung cancer. And he didn't even smoke. How's that for a big F-you from Fate? He'd tried his best to keep in shape after college. Sure, his eyesight wasn't what it used to be, and most days his back felt stiffer than cold taffy when he got up in the morning.

Compared to his friends, though, with their cholesterol pills and heart medicines and whatnot, he'd done okay.

And where did that get you? Decades of loneliness and no one to shed a tear now that it's time for you to kick the bucket.

Ah, well. At least he had tonight.

He checked his watch. Almost six o'clock. Juliana should be here by now. Her and her Yellow Hat Club friends. He'd heard them talking in the diner earlier, that there was a carnival in town, the first time anyone could remember that happening on Halloween since high school. And they were all going together. A girl's night, just like the old days.

With no idea where Juliana Theobald—who'd once been Julian Caplewood before she married that asshole Matty Theobald—might be, Hank wandered the carnival. As befitted Halloween, all the rides had scary names: the Wheel of Death, the Alpine Slide to Hell, the Terrifying Mirror Maze. Waist-high gremlins and trolls roamed the grounds, and Hank wondered where the carnival had found so many little people to employ.

A flash of yellow caught Hank's eye. There, off to his left. A group of women, their faces hidden by garish bonnets of lemon, sunshine, and daisy. Standing in line for the Time Tunnel. Despite the name, Hank recognized it right away. In any other fair, it'd be the Tunnel of Love. Cheap pontoon boats decorated with clock faces floated on hideously artificial blue water and entered a dark opening cut into a plywood wall painted to look like a grandfather clock.

This might be my only chance. Time to act while opportunity beckons.

Hank pushed through the throng and got in line behind the women. As luck would have it, Julian was near the back of her group. When it came time for her to climb into one of the boats, Hank cut in front of her partner and sat down.

"Who—oh, Hank Romanov. What are you…?"

"I'm sorry to surprise you like this," Hank said, ignoring the protests of Alice Monroe and waving for the wart-covered carny to push them off. "I needed to talk to you, in private. It's important."

Juliana frowned but didn't object. Her blue eyes, no longer crystalline but still just as beautiful, regarded him with a mix of confusion and concern.

"All right. What's the matter?"

Hank paused as the boat entered the tunnel. Day turned instantly to night, with only tiny red and green bulbs set into the walls preventing total darkness.

"Juliana, I have a confession to make. I've always loved you, ever since—"

A metallic clank sounded somewhere and the boat shot forward fast enough to throw them back against the hard seat. The lights blinked on and off like flashbulbs. The boat rocked from side to side. The effect was disorienting. The boat rocked again and spun in a circle. The flashing of the lights grew faster, leaving purple images in his vision. Hank instinctively reached for Juliana and found her doing the same. They held each other tight, and she gasped as the spinning grew worse.

His mind went back to high school, and her body was no longer frail and trembling in his arms; it was supple and soft and warm. Her breath smelled of cigarettes and beer instead of hot chocolate as it passed his face. And she was laughing instead of crying.

Bright light exploded all around them and Juliana gave a delighted shriek as the boat dropped several feet and rose up again.

Then everything was calm and they were exiting the tunnel. Hank leaned back to ask if she was all right, knowing the mood had been spoiled, that now his admission would end up being an awkward apology.

A teenage girl sat next to him, grinning from ear to ear.

Juliana.

"That was bitchin'!" she said. "Let's do it again!"

Hank squeezed his eyes shut and opened them again. Nothing had changed. Juliana wore the same exact outfit as she had that night he sent his life down the wrong track. Plaid trousers, a white blouse, a heavy red cardigan. The carnival lights reflected from eyes as blue as jewels, and her hair was blonde again, cut in a neat bob that just touched her shoulders.

"C'mon, Hanky, one more time." She grabbed his hands. Hers were creamy and smooth, unmarked by liver spots.

And so were his.

He looked down at himself. The blue-and-white letterman jacket with the red "P" for Polk High was as familiar as his own face. His black slacks were pleated crisply down the front and his feet were tucked comfortably into his favorite loafers.

"Uh, no," he managed to say. "Let's, um, get a soda."

"Okee-dokey." She waited for him to climb out and then help her onto the rickety platform. The same wart-faced gremlin glared at them as they walked away.

With his thoughts reeling, it took Hank a moment to realize everything was different, yet weirdly the same. The rides and carnies hadn't changed, but the people had. Everyone wore clothes from a simpler time. Skirts, fuzzy angora sweaters, cardigans, and wool coats surrounded him. Here and there, the occasional pair of jeans or a leather jacket identified someone from the northside of town. The kind of kid who'd hang out behind a ride and shake you down for some change, or maybe sell you a marijuana cigarette.

A kid like Matty Theobald.

"Look! It's Alice and Debbie!" Juliana took him by the hand

and he let her lead him through the crowd. As they walked, he noticed the music had changed, too. No more rock or rap blasting from the speakers. Instead, the raucous chords of "All Shook Up" and "Jailhouse Rock" motivated kids and adults alike to play games or take a chance on a crazy ride.

"Julie!" Alice Munroe and Debbie Walker squealed and Juliana echoed it. The three of them clasped hands as if they hadn't seen each other in years rather than just a few hours earlier at school.

School. If this really is senior year all over again, then today's Friday...

The rest of the memory jumped the gap of sixty-five years like it was brand new. Seeing the flyers for the carnival. Every kid at school excited to go; there'd never been a Halloween carnival in Polk City before. Him and his two best friends, Jarrett Holmes and Carl Vernon, going there right after football practice.

Seeing Juliana standing alone by the Tunnel of Love and getting up the nerve to ask her if she wanted to try the ride. To his shock, she'd said yes. And then...

"What the hell's going on?"

Right on schedule. Matty Theobald, looking the same as Hank remembered. Textbook greaser: hair slicked back, leather jacket over a white T-shirt, jeans. To look at him you'd never believe that by the age of fifty he'd own three successful tire stores, live in one of Polk City's biggest houses, and have the perfect family with Juliana and their two kids.

"Hey, Matty. You didn't show up, so Hank here filled in." Juliana looped her arm through Hank's. His stomach clenched with the knowledge of what was about to happen.

"Yeah, well, take a hike, jerk. Playtime's over." Matty took a pack of Winstons from his jacket pocket and lit one with a practiced flick of his Zippo lighter. That was Hank's cue. Sixty-five years earlier he'd turned to Juliana and said they should leave. She'd called him chicken, and he'd slunk away to the sound of their laughter, his reputation ruined.

I don't know what brought me here, or why, but this is a chance to do everything over again. The thought occurred to him that maybe he'd had a stroke and died, that this was just his life repeating before darkness claimed him. Then he decided it didn't matter.

There's nothing to lose.

He swung his fist, putting every bit of his seventeen-year-old muscles, hardened by years of playing football, into the punch.

It landed square on Matty's cheek. The cigarette shot away like a miniature comet and Matty fell to the ground. The three girls gasped, and Hank had a moment to bask in the glory of decking Polk High's biggest dirtbag.

Then two pairs of hands grabbed him from behind and he remembered too late that Matty never went anywhere without his sidekicks, Lou Barkley and Ken Pedlow.

Matty stood up and rubbed his jaw while Hank struggled to break free.

"Sucker punch, huh?" Matty spat blood and smiled, his teeth still covered in red. He drove his fist into Hank's stomach. The pain exploded through his body and he doubled over, fighting to breathe and tears filling his eyes. Lou and Ken let go of him, and he reacted on instinct.

He lurched forward and tackled Matty.

They landed in a heap on the ground, both of them swinging wildly. Someone shouted his name, and multiple voices cried out "Hit him! Hit him!"

Then strong hands were pulling him up and away. He jerked his arms free and was about to leap forward again when a deep voice said, "I wouldn't do that, boyo."

Hank paused and saw two cops holding a furious-looking Matty in their grasp. He had a sick feeling he was in a similar position. The authoritative voice confirmed it a moment later.

"Unit Seven here. Got a couple of punks fighting at the carnival. Bringin' them in now."

At the police station, he and Matty were taken to separate rooms. Hank's father showed up twenty minutes later, his face beet-red all the way to the roots of his crew cut.

"What the damned hell were you thinking, boy? Fighting in public? With some piece of shit from Northside? What if you get suspended from the football team? For what? That no-good Caplewood girl? She's nothing but trouble. Hangs out with a bad crowd."

"She's not like them," Hank muttered, falling into old patterns even as the older, current version of him was still trying to grasp everything that had happened.

"You're grounded, you know," Yuri Romanov said as they pulled into the driveway. Another blast of nostalgia-slash-déjà vu washed over Hank and he had to wipe tears from his eyes at the sight of his old house. The one he'd sold back in '97 to pay for the nursing home his father ended up in.

Inside, it smelled like Friday: filet of haddock with peas, courtesy of Swanson. He knew without looking that there'd be a crumpled frozen dinner tray in the garbage and two empty cans of Budweiser on the snack table next to his father's recliner in the den. No Schlitz or Black Label. Only the best for Yuri Romanov. Just like the TV set had to be the biggest one on the block, a massive square monster enclosed in a cabinet that came with speakers and a side compartment to store liquor in. Or the car he drove, a brand-new Chevy Bel Air.

By habit, Hank headed up the stairs to his room, where he froze, confronted by his own youth. The shelves over his desk held all his football trophies. Pinned to his closet door were two triangular Polk High pennants. If he opened that door, there'd be a neat row of slacks, white button-down shirts, and jackets on hangers. Shoes would be laid out in a neat row, brown on one side, black on the other. In his dresser, all the socks, ties, underwear, casual slacks, sweaters, and short-sleeved polo shirts were properly folded.

A single picture decorated one wall, the only thing his father allowed: Johnny Unitas, in full uniform, rearing back to throw the ball. It was actually signed by Johnny himself; Hank's father had bought it special. "Motivation," he'd said, when he hung it.

Past and present collided with each other and Hank felt a scream coming on. He threw himself onto the bed and pressed his face against his pillow. Maybe if he just went to sleep, he'd wake up in his own chair. Because it had to be some kind of nightmare or hallucination. God couldn't be so cruel as to make his afterlife an awful repeat of—

Something tapped against his window. Once. Twice. He sat up. A third tap. He went over and peered outside.

Juliana stood in the lawn, ready to toss another pebble. When she saw him, she waved for him to come down.

This never happened in real life. Once again, the idea of creating a new path came to him. He had a second chance. Real or not, he'd be stupid not to take it.

Sneaking out was easy. Like so many other things since the magical transportation, muscle memory guided him down the stairs, avoiding all the spots where the wood creaked. Not that it mattered. His father was in the den, the TV blaring, engrossed in *The Adventures of Jim Bowie*. Just like every night since Hank's mother died a year ago. Hank eased around the corner and out the back door.

Juliana was waiting for him.

"Are you in trouble?" she asked.

"Yeah," he said. "Grounded. My dad's afraid I might get suspended from the football team, too. It was worth it, though."

She looped her arm through his. "It was bitchin' cool, that's what it was. Two guys fighting over me. Like in a movie."

Hank's heart pounded and his head felt light. Juliana Caplewood, hitting on him? He no longer cared if it was real or a dream. This was it. Time to live the life he should've had.

"Well, if this is a movie, did the good guy get the girl?"

She smiled and it lit up the whole night. "Let's find out. Wanna go to a party?"

He looked back at the house. "I don't know. I'm already in big trouble…"

"How much more can you get in? C'mon, it's gonna be a real blast." She batted her eyes at him, and even though he knew it was a calculated move, he couldn't say no.

"What the hell. Let's go."

"Yeah! Now we're cookin' with gas!"

It turned out the party was a bunch of kids hanging out in the town park. Some of them had brought beer. He recognized most of the faces, although he couldn't put names to them anymore. Alice and Debbie were there, and some other girls. Someone called out his name, and he turned. Jarrett Holmes was approaching, a beer in each hand.

"Hey, Brando! Didn't think I'd see you here."

Hank accepted the beer and took a sip. The crisp, clean taste surprised him; it was so much better than the beer he drank in his own time. Fresher ingredients? A younger, healthier tongue? He took another sip, savoring the bite as it went down.

"A pretty bird convinced me," he said, motioning toward Juliana. She smiled and gave them a wave.

"Guess showin' that bum some what-for worked out for ya."

"I hope so." Hank had to fight back tears as he gave his old friend a slap on the back. Jarrett ended up joining the Marines after high school and died fighting in Vietnam, a war Hank missed thanks to ruining his knee playing college football. "Tell you tomorrow."

An hour later, everything was working out better than Hank could've hoped. Juliana let him lead her away from the party to a secluded section of the park. He laid his jacket on the ground for them to sit on and she didn't even pretend to object as he leaned over and kissed her. When he placed a hand on her breast, she moaned into his mouth and ran her fingers down his chest and past his belt.

And just like that, sixty-five years of fantasy came true.

When they were done, he stared at the sky while Juliana pulled up her underwear and pants and lit a cigarette. He was afraid that if this really was a dream, or a stroke-induced hallucination, closing his eyes might return him to the real world.

"That was pretty crazy. Guess you're not the square everyone thinks you are." Juliana raised an eyebrow at him and passed over the cigarette.

Despite the insult, Hank smiled. His teenage body might have been virginal, but he'd learned some things during forty-odd years of marriage, even if it wasn't a great relationship. Plus, there'd been porn.

Lots of it. He felt pretty sure of two things: one, Juliana Caplewood was definitely not a virgin. *Secretly fast* was what they called her kind back then. Two, he'd bet good money Matty Theobald had never done some of the things they just had.

Score one for Hank.

"That ain't nothing," he said, surprising himself by falling into the speech patterns of his youth. "Stick with me and I'll show you a real good time."

Her eyes twinkled in the moonlight. "Sounds bitchin'. Maybe when you get sprung from house arrest, we'll play a little back-seat bingo." She leaned forward and kissed him. Her mouth tasted of cigarettes and bubble gum. Then she stood up and brushed off her clothes.

"Gotta split before my parents freak. See you Monday, big boy."

She hurried down the path, leaving him in a weird state, his adult brain ecstatic from fulfilling his lifelong dream and his adolescent body already pumped up to go another round.

He had no desire to return to the party, so he dressed and headed home. As much as it was a disappointment to find out his teenage crush hadn't been the pure young girl he'd always believed, he was kind of glad in a way. There'd been no fumbling, no awkwardness on either of their parts. In fact, sex with Juliana had been better than he'd ever imagined.

He couldn't wait to do it again.

The weekend went by agonizingly slow. There was the football game on Saturday, where Coach Moffit told him he was benched because of fighting. Secretly, Hank was glad of that. Muscle memory was one thing; he was afraid it wouldn't be enough for him to compete in an actual game without getting hurt. He spent the rest of Saturday and all day on Sunday doing chores around the house, part of his punishment. And he was still grounded at night.

He did everything without complaint, while in his head he kept reliving the feel of Juliana's body under his. With each passing hour, the squirming ball of anticipation in his stomach grew larger. By the time he went to bed on Sunday night, he felt like he'd jump out of his skin. And he'd decided three things: One, this wasn't a dream, or a near-death experience, or a coma. It was too long, too real. The only explanation was he'd been sucked into some kind of freak time rip, like in the movies. Why just him, he had no idea. And he didn't care. He'd been given the chance to relive his life and this time he'd do it right. The way it should've happened.

The second thing was quitting the football team. No ruined knee, no crippling arthritis when he got older. His old man would freak, but too bad. After high school, he'd get a job. He'd already started thinking about what stocks to.buy and bets to make, things that would earn him millions later on.

Three, he was going to ask Juliana to go steady. She was obviously into him, and it drove him crazy knowing that if he'd just asked her out back then, she'd probably have said yes.

His brain filled with visions of her wearing his school jacket, he drifted to sleep.

The first thing Hank saw when he got off the bus Monday morning was Juliana and her girlfriends standing in front of the school. With a new confidence, he strode right up to her.

"Hey, Juliana. I missed you this weekend. But I'm not grounded anymore. Wanna go out tonight? We can grab a—"

Someone shoved him in the back and he stumbled forward. Juliana jumped away, her hand going to her mouth too slow to cover a smirk.

"I thought I told you to stay the hell away from my girl," Matty Theobald said, his fists clenched.

"She's not your girl anymore," Hank shot back. Students started gathering, their teen senses alert to a potential fight. Hank reached out to take Juliana's hand and she stepped back.

"I never said I was dumping Matty. He's ready to fight for me. Are you?"

Hank knew in that moment she'd screwed both of them, and not just on her back. She had planned this whole thing. And if he backed down now, he'd lose any chance with her. Matty's face darkened; he was pissed at her, too. But he couldn't say no. His reputation would be ruined.

And I'm in the same boat, Hank thought, seeing his football teammates in the crowd.

"After school," Matty said, glaring at Hank. The way the crowd was going, they had only minutes before a teacher showed up to chase them away. "The Fields. You and me, Hanky-panky."

"I'll be there," Hank said, his own anger rising.

"Break it up," a male voice called out. Mr. Evola, the vice principal, pushed his way through the throng of students. "What's going on here?"

"Nuttin'." Matty gave an evil smile. "Just havin' a chat." He pointed at Hank and then stormed off.

When Hank turned around to ask Juliana what her problem was, she was gone as well.

For Hank, the day sped by too fast. It took only a few minutes for the reality of what he'd gotten himself into to sink in. The jitters he'd had earlier grew into full-blown sweats and his hands trembled as he opened his book during first period math. Things only grew worse when he went to his locker after first period and realized he couldn't remember the combination. For the rest of the day, he had to pretend he'd left his books home, earning several scoldings from his teachers.

When the final bell rang, his stomach cramped so bad he thought he might throw up right on his desk. No one seemed to notice; Jarrett and Carl pounded his back and practically shouted with excitement over the *bruising* Matty was going to receive.

With no way to back out, Hank walked with Jarrett and Carl to The Fields, an empty section of land at the north end of town that served as an unofficial dividing line between the nicer part of Polk City and the section everyone called Dirtville. Dirtville was comprised of two trailer parks, some run-down shops, and a few neighborhoods where the houses were mostly bungalows and the lawns were rarely mowed.

Matty, Lou Barkley, and Ken Pedlow were waiting, along with a bunch of their friends and way more kids from school than Hank had expected. Juliana was with them, holding Matty's leather coat and wearing an anticipatory expression that reminded Hank of a big cat eyeing its prey.

She still looked beautiful.

And despite his feelings of anxiety and a growing certainty she had a bit of a mean streak, he wanted her. After all, she'd married Matty and they'd stayed together for more than fifty years. Given him two beautiful, smart kids. She couldn't be that bad.

Besides, he'd be the laughingstock of the school if he didn't fight. He'd already gone through that once in life. He wasn't living it again.

"Let's rumble," Matty said, stepping forward. Hank took off his jacket, feeling stupid in his slacks and button-down shirt compared to Matty's jeans and white T-shirt. Hank raised his fists, trying to remember the few fights he'd been in back then. Matty didn't allow him the chance. He rushed forward and swung for Hank's face. Hank managed to dodge it and grab Matty's arm, intending to throw him to the ground. Instead, he got an elbow in the stomach and Matty broke free.

There was a *click*, and suddenly a switchblade glittered in Matty's fist.

"Gonna cut you good, pretty boy," Matty growled.

Something got pressed into Hank's hand. He glanced down. It was a knife, with the words Carnival of Fear etched on the blade. Before he had time to wonder at that, Matty charged him again. Hank sidestepped, and then they were dancing around each other, Matty thrusting with his knife and Hank doing his best to avoid getting stabbed. A voice shouted at them to stop before someone got hurt. But all he saw was Juliana, her eyes brimming with excitement, licking her lips as she watched.

If I win this fight, she'll be mine forever.

And on the heels of that: *If I die, who cares? I was dying anyhow.*

He sprang forward, thinking he'd swipe at Matty's arm and maybe make him drop the knife. Instead, Matty was caught completely off-guard by Hank's attack and stumbled. His arms went wide as he tried to maintain his balance.

Hank's blade plunged right into the center of his chest.

Matty's eyes went wide and his mouth fell open.

"Whu…uh…?" The rest was lost as blood bubbled over his lips and he collapsed to the ground.

"Matty!" Juliana fell to her knees next to him, cradling his head. He tried to speak but only spat out more blood. "Matty, I'm so sorry. I didn't want this. I was just trying to make you jealous. Don't die, I love you, I always loved you."

Her words cut deeper into Hank's heart than any knife. All he could do was stand there while Matty died in her arms. The angry wail of a siren started up in the distance, meaning someone had gone for the police. They'd be arriving soon, and then he'd be arrested and convicted of murder.

This shouldn't be. We were going to get married. Have children. That big house would be ours…

He couldn't stay in this time. Better to go back, let the cancer take him, than rot in prison for the next fifty years. He reached for the knife.

Juliana already had it poised over her heart.

"No!" He grabbed for it just as she pushed it in. She uttered one scream, a terrible cry he knew would stay with him forever, and then slumped over. He caught her before she hit the ground.

"Juliana, no, no, no! It was supposed to be different this time." Hot tears ran down his cheeks. How had everything gone so wrong? This was their second chance. He—

Red and blue lights filled his vision as three police cars pulled up. Someone shouted for him to—

"Back away. You hear me, asshole? Right now!"

Hank's whole body suddenly hurt and it was hard to breathe. He looked up. Two police officers stood there, guns aimed at him. Behind them, lights flashed against a night sky. Wide-eyed people and leering monsters stared at him from behind the cops. The sirens were gone, replaced by calliope music and clanging bells.

A sign on the fake dock read, "End of the Ride. Exit to the Left."

Hank looked down. A gray-haired, wrinkled Juliana lay in his arms, a knife protruding from her chest. On the handle, the words Carnival of Fear were visible beneath a film of blood.

"Get out of the boat, slowly, with your hands in the air," one of the cops said.

This can't be real, Hank thought. None of it. He had to make it go away. Start over. There was only one way to do that. He pulled the knife from Juliana's corpse and held it up.

Gunfire exploded and a massive weight struck his chest. He fell over the side of the boat into the water. The lights faded and icy cold filled his body as he sank.

Juliana, I'm coming. And this time I'll do everything right.

(My inspiration for "A Timeless Tragedy": I saw Romeo & Juliet described as a timeless tragedy. Right then, the concept popped into my head. Elderly people. Unrequited love. Time travel. Second chances. And around again. —JG)

Brothers in Arms

Kenneth W. Cain

I t was the summer I lost my virginity to the woman I would marry. Bootcamp in New Orleans was brutal, the humidity so thick it felt like you were carrying a whole other person when we went for our daily jogs. Most of us were still very wet behind the ears; green, as in we hadn't seen any action other than what we experienced during our daily drills. That night I was lying in my bed in our bunkhouse, writing a letter to Susan, when the commotion broke out.

I knew what was going on. Why? Because I was one of the "informed," the unlucky few who lent an ear to Benny Schwarber's constant complaining. Mostly, I'd only been humoring the guy. He was a massive specimen, but not too bright in the head. But that wasn't why I did it, out of some sort of fear. No, there wasn't much to do on base during off hours, and Schwarber could prattle on like the most annoying "Becky" in the world, when he wanted to. I'd come to understand his way, how every matter to him was simply black or white; there was no gray area. His strict Southern Baptist upbringing along with the hardcore reality of bootcamp only seemed to reinforce his beliefs. You'd sooner see a blue moon than Benny let his guard down, though it did happen on occasion. But this… Whatever was going on, it wasn't a prank.

"Damn it, Hernandez. We told you to stop!" said Yarnell.

I tried to ignore the turmoil but failed repeatedly.

Yarnell and Yates held Levi Hernandez up. Schwarber moved back, took a bold step forward, and socked Hernandez in his gut. "We told you to keep that shit to yourself!"

Hernandez hung from the two men like a wet towel. And when they let him drop, he sounded more like one, dripping in sweat and blood as he splatted against the cement floor. There he lay prone, visibly emotional, when he caught me looking. I stared at him for a long moment, watching the tears well up in his eyes, wishing I was brave enough to do something...anything.

Thinking better of the situation, I diverted my gaze elsewhere. Even then, my eyes betrayed me, returning to the group of soldiers standing above Hernandez. I rolled over in bed, facing away from the chaos, and closed my eyes.

"Kansas!"

I ignored Schwarber.

"Kansas. Get up, damn it."

This was something I had no interest in, but what choice did I have? I rolled over and saw Schwarber's toothy grin. The guy must not have brushed his teeth enough as a kid, given so many were missing.

"Here. Take this and follow me." He threw a sock on my stomach. It felt unusually heavy.

I picked up the sock, noticed there was a bar of soap in the toe. "What the fuck, Schwarber? What are you planning on doing with this?"

"Just be quiet and follow."

Like it or not, I did as told.

Schwarber led me down the hallway to where they had Hernandez surrounded. Some of the others had socks now, too.

It all happened too fast.

They were but cogs in some complex piece of machinery. Up and down like pistons their arms went, those socks raining blows against Hernandez's back, thighs, and head so fast I couldn't tell how many times they connected. Seeing it stunned me, and the sock slipped from my hand. It landed against the floor with a *thump thump*.

"What are you doing?" Schwarber was staring at me in disbelief. "Hurry up. Get in on this."

But I didn't. To say I was in shock would be an understatement.

"Kansas?" Schwarber's face twisted into a mask of anger, the ugliest and most disturbing thing I'd seen in a long time. "I swear, if you don't—"

"That's enough." Dern had both arms out, was working to back the others up. "He's had enough."

Schwarber's anger intensified. "No, he hasn't. Ain't no queer that deserves any reprieve, got it? Not in my platoon." He pushed his way through the crowd and riddled Hernandez with a dozen blows. The entire time, Hernandez barely moved, and I worried he'd lost consciousness.

"Benny, stop," I said.

He snubbed me, of course.

"Benny!"

He froze, arm raised high, that sock dangling precariously from his fist. I felt his eyes burning a hole in my skull.

"Dern said he's had enough," I said.

Benny stomped toward me, and if not for several others filing out of the bathroom all at once distracting him, he may have come after me. I stood in disbelief, watching the door swing shut, then open… shut, then open. Inside the bathroom, I saw someone lying on the floor. Just a peek, but enough to see streaks of blood all around him, the foam-green tiles painted red.

"This isn't right," I said without thinking.

"What?" Schwarber clenched his fists. "You're a fucking idiot. He deserves every bit of this and more." He jabbed a finger at me. "Is this…" Now he pointed at Hernandez. "Is this the sort of man you want protecting you? To have your back?"

"More like backside," Hill chided.

Most of them laughed. Schwarber was boiling over with rage, and I had no idea what that might look like. This was dangerous ground. A war zone.

Thing was, I didn't care who defended our country, so long as their focus matched my own. What they did in their private lives, who they chose to sleep with—how did any of that play into it at all? We were brothers, all of us. Through thick and thin, we'd have each other's backs, now through the end of time. That was the code, the creed we lived and died by. What was going on tonight…this… This wasn't only wrong; it was against the rules. *Our* rules.

"I can't be part of this." I turned and headed back to my bunk.

Before I took more than three steps, Schwarber rushed me. He leaped onto my back and had me pinned against the ground. I tried to escape, tried to wriggle out from under him. When that didn't work, I flailed my one free arm back. Why, I had no idea. It was all I could do…until he got his knee on it, too. That sent a bolt of pain through my arm, but that was nothing. Blows rained down on me faster than I could process.

I thrust my head back and made contact with his nose. That only exacerbated matters. By the time he had exhausted himself, I felt welts rising on the back of my head. He released me, and I rolled over, breathing heavily, trying to see straight.

Schwarber stood back, pride seemingly dripping off of him as he glowered down at me.

I sat up warily, stared him straight in the eye, and said, "Fuck you, prick. You might be bigger and stronger, but you're far weaker than anyone here." I jumped to my feet and poked a finger into Schwarber's chest.

He only grinned. "Whatever, queer lover."

The others laughed, but I ignored them. Using the wall as my guide, I went to check on the man lying on the bathroom floor. I saw right away it was Lofgren, that he was out cold. Without hesitation, I pawed out several paper towels, wadded them up and soaked them with water. I used the wet mass of soppy paper to clean Lofgren's face free of blood. The cool of the water must have shaken him out of his daze.

"Where… Where am—"

"Just relax," I said.

"What... What happened?"

The door busted open, which made me jump. I was instantly on guard, relaxing only once I saw Hernandez standing there. Tears streamed down his cheeks. He looked like he'd been through hell. All of us did. But there was a special sort of pain Hernandez was enduring in that moment. Something far worse than being beaten within an inch of his life. I could see then he'd been broken.

I had no idea how badly until later.

The two of them said not a word to each other. Everything they had to say had already been said. I could see it in their eyes, those unspoken truths that express love in a way few can fathom. Having just found love myself, I was blind to it then. Now that I'm much older, I can see it in my memories plain as day, and it still haunts me. Theirs transcended time, bigotry, the impossibilities of their profound caring for one another. To them, this was just another obstacle to suffer through. Or so I thought.

And perhaps that would have been enough, if this had been the first time. Or even the second. I should have known right away. After all, I hadn't always refused to take part in this crap. No, I'd been goaded into being an awful human being more than once. My heart aches to this day for the stupid shit I've done, all at the behest of some behemoth tool. And while I am quite certain neither Hernandez nor Lofgren ever blamed me for any it, that never washed the guilt away. If anything, it only made it worse, because they wouldn't hate me. It would take a lifetime of apologizing to make up for it, too, one I was fully ready to embark upon after the night's events.

Things settled fast. Hernandez and I finished getting Lofgren cleaned up. Then we cleaned up ourselves. Soon after, everyone went to bed. It was late, and we would be hitting the trails hard come 0500 hours. The time for...*play* was over. As far as I knew, everyone was asleep within fifteen minutes. But if I knew anything about myself at that young age, it was that I didn't know near as much as I thought I did.

I made a habit of waking early. That way I had a chance to get myself sorted before the run. Half asleep, I staggered into the bathroom. I was the only person up, and I wanted to get some water splashed onto my face, a means of jolting myself into the here and now. And that's when I saw him.

While everyone slept, Lofgren had hanged himself inside one of the bathroom stalls. He was stripped down to his bed shorts, the bruises and sores still very visible on his graying body. Lofgren wore a makeshift sign around his neck that read "Your gay brother." Seeing that was enough to break anyone, let alone the man's lover.

I immediately sought out Hernandez, but he was nowhere to be found. The day was filled with bedlam, and for some reason, I wondered if he'd already found his dead lover and gone AWOL. That's what I would have done, after all.

While they were taking down Lofgren's body and removing it from the bunkhouse, a patrol found Hernandez. Many of us rushed out to the lake, where we found several soldiers, men and women alike, diving. They were taking turns bobbing under the water, staying down for a few minutes and then popping back up. I couldn't fathom what they were doing.

And then Hernandez's body floated up to the surface.

Apparently, he'd drowned himself.

I stood there in disbelief, staring at Hernandez's dead body, feeling cold and confused. It was Schwarber who broke the silence.

"Good riddance," he said under his breath.

"What?" I turned to him. "How fucking dare you?"

"Shut up, Kansas, or we'll come after you next."

"Fuck you!" I pressed my finger into his chest. "Don't you get it, moron? They didn't kill themselves because of the things *you* did to them. They did it because you idiots wouldn't let them be who they were. You morons killed our brothers, and why? Because you couldn't stand the fact that two men could love one another. You might be big and strong on the outside…" I ground my finger harder into his chest. "But in here, in your heart, you're so very weak. They killed themselves because of their love for one another." My eyes bore into his. "Never forget that. What you caused."

I left them there to chew on my words.

Benny Schwarber and I, we never really saw eye to eye on any-thing after that. So be it. That didn't change what we were to each oth-er. No, that was a brand that had been seared deep into our hearts, like it or not. There was no escaping that brotherhood, no matter what any of us did or said. But make no mistake about it, what he did to Her-nandez and Lofgren, that changed everything. It strained that bond, to say the least.

As I stand over his coffin, reading the scripture I earmarked, I'm reminded of those days. Momentarily, my thoughts are disrupted by seeing Benny's partner. After all these years, only now do I understand. It took this long to figure out the *why*.

How torn my "brother" must have been to make those choices back then. How tortured to carry that weight for a lifetime afterward. It is clearer to me now more than ever; we are all broken. Some of us ac-cept that fate and strive to become better men and women. Others never really learn how to deal with it. And for those folks, it's always hardest.

In a way, we are all a brotherhood. An island of misfits. We walk around this earth, looking for peace, and often we don't even know when we have found it. Meanwhile, while we embark on this never-ending quest, there are forces who would rather keep us in the dark. Some of us overcome, but so many more succumb to their will day after day. We are poisoned by old, outdated beliefs.

After years of crying myself to sleep, of begging God and my brothers for forgiveness, I am left with a single thought. Now is the time for change.

(Inspired by Romeo and Juliet, a classic I'm thankful for having read back in high school, because love is a hard thing to come across, and it comes in many forms. When you discover it, don't let others define it for you; grab it with both hands and hold tight. – Kenneth)

A Lover's Pinch

"The stroke of death is as a lover's pinch,
Which hurts, and is desired. Dost thou lie still?"
—Cleopatra (Antony & Cleopatra)

Ahlissa Eichhorn

Rage weighs my heart against yours as blood glides
Over the gilded armor of your skin.
That contemptuous vow made with the tides,
A vexed knife giving your flesh a new grin.
A proper burial, my last good deed
Before I send for Death and its sweet bite.
Choking on this anguish, soon to be freed
Of the dance between jealousy and spite.
I sit under my crown slick with venom.
Breath feeble, a demon for company.
Mesmerized by fangs, a tongue like vellum,
Its low hiss an eternal symphony.
     I can see the reeds now, swaying in flames.
     Love, pain, hate; the syllables of your name.

Showtime

(inspired by The Winter's Tale)

Lee Murray

The Oracle Online
From our Entertainment Desk:

A stainless steel memorial to screen icon Hermione Gallant will be unveiled this coming weekend in a new addition to the Grecian-themed Four Ladies of Hollywood gazebo, city officials announced on Monday. Designed by acclaimed sculptor Paulie Nathan, the Gallant statue, which depicts the star in her most famous role, Queen Hermione from Shakespeare's *The Winter's Tale*, will replace the Marilyn Monroe figurehead stolen in 2019.

eon Sicilia throws open the double doors to his executive office at Leontes Enterprises and ushers his childhood friend, now partner, Xavier Pollard, into the room.

"Come in, mate," Leon says jovially.

The English oak doors close automatically behind them, muffling the saxophone solo drifting up from the soirée in progress in the atrium three floors below.

"Let me get you something with a little more bite," Leon says, crossing to the office bar, his patent-black shoes, dusted with the evening's glitter, barely whispering on the polished wooden floors.

"Thank God," Pollard whines. "I bloody hate these events." He yanks at his tie, loosening it from his bull neck, and sinks his bulk into one of a half-dozen leather armchairs strategically placed to take in the Hollywood lights in the office's floor-to-ceiling windows. "Stupid fucking penguin suits."

Leon pours Black Label whiskey into two crystal glasses, offers one to his friend, then pulls up another of the armchairs. Settling into the soft leather, Leon raises his glass. "Here's to us, and our ongoing partnership."

"Too right." Pollard, who's already had more than a few tipples from the champagne tower downstairs, lifts his glass clumsily, sloshing amber liquid on the distressed leather.

Leon frowns. That splash would leave a stain. He would have to replace the chair. Sourced from a famous New York speakeasy, these armchairs had cost him a fucking fortune, not to mention a role in one of his productions for the interior designer. The thing is, in this business, storytelling, even down to the selection and placement of the furniture, is significant. Hollywood is all about aesthetics.

"Tell me again why we were estranged for a decade?" Pollard gushes. "What a couple of idiots. We could've done this deal years ago."

It was true; theirs was one hell of a deal. Showcasing two of Hollywood's hottest properties—Leontes starlet Perdita Johnson, purportedly the secret lovechild of a controversial U.S. senator and chiseled former pro-football star turned leading man, D. Floyd Kitowski—the three-picture venture between Leontes and Pollard's Boho Productions was already proving lucrative. The first film had broken box-office records, with merchandising for Black Friday week bringing in many times that, and the second two movies looking set to follow suit. Even more so now their respective starlets have fallen in love. What a fucking coup. In time for the holiday parties, too. Leon expects another uptick in sales when the movie goes to streaming. Pretty soon he'll be rich enough to replace the water in his swimming pool with tequila.

"Although, I can't help but worry," Pollard drones on. "It's looking sweet for us now, but you know how screen romances are. They rarely work out. What if Perdy and D. Floyd split up? There'll be temper tantrums, delays, and God-knows-what-else. If that happens, it's going to create a monumental headache for us."

"It'll be fine," Leon says, nudging the cigar box on the coffee table toward Pollard with his toe. Leon's hoping the couple *will* split. In fact, he's counting on it for the free publicity. He can't wait to read the clickbait social media posts:

—Perdita and D. Floyd: Is it Over?
—Perdita Dines With Sexy Stuntman
—D. Floyd Has Regrets, Friends Confide

Then, amid the media maelstrom, Johnson will gain maybe a pound, stress eating about the breakup, and the press will hound about her "baby bump" every time she leaves the house for coffee...

Leon takes a swallow of his whiskey. "Chill, mate. The contracts are ironclad, and even if they aren't, well, things have a way of working out."

Pollard grabs a row of cigars and slips them into the inside pocket of his suit jacket. "You mean like that business with Hermione?"

Lifting his glass to cover his alarm, Leon considers his friend. Does Pollard suspect him? Well, even if he does, it isn't in his interests to cross Leon, not now that they're in business together. Still, the story of Hermione's disappearance at the height of her career has been the making of Leontes Enterprises. Not since Natalie Wood's disappearance on that yacht trip in 1981 had there been such a media furor. For years, Leon has exploited the news to the full, even fueling speculation about her fate whenever the buzz died away, at least he *had* done, up until the point the detective assigned to the case had been mowed down by a postal truck.

"You know I never tried to poach Hermione, right?" Pollard says, while swirling the liquid in his glass. "I know back then you thought I did, and I'll admit it was tempting..."

There's a brief knock. Pollard trails off as that intern—whatshisname—pops his head around the door. "Excuse me for interrupting,

Mr. Sicilia, but things are winding up, and Paulie asked me to bring this statue of Miss Gallant back. Said she belongs up here in your office."

"Yes. No problem." Leon waves him in.

Pollard raises an eyebrow as the youngster struggles to maneuver the bulky prop through the double doors, which keep closing on him like a sitcom gag. "Speak of the devil," Pollard whispers. He tips his glass to slurp up the last drop of whiskey.

"Sorry." The intern wiggles the statue through the door. "I'll just be a minute." Through a mix of shuffling and twisting, he gets the statue back in its place behind Leon's desk.

"Oh. Looks like someone spilled wine on her. I'll just give her a wipe—" The boy puts his hand in his jacket pocket and lifts the corner, about to rub the statue's breast…

Leon leaps up. "Stop! That'll do. I'll deal with that," he barks. "I need another drink anyhow."

The intern, another brownnose whose name still escapes Leon, bows profusely. "Yes. Thank you, sir. I'll leave now. Wonderful evening." Still kowtowing backwards, the jackass hits the double doors, then turns and fumbles with the latch. "Sorry."

"I hope that lad plans to be a comedian, because his timing is impeccable," Leon says when the boy has finally left.

Pollard hauls his bulk out of the chair and joins Leon at the bar. He holds out his glass and tilts it provocatively. "What makes you think he's a performer?" Pollard says. "He could just be an intern."

They both cackle at that. Leon fills his friend's glass, and together they stroll over to examine the statue. The actress is clad in the gauzy Greek attire of her namesake, long-suffering loyal wife, Hermione, from Shakespeare's *The Winter's Tale*. Its face, tilted upwards, is fixed in an expression of wonder, as if she is mesmerized by the lights pixelating in the windows. Her eyes, however, follow Leon in that creepy-as-fuck way they always do. Leon hates it. The statue had been a gift from Paulie, Leontes' long-standing prop girl, who'd made it as a tribute to the star. Leon wouldn't tolerate it in his office if it weren't for the media interest in Hermione's fate. Always good to be able to roll out a tragedy when negotiations aren't going your way.

"So, here she is—Hermione Gallant in all her splendor," Pollard says, breathing whiskey fumes in Leon's direction. Pollard gropes the statue's rump. He leans in. "Are the rumors true then, Leon? Did you do her?"

Leon grins. "In this very dress, in fact."

"I knew it," Pollard says. "Can't say that I blame you." He lifts his glass in mock salute. "She was one of the best."

"She was indeed."

"What do you think happened to her?"

"She passed into legend, Xavier."

"No, I mean *really*."

Leon shrugs. "Who can say?"

"She should've been here to see all this," Pollard says.

Leon cups the statue's breast salaciously. "She should indeed. Do you hear that, Hermione, my angel? Xavier and I wish you were here."

All at once, a spool of black smoke emerges from beneath the statue's feet.

So long, I've dwelled here in this deathly darkness
Sifting through my nightmares for the brazen truth
When at last it assaults me with its starkness
Your words and actions offering up the proof

No one doubted your description of events
You, the undisputed king of stage and screen
An oracle can't convince you to repent
So, I'm forced to re-enact the final scene

I imagine all you'll say in your defense
Perverse and effusive with your lousy charm
Yet you've soared to heights unheard at my expense
While pretending that you never wished me harm

Long I've waited, patient for this perfect role
Angel, now avenger of the truth you stole

"Holy fuck!" Pollard snatches back his hand. "The statue's on fire!" Startled, the buffoon stumbles backwards, hitting the wall and flinging his whiskey at the statue. There's a whoosh and the whole thing goes up like flambé, the statue-woman burning at the stake.

What the hell? Props aren't supposed to be flammable.

Leon jumps back, narrowly avoiding being caught up in the inferno, but Pollard isn't so lucky. His tie, flapping loose about his neck, is swallowed in flames.

"Help," Pollard gurgles. He lurches sideways, flapping his arms like a chicken. Leon hesitates. Why should he risk it? The idiot brought it on himself. But by now Pollard is a human torch rushing about the room. He's going to set the whole place alight, which would be mightily inconvenient. Why haven't the sprinklers activated?

Damn it. Leon knocks the panicked Pollard to the ground with his shoulder, then folds the corner of a Persian rug over him, smothering the flames, but the curtains are already alight. He grabs Pollard by the shoulders and drags him across the floor. "Stop fucking around, Xavier. We've got to get out of here."

Pollard's scream, hampered by swelling and smoke, is little more than a rasp. Using a foot to hold one of the double doors open, Leon yanks him, choking and spluttering, into the corridor. Releasing him, Leon clutches at the balustrade, snatching a second to catch his breath. Any fatter and Leon would've left him there to roast.

As the automatic doors close, Leon watches the fire climb to the ceiling. Made of foam or plaster of Paris, or whatever it is they use these days, the statue is burning merrily. Behind a wall of dancing flame, Hermione's face blackens. Those damned eyes follow him. *Fuck.* The bitch is smiling. Then the doors click closed on the barbeque. Leon stumbles across the corridor and thumbs the fire alarm. Immediately, sirens blare. Leon turns to Pollard and winces. The man is still lying on the floor, his neck charred red and swollen with yellow blisters.

"You saved my life," Pollard sputters.

He had, hadn't he? Leon revels in the frisson of excitement. "Well, we're partners," he says, already composing the story he'll tell the press. "Can't have you backing out now, can we?"

Leon nods at the gray smoke seeping under the double doors, billowing into the corridor.

Pollard's eyes widen. "Leon!" he croaks. "Look. It's Hermione!"

Leon whips his head up. In the gray haze, a thick curl of black smoke swirls upwards in gauzy swathes, like the folds of the Grecian dress that had draped the statue. *Jesus.* Leon's skin crawls. It does look like her.

Quickly, he lifts Pollard by the shoulders of his tuxedo, bursting the blisters and causing Pollard to bellow in pain. "Don't be ridiculous, Xavier," he says. "You've had a shock is all. Let's just get the fuck out of here."

They take the mezzanine stairs, Leon supporting Pollard on one side. Struggling to breathe, Pollard's progress is painfully slow. The infernal blast of the fire alarms is doing Leon's head in. More than once, he considers dumping Pollard and making a run for the exit, but some of the press corps might still be in the atrium, so he perseveres.

Waste of time. When at last they reach the ground floor, the atrium is hazy with smoke and there isn't a camera to be seen. The blurry shapes of musicians caterers, interns, and a bedraggle of drunken guests dart in and out of the murk, all searching for the exits like lost spirits in a gothic horror movie.

"Hey, we need a paramedic here!" Leon shouts. The din is excruciatingly loud. No one hears him. Leon makes a grab for someone. "A little help here," he barks. Only, it isn't a person. It's a foam prop. A satyr—one of many the event planner had hauled up from the basement storeroom and placed around the atrium to enhance the evening's Dionysus's Kingdom theme. Bloody unnatural things—hairy man-apes with goat horns and legs, clawed appendages, and their equipment on display.

Leon is about to turn away when a stream of black smoke speeds away from the ceiling and curls around the flute pressed to the creature's bulbous lips. A moment passes, and the satyr blinks.

The fuck?

Leon rubs at his eyes. Damned smoke. He's seeing things. But there's no doubting it when the satyr lowers the flute and grins, flashing its dog teeth.

Behind Leon, Pollard squeals in fright, his shriek carrying over the clamor of the alarms. Not a bad effort for someone whose neck looks like a piece of rare steak, complete with blobs of hollandaise.

Leon turns and grips Pollard by the arms. "It's nothing," he says. "A new tech, a special effect Paulie's been working on. We were just too busy schmoozing to see it before." That has to be the reason because when Leon looks again, the beast is gone, probably whisked away by the prop specialist. They must have missed her in the rolling smoke. Still, that drooling canine grin put the wind up Leon more than he wants to admit.

A sharp crack carries over the siren, making Leon look up. Even through the smoke, it's clear the atrium's roof is alight.

"That way," Leon says, pointing toward the swirling fog. "It's our quickest route. The main doors are opposite the staircase. The ambulances, when they get here, will be out there."

Pollard is struggling too hard to breathe to put up much of a fight. They hurry into the gray. That distinctive cloud of black smoke is back, too, lurking above them with fingers that snake outwards, probing and searching...

It's shaped like the statue, *like Hermione.*

Leon pulls at his collar. It's the smoke and the noise playing tricks on him. He just needs to get outside. A couple of gulps of fresh air and a visit to the insurance broker and this will be all over.

But the creepy satyr has been waiting for them. It braces its hooves on the marble floor and swings its flute like a baseball bat, arcing wide to smash what remains of the central champagne tower.

Crystal shards fly in all directions. Leon turns away, the vicious hail smattering the back of his jacket and crunching beneath his feet. A sliver nicks his face, warm blood rolling down his cheek.

Pollard grabs Leon's sleeve. Pulls up. He gasps and grasps his stomach. Talk about unlucky; there's a champagne stem sticking out of Pollard's guts. Pollard moves to rip the flute out, but Leon stops him. He's made enough movies to know how *that* ends.

"Leave it for the paramedics," he says, pointing towards the exit, but they haven't even taken a step when the building shakes.

Leon looks up again. Neon sky shows through the drifts of smoke. The fire is eating away at the building's timber framing. No time to think, Leon dives to one side, covering his head with his hands as the ceiling plummets in a torrent of lumber and ceiling tiles. Abruptly, the internal sirens stop their wailing, replaced by the crash of timber, and still later by the distant whine of ambulances. When the raining stops, or near enough, Leon sits up gingerly. His hip and knees are ravaged by bits of glass. The fire has gone out, choked by the debris, and the atrium is cloaked in white dust.

Somehow, Pollard is still beside him, the man's face as white as the proverbial ghost. How he can still be alive, Leon has no idea.

Pollard wipes grit—probably asbestos—from his eyes. "What now?" he rasps, since there is no getting out through the atrium.

"The stairwell," Leon says. "There's an exit through the basement."

Dashing back the way they came, Leon sets his shoulder to the fire doors into the stairwell, Pollard hard on his heels. As Leon turns to close the fire doors, he glances through the glass insert at the ruined atrium.

Hermione's visage bursts into view.

Leon takes a step back, almost toppling off the landing at the sight of that wretched masque of coiled smoke and black shadow. She isn't real. It isn't possible. Just a cinematic phantom born of smoke and tinsel. Then her spark-red eyes glitter and suddenly Leon isn't so sure. The smoke wraith cracks a smile. Leon quivers at her malevolence, a pang of fear seizing him.

Just as quickly, the visage dissipates. Leon breathes out in relief. But when he looks down, fingers of black smoke are rolling under the door.

How like you two to save your royal flesh
Ignore, abscond; they are your best defense

Then rise unencumbered to corrupt afresh
Sans guilt, and with no chance of consequence

But now sequestered in this under realm
Your puissance wanes with every putrid breath
Rudderless, ripped untimely from the helm
Confronted with the threat of violent death

In truth, I think yours is the fairest path
Than years lost languished in a stony shrine
A sad mishap and newsworthy bloodbath
Leontes Burns; makes a striking headline

For now, I'll have my gaiety restored
A moment spent with kings I once adored

"Quick! Downstairs," Leon roars.

"What's happening?" Pollard croaks, one hand on his belly and the other clutching at the railing.

"Smoke!" Leon shrieks.

"What?"

"Just go!"

Black tendrils seep around them, making Leon's spine crawl with unease. He itches to shove Pollard down the stairs; the clown is moving so damned slowly.

At last, they reach the bottom; it's a stub, this corridor previously shared with the building next door. Now, the only egress is through the prop department's myriad aisles and alleyways and out onto the next street. Leon bustles Pollard into the basement, then, snatching up a model cudgel, slips the wooden shaft through the door's handles. He checks the gap at the bottom, waiting for the telltale curl of black smoke to slither underneath, but the space remains clear.

"Good. Looks like the fire doors should keep her out; still, we shouldn't linger."

Pollard coughs. "Which way's the exit?"

There doesn't seem to be any signage. Leon waves an arm vaguely south. It has to be somewhere that way, although he can't be sure. It's been ages since he came down here. Not since the days of Hermione's disappearance.

"Is it far?" Pollard is looking green around the gills—or he would be if his neck wasn't a glistening patchwork of burst blisters.

"Nah," Leon replies. "We just have to find the right aisle." Which could be easier said than done. The basement is a vast warehouse of props and costumes used in Leontes productions going back decades. Aisle upon aisle of stuff is stored here. From where they're standing in the doorway, Leon can see bits of a spaceship, some model T-Rex bones, a couple of church pews, and the shanty town backdrop for a cowboy film that flopped—every manner of thing. But because the contents are so varied, one aisle doesn't run parallel to the next. In fact, this basement is a labyrinthine nightmare.

Which was why it had been the perfect place to stash her. Even Leon couldn't tell you where she is exactly, not that anyone had looked. Not even the police. They'd been too busy searching Hermione's apartment, her beach place in the Hamptons, and following up rumors about a possible trip to Greece, reports which Leon may or may not have seeded.

He tries to visualize the tiny cell he'd locked her in. A ship's cabin if he recalls. Or maybe a dungeon. Not certain. It was all so long ago. Water under the bridge really. He'd brought her down one evening to borrow a piece of paste jewelry for some awards show. Well, that had been the *pretext*. And then she'd gone and ruined it all, hadn't she? Never trust a woman. Feckless creatures.

"This way." With a final glance under the door, Leon sets off down an aisle leaving Pollard to tag along in his wake. The first aisle is a gloomy affair, although the shelves are stacked with period lighting. The glinting gas lamps give Leon the jitters. It's the statue going up in flames that's unnerved him. That, and the glass in his hip. Having to navigate this basement where Hermione had taken her last breath isn't helping, either. Not that there's anything to worry about. It's not like she could hurt him. She'd be mummified by now, her skin all black and leathery, her skull shrunken to the size of a monkey, and her beautiful face twisted in a howl behind the dried-up gag.

Halfway along the aisle they hit a dead end. Leon and Pollard segue into an even gloomier passageway, at an angle to the first, the yellow overhead lights casting ominous shadows before them.

How long had it taken Hermione to die down here in the darkness, Leon wonders? A week? Maybe a month? It's not like he really meant to leave her. Just teach her a lesson, you know? He'd even resolved to let her out once, then lost his nerve when he'd got down here. Women bear grudges for the tiniest things. She would've said something. He could've undermined her, spun it to his advantage, for sure, but he didn't have the energy. So he'd stopped coming down to the basement, and after a while, well, the problem became moot. She was obviously dead. Best to leave her in peace. Besides, he couldn't afford to rouse Paulie's suspicion; the prop supervisor was always in the basement, and there'd been a time when she'd been starry-eyed for Hermione.

"Jesus," Pollard whispers.

"Yeah, no kidding." Leon is creeped out, too. On either side of them, the stacks here are crammed with taxidermied animals. Graded from small to large, there are stuffed falcons, porcupines, and wolves, the dusty creatures following them with their clouded dead eyes—just like that stupid statue.

"Look at that," croaks Pollard. "Hermione's back."

Leon glances about. "Where?"

"Up there."

Leon sucks in a breath. Pollard might be riddled with pain, but there's nothing wrong with his eyes. The Hermione smoke-wraith is hovering over the stacks.

"What does she want with us?" Pollard asks.

Leon can guess. "You want to hang around and ask her?"

"No," Pollard says.

"Let's piss off out of here then." But before they can hurry past the last of the stuffed animals, the smoky apparition sweeps down from the ceiling and merges with a massive grizzly bear, Hermione's black limbs fingering down its throat.

Leon's heart sinks to his shiny leather shoes as the animal shakes the dust off its coat and steps into the passageway. It roars hot breath in Leon's face, and its eyes, once clouded, glow yellow. Leon wants to deny it, but the stench, the sound, is all too real.

"Back up, back up," he screams. "Run!" Pollard doesn't have to be told twice. They run for their lives, the bear lumbering after them in the gloom.

"Where do we go?" Pollard gasps. It's been like this since their childhood. If only Pollard could think for himself. Leon's already saved his skin once tonight. The bear's jaws could close on Leon's throat at any moment.

"Just keep going!" Leon screams.

Dammit, if Pollard doesn't slow. *What the hell?* "Keep going, I said." Leon looks forward, over Pollard's shoulder. That blasted satyr is blocking the end of the aisle. It's eyes twinkling maliciously, the creature twirls its flute.

"Keep going," Leon insists.

"No," Pollard says. All right for him. The bear would get Leon first.

Hang on. This passage looks familiar… "Go right," Leon yells. "There's a crypt about ten yards in."

In the narrow aisles, they can turn more swiftly than the bear.

"I see it," Pollard shouts. He throws himself at the door. It doesn't budge.

"Move," Leon shouts, thrusting Pollard out of the way. Throwing across the lock, Leon dives through the wooden door into the fake tomb.

Pollard, hampered by his injuries, clambers through the gap after Leon, but he's too slow; the bear is there, its daggered claws raking at his thigh. In the small space, Pollard's scream is deafening, but he kicks off the attack and rolls inside.

Leon slams the door shut.

Outside, the bear hurls itself at the crypt. It's all Leon can do to hold it off, his weight insufficient to keep out a bear—even one stuffed with kapok. "Help me," he hisses through clenched teeth. To his credit, Pollard crawls over, slumping with his back to the door. On the other side, the bear roars its frustration. It thrashes at the crypt a couple more times, then moves away to smash at the stacks.

The passage goes quiet.

Leon feels around, finding a metal candlestick to brace the door. "It's gone for now," he tells Pollard.

Pollard grunts. His leg is bleeding in great gluts. Trembling, he wraps a length of grubby fabric around his thigh in a makeshift tourniquet. "Give me a hand to tighten this, will you?"

Recognizing the scrap of fabric, Leon jumps, but he braces his hand against Pollard's hip, inhaling the metallic stench of blood, and yanks the fabric tight. Pollard groans. Leon ties it off. The blood slows. That done, they lean back against the wall to catch their breath.

Pollard grasps Leon by the leg. "Wait. Is that…?" His gaze strays to the wizened cadaver. Not much larger than a child, it is facing away from them, curled in the fetal position, its bony arms cradling its shoulders.

Leon wipes the blood from his hands onto his dress trousers. "A body. Yes, yes. Don't worry. It's a fake."

"That isn't fake. It's Hermione Gallant."

"Nonsense, man. It's the pain talking. You've lost a bit of blood and it's making you light-headed. Those bones just *look* real. Paulie, our props girl, is da bomb."

"Leon, I know that ring. I gave it to her."

Leon looks up sharply. So Pollard had lied; he *had* tried to poach her away. Birds of a feather. Leon has to admire him for keeping the secret so long.

"I tell you, this is Hermione's body," Pollard rabbits on. "Don't you see? It explains everything. It's the reason the statue went up in smoke, why she's been following us…"

"Now look, Xavier, I don't know—"

"She wanted us to find her," Pollard says. "She must have accidentally locked herself in here, so she's created a trail for us to find her." His shoulders shake visibly. "Leon, what if we're locked in, too?" He scrambles for the door.

"No, Xavier. Don't go. The bear…"

"I'd rather be mauled by a bear than die slowly in this fake crypt," Pollard says. He removes the candlestick and cracks open the door, then glances at Leon and exhales heavily.

Leon had known they weren't trapped, but he feigns relief for Pollard's sake.

"The bear's gone," Pollard says.

"Okay, let's go then."

They exit the crypt, listening for the bear, Leon checking the ceiling for smoke. They hobble down an aisle lined with armaments: from blunderbusses to machine guns. Let the bear come for them now.

Instead, it's the satyr that appears before them.

Leon's had enough of this shit. Time to wipe the smirk off that prancing man-beast. Grabbing a machine gun, he uses the butt to break open the padlock of the munition store, and snatching a pistol from the shelves, loads it with shaking hands. He raises his eyes to Pollard. "Run, mate. I've got this."

Pollard nods, then staggers back the way they came.

The satyr too, dances away.

Not so fast. Leon dashes after it into the next aisle. Mocking him, the satyr prances before him, playing its flute with those flapping lips.

Leon lifts the gun. Groans.

He can't shoot. Beyond the man-creature, Pollard is also in this aisle.

A finger of black smoke coils away from the ceiling and enters the barrel of the pistol. *No!* Leon recoils in horror. He tries to release the gun, but his fingers won't open. They tighten on the trigger.

"Stop this, you bitch!" Leon grasps the gun with his other hand, but the weapon has a mind of its own. Leon grapples with it, even as his fingers squeeze the trigger.

It fires.

At the end of the aisle, Pollard stumbles, then crumples in technicolor slow-mo, his brains splattered across the stacks. The satyr giggles and waltzes out of view. Smoke crowds the corridor. Leon staggers backwards into the stacks. His pulse thunders in his temples.

She killed him. *She* did this.

"Mr. Sicilia! Are you in here?"

Paulie's voice. *Thank heavens.* "Paulie! Where are you?" Leon shouts.

"I'm here, near the exit. The paramedics are here with me. Follow my voice, sir!"

Homing in on Paulie's voice as if it were a puffer fish light, Leon ignores the damage to his shoes and races through the blood and brain matter. He takes the next left-hand angle—and is confronted again by the satyr. Leon swivels and sprints into the next passage. The smoke twists and coils above him, Hermione's face drifting over the tops of the stacks, cackling with mirth.

"Paulie!" Leon gasps. He has to make it before that bitch Hermione inhabits something else.

"Here. I'm here, sir," Paulie coaxes. "Keep low, the smoke is less dense near the floor!"

Leon runs at a crouch. He's close now—Paulie's voice is getting louder—but Hermione is close, too, her smoke-tendril limbs playing with his hair, tugging at his clothes. *Oh God...* His lungs burning and his nostrils full of smoke, Leon dashes around the corner.

No! That fucking satyr again.

"Mr. Sicilia!"

Hermione tickles at Leon's neck in a tendril of black smoke.

Leon sprints the length of the aisle, then turns down another alley. Stops.

What the fuck?

He's back where he started. At Pollard's cadaver, the champagne flute still protruding from the poor bastard's stomach. On the plus side, he's found Paulie, the paramedics, *and the police.* But the black smoke pulls up, too, twisting in a cloud above the stacks.

"Paulie, thank fuck," Leon says.

The prop specialist pales at the gun still in Leon's hand. She draws in a breath. "He's armed," she whispers.

A burly hero in a Kevlar vest steps in front of Paulie, his gun raised. "Put the weapon down, sir," he says calmly.

Leon stares at the gun, at the blood smeared over his hands, and realizes how it must look. "No, no, you don't understand," he insists. "I didn't fire this gun. You've got it all wrong. It wasn't me. It was Hermione Gallant!"

Behind the police officer, Paulie clucks her tongue. "That's not possible. Miss Gallant has been missing for more than a decade."

"No! She's not," Leon shouts. "She's down here. In the smoke."

Paulie's voice, so comforting before, has a hard edge to it. "I've worked in this basement for years. If Hermione Gallant had been living down here, I think I'd know…"

Leon lurches forward. "She's here, I tell you!"

"Put the gun down now!" police officers yell, their guns aimed at his face.

Leon trembles. Talk about out of the frying pan and into the fire. He'd eluded Hermione only to face down a bloody firing squad, and the irony is, the only person who can verify Leon's version of events has his brain matter spattered all over the concrete floor. His adrenaline still racing, Leon opens his fingers, marveling at the stickiness of Pollard's blood, and lets the prop gun drop to the floor. Then he raises his arms, slowly, slowly, in case one of the officers is feeling trigger happy.

The police crowd in, one of them cuffing Leon's wrists.

Not to worry. He's escaped Hermione's wrath. It'll be okay. Leon has built an empire in this town. A king of the screen, he has money, insurance. Everything is optics anyway. He'll hire the best lawyers to get him off. Things have a way of working out.

Above him, the black smoke drifts in an angry haze.

Too long I'd hungered for this interlude
Eye for an eye, or so the scholars tell
And well enough to mend a simple feud
Yet, in my case, there was no parallel

Ruined by your wont of assignation
I spurned and burned you is the reason why
O, I represented a vexation
Now, tooth for a tooth; it's your turn to die

Then, sudden thought—my attitude inversed
I would not kill you as I'd first surmised
Our final scene played not as I'd rehearsed
Too gentle for the man I so despised

Leontes, my whole life was spoiled by you
I would not let you haunt my death-sleep, too

The Oracle Online
From our Entertainment Desk:

Movie mogul Leon Sicilia, CEO of Leontes Enterprises and mastermind of the *Death Watch* movie franchise which features actors Perdita Johnson and D. Floyd Kitowski, has been jailed for life for the murder of his business partner, Xavier Pollard, at a Hollywood party last year. Sicilia shot Pollard dead when the latter discovered evidence that Sicilia had kidnapped and killed screen legend Hermione Gallant. The desiccated corpse of Gallant, who disappeared at the height of her screen career, was discovered in the basement of the Leontes building, putting an end to a decade of media speculation regarding her whereabouts and closing the unsolved cold case for Hollywood police. Counsel for Sicilia, Thomas King, had previously argued that Sicilia's deteriorating mental state meant he should not be brought to trial, but Judge Florizel, under advisement from medical experts, claimed the screen mogul was "playacting in a deliberate ploy for sympathy" and sentenced him to cumulative life sentences after a jury took just two hours to deliver the guilty verdict. Sicilia will not be eligible for parole until 2066.

In true Hollywood fashion, Ms. Gallant's previously un-discovered diaries, released by her nephew Mamillian Gallant, are currently the subject of a bidding war by publishers. While industry commentators have criticized the timing, Gallant's agent, Emily Camillo, says the diaries, written in Hermione Gallant's own hand, are both "shocking" and "a sad indictment on today's society" with the #MeToo story expected to attract a six-figure fee.

Meanwhile, Clio Dillon, spokesperson for Pastoral Productions, the new owner of the blockbuster *Death Watch* franchise, announced today that the next movie in the much-anticipated series, *Death Interrupted*, is expected to release in the new year after a delay of sixth months, fueling rumors of a pregnancy for star Perdita Johnson...

Fortune

Philip Fracassi

I

Thomas stares at the gaudy neon sign through the smoky tint of the Cadillac's window. Rivulets of rain shimmy down the dark glass, giving the sign's garish colors a smeared, dreamlike quality. The driver turns his head, his face a silhouette against the windshield's glow, soaked by streetlights. "Sir?"

Thomas scowls. He doesn't like being rushed.

"Let's go," he says.

A moment later, his door opens to a world of heavy rain on dirty pavement. An umbrella, held aloft by his driver, keeps the rain off as he exits the sedan. The men walk step in step toward the large window that frames the neon, the sign a circle of occult symbology—a yellow hand, palm-up, at its center. Just above the circle a buzzing, bright red word:

PSYCHIC

"Sir, are you sure…"

Thomas glares at his driver with such malice that the larger man (a war veteran who could disassemble Thomas's slim body as if it were made from sticks and tissue paper) jerks away with a wince, then jams a finger into the buzzer beside the iron-mesh outer door.

After a moment, the interior door opens. Broken white light spills over the men.

The woman pushes open the security door, then disappears into the room behind her.

"Wait in the car," Thomas says. "This won't take long."

The driver nods and pulls open the mesh door wide for his boss, careful to keep the umbrella positioned so the rain doesn't tap the older man's narrow shoulders.

Thomas steps inside, then looks back at the driver's hulking shadow through the metal grating. Scowling, he shuts the inner door, blocking out the night.

"Please sit," the old woman says, her short, thin body draped in colorful silks. Her gray hair is swept back, giving her severe nose a beakish appearance. Bright brown eyes glisten like stars within folds of wrinkled skin.

Thomas sits at a small round table, its surface draped in purple velvet. Dark crimson rugs cover the floor, the walls and ceiling painted a rich chocolate. Flickering orange sconces give the space a hellish glow. Thomas waits silently as the psychic nestles down across from him.

Without preamble, she pulls an oversized deck of tarot cards from the folds of a sleeve, begins laying them out, one by one.

Thomas slaps his hand down atop the second card, long fingers covering the image of a robed woman. The psychic jerks back in surprise, looks at him with eyes that are initially wary, then curious. "Not yet," he says, meeting her glare, then removes his hand slowly. "I'm sorry to startle you, but I have a very specific request, and a very specific offer."

"I'm listening," she says.

"You see, Ms. Santos…may I call you Camila?" Thomas allows himself a smirk, but the old woman is unfazed by the fact he knows her first name. She only shrugs, and his smirk dissolves before he continues. "Camila, then. You see, Camila, I'm a very wealthy man. I have"—his eyes move around the room, as if searching for the right word—"*resources*. And, after a year of having those resources gather information for me on every psychic, every fortune teller, every crystal-ball-staring, tarot-card-flipping, palm-reading nutjob in the city, I've learned something very interesting."

Camila crosses her arms and waits. Thomas leans forward, his smirk returning.

"I've learned that a few of you—not many, but a few—can actually *do* some of the things you say you can do. Of course, you don't waste your real talent on the tourists, or drunken bachelorettes...or even those who might really believe. You save it for special occasions, don't you? For loved ones who might be in trouble. Or even"—Thomas's smirk spreads to a full grin, white-capped teeth slick between dull lips—"for that little girl you helped find a few years back. It was you who tipped the police, wasn't it?"

Camila says nothing, and now it's Thomas who shrugs.

"I know all about you, Camila. And I know," he says, waggling a finger in her direction, "that you're the *real deal,* as they say. When motivated, anyway. And that's what I'm here to do, Camila. I'm here to *motivate* you."

The old woman crosses her elbows on the small table, silky sleeves glistening in the room's weak orange light, her eyes shiny pits in her skull. "You rich white men like to talk," she says, "but you don't like to say anything. Why don't you say something instead of all this talk. Say what you want and let's be done with it."

Thomas settles back in his chair. "Well spoken. To the chase, then." He takes a steadying breath, places a hand gently on the table-cloth in front of him, studies the patterns his fingertips make in the velvet. "I'm here with good news, Camila. I'm here to pay you more than you ever dreamed possible. But in return, you must not only read my fortune...you must guarantee it."

Camila shakes her head, brow furrowed. "What do you mean? The future is the future. Money or no money."

"I will pay you half a million dollars," he says, continuing as if she hasn't spoken a word. "Wired to a tax-free, offshore account in your name, in exchange for the promise of a good future. I want to live the last years of my life in blissful, carefree happiness. I want my finances to remain rock solid, my health to stay intact." He rests his arms on the small table, fixes his eyes on hers. "I want to die peacefully, in my sleep, at the ripe old age of ninety-something. And when I pass, I want there to be a big fucking smile on my face. Do you understand?"

Camila nods slowly. "I understand."

"So," Thomas says, wiping a streak of saliva from his lower lip, "you'll do it? You can do this for me?"

Camila looks down at her hands for a moment, as if debating. When she looks up her eyes are steady, her face determined. "For half a million dollars I will do everything in my power to guarantee these things you ask for. You will be happy. You will stay rich. You will live long and be healthy. You will die peacefully. With a fucking smile."

Thomas, breathing heavy with excitement, splays his fingers flat on the velvet tabletop. "How? How will you do it?"

Camila waves a hand in the air, as if the question is of no importance. "With charms. A protective spell. It will not be easy. These kinds of spells come at great cost. I will lose several years of my own life. But, for the money you offer…"

The old woman grins broadly. "It's a sacrifice I'm willing to make."

Twenty minutes later, Thomas steps into the night. The rain has stopped. A breeze rides up from the waterfront and he takes a moment to inhale the briny scent. The sweat of a coastal city.

The driver approaches, umbrella in hand.

"I'm all right," Thomas says. "There's no rainfall to hurt my bared head. Just get the door, please."

The driver opens the car's rear door and Thomas climbs inside. The leather seat smells divine, the car's interior a warm balm against the night's chill. When the front door closes, he settles back, comfortably tired.

"Home, sir?"

"Afraid not." He clutches the heavy coin in his pocket, the one given to him by the psychic. "We have two more stops this evening."

The driver turns around to face his longtime employer. "With respect, sir. You should take it easy. It's late."

"Don't worry about me," he says too loudly. "Now look, the second address is 410 East Lorenzo Avenue. Just east of the park."

As the car pulls away, Thomas closes his eyes. He tries to relax but finds himself agitated. Remembers the nightmare. Or as he thinks of it: the *vision*.

A vision of his future. Old and broken. Penniless. Destitute. Disfigured.

Mad.

He'd woken from the horrible dream weeping, unnerved. Unable to shake it in the weeks to come, he vowed to do something. To assure his fate, no matter the cost.

In his pocket, the coin grows pleasantly warm against his palm and the memory softens, dissolves. He smiles in relief as the car carries him like a shadow through the night, a rider on a dark horse.

The apartment building is old but surprisingly tidy. Metal shingle eyebrows crest two stories of street-facing windows, the brick walls unmarred by graffiti. Across the street a group of men sit on the steps of a dilapidated house, a mimic of the ones staggered side by side up the narrow street. The men wear soiled T-shirts and loose jeans, drink from bottles and speak loudly enough to carry past the sedan's tinted windows and into the backseat, where Thomas watches them, frowning.

He notices the rain has started again, but it's mild enough not to drive the men into their homes. A cold mist coats the sedan's windows. When the driver opens his door, Thomas says, "I think you better stay with me until I'm inside."

They approach the apartment closest to the street, a metallic "1" stuck to its surface like a chrome leech, petrified and aged with rust. Thomas knocks and there's a clatter from inside, as if a cabinet of pots had leaped to the linoleum—a culinary suicide pact—at the sound of his knuckles rapping wood.

Heavy footsteps pound toward the door and Thomas arches an eyebrow when his driver takes half a step backward, as if fearing whatever will appear in the opening.

The door opens, however, to reveal nothing but a middle-aged woman in a pink terrycloth robe, beneath which Thomas spies white long johns reaching from throat to ankle. She scowls at the two men, frazzled hair pulled into a bun, blue eyes narrowed with hostility.

"Ms. Evans?" Thomas does his best to appear docile but not afraid. He thinks a woman like Ms. Evans would smell that fear. Smell it and attack.

"You Halstead?" she asks, eyes darting side to side, as if there might be more strange men in hiding, looking to pounce from the shadows.

"That's right," Thomas says, and tries a tepid smile, one he hopes the woman will find innocent. "May I come in? My driver, of course, will wait in the car."

The woman taps her dirty bare foot against the hardwood floor, as if debating. Then, without a word, turns and walks into the house.

Thomas follows.

Martha Evans is a witch.

When Thomas first heard this he laughed, asked the lead investigator if the amount of money he was making allowed time for stupid jokes.

But then Thomas listened, and by the time he ended the call it was understood that Ms. Evans would be on his short list of candidates. The witch had proven, time and time again, that she could perform undeniable feats of magic.

One story told of a neighbor's teenage son who'd been shot in a gang-fueled crossfire. Two bullets caught his chest, sending him to the ground in a heap. Bleeding onto the street. An ambulance was called, of course, but locals knew it would take time, that police and emergency units would hold back until the danger had passed, the streets safe for someone wearing a badge.

Instead of waiting for her son to bleed out, the mother had two men carry the boy to the door of Martha Evans. According to witnesses, Martha first stopped the bleeding with a foul-smelling poultice she'd spooned from a dusty jar, one of many kept in the pantry of her kitchen. She followed with a *ritual,* a babbling of words so foreign that none in attendance could agree on the language. The child's shirt was cut away, strange symbols drawn across his body in white paint that turned quickly pink with blood.

After that, everyone but the boy's mother had been pushed from the apartment.

By the time the ambulance arrived, the child was walking across the street, unsteady but upright, and seemingly uninjured. His mother held his elbow, crying the whole way.

When seen the next day, the boy was completely healed. As far as folks in the neighborhood know, he never even saw a doctor.

And there are other things Thomas knows about Martha Evans.

He knows, for instance, that she hasn't paid her rent in years. That her apartment, despite being in a rough neighborhood, has never been broken into. He knows that when she walks down the street, people wave, or nod, but she's never harassed—her purse isn't snatched, teenagers don't make fun of her as they pass. Some locals even offer small gifts, as if in tribute. A bottle of wine, a home-baked pie.

It's said she offers tonics that regrow hair and cure disease. That she once cast a spell on a man who beat his wife. It covered his skin in boils.

So now Thomas sits in her kitchen, fingering the coin in his coat pocket while she lights another cigarette. "You sick?" she asks, blowing a plume of smoke into the air.

"No," Thomas replies, taking in the fastidiously neat kitchen, how it seemed at odds with her stringy hair and disheveled clothes. *She looks like a hag.*

Abruptly, she laughs (*a cackle,* he thinks). "I could look like a runway model if you'd prefer," she says, grinning. "It'd be an illusion, of course, but maybe you'd be more comfortable."

"That's not necessary," Thomas replies evenly, raising an eyebrow. "But impressive."

The witch shrugs and bats her eyelashes playfully, then sucks on her cigarette as if it were oxygen. "So what can I do for you, Mr. Halstead? A love spell, perhaps?"

Thomas wafts away the clove-scented smoke. "It's about my future, Ms. Evans. I'd like some guarantees about my future."

Martha remains quiet as Thomas explains his position, then makes an offer of money, the same amount he'd given Camila Santos. When he's done, she considers him a moment, then stares into a high corner of the room, mouth moving silently, as if speaking to someone—or something—Thomas cannot see.

When she finally turns her eyes back to him, she nods. "Okay, Mr. Halstead. I can do what you want. I'll work you up a spell. But it's gonna take some time and some doing. I'm what you'd call a cradle witch, which means I don't have a contract with a higher power and I don't suck demon cock; you get me?"

Thomas doesn't, but waits for her to finish.

"Point is," she says, "I gotta do it all myself and it can be draining. On the plus side, you don't need to be here for it. Just leave me some blood and some hair and I can do the rest. Oh, but there is one thing…"

Martha stands abruptly and walks to a kitchen drawer. She rifles through the inner contents, then pulls out a narrow box and a jar of dark liquid. She sits down, taps the box with a blood-red, chipped fingernail. "Inside here is a very long, very sharp needle. And this," she says, waving her cigarette at the bottle, "is…well, let's just say it's ink." She cackles again, but it's short lived, and when her smile fades her expression is serious. Intimidating, even.

"I need to mark you."

Thomas straightens, eyes widening, but the witch only shakes her head, stabbing out her cigarette in a tin ashtray.

"Don't worry. I don't need to put a pentagram on your balls or nothing. I just need to give you my mark so the spell holds. No bigger than a dime, I promise."

Thomas thinks a moment, absently taps his chin with a bony fingertip. "All right, Ms. Evans. I'll agree to the tattoo, and you'll have your money before I walk out the door." He leans closer, offers a sly smile that doesn't meet his eyes. "But please take this as fact: If your spell doesn't work, and you've marked my skin and taken my money, witch or no witch, you'll be dead within the year. My people are very good, and very…curse resistant."

But the witch only grins, and Thomas notices the tongue inside her mouth is black as an eel, a realization that makes him shudder.

"Understood, Mr. Halstead," she says, opening the box. "Now, where do you want it?"

Thomas winces as he settles into the backseat of the Cadillac. His left heel throbs where the witch had stabbed him—repeatedly—with her needle. He'd opted for a part of his body that would be hidden from anyone who may see him, dressed or otherwise.

"One last stop, and it's home to a brandy and a good night's sleep," he says to the driver, hating how exhausted he feels after the night's excursions. In just over two hours he'd become a million dollars poorer, and he still wasn't done. The money meant nothing, of course. He'd make it back collecting a week's interest on his brokerage account. And if things worked out as he hoped, and the psychic and the witch were true to their word, it would be more than worth the expense.

As the sedan cuts through the sleeping city, Thomas takes time to regroup his emotions, center himself for this final stop. His heel has stopped throbbing, but now it itches. He fights the urge to rip off his shoe and scratch at the witch's mark. Instead, he thrusts his hand into his coat pocket, fondles the heavy coin. It's warm, comforting, and he feels better touching it.

As streetlights strobe past his window, pulsing like the city's sulfurous heart, he studies the buildings sliding by—the skyscrapers and mixed-use structures, the museums, the restaurants. His company owns so much of the property he can't help but think of the city as his own. A kingdom of concrete and steel. And now that he's secured his future—bribed fate—he could relax and enjoy his wealth, his power.

A sudden warmth spills upward from his heel. A rush of

euphoria that fills his body, makes his heart swell, his scalp tingle, his cock stiffen.

The spell, he thinks. *That damned witch has cast the spell.*

Thomas closes his eyes and smiles. The tires hum soothingly against the wet road, and he lets himself have a few moments' rest before finishing what he started.

II

For the third time that night, Thomas knocks on a stranger's door.

A tall, heavy man answers, his eyes wide and wary. He's old, older than Thomas by a decade, at least. His close-cut hair is gray against his dark scalp, his cheeks and chin stubbled with white. "You him?" the man says, his substantial presence filling the doorway. Thomas turns to make sure his driver is near at hand, then smiles as best he's able given his tiredness.

"I'm Thomas Halstead. And I'm sorry to be late. I got here as soon as I could."

The man's eyes flick over Thomas's shoulder to the driver, the previous wide-eyed wariness narrowing to full-on skepticism. "Who's that?"

Thomas sighs. "My driver." He turns. "Wait in the car, please."

Only when the driver has left the small house's porch, and secured himself into the black sedan, does the old man step aside.

"All right."

Thomas nods, takes a breath, and enters.

"She's brushing her teeth. You can sit down at the table. There."

The man points to a wooden chair placed at a round, four-seat kitchen table.

What's with people sitting in their goddamn kitchens? he thinks, settling into the uncomfortable chair.

The lights are fluorescent, buzzing and bright. The yellow cabinets and white tile countertops give the room the feel of an elementary school teacher's lounge, and Thomas has to massage out a building ache in his right temple as he sits and waits.

"You want some water? Coke?"

The man points to the sink, then the refrigerator. "I'm fine," Thomas says. "Maybe we could sit in your living room? The lights in here are very bright."

"You want something to drink or not?"

Thomas shakes his head and the man nods, then saunters down the hallway. Thomas hears him knock on a door and murmur something when it opens.

A few moments later the man reappears. Behind him trails a young girl wearing pajama bottoms and a Minnie Mouse T-shirt, braided hair pulled away from a cherubic face. She sits in the chair opposite Thomas, raises her elbows in order to perch them on the tabletop.

Cute kid, Thomas thinks, noting her round cheeks and large brown eyes. *But there's something else going on in there…something very old, and very serious.*

The old man finds a chair along a wall, where he sits and watches, hands on knees. Poised. Thomas makes an internal note not to make any sudden movements. He clears his throat. "My name is Thomas Halstead. I appreciate you seeing me."

The girl watches him a moment. *Studies* him. Her eyes gaze deeply into his own. Then she smiles, rubs a finger along the side of her nose, and looks like a kid again.

"I'm Angie."

Thomas nods. "I know, I know," he says, and chuckles. "I know all about you. About the wonderful things you've done. The…miracles you've performed."

Angie says nothing.

"It started in your church, is that right? You healed a man?"

Those big doe eyes flick around Thomas's face in a way that makes him uncomfortable. Sweat beads on his brow. He doesn't like to be scrutinized.

"Yes," the girl says, finally.

"And other miracles," Thomas continues. "You've appeared at revivals in the country. Tell me, Angie, do you get your power from God?"

The girl wipes her mouth, then looks to the old man. "Gramps, can I have some milk?"

The man nods and stands, moves to the refrigerator. Thomas almost wishes he'd agreed to the offered soda, but holds his tongue.

Angie gets her milk, takes a long sip, then smacks her lips with an *aahhh* that feels over the top to Thomas, as if this is part of an act, a way to gain control of a conversation using a tactic he'd never imagined.

Innocence.

Like a wolf in sheep's clothing.

"I'm not religious," Angie says. "I don't know what I believe about God, or the church, or whatever. When I do stuff to help people, it's like…" She purses her lips, thinking. "It's like there's a door inside of me. And if someone asks for help, I knock on the door. Sometimes the door opens, and I can help them." She shrugs. "Sometimes no one answers at all."

"I see," Thomas says, not seeing at all but happy to move onto business. "Well, I'd like you to knock on that door for me, Angie. I'd like you to use that power of yours to secure my future. Keep me healthy. Keep me rich. Let me live happily for the remainder of my life. If you do this for me"—Thomas glances toward the grandfather to make sure he's listening—"I'll pay you half a million dollars. Tonight. In a tax-free account that your grandpa can access the second I leave. He just gets on his computer, puts in the information, and—voila!—you're set for life."

Angie smiles at his pitch, but not in the way Thomas had hoped. It's not a smile of excitement, or greed, or even satisfaction. It's a mix of sweetness…and pity. The smile a mother gives her child when he asks if the moon is made of cheese. The look you give someone who is so naïve it breaks your heart.

"Mr. Halstead," she says slowly, carefully.

Pityingly.

Thomas feels his face flush with blood and rage; lips tighten over clenched teeth.

"There are no guarantees in life," she says. "There are no spells.

No talismans. No gifts of grace that will give you what you want. You can't control fate, Mr. Halstead. You can't dictate the future." She laughs a little, her childish giggle belying the maturity of her words, her lecturing tone. "And you certainly can't *buy* it. It's like buying your way into Heaven." She shrugs, the image of Minnie Mouse's smile suddenly mocking. "It just can't be done."

The hand Thomas rests on the tabletop twitches, fingertips tapping the wood. It takes every ounce of restraint not to reach out, grab the brat by the collar, and shake her; slap that smug little smile off her chubby-cheeked face.

"Angie," he says, growing even more enraged at hearing the shakiness of his voice. "What you know of the world would fit into the tip of my little toe. You're a silly child with a silly child's ideals of what is—and what is *not*—possible in this world. So, I'm going to ask you again, politely, to think about my proposal. I'm confident you can offer me a blessing, perform one of your miracles on my body, my mind...my *future*."

Thomas leans close and lowers his voice, as if relaying a secret. "Look, I'll make this easy on you. The truth is I don't really give a shit if you believe."

Angie's eyes go comically wide, but Thomas senses Grandpa's tension from across the room. His voice drops lower. "To be honest, you're nothing but a fail-safe. A redundancy. But I pride myself on not taking chances, so..." Thomas sits back, does his best to appear relaxed, in control. He shoves his trembling hands into his lap, curls them into fists.

"Tell me what I want to hear, and I'll go."

Angie glances at her grandfather, then shifts her eyes back to Thomas. Her smile is gone, and she looks much older than her ten years. Her eyes, energized and sparkling only a moment before, are now lifeless. Sad.

"I'm sorry you came out here tonight, Mr. Halstead," she says. "More sorry than you'll ever know. But I can't help you. The truth is no one can help you. No one can give you what you want. And I won't take your money for a lie."

With that, she picks up her milk and drinks the last of it as Thomas watches, mind racing with options, with dark thoughts.

Angie sets down her glass and slides off the chair. Her grandfather shifts forward but she waves a small hand in his direction. "It's okay, Gramps. I'm going to bed."

The old man nods, watches as she disappears down the hallway. Both men remain seated as the bedroom door clicks shut, then the big man stands.

"Time to go."

As the sedan pulls once more into the dripping night, the moon red as blood, Thomas sits forward. He wants the driver to hear him clearly. "When we get to the house, call a couple of the boys," he says. "Burn that bitch's house to the ground."

The driver nods and eases the wheel to the right, glides the car smoothly, effortlessly, onto the highway on-ramp.

"The occupants?" he asks.

Thomas waves a hand in the air, settles back into the seat with a sigh. "Let fate decide."

III

In the months that followed Thomas's auspicious night of guaranteeing his future through mysticism and magic, things went from good to better to incredible. His lucky coin never left his pocket as he watched his value increase exponentially. Everything that could go right, did go right.

The tattoo on his heel, a strange symbol that meant nothing to him when he finally decided to study it more closely, continued to send warmth and pleasure through his body. His vision improved. His energy matched that of a man twenty years younger. His sex life was reborn, his business acumen inspired.

As for the little miracle worker and her guardian, he'd been informed that the old man had died in the fire—a tragedy caused by an electrical mishap in the old house's wiring. At least, that's the report Thomas had paid for.

The child, however, escaped unharmed. She'd been placed in an orphanage run by the nuns of St. Andrew's—a dilapidated old church with a single room to house two dozen orphans, boys and girls made to work long days cleaning houses and offices, the owners of which in turn made donations to the church. Social Services turned a blind eye, noting their ineffectual position due to the work being deemed "voluntary."

But at the end of those blissful first months was a black mouth. A gruesome, hungry monster hulking on the decrepit stage behind the flimsy red curtain, waiting for the real show to begin.

And so it did. With a fury.

The first twist of fate came while Thomas was sitting in a board meeting.

He'd been fondling the heavy gold coin in his pocket, bored by a presentation about international expansion, when he felt a sharp *burning* in the palm of his hand—a pain so severe he gasped aloud, causing the heads along the glossy conference room table to turn in unison and stare at him, their leader, suddenly wheezing at the head of the table like a sick king.

Thomas stared down at his hand—yanked free from his pocket, fingers spread wide—in shock.

The coin was melting *into* his palm. The gifted talisman had liquified, turned to flesh-eating gold. The bubbling metal spread along his hand, tiny flames bursting like sprites as it ran over his fingers, his wrist...seeming to *expand,* as if the coin, once molten, had tripled in mass.

Within seconds his entire hand was covered. Melted to a sizzling, smoking lump.

Thomas screamed. Screamed and screamed as board members sprang up and away from the table, some knocking the padded leather chairs to the floor in their haste.

By the time paramedics arrived less than ten minutes later,

Thomas's hand was a bright stump, fingers curled inward or dropped away—soft noodles of flesh; sodden lumps in the plush carpet.

Thomas passed out from the pain, and when he returned to consciousness, he'd not only lost his hand but a fortune. During those fateful minutes, his company's stock had plummeted due to a report of company-wide illegal activities, activities brought to light in a bombshell report by the FBI.

While at a local hospital—during which what remained of his hand was cut off from the wrist down, and his corporation's stock price fell to an all-time low—Thomas lost his company in a hostile takeover by a competitor, one who smelled blood and moved with the voraciousness of a killer shark. The board (proceeding without Thomas's ability to establish a proxy or vote in absentia) inexplicably voted unanimous approval for the takeover.

Less than a week after he left the hospital, the witch's mark on Thomas's heel also turned sour.

Hearing an inhuman shrieking from the bedroom, a nurse found Thomas naked on the floor, clutching at his ankle. The foot below his clasped hands, she saw with horror, had *shriveled*. She later told a friend it looked like "the dying root of a sickened tree." The flesh turned black, the foot nothing more than a twisted, gnarled kink at the end of a ghost-white leg.

Once again Thomas was rushed to the hospital, where the befuddled doctors had no choice but to proceed with an amputation.

During surgery, Thomas suffered a minor heart attack, his survival due solely to the actions of the quick-thinking medical staff. Once stabilized, he was taken to the hospital's intensive care unit.

Three days post-surgery—due in large part to the blood-thinning medication fed intravenously to ease the pressure on his heart—a blood vessel ruptured in his brain, causing him to have a severe stroke.

His full recovery, thanks to a span of tragic (and partially unexplainable) health issues, was now an impossibility.

While Thomas was losing use of the right side of his suddenly frail body, he continued to be investigated by the tenacious agents of the FBI.

By the time he was discharged from the hospital—less than a month after his most recent admission—the government had seized a majority of his assets and enforced penalties rivaling more than triple his net worth. In addition to the impossible financial setbacks, he was also notified—as a last favor by his lawyer of more than twenty years—that criminal and civil charges would be waiting for him upon his recovery, and that he would need to find more affordable legal representation.

IV

The creepy man stares at the kids as they play in the yard.

The children have created a chaotic, makeshift form of soccer, using baseball hats and discarded jackets as goals, the soccer ball itself scuffed, half-deflated.

By now, the orphans of St. Andrews are used to seeing the creepy man.

He's stood in the alleyway across from the church's side yard every day for the past two weeks, watching them. At first, a few older boys shouted insults; called him a pervert, a dirty old man. Soon after, having had time to study him properly, the children noticed his deformities—the droopy, lined face; the crutch supporting his body due to his left leg missing from the knee down. The metallic gold stub where a hand should be.

It's only when the creepy man ventures closer, onto the sunlit sidewalk and out of the shadows, that Angie recognizes him. Later that day, she asks one of the sisters to ask him inside, offer him food and water.

Angie watches from the dormitory window as the nun approaches Thomas and beckons him to follow. As he limps after the black-robed nun, he glances toward the building and spots her. For a moment, their eyes meet, and he grins.

"He wants to see you," Margaret says, the youngest of the nuns who live in the orphanage wing. "He says you know him."

Angie nods, already moving toward the door. She's a year older than when she first met Thomas Halstead in her home, sat with him in her kitchen, her granddaddy nearby, alive and cautious.

But alive no more.

Angie enters the common room, empty now except for Sister Margaret and Thomas, who slumps in one of the oversized wooden chairs the priests use when seated behind the altar for mass. When she's within a few feet of him, she realizes just how far he's fallen.

His face is slack on the right side, as if boneless. He's unshaven and dirty. He smells, she can't help notice, of shit and sweat. Of piss. His hair is long, gray where it had been black and so infested with lice she can see the tiny bugs crawling along the edges of his scalp.

Margaret sits a few feet away, pretending to crochet a scarf while carefully watching the man's every movement, hearing his every word.

When he smiles at Angie, she wants to scream. His teeth are caked with grime, the straight white tombstones she'd seen just a year ago now gone. One of his front teeth has gone missing, a black rotting hole in its place.

"Hello, princess," he says, voice slurred, that dark grin widening, cracked lips bleeding where they stretch. "It's been a minute."

Angie sits on a plain folding chair, facing him. She meets his eyes, but says nothing.

"I wanted to see you," Thomas says. "I *needed* to see you. To, uh, to show you what's become of me. I wanted you to have the satisfaction, you see. I owe you that, yes, yes…for what I've done."

Angie shakes her head, dismissing this. Her brow furrows. "What happened to you?"

Thomas sighs heavily, and Angie forces herself not to shirk away from the stench of his breath. "Well…" he begins, studying his grimy hands, the broken fingernails. "While I still had the means, I had my people look into a few things."

He leans sideways on his chair, rests the tarnished gold stump of a wrist on the armrest's worn varnish. Margaret stiffens but makes no move to intercept. Angie stays still.

"Turns out you were right, about what you said that night. The psychic I paid to secure my future? She died from an aneurysm. Much worse than mine, I assure you." Thomas taps the paralyzed side of his face with a finger. "According to my sources, the physical trauma of casting her charm nearly killed her. Then, a few months later, it did. She died bleeding from her eyes."

Thomas wipes a line of drool from the corner of his mouth with a filthy handkerchief, then continues.

"The witch who marked my heel did all she could to create the spell needed to fulfill her promise. She was successful, at first. But in the end, she was forced to conjure a spirit, demon, whatever..."

Thomas meets the young girl's eyes, and she shudders at the shadows hiding there.

"She was possessed," he continues, shrugging his functional shoulder. "Her mind...her body, torn to shreds. In the end, she leaped in front of a train, naked and mad. The second her soul left this plane..."

Thomas raises a pant leg, shows off a reddened, infected stump.

"This happened," he says, chuckling. "Now I am surrounded by enemies. Oh...the things I have done, young one." He looks at her knowingly, his tone solemn. "The murder of your grandfather? The loss of your home? It doesn't scratch the surface of my misdeeds. My evil. But I am not mad, child. No no...not mad. Not yet."

Angie absorbs all this quietly. After a moment, she moves to stand before him. She takes his remaining hand, picks it up, holds it between her own. "Do you want a miracle, Thomas? Do you want to be healed?"

A tear runs down Thomas's dirty cheek, a clear river through blackened ground. "The time for miracles is past for me," he says quietly. He pulls his hand free from the child's small fingers, shoves it into the pocket of his worn coat. "There's only one thing left on this earth for me to do."

Thomas pulls a curved knife free from his coat and stares at it, eyes wild.

"A serpent's tooth," he says.

With a sharp intake of breath, Angie plants her hands on his bristled cheeks.

The nun, realizing, begins to scream.

Light boils from Angie's eyes as the door inside her heart blows open. A surge of power passes through her body and into the man she holds tight.

The knife springs upward, into his soft throat, and is swallowed by the light.

(inspired by the daughters of King Lear, and dedicated to witches everywhere)

The Final Silence

Sara Tantlinger

Cordelia: "What shall Cordelia speak? Love, and be silent."
– (King Lear 1.1.68.)

Sweet Cordelia, do your words haunt you yet?
Love may have once been richer than the tongue,
But to the king, your name an epithet
Never to be whispered, spoken, or sung.
Your sisters disfavor you with their greed
And laugh as truth leads to your prison rope.
Repentant father, too late with his plead,
So come with us, we ghosts of vengeful hope.
Heed the cry of women from horrors past;
We send poison to plague upon them all.
You defied man's whims, so be free at last.
Shed the shame of fear, that shadowy caul.
　　　They snapped your neck, thought it a justice knell—
　　　Go, haunt them into madness, into hell.

Kingbreaker

Simon Bestwick

I.

It's fair to say things have been a bit shit here in England, lately.

And yes, I do mean England, I'm afraid. Among recent developments, Scotland made a unilateral declaration of independence, and more surprisingly, so did Wales. On a personal level, that came as a particular punch in the guts, as I'm half-Welsh on my father's side of the family and I'd always hoped to live there. (What can I tell you? I've always been a Daddy's girl.) And don't even get me started on Northern Ireland and the mess that's going on there.

On top of all that, record levels of unemployment and homelessness, skyrocketing food and energy prices—so you no longer have to choose between freezing or starving but can do both at once—and, unsurprisingly, a great deal of civil unrest. Protests which have been met with baton charges, tear gas, rubber bullets and eventually real ones. Followed by riots.

Oh, and we're currently on either our eighth or ninth prime minister in two years. I've actually lost count by this point. All from the same ruling party—which consists exclusively of crooked, inbred, brain-damaged incompetent sadists (to cite their better qualities)—and each apparently determined to be a bigger disaster than the last. (They've made a roaring success of *that*, if nothing else.)

And they squabble among themselves, as well, each one scrabbling for the biggest share of the budget, or the most power for their own little faction. I'm not sure they even realise there's a country outside their little bubble that actually, God help us all, has to depend on them to run things.

At least the COVID pandemic isn't an issue any longer. Or rather, it's less of one than the outbreaks of cholera and actual polio that are now rife.

So yes, the green and pleasant land is currently neither, and people are unsurprisingly unhappy about it. As a result, the government has finally begun to listen to people's legitimate grievances and address them.

Just kidding.

No, what they do instead is come up with new Emergency Powers, kick down people's doors in the dead of night, and haul them off who knows where for indefinite detention in the name of "national security."

Which, having set the scene, brings me to the latest and shittiest development of all:

They've just gone and done that to *me*.

The cell is tiled and white. There's a bed and a toilet. So, to that extent, I suppose it could be worse. Not much, though. I'm not sure how long I've been here, because the lights are very bright and never go out. And there's a lot of noise from the corridor outside. Screaming, mostly.

I'm not sure if that last bit's been staged for my benefit; either way, it's ensured I haven't slept since getting here.

They came at two a.m. I know that because, when I was woken up by the sound of the front door being smashed off its hinges, the first thing I saw was the digital clock on the nightstand. That was about all I had time to take in before they stormtroopered their way into the bedroom, hauled me out of bed, kicked me down the stairs, and dragged me to the police van in my walrus onesie. (Don't judge me; it's very warm and comfortable. I'm still wearing it now.)

I am, for the record, cold, tired, hungry, pissed-off, sore (I'm probably black and blue under this outfit) but, most of all, I'm scared.

I've been racking my brains trying to work out what exactly I did or said to land me here, and I've alternately come up with everything and nothing. Some of my social-media rants have been a bit intemperate, I admit. But a girl has to vent. It's not as if I've been involved in any real anti-government activity. I signed a few petitions, even attended a couple of rallies before it began to feel a little too life-threatening an activity. The trouble is, any of those things could be reason enough, if the wrong humourless busybody or petty little power-tripper comes across them.

So even if I'm not sure what day of the week this is, I know it has not been a nice one.

A click of locks rings out, and I look up. The cell door opens, and two big men come through.

The interview room's a bare place—rough carpet, pale walls, plastic chairs, a table with tubular steel legs, and a composite wood top. It could be a room in any office building in the country. Although the stains on the carpet spoil the impression a bit, and don't bear close inspection.

The man behind the desk is stocky, red-haired and brutal looking, with small narrow eyes and a rumpled suit. It looks like an expensive one, though, and he speaks with the kind of clipped public-school accent that so many of the yobs in charge have these days.

"Ms…" He looks at the papers in front of him, smirks and then looks up. "Hoodless?"

"That's my name," I say. "Don't wear it out."

You'd think that would get a laugh, especially as I'm still wearing that fucking walrus onesie. But it doesn't, and I flinch because I meant it as a joke—when I'm scared, I babble and say stupid shit like that—but as soon as I heard myself I realised it sounded like defiance, and this is very much the kind of place where they beat that out of you.

To my relief, he just shakes his head, looks down at his papers again, and motions to a nearby chair. "Sit."

I do as I'm told, hating myself for feeling grateful he's a) invited me to sit and b) hasn't had anyone punch me yet. *What can I do for you?*

I almost ask but manage not to. I always crack jokes when I'm nervous, but I really need to kick that habit now. In this place, they break people. People come into places like this and either never come out or come out looking like their own ghosts.

"My name is Latimer," he says. "Do you know why you're here, Ms. Hoodless?"

I shake my head, really wishing I did so I could have some sort of grovelling apology prepared. I'll say or do whatever he wants to get out of this place, despite all my big talk on the internet: if I hadn't already known I was a coward, I'd be in no doubt by now.

"All right," says Latimer, and leans back in his chair. "I want to talk to you about Shakespeare."

I stare at him, then finally get my voice back. "Shakespeare?" I say.

"Yes. Something of an interest of yours, isn't he? The Bard of Avon and all that?"

"He was, yes."

"Used to be an actress, didn't you, before you went back to school?"

I really don't like his tone, but there's not much I can do about that. "Yes. Stage magician, as well, if you're interested—"

"I'm not. Tell me about Jack Cade."

I stare at him, because of all the questions I was expecting, this wasn't one of them. "He's a character in *Henry VI, Part Two*."

"One of Shakespeare's history plays, yes?"

"That's right."

"Good. So tell me the history."

"Cade led a rebellion against Henry. No one really knows much about his origins or background. It started in 1450—England had just lost France, people were afraid of an invasion, the kingdom was bankrupt, and the king's court and the law were completely corrupt. Cade wrote a manifesto called *The Complaint of the Poor Commons of Kent*, listing people's grievances—that's why they also called him 'John Mend-All.' Eventually, they marched on London…"

"Where they were put down," says Latimer. "Now Shakespeare portrays Cade's Rebellion as having been planned by the Duke of York, yes?"

"Yeah."

"Well, he was nearly right, except it wasn't York. It was York's closest ally: Richard Neville, the Earl of Warwick—otherwise known as the Kingmaker." Latimer smiles. "But you know that very well, Ms. Hoodless. What I want to know is where Jack Cade is now."

II.

I've had some batshit-crazy requests in my time. It happens when you're an actor, especially given the amount of improv-related stuff I've done.

This particular one, though, takes the cake.

Although admittedly, it's not *quite* as mad as it sounds.

"How am I supposed to know *that*?" I demand.

Latimer tuts and shakes his head. "No need to be so modest, Ms. Hoodless. Your PhD thesis explicitly focuses on the depiction of the Cade Rebellion in Shakespeare's *Henry VI* plays, versus its historical reality. Your understanding of existing source material is second to none, and you've conducted extensive original research, too—in which you determined Warwick's role in fomenting the uprising. So if anyone can answer this question it's you."

"You been talking to my PhD supervisors?"

"They were most informative," says Latimer.

Thanks a bunch, guys. Although I daresay they hadn't much choice. I'd probably have sung like a canary as well.

"Well?" says Latimer.

"I don't know what you want me to say," I tell him. "Cade was captured in Sussex but died of his wounds on the way back to London. They still wanted to make an example of him, so they held a mock trial at Newgate. The corpse was dragged through London, then hanged, drawn, and quartered. His head was mounted on London Bridge, and the other pieces were posted throughout Kent to send a message to any other unruly commoners. They'd have been left to rot and fall apart."

"So you can't help me?"

I really don't like the way he says that, all low and silky-voiced, the way bullies always do when hoping you'll give the wrong answer. If I had more sense, I'd bullshit him, spin things out to buy time. But like a fool, I'm honest, and say, "I don't think anyone can."

"Pity," he says, then reaches inside his jacket, draws a Glock automatic, points it at my face, and fires.

I scream out loud and fall on the floor, then realise I wouldn't have been able to do either had the gun actually been loaded—which it isn't, as it only clicked. He only wanted to scare me. He succeeded, too; I very nearly just added to those stains on the floor.

Latimer disassembles the Glock and lays the parts out carefully on the table, including the empty magazine. Then he puts a small cardboard box beside it.

"Let's see if we can clarify your thinking a little," he says. One by one, he takes bullets out of the box and stands them on end on the table. When he has enough, he begins thumbing them into the magazine.

"Warwick's family," he says, "the House of Neville, is a very old one. Goes back to Norman times. Also married into an old Saxon noble family, the FitzMaldreds. One of the things that made the FitzMaldreds so useful to the Normans—they were among the few Saxon nobles to retain their positions—was their facility with what would now be called the Dark Arts."

"What?" I say, completely dazed now.

"Jack Cade," continues Latimer, "wasn't really a man at all. One reason his origins are so obscure. No, he was something far more powerful and elemental. He was Jack-of-the-Green."

This is outside my whole field of expertise, but I do my best to remember what I can. "Jack-of-the-Green," I mumble. "That's the Green Man, right?"

"Exactly!" More bullets click into the magazine. "A sort of nature spirit, or demiurge."

"A force of rebirth and renewal," I say. "That's what he symbolised, if I remember."

"Quite." Latimer puts the reloaded magazine aside. "The death and destruction of the old year—old things and old ways—and the birth of the new. Also, a warrior of tremendous power, embodying the spirit of the land itself."

He begins reassembling the pistol. "With Jack-of-the-Green at their disposal, the Saxons could have defeated the Normans, or thrown off their yoke after the Conquest. King Harold could have used him at Senlac Hill but baulked at 'trafficking with demons.' Later, Saxon rebels were less scrupulous, but by then the FitzMaldreds had allied themselves to the Normans."

I am now absolutely terrified, since I'm stuck in a room with a man who appears to have the power of life and death over me while also being completely barking mad.

Latimer puts a heavy gold amulet on the table, on a thick gold chain. It's in the shape of a man's face—a heavily bearded man, with ears of barley sprouting from his nose, mouth, and ears. The symbol's instantly recognisable; I've seen it on church architecture, even on Victorian-era buildings in my home city, Manchester.

"The Green Man," I say.

Latimer runs a finger round the edge of the amulet, which is inscribed with various symbols I don't recognise. "This enables the holder to control Cade," he says. "Or whatever you wish to call him. You see, we learned to use him in a controlled way. Whenever there was discontent, we let him loose. He'd assume human form, start a rebellion, gather all the malcontents around him, and set out to overthrow the established order; it's what he *does*, you see. But of course, we never let him get that far. When the time was right, we'd ensure he 'died' or made some catastrophic error of judgement, then put his followers down."

I swallow because my throat's dry. "So that's what Jack Cade's Rebellion was all about?"

He nods, beaming. "My illustrious ancestor, the Kingmaker, turned him loose back in 1450, and then switched him off again. After Cade's 'death' and dismemberment, Warwick gathered his remains again, ready for the next time, and transported them to one of his estates in the North. So far, so good—but then came the Wars of the Roses, and when Warwick died at the Battle of Barnet in 1471, the location of Jack's tomb was lost. Our family's fortunes were much reduced thereafter, and my branch of the family, within a few generations, quite left out. But we did hold onto one thing. This." He holds up the amulet and smiles. "So, as you can imagine, I'd very much like to find Cade's tomb. With him at my command, I could rather write my own ticket."

"How do you expect me to know where they buried him?" I say at last.

"I'd have said you're perfectly qualified to find out," he says. "And very well-motivated. You've got a week."

"What? A week to—"

"A week to find the tomb," he says. "After that it'll be too late to do me any good, meaning you'll be of no further use to me. You see, Ms. Hoodless, just now the government requires a good old-fashioned rebellion, something they can come down on like a good old-fashioned hammer. Perfect opportunity to settle accounts with anyone and anything our party doesn't like. Remake the country in our image, once and for all. Rebirth and renewal and all that—as symbolised by the Green Man."

I'm pretty sure that's not what Jack-of-the-Green was supposed to represent, far less what he'd be trying to achieve if he ever got off the leash. But then again, he wouldn't get off it, not for long. Just long enough to serve Latimer's purposes. (If he existed in the first place, and of course he doesn't. He can't.)

"The trouble is, we've done far too good a job in years past," says Latimer. "Propaganda, distraction and all that. There just isn't enough of a real enemy within. Nothing with the numbers and organisation required to pose a genuine threat to us. And it's rather hard to create something like that out of whole cloth. But turn Jack Cade loose again, and he'll have everyone for miles around who's even slightly discontented whipped up into a raging mob and marching on London, and then—" Latimer slaps his fist into his other hand. "There we go. If I can pull that off, things will look very rosy indeed for me, but I only have a week. And that means, so do you. So..."—he clicks the last pieces of the pistol together, slams the magazine into the grip, and racks the slide—"going to help me or not?"

It's really not much of a choice, put like that. Christ knows what I'm supposed to do, given the whole story's complete raving lunacy. Even if I can find Cade's tomb, what's Latimer going to do when all he finds inside is a heap of old bones? But at least this way I've got a week to find a way out of this mess, and saying no is most likely a shortcut to a bullet in the brain. So I give him the brightest smile I can, and say, "Where do we start?"

Latimer smiles and puts the Glock down.

For now.

III.

A week can go by very, very fast, especially when it's the last one of your life.

I really underestimated a few things. Such as the sheer volume of documents and records Latimer would produce for me to wade through—under normal circumstances, a historian's wet dream—and my ability to come up with an escape plan.

Having completely failed on that score, the only strategy I'm left with is "do anything and everything I can think of to find where the Earl of Warwick interred Jack Cade."

Which is not ideal.

To give you an idea of the problem, let me explain: Richard Neville, the 16th Earl of Warwick, was known as "the Kingmaker" because he was the single most powerful magnate in the country. Originally allied to the Yorkists during the War of the Roses, he switched sides after falling out with Edward IV and joined the Lancastrian cause, trying to put the deposed Henry VI back on the throne. He was hugely popular with the public and very skilled at riding the currents of popular opinion, but most of all he had the wealth and fighting men to tip the balance in favour of whichever faction he sided with.

Both of those factors stemmed from the sheer size of his family's holdings. The Nevilles at that point owned huge tracts of North and

Central Yorkshire, County Durham, Cumberland and Northumberland, and bits and pieces of Lancashire. And that was just their Northern holdings—they'd smaller, scattered estates all over the Midlands and the South, too.

At least I can discount those, if Latimer's sources can be trusted, and I sincerely hope they can as otherwise I'm completely screwed.

Though, let's be honest; I probably am anyway, aren't I?

Not only am I exhausted, I'm *still* wearing this frigging onesie, which has begun to honk mightily. You'd think a change of clothes would be a reasonable request, but apparently not. Maybe it's so I can't try sneaking past the guards; even the slowest of Latimer's goons couldn't miss a woman dressed as a walrus.

I've spent the past week cooped up in this room—another cell, basically, but slightly bigger and less uncomfortable than the usual, with a desk to work at and even internet access (albeit strictly monitored,) sustaining myself on coffee and food from the staff canteen (not exactly cordon bleu, but better quality than what they normally feed prisoners, I'm sure) and catching odd hours of sleep on a cot-bed in the corner. Anything I need for the job is brought by Horner and Vernon, the two heavies who fetched me from my cell a week ago.

In that time, I've pored over every record I can find pertaining to the Nevilles and their Northern holdings. Any location, no matter how obscure, that they owned. My one clue is that I'm looking for some sort of sacred site, be it a church, chapel, cemetery, abbey, priory, or monastery. They'd need that to contain Jack Cade, or so Latimer says.

Plenty changes over nearly six centuries. That's not counting the big, seismic events, like the dissolution of the monasteries or the civil wars, which would have wiped dozens of such places off the map. Or the Industrial Revolution; cities, especially in the North, expanded massively, leaving other locations buried under office buildings, motorways, or carparks, like the one they found Richard III under.

I'm now on the last day of my week. Latimer's been in a couple of times, looking ostentatiously at his watch and "accidentally" showing off the pistol in his holster, the absolute prick. Like that's going to help. If I get any kind of chance to before they kill me, I fully intend to kick him in the balls as hard as I can. Give him a ruptured testicle to remember me by, if nothing else.

My one hope, right now, is a bunch of household accounts from some of Warwick's estates, covering the period after the end of Cade's Rebellion. It's an incredibly slim hope, that there'll be something there that might stand out, but—just assuming there's an ounce of truth in any of this demented story—if Warwick *did* get hold of Cade's remnants, he'd have to seal them up somewhere safe. That would take work, and that work would have to be paid for. No one works for free.

Just as I'm about to give up hope entirely, something jumps out. I rub my sore eyes and cross-check with the other relevant records. I've no time to spare, but nor can I afford to rush.

At last, I'm sure. Or as sure as it's possible to be. So I take a breath and shout for Latimer.

He comes through the doorway within ten seconds of my shouting his name. His life might not be at stake here, but his career is. Or at least whatever power-mad daydreams he's nursing.

"Well?" he says. He's always pale, but he's whiter than ever now.

"I think I've found it."

"You *think*?"

I push a document across the desk. "Here."

Latimer frowns down at it. "What am I looking at?"

"Warwick's accounts for November 1450," I say. "*To Master Holloway, stonemason, the sum of one hundred marks for repairs to tombs and other stonework at the Priory of Thorpe Halsey*. Cade died around July 1450, and then his quarters were despatched around Kent. Warwick waits for the initial hubbub to die down, then retrieves the remains. Two months, say. That takes us to September. He transports them to Thorpe Halsey, right in the middle of his estates, the following month. Hires a mason to entomb them under the guise of repair work—or maybe this is where they've always been kept when they're not in use. And one month later—November—he pays the bill."

Latimer holds the document up, and I can see his hands shaking.

He wants to believe it, I know, but he can't be sure. "Is this all your evidence?"

"Not quite." I produce another document. "From the priory's few surviving records: delivered to us this day, *14th October 1450...* casks of wine, loaves of bread, wheels of cheese blah blah blah, and then here, see? *And a chest containing certain privy matters from my Lord the Earl of Warwick.*"

Latimer looks at the two documents for a very long time, and finally he smiles. A genuine one, for the first time in our acquaintance-ship. "You may have just bought your life, Ms. Hoodless," he says, then strides out without another word.

I lean back in my chair, and I smile, too.

Maybe I have, at that.

But...apparently not.

At least, that's not how it looks a few hours later when I'm on my knees in a different room, contemplating a drain in the middle of the floor. There are rusty stains on the tiles around it, and hair caught in the grate, along with white chips that might be bone.

I'm somewhat sore. Horner and Vernon booted the cell door open about ten minutes ago, hauled me from the cot-bed, and threw me in the general direction of the doorway before alternately dragging and kicking me along the corridor.

From which, with my amazing powers of deduction, I conclude Mr. Latimer isn't best pleased.

Horner and Vernon—the Tweedledum and Tweedledee from Hell—stand flanking the door and saying nothing, faces utterly blank. That's pretty frightening, I have to say, but infinitely preferable to the look on Latimer's face when the door flies open and he walks in.

He already has the Glock in his hand.

"Empty," he says at last. "Dug up every inch of the ruins, Ms. Hoodless, and there was nothing there at all. Only an empty tomb."

Horner and Vernon grab my arms and push me forward, so I'm kneeling with my face above the grille.

"Did you enjoy arousing my hopes, only to dash them?" Latimer says. "I sincerely hope you did. And I sincerely hope it was a joke worth dying for."

This isn't a bluff; he isn't going to punish me by pulling the trigger on an empty gun this time. This time there'll be a bullet in the chamber.

"I don't get what I want," he says, "but, at least, neither do you."

The worst part is that I don't understand this. My brain was still running after he'd gone, having been revved up so long, like a machine. I practised some of my old conjuring tricks to try and wind down—palming a coin, walking it over my knuckles—but even so, I went over this again and again, and each time I came to the same conclusion: Cade's tomb *has* to have been at Thorpe Halsey. There's nowhere else Warwick could have sent the remains. I'd have found some clue otherwise. They have to be there.

I hear him pull back the pistol's slide, chambering the round that's going to kill me, and then—

It doesn't matter how well you know a subject: if you focus too narrowly on one specific part of it, you can miss something. Something that, when you step back and look again, becomes blindingly obvious.

In that last second before Latimer pulls the trigger, my focus goes wide and I see the big picture. I make the connection and scream at the top of my lungs. "Robin of Redesdale!"

IV.

It's the dead of night and pretty chilly for the time of year; I can see breath hanging like cigarette smoke in the air as Horner and Vernon manhandle me out of the helicopter and march me across the playground.

And yes, fashionistas, I'm *still* wearing that wretched onesie.

The whole school's been cordoned off; the playground and playing fields have been dug up, and several buildings knocked down. No doubt there'll be some suitable cover story for the parents, teachers, and kids. Or perhaps there'll be no explanations at all, just *Because fuck you, that's why.* If not tomorrow, then the day after. Once Latimer has his way.

I remind myself that the whole idea's ludicrous. Even if there is a tomb, Latimer won't find what he's looking for, because it's an impossibility. There'll be bones, but they won't be—can't be—Jack Cade's, because the dead can't return to life. And they won't now.

All that's happened is that for a moment I bought into the logic of Latimer's madness and followed it, so now here we are. That said, it's better than where I'd be if I hadn't; that is, en route to a crematorium or landfill somewhere.

Most likely, though, I've just delayed the inevitable, especially with Horner and Vernon in attendance, and a larger brood of armed thugs all around the site.

Latimer's standing over a hole in the middle of the playground, smoking a cigarette. He turns and smiles. "Ah, Ms. Hoodless. Come. Come. I thought you'd want to see."

Horner and Vernon prod me down a ramp after him, down into the earth underneath the school, and the long-buried remains of St. Mary's Chapel, a few miles outside Towcester.

Remember how I said earlier that Warwick's family, the Nevilles, also owned estates in the Midlands and the South, but none of that was relevant to finding Cade's resting place? Well, I was wrong, and the reason I was wrong was because I forgot about Robin of Redesdale.

Before breaking out into open rebellion against Edward IV, Warwick the Kingmaker fomented an insurrection in Yorkshire in 1469. As in 1450, he used a proxy. Nobody's really sure who the man was, any more than they are about where Jack Cade came from twenty years earlier, but he went by the name of Robin of Redesdale.

People also called him "Robin Mend-All." Sound familiar? It should.

If you've paid attention.

Robin of Redesdale was killed in a battle with the Yorkist forces…but the battle didn't take place in Yorkshire. It was in Oxfordshire, way to the south—at Edgecote, near Banbury.

Warwick had to flee the country for a spell after the battle, meaning he'd have been in something of a rush. Which meant, in turn, there mightn't have been time—assuming Robin and Jack were the same creature, the one Latimer's convinced exists—to ship the remains back to the Nevilles' heartlands in the North.

But Warwick had estates nearer the battlefield, just over the county border in Northamptonshire.

Once I worked that out, it was just a case of going through yet more records (fuelled by industrial quantities of energy drinks—I'm pretty sure my pee's fluorescent by this point) till I found St Mary's.

And now, here we are…

Latimer leads the way through a tunnel into the chapel crypt and stops to point dramatically, but the effect's spoilt slightly when I bump into him. Horner and Vernon drag me back. Latimer smiles.

"Feast your eyes, Ms. Hoodless. Jack Cade, Robin of Redesdale, and many others before. Jack-of-the-Green himself."

He motions me forward and—having little choice—I do as instructed. It isn't hard to work out where he wants me to go. There are several sarcophagi in this crumbling vault but only one has the lid removed and is surrounded by arc lights.

What do I expect to see? Bones, I tell myself; it can only be bones. But I've fallen, a little, under the spell of Latimer's madness. I don't quite believe that's all I'll see. Not least because Latimer wouldn't be looking so pleased, otherwise.

And I'm right. The body is whole, and mummified. At least, that's the best term I can find for it. It's brown and dry and wrinkled and cracked, like tree-bark. Withered leaves cling to it; dry dead barley-husks protrude from the ears and gaping nostrils, and are caught in the lipless slit of its mouth. There's wispy hair and a beard, both tinted green as moss.

"You see him in his natural state," Latimer says behind me. "He can, of course, assume a more fittingly human semblance, but for now he's still asleep. Fortunately, he's easy enough to revive. All we have to do is—"

As he speaks, I hear the swish-click of a spring-loaded blade and start to turn, but he's too fast for me. There's a sting as the knife bites into my throat, and then a welter of blood splashes across the form in the sarcophagus.

"This," says Latimer.

He holds me over the sarcophagus, letting the blood gush out, then lets me fall. My mouth and nose are full of a coppery taste and smell, and I can't breathe. I push myself feebly backwards against another tomb until I can sit up.

"Nothing personal." Latimer cleans the knife. "But you should have realised I couldn't possibly have let you live."

To be fair to him, he's right. But then, to be fair to me, I did.

Something stirs inside the sarcophagus. Latimer looks away from me, and ecstatic joy fills his face as, for the first time in six hundred years, Jack-of-the-Green walks.

Out he springs, lithe and limber—not tall, only slenderly built, but alive with power. Even in the state I'm in, I can feel it crackle off him, like static or waves of heat. Glossy green ivy now clothes him neck to ankle; tufts of fresh green barley jut from nose and ears and tumble from his grinning mouth. His hair is a shock of grass; his eyes burn emerald.

This is Jack Cade. The real Jack Cade.

"Jack-of-the-Green," says Latimer. "I command you."

"Hey." If I put enough pressure on the wound, I can just about manage a faint, whispery croak. "Jack."

Cade turns to me.

"Jack-of-the-Green!" Latimer shouts, but there's unease as well as anger in his voice.

Good.

One of the reasons I always liked this onesie—before being forced to wear it nonstop for a week, anyway—is that it has pockets. I put my free hand into one of them now and take it out again.

Remember how I bumped into Latimer before?

To perform magic tricks effectively, you have to be very good at sleight of hand. And—even out of practice as I am—I am still, in all modesty, more than just "very good." I'd have made a hell of a good pickpocket if I hadn't gone back to college.

Exhibit A: the gold amulet hanging by its heavy chain from my fingers.

I hold it out to Cade.

It can hardly do me any good, after all, can it, even if I wanted the thing? And this should piss on Latimer's chips from a great height, which is the best result I can hope for at this stage.

"No!" Latimer runs forward, but Cade sends him flying with one sweep of his arm. Latimer hits the stone wall with a crackle of snapping bones.

Horner and Vernon draw their guns and open fire as Cade takes the amulet, but if they hit him, he doesn't seem bothered. He grins at me instead and winks, then reaches out to touch my throat.

Then he's gone, and there are only screams.

V.

When I open my eyes again, I can breathe, and when I feel my throat, there's no wound.

"Fuck," I say aloud, and my voice is normal, too.

Renewal and rebirth.

A faint sound from the corner turns out, on inspection, to be Latimer. By the look of it, his spine's broken. Along with pretty much everything else about him, as far as I can tell. He looks up at me, but I don't know what he's asking for. Help? A merciful death? It doesn't matter; a moment later, there's a rattle in his throat, his eyes grow fixed, and he lies still.

I make my way through the tunnel, over the scattered remains of Vernon and Horner (now Tweedledead and Tweedledeader) and up the ramp.

There are bodies everywhere.

In the distance, fires burn, and voices chant and cheer.

Jack's his own master now, and he's wasted no time. The disaffected and the dispossessed, the angry and the malcontent, flock already to his banner.

Cade's army is marching on London once again, on his way to pull down a king. But this time, there'll be no one to switch him off, and he won't be helping to put a new one on the throne.

This time, all the kings are falling.

Still, Jack Cade can attend to that side of things. I have more pressing concerns. The main one being how the hell a girl's supposed to get back to Manchester with no money, while wearing a walrus onesie covered in blood.

Still, somehow, I think I'll cope. Maybe it's the near-death experience, but I'm feeling weirdly optimistic, just for once.

Rebellion, rebirth, renewal: things may get worse before they get better, but England's future might no longer be so bleak.

Or Wales', come to that.

(I've always loved the Henry VI plays, clearly a young man's work with all the energy that goes with it, and in particular with the character of Jack Cade, especially as I began to wonder if he really was the villain Shakespeare painted him as. 'Kingbreaker' was also inspired by the ongoing horrorshow of contemporary British politics, and was written during Liz Truss's brief but catastrophic prime ministership.

Halfway through the writing of this story, the Queen died. As far as I know, this was a coincidence. If not, you'll find me in the Tower of London. – Simon)

The Third Murderer

(inspired by the weird ladies of Macbeth)

Jessica McHugh

Moonlight pacts carve new fates upon the heath:
A life denied to me by noble chains,
Cursed with one purpose—a bauble, a wreath—
Doomed to be cherished, to reign, and be reined.
No more can I suffer this mortal cage.
I'll pay the tribute the Sisters demand.
I'll lead these instruments across the stage,
Where their blood shall stain and cocoon my hands.
My skin will then spoil and wither away;
I'll claw my counterfeit muscle from bone.
With every soul on my coven's list slain,
They'll drink their fill, and they'll welcome me home.
       Come, Lords of Scotland. I'll make thee revered.
       Kneel for thy Lady; it's time to get Weird.

When shall *We Three* meet again

"IN *THUNDER, LIGHTNING,* OR IN *RAIN?*

—Macbeth

The Case of the Bitter Witch

(inspired by Macbeth, who ended up a real bastard)

Kasey Lansdale & Joe R. Lansdale

Mercy, Oklahoma is a small town with a small community theater, and one hell of a large problem that someone like me and my boss, Dana Roberts, were perfect to solve.

Come to think of it, who else could? And this whole business, once we had a look at it, seemed easy enough. It was less than a bump on the ass of other cases we had unraveled, so we felt cocky.

Actually, and this is between you and me, Dana got cocky. She's so good at what she does—and together we are even better—she took the job more out of boredom than deep interest. Any other day, she might have passed. It wasn't like the money we were being paid was all that rich.

Who'd think dealing with spectral events could, at least to some extent, become as everyday as changing underwear?

"Hey, we got a ghost to get rid of."

"Okay, let me have a coffee first."

It was the unusual cases you got excited about, that you remembered.

This one didn't seem all that exciting. An annoying spirit in a community theater. (Most likely a stagehand leaving the lights on at closing, or so I first thought.)

Just in case you're one of those who doesn't know who Dana Roberts is, she is an investigator of the supernormal. As am I, her assistant, Jana Davis.

That's right. We are ghost and ghoolie hunters. Though she wouldn't like me saying that. You probably know about Dana due to her many bestsellers about her adventures. Hard to go in any bookstore and not see something of hers on a table display. My name is there, too—in small, ant-sized print at the bottom of the page. Sure, her name and the title of the book stand out in elephant-sized letters, but at least I'm on there. Ant sized or not. We ants are strong for our size.

There was a short-lived reality television show about our events, and though Dana was terrific on camera, the whole day to day making of a reality show bored her. They kept wanting to set up false events and pretend they were real. And I don't mean just the cases, but silly stuff where she and I were supposed to not get along and argue about this and that, and there was supposed to be some rivalry between us.

We have our moments, but this stuff was bullshit of the first order. Whatever first order bullshit is like.

Also, we had enough real stuff that making up things didn't make sense. We had material for ten seasons. We did one.

So, there you have it. Reality show over. Dana didn't need it for money or confidence. She's as self-assured of herself and as fearless as the Pope receiving a hand-delivered invitation from the Devil to tea. Dana was the Pope; she'd accept the invitation, make the Devil pour the tea, and serve angel food cake after insisting Satan say the blessing. Even the Pope might balk at that.

That's if she believed in God. She's an atheist and doesn't believe what we do, what we explore, has anything to do with the supernatural. She calls it supernormal. Something extraordinary that we don't quite understand yet, but in the end, though fantastic, explainable.

Dimensions and pocket universes have something to do with it. However, you look at it, there's some creepy business goes on out there, and it's all just a dimensional fraction away from your face.

Fact is, how dark and deep this all became may actually have been our fault. It might be the first time I truly saw Dana knocked off her stride. Mistakes were made. Bad things were discovered, and we made it worse.

Unintentionally, of course.

I did buy a nice pair of cowboy boots to wear on our mission, so there was a silver lining.

Just thought I'd mention that. They're super cute.

Mercy, Oklahoma has all the appeal of a leftover carrot salad. It was the kind of town you didn't go to, but passed through, or broke down in.

Except for the nine hundred people who lived there, of course, and I'm not sure what they were thinking. Perhaps the founders broke down there, too, had a wheel come off their covered wagon or some such, and their descendants were too depressed to leave.

Mercy is a series of brick buildings split by what had once been an important path to Texas, but was now a cracked concrete strip. The wider interstate had replaced it, and there were even fewer people just passing through than when it was first founded. It was more of a wrong turn now.

Even more peculiar, railroad tracks ran just to one side of the highway, and next to that was a row of those brick buildings.

The rail is no longer used, but back in the day, serious caution would have been needed to cross from one side of the street to the other. You had to not only make sure you didn't get hit by a car, but you might have a train to worry about.

Anyway, we showed up in Mercy, Oklahoma with our rental car and tooled right over to the theater.

Millicent Browning met us there. She was a thousand years old if she was a day. Wore an enormous amount of blood-red lipstick, and enough rouge to keep a trailer full of clowns in full paint. Her hair looked like red wire. She had a white worm of a hearing aid fastened to the back of her ear and wore glasses with a chain attached to them that went around her neck.

She was waiting in a powder-blue Lincoln when we arrived, but was out of the car before we could park, leaning on one of those canes with the claw foot at the bottom. She was old and over decorated, but she was spry.

"You got my email," Millicent said.

Since we had sent emails back and forth, talked to her on the phone, this seemed an unnecessary observation.

"Should we step inside, out of the heat?" Dana said.

"Yes," Millicent said. "But I tell you, I'm a little nervous in there."

We sat in chairs in the dimly lit foyer where you bought tickets and snacks at intermission. I could have used a snack then. Breakfast had been hours ago for us. Dana never seemed to be all that hungry. She ate, but she was regimented, on a schedule. I have blood sugar issues, so I don't pass up snacking opportunities, lest I become irritable.

"It's the stage that's the problem," Millicent said, "but that doesn't mean I don't think it could be elsewhere in the theater. But that's where the bad stuff is. That's where it's been seen. That's where it started."

"Where what's been seen?" I asked.

"The witches," Millicent said. "Three of them. I know how it sounds, but that's what I saw. Not just me, by the way. Others have seen 'em, too. Witches just like you'd imagine them. Huddled around an iron cauldron, speaking spells and all manner of mumbo jumbo. Wearing ragged black gowns and tall pointy hats. A big black cauldron with one of them stirring in it. Thing is, we're performing the Scottish play on weekends, and it's as if those witches from the play have come alive, except they make our actors look just like what they are. Local half-ass thespians in Halloween costumes."

I had learned long ago that *Macbeth* was not to be mentioned aloud in a theater where it was performed. Supposed to be bad luck. Hence her use of *the Scottish play*. But if they were seeing witches, sounded to me like bad luck had already set in.

"You say bad stuff," Dana said. "What sort of bad stuff are you referring to?"

"Wiring rigs falling. False walls collapsing. Janitor was chased off the stage by them, fell, and broke his ankle. Crawled out, he did. Course, cops got here, nothing. They think we're loony, and Natalie Crawford doesn't help. Going around with a pet duck dressed up in khakis and beret. You know how much work that must take to get that duck in uniform?"

"I can only imagine," Dana said.

Dana nodded, impervious to this ducky information, stood up from her chair and walked over to the concession area. She went behind the counter, poked around for a minute where we couldn't see, then made her way back around the counter and through the double doors in the direction of the stage, leaving me behind with Millicent.

Millicent was a bit goofy, but she was scared. Really scared. Whatever it was that was happening at the theater, Millicent was convinced it was born of true evil.

When Dana joined us again, I could see her eyes had started to glaze. It was obvious to me that she didn't think there was as much to this business as our friend Millicent did. I was also guessing she regretted hopping on a plane to Oklahoma without first vetting the client.

Knowing Dana wasn't skilled at tactful conversation, and also knowing my bank account was not nearly as padded as hers, I spoke before she could.

"I think it best Ms. Roberts and I come back at night and check these things out for ourselves."

"All alone, just the two of you?" Millicent said.

"All alone," I said. "Except the three witches of course. That'll make five of us." I couldn't be sure, but I thought Dana might be trying to suppress a grin. Or she needed to pee.

Dana didn't love it when I beat her to the punch like that, but she was used to it by now, and I was glad to see, or at least think, she might have been amused. I believe that a certain amount of my impulsiveness was something she liked about me. Liked that I wasn't afraid of her.

Actually, I was, but I didn't want her to know.

"We will be back at nine o'clock this evening to set up. You have the extra set of keys for us?" Dana said.

Millicent handed over the keys and we thanked her for her time. We then headed back to the hotel room to gather supplies for the night ahead.

"Why are you bringing that?" Dana asked.

I looked down at the thick sleeping bag rolled up on the floor next to a few other supplies. Mostly fruit gummy snacks I had brought from home. I like when they're in the shape of bears. Taste better that way. I can't explain it.

"I can tell by the way it went today you don't think it's anything more than old rafters and a breeze," I said. "That the idea of three witches and a metal cauldron is a little too on the nose for a haunting. So, I thought I'd catch up on my beauty sleep tonight."

"I'm not saying there is nothing there. Only that whatever it is will be easily managed. It feels fairly innocuous. I have a few suspicions that will need to be confirmed. Did you say, beauty sleep?"

I didn't answer, expecting a trap.

We sat around the hotel room table and ate our respective lunches. Dana ordered a watermelon salad, which seemed to be mostly watermelon, and I had a bacon cheeseburger, cooked medium. Mostly bacon, cheese, and burger.

I didn't need a pep talk on what we would be doing that night, as it was pretty clear it would pale in comparison to our other cases, but I did feel like I was going in a bit blind. Dana seemed to know all the answers and wasn't sharing. Usually, she had good reason for this sort of behavior, but when you're facing life and death as often as we do, a recap wouldn't hurt my feelings. I also suspected that sometimes she wanted me to think she knew all the answers, but like me, at least in certain situations, she didn't know owl shit from axle grease.

"Our next step?" I asked.

"I'm going to do some research. You should brush up on *The Lesser Key of Solomon*. Specifically the *Ars Notoria*."

"You think I packed that in my carry on?" I said.

"The magic of the internet, Jana."

Good point.

You could find most anything on the internet nowadays. I knew some of the nitty gritty of the text would be absent, but that was okay. Dana had the really important stuff memorized, and if she didn't, she had a stack of books with her for just such an occasion. I couldn't speak Latin anyway and spent a lot of time researching things via Google Translate. That can result in some strange and erroneous interpretations, but it was usually enough for me to get the gist.

We spent the next several hours studying, until it was time to load up and head back over to the theater. By then I was already sleepy.

"Load up," Dana said.

By load up, Dana had me take everything she'd set aside and Tetris it into the back of the SUV we had rented.

I was getting pretty good at fitting everything in when we traveled, and trust me, that's saying something. Dana was not a light packer. Not only was she carrying her spook supplies, but she had a different outfit for every possible occasion. Never know when you might need your best runway look in Mercy, Oklahoma. She also was more than willing to let me do all the tote and carry.

Once we arrived at the theater, I did the same thing in reverse while Dana stood there watching. She didn't even offer moral support.

I had everything just about set up in the wings where we could see the stage but still be hidden behind a pile of stacked frames for constructing stage sets.

I rolled out my sleeping bag next to a pile of Dana's books, laid out my snacks where I could see each one, stretched out, and waited for further direction after chewing a few gummy bears. The orange ones are my favorite.

I planned to shut my eyes for a moment, just relax, but I must have fallen asleep, because the next thing I knew, Dana was nudging me with an Italian leather adorned foot like I was a stray dog blocking her path.

"Do you mind?" I said.

When she didn't answer I sat up, coming into the moment and

realizing where we were. I could feel the strangeness in the theater the same way people in the Titanic's steerage must have felt the rising of the freezing ocean water. I peeked over the stage materials, and saw what Dana saw.

On the stage was a thin swirl of mist, and then the mist expanded and thinned. Shapes were in the mist, and no matter how often I had seen weird business in my adventures with Dana, the hackles on the back of my neck began to prick.

Gradually, three women came into view at the center of the stage, and calling them women might be a generous term. They were spectral in black clothing, and as Millicent had said, they looked like witches but not in any perfect sense. Withered and unkempt, their clothes draped like torn rags down to their bare, grayish feet. A silent wind swirled their robes and their pointy black hats wavered but maintained their positions. Their faces were hollow-cheeked, leather-like, and bearded with scraggly hair that could easily have been mistaken for wire. The beards almost covered their wormy lips and papier-mâché skin. They had warts, of course, some big enough to scale with mountaineering equipment. The hands, visible at the bottom of their dark sleeves, appeared to have been boiled until they were the gray color of steam. The air smelled like something dead and coated in manure.

I watched, stunned as the witches traded off stirring a big black metal pot with what looked like a black scepter adorned with a human skull as its handle; they used the eye holes as a grip. That cauldron had to weigh a hundred and fifty pounds if it weighed an ounce.

They were muttering something as they passed the skull handle off to one another. They were too far away to understand clearly. Dana seemed unimpressed with what was happening on stage. They may as well have been cartoon witches.

"Can you stand up? I need you to do something for me?" She said this as calmly as if she might be asking for me to pass the biscuits. If she ate biscuits. "Hold this book open while I read these passages." I made a mental note to add *podium* to my resume, then turned my back on the witches as instructed. "Azzalamatè, Azzè, Lematè, Azzubiè. Keep the book level."

It took a moment to realize that wasn't part of the spell. She started over with what sounded like gobbledygook to me, nodding when she needed me to flip a page.

Way I was positioned, I was facing Dana, the witches behind me. There was a cold wind at my back, and though I tried glancing over my shoulder a few times, I didn't see much.

Finally, she ceased chanting, told me to stop turning pages, and I turned to look.

The mist that had started out soft and fog-like was starting to swirl and darken. Nothing good comes from witch-haze, I was pretty sure.

Although it was a creepy event, the urgency that usually hung in the air wasn't there. A thought that put me at ease.

"That should do it," Dana said.

"Do what?"

"Seal us in here together while we check things out."

"Wait, you just closed us in here together with those things, behind some mystical door?"

"I only sealed the stage. You and I can come and go freely. They can't. Flip a stage light. That metal box over there, and then grab my bag."

The box was on the wall. I used my penlight to examine it, flipped it open, and hit a switch. The stage was now lit in a sad honey-colored light that would have been hard to read by.

I picked up her bag, the one that held spells and magical items, and followed behind her, filling her every footstep with my own until we were both standing behind the tallest of the three witches like a conga line.

The whole thing felt a little too close for comfort, specifically my own. Dana seemed unfazed. I reached up, grabbed the pendant that hung from my neck, and rolled it between the meat of my forefinger and thumb. I let it drop against my chest behind the collar of my linen button-down top, cool metal smooth against my skin.

This charm had become something of a security blanket since saving me on a prior case. I liked knowing it was close at hand, even if it was nothing more than a magic shop trinket under most circumstances.

"Reach in my bag and pull out that small, glass bottle." I rummaged around in the leather satchel, pulled out a blue-tinted bottle filled with liquid.

"What's in here?"

"A combination of things. Mostly urine."

"Naturally."

The witches didn't look up as Dana inched in closer between them. They were frozen firmly as popsicles. Dana uncorked the lid to the container, poised for action. The smell of ammonia wafted up from the bottle, making me gag.

Dana was now standing between two of the old, immovable hags.

I took in a deep breath—a mistake when you're holding an open jar full of odiferous witch repellent—and waited.

Dana shuffled her feet like she was doing the electric slide, reached for the scepter. Dana's fingers passed through it.

And kept going.

Down into the cauldron, through whatever liquid was inside of it. She clenched her hand a few times.

I waited.

Nothing.

She turned and grinned at me.

"You little shit," I said. "You had me going."

"I know," Dana said, clearly proud of herself.

I let out a sigh of relief and put the lid back on the jug of urine. "And this," I said. "Nice touch. You pee in this yourself?"

Dana didn't answer.

I liked this side of her. It didn't come out often. I think she was finally beginning to feel comfortable with me and, what could be called on a good day, our friendship.

"So, what now?" I said.

"Not much, actually. Clearly there's something happening here. These witches didn't manifest themselves. If my theory is correct, this should all be over by morning."

"What's your theory?"

"Come with me."

We left the witches to their stirring and wandered back over to our things. I followed her like a little baby duck back to our mountain of supplies, realizing I hadn't needed to carry and unload so much stuff.

I noticed immediately that several bags of my fruit snacks were missing, and the book was no longer on my sleeping bag. Even a big rat wouldn't be able to drag that book out of here.

"What's going on?"

"You see," Dana said. "When I inspected the concession stand earlier today, I saw what looked to be dusty prints on the snack drawers underneath the glass enclosure. The lock was clearly broken on one, and it was bound in place with a rubber band."

"A rubber band? You solved this case because of a rubber band?"

"That, and the sleeping quarters I found nestled beneath the stage." Dana took a step down from the wings and made a hands-off gesture. "Come on out. You're not in trouble."

Dana pulled a flashlight out of her bag and flicked it on, pointed it at the edge of the stage.

To my surprise, I heard an immediate rustling sound followed by a few grunts and what looked from a distance like a floating head behind stage left.

"I can't believe it," the old woman said. "Been hiding out here for three months, none the wiser."

She wiped at her nose with the back of her hand. "You two come in here with this rubber band nonsense and sniff me out like a dog in heat."

"Listen," Dana said. "Truth be told, if it were merely you sleeping under that stage, I wouldn't say a word. The problem is them."

Dana pointed to the frozen witches.

"I'm lost," I said. "What's your name, ma'am?"

"Persephone, but friends call me Percy." It was unclear if that was an invitation.

"Percy. Did you take my gummy snacks?"

"Jana," Dana said. "We have more important issues at hand."

Speak for yourself, I thought.

"What Jana means is, why do you think these witches are here, and why is it that you seem unafraid?"

Good questions, but don't think I had forgotten my gummy bears.

"What's there to be afraid of?" Percy said. "I had a nice warm place, got to listen to plays beneath the floorboards. Not the best diet, the stuff I stole, but it kept me perky."

"Would you like a real meal?" Dana said.

I could see the gummy bear situation had sailed.

"What do I have to do for it? Nothing while wearing leather, I hope? I'm allergic."

"Talk is all," Dana said. "Just a nice talk over a meal."

Percy studied us carefully. "All right, then. Let me get my carpet bag."

Back at the hotel, late-night room service was out, but Dana ordered delivery, a pizza, hamburgers, and tacos from three different places. They brought it up to our room about thirty minutes later, and I laid it all out on the table.

Percy was in the shower, and Dana had determined our guest would fit better in my jeans and one of my tops than anything she had. I had to admit this was true, but I didn't like it. Now I was clothing my gummy bear thief. All I was interested in now was why was she under the stage, and exactly what did she have to do with the witches?

Percy came out of the bedroom carrying her carpet bag. She had never let it out of her sight. Steam from the bathroom followed her. She was tall and actually quite elegant for a woman who had to be in her eighties, though now, clean, her gray hair hanging over her shoulders, her eyes bright and alert, she looked like an aging goddess. Come to think of it, she had the name for it.

My jeans and shirt fit her well enough, and she was barefooted and walked spry for someone who had been living under a stage and subsisting off stolen candy from the concession stand, and my gummy bears.

"Come, sit down," Dana said.

She did, and tucked into the food on the table like a grizzly bear preparing for winter hibernation.

I couldn't believe how much she could eat. I barely rescued a few fries and a slice of pizza for myself. Dana didn't seem interested in the food at all. She watched Percy eat.

"Where are you from?" Dana asked, as Percy leaned back in the chair and let out a burp that would have caused a mating frenzy in dinosaurs.

"I'm from pretty much everywhere. Born in Mercy."

"You knew about the witches, of course," Dana said.

"Yes."

"You are connected to them, aren't you?"

"You're a smart one."

"Smart enough."

"You say you know about the witches, so tell us about them," I said.

"Missy here is not a smart one, is she? She actually work for you? Or is she some kind of family charity case?"

There was a pause as Percy practically slurped a taco.

Wiping her mouth on the sleeve of my shirt, she said, "And I know who you are. I've seen your pictures, read a couple of your books. Dana Roberts. The Spook Hunter."

"I prefer investigator of the supernormal."

"Do you? Well, I don't think you're such hot shit, Dana Roberts. You think you know things, but I've been in the fire, so to speak, and a brighter and hotter one than you've ever encountered."

"Opinions vary," Dana said, smiled, crossed her legs and kept her cool.

Me, I was angry at the way Percy had talked about me, how she talked to Dana, and how fast she could eat. And there were, of course, my gummy bears digesting in her stomach and the taco stains on my shirt.

But cool was Dana's first name. I had a hard time envisioning Dana as a child. And when I did, I saw her wearing little pantsuits, being able to recite the alphabet backwards. Maybe she carried a little tablet around with her to take notes on unusual events. Normally, someone like that would have been a target for bullies, but I had a feeling bullies may have learned from experience that Dana could come out of nowhere, like a shark attack.

"I suspect," said Percy, "that Macbeth and me are the cause for the witches. And don't think you got rid of them tonight. They'll be back. I've been watching them, not wanting to leave my cozy hideaway until I had to. Hard out there on the road for an old lady. I can feel the gate closing. Short time from now, they'll really be powerful. I won't mind. I think they like me."

She gave a coy smile.

"You certainly talk with confidence," I said.

"I know shit, Missy. I been around. I've lived on the edge for years, since I was a teen. And don't let my comfortable and folksy manner fool you. I was traveling the world, learning about the occult when you were still pooping in your diapers. Me and my husband, we married young. He thought of himself as a wizard, or some such, and I suppose he was. Me, I was a descendant of witches, so I think that's how we came together. We were meant to be together. He awakened in me my libido, and my connection to the craft. We traveled in an old car he had. The backseat was full of our clothes and goods. Had a bottle of holy water in the glove compartment, and a trunk full of books about spells, ghouls, and ghosts and nasty things that go bump in the night. We had a pistol, too. Holy water doesn't do shit against assholes, just spirits and demons and such. At my age, I don't mind telling you I used that pistol a few times to rob service stations along the way, some mom-and-pop stores. I shot a man once, and like the old Johnny Cash song, did it just to see him die. Are you shocked?"

Neither Dana or I replied.

"Eventually sold all our goods, except for a couple of books. We stole passage on ships, climbed mountains, lived under the roughest conditions possible. Ended up in Tibet, lived with some monks there. That's a hard life, girls. And from the looks of you, neither of you have had that kind of experience. I'm talking living on nearly nothing, eating little to nothing, the cold wind up your ass and the heat scalding your face. There were times when I wanted to quit. I loved my husband, Drake, but damn. I was worn out with the life. Worn out looking for the truth, whatever that was. I decided there was no real truth. There were other realities, but truths? I don't think I'd use that word. I was beginning to suspect that the truth, the nature of the universe, was all bullshit and bottle flies, and I knew, too, I had changed. I had lost my heart and gained a lump of coal. I wished everyone dead. And I mean that. Including Drake and myself.

"I'll be honest, I discovered in time I was a lot more material than I thought. I was a nice-looking woman that had wanted all the standard things. House. Kid. Restaurants. Cars. A flush toilet and a shower with hot water. A bar of soap wouldn't hurt my feelings either. I never did get any of that. I had to keep moving, even after we crossed the desert, which is where Drake died. A man twice my size, tough as a boot, and he went toes up in the sand. I hated him for it, and in a way, you could say I wouldn't let him leave me. Not completely. Next day, while I was being cooked by the sun, Bedouins showed up and took me in. And as the saying goes, only I survived to tell the tale. Of course, in a way, Drake is still with me. I didn't give him up completely, even though his body was buried by the blowing sand."

"What are we talking about here?" I asked. "This is starting to sound like children's story time at the public library."

"Keep it up, Missy," Percy said, "and I'll give you a knuckle sandwich you'll never be able to swallow."

Then she fell into a violent coughing fit. She was hunched down, hands gripping the tops of her knees, spittle flying in all directions.

"Easy," Dana said.

Her eyes were no longer bright, and in that instant, she appeared far less regal and a lot more like a dying woman.

"I think it's the walking pneumonia," Percy said between coughing jags. "Had it before. Happens from the damp. Being on the road. I steal a bottle of cough syrup, few things at the drugstore, take that for a few days, slug it down with a bottle of stolen vodka, and I'm right as rain."

"I don't know about that rattling sound in your chest," I said. "That doesn't sound right. I think vodka with cough syrup and the like isn't such a good idea. We can call a doctor."

"I need the desert, dry air. Besides, my time is wrapping up, and truth be told, I'm tired, worn out. I'm ready to put a bow on things. Still, I want old age, disease, an accident to take me. But not it."

"It?" I said.

"It follows his scent."

"His scent?" I asked.

"Drake," she said. "I can't let him go, though he sure isn't the same anymore."

"Who is following?" Dana asked.

"You might say the past. Anyway, I been on my own a while. I come up to that theater late one night, found I could jimmy the lock on the back door with a hair pin. Inside, I discovered some old tarps and such, made myself a bed under the stage. They only have rehearsal couple days a week, performances on the weekend. So, it was pretty much me and the theater. Nice and cozy under that stage. And I got the chance to listen to one of the greatest plays ever written. The other great ones, well, Shakespeare wrote those as well. Not saying those community actor hacks could act their way out of a paper bag with a hatchet, but the play pretty soon overpowers the performer. I could lay there and recite the whole damn thing, line for line. Want me to show you?"

"Not necessary," Dana said.

"I may not have a photographic memory," Percy said, "but I can remember damn near everything ever happened to me, told to me, if I take a real interest in it. That's a problem. It's why I feel such hatred for the world, and for myself. But still, I keep moving."

On that mysterious note, Percy's remaining energy drained, and she melted into the chair like a popsicle, spilled out over the faux maroon leather, dripped from the chair, and lay puddled up on the floor, snoring a rattling cough like someone shaking dice in a cup.

"She needs a doctor, and I'm not giving her a choice," Dana said, pulled out her phone, and dialed 911.

Though the waiting room wasn't all that crowded, there were people coming into the room on stretchers, limping, or moaning. For a population the size of the town, there were a lot of sick and injured folks.

We were waiting to find out about Percy, of course. To talk, we practically had to yell over a riding waxing machine. The janitor operating it wore headphones to keep from having to hear that racket, but we got it full force. I doubted breathing in floor wax was doing any of us good.

"What do you make of all that talk?" I asked.

Dana said, "She's got a powerful spirit about her, and not a natural one. I assumed the witches tonight were merely battery images. I'm less certain now."

"You know I'm going to ask it, so what are battery images?"

"Sometimes, when situations are right—and it can be weather or location, minor spells, powerful thoughts—imagery can become solid. To some extent, anyway. A powerful play like *Macbeth* can manifest itself from the stage performances, the actors' dedication to the roles. Those kinds of manifestations are harmless. Unless the battery is particularly powerful."

I thought on that a moment. Dana was waiting to see if I could fill in the rest of it.

"Percy is the battery." I said this just as the waxing machine was cut off and my voice echoed loudly throughout the waiting room.

Occupants of the room looked at me wondering what the hell that meant. I smiled at a seated man wearing a cowboy hat with a crooked crease in it, his leg in a cast, crutches beside him.

The physician came out. He looked like a twelve-year-old playing doctor. His white coat almost trailed the ground. He gave us the scoop.

Turned out Percy was going to be in the hospital a while. She had grown worse, and the doctors, for her protection, had induced a coma. Bottom line, whatever it was, it was worse than walking pneumonia. The doctor gave a list of things he thought were plaguing her.

Dana gave her information, slipped them a blank check, said, "For expenses."

I assumed this was my cue to hand the receptionist a card with our information on it. Dana had already started out the door. She can be considerably more thoughtful to the dead, or in this case incapacitated, than to the living. General discourse she could manage well when she chose, but it wasn't a big interest of hers, and most of the time that was pretty obvious. Money does in fact give assholes leeway. I wanted to be an asshole with leeway.

We went back to our hotel. When we were in our room, Dana looked in the carpet bag Percy had been carrying.

She pulled out a few foul-smelling clothes, a sweater that wouldn't have warmed a flea due to how many holes were in it, a few toiletries, one of my bags of gummies, and then, a Mason jar with a lid on it. There were little holes punches in the lid. It was like a carrying jar for a butterfly specimen.

Thing was, there was something in the jar. And it wasn't a butterfly.

It was small and withered, leathery, and was obviously something shaped like a human; a man specifically. It had a wad of dark hair stuck to its head, and pieces of it had flaked off onto the bottom of the jar. I determined that the shape had been made out of animal hide with the fur still on it. Most likely that leather had been wet with blood when the thing was twisted into form. It was about six inches high, had a little nose, a gash of a mouth, and slits for eyes. And as I was looking at it, it opened its eyes, black as obsidian, as round as little olives. The eyes sparked.

"Jesus," I said, "it's alive."

It didn't move, just stared. Dana turned the jar and examined the creature more closely. She took a deep breath and returned it to the carpet bag.

"What the hell, Dana. It's alive."

"Now I understand."

"Good someone does."

"I'll venture to say it's Drake's dark spirit. The spirit is inside that doll. It's a kind of manitou. A voodoo force, a Tibetan talisman. Percy's love for Drake, her obsession with keeping him in some form or another, his poor old withered soul inside of it, craving to take off into the sweet unknown like some bird that wants to fly out of its cage, but held here by that doll and Percy's spells. She's trapped him because she both loves him and hates him. Also, if he had the knowledge she claims, he gives her more power than she would have on her own. She controls him. Or did. Maybe now that she's separated from him, not so much. Hard to say."

"It's alive, Dana."

"In a manner of speaking."

"I know alive when I see it."

"She exorcised the soul, for lack of a better word, while he was dying. Preserved it in this jar."

"What do we do with it? Him?"

"Take advantage of it," Dana said.

"That sounds horrible. Not to mention icky."

"Not as horrible, or as icky, as things are about to be. Percy was feeding off the power of the play. And I will bet you a pastry to a dollar, where the theater is located is a power point; a location where the alignment of certain energies feed supernormal activities. Why some houses are haunted, others aren't. Why some places seem to generate more unusual events than others. Ghosts. Spirits. Poltergeist. All of those things have more power at those points. A powerful play. A bitter sorceress under the stage led to the witch's manifestation. I think they were weak because she was weak."

"So, we didn't get rid of the witches?"

"Only for the moment. They are a kind of tulpa for Percy. Thought forms, auras, that come into existence by the power of astral projection. Most tulpas are good. Children sometimes create them when the situation is right. Invisible friends, but real to the child."

"But not in this case," I said.

"Not in this case. We can see the thought forms Percy's created. They are more than ethereal objects. So many bad things have come together, that tonight I doubt we really changed things at the theater, just pushed it back a bit, but my deduction is that—"

Dana checked her watch.

"—like so many things in the supernormal world, when it's midnight they will grow stronger."

"But Percy is in a coma. Surely, she can't generate power to those witches."

"Completely lost in her mind, and that's where her power is. Physically, she is frail, but in the coma, she's more powerful than she would be in normal sleep. And if she's as bitter as she seemed to be, even unconsciously, it's possible she will project some pretty mean witches. And come midnight, and with the location—and that's a guess, but I make good guesses—a very powerful and very dangerous force will be released. Percy never realized that to have the power she wanted, she had to let everyday concerns go, even if it was only about finding food and a warm place to sleep. She has that now. There's nothing now but her primitive sensations and what slithers in the dark of her id."

"Holy cow," I said, not being able to find anything better to say.

"The most assured way to be protected from what will happen tonight, what will be let loose from the theater and into the world, would be to smother Percy in her sleep. But since we aren't murderers, we'll have to put that idea in abeyance. Grab the bag, make sure the Book of Solomon is in it, and if you want a snack, please do have one before we get there. Once there, we haven't time for you to stop and devour a granola bar."

We gathered up the goods, including the living doll that may well have been Drake, and hightailed it to the theater. When we arrived, slipped inside, Dana checked her watch in the beam of her little pencil-sized flashlight.

"Eleven forty-five. Jana, if you've ever considered another line of work, now might be the time to make a career change. I won't blame you if you walk out that door and keep going."

"In for a penny, in for a pound."

"No, dear," Dana said. "You're in for a ton."

I imagined Percy, deep in her coma, down there in the dark world, turning all her anger, disappointment, into something that could only be described as evil. It gave me the willies.

The closer we came to the stage, the more I considered Dana's offer to make an exit. But I didn't. My mama had most definitively raised a fool.

"It's beginning," Dana said. "Twelve midnight, the witching hour is in sight."

There was a slight wind where no wind should be. The edges of the pulled curtains shivered slightly, and then there was the mist. More yellow-colored this time, and thicker. It was like breathing pea soup if pea soup tasted like sulfur, something long dead, with just a decorative hint of rosemary and thyme. Possibly some cinnamon.

The mist began to swirl and the wind became so strong I had to lock my knees to make sure I wasn't blown over.

I could feel the essence of the witches in the wind, but it was as if they were feeling me instead of the other way around, and it was a bad touch, let me tell you. Way down inside of me, everything negative I had ever felt. Disappointments, anger, every slight I had ever experienced, heated up and boiled over. I found myself growing angry. The way I figured Percy was.

Dana pulled Drake and his jar out of the bag.

"If you pee yourself, don't be embarrassed," Dana said. "Pull your amulet into view."

I reached into my shirt, pulled the amulet out, dropped it on my chest. The chain that held it, the amulet itself, felt strangely heavy.

"Will the amulet stop it?"

"No, but it might give it hesitation, if it can be seen. Bring out the Book of Solomon, turn to page three-sixty."

I pulled the book from her bag, along with my penlight, and thumbed furiously until I found the page. The page was dotted with something dark and something wine colored. I didn't want to know what that was. The letters were large, and with my penlight clenched between my teeth, I could see to read, but I couldn't understand the language.

"Shit," I said.

"I'm going to do the reading. Hold the flashlight."

She took the book and handed me the jar of Drake, like we were two winos sharing a bit of homemade hooch.

"When I say, unscrew the lid and let Drake out—do so, and pronto. He may come out on his own, or he may have to be poured."

While I was studying on that, the wind ceased. I turned off my light and dropped it in my coat pocket. The air had the feel you get when a tornado is about to strike—muggy, thick as amber. The world feels empty. The birds don't sing, the frogs don't croak, not a leaf stirs, and then you hear that sound, like a big train balling the jack, and if you hear it too late, you can kiss your ass goodbye.

On the stage the witches were back, along with their cauldron. They formed quickly, the mist dripping black tendrils and green, the dark and the bright blending and whirling into shapes. If those witches had previously looked like death warmed over, they now looked like hell in a garbage dump. Their dark clothes were ragged, their hands near skeletal, with nothing more than a transparent coating of frog-colored flesh, their faces the same hue. Their noses were long and beaked and wart-covered, their teeth black nubs. They were, as we used to say as kids, the same but different.

The pot coughed blue smoke and the smoke rose up, and in it, there was a shape so terrifying as to be beyond perfect description. The air trembled and I felt my knees wobble like a rickety step ladder. My skin was swollen with goose bumps.

I think even Dana, who had seen most everything, and some of it twice, was taken aback. It took a couple of heartbeats before she started to read.

Read she did, practically coughing out the words, but still the tulpa, or whatever it was, rose high and became solid. It slithered out of the cauldron, and in the mist around it, I could see the stage characters from *Macbeth* had taken form. The old boy himself, sword in hand, covered from head to toe in blood. His wife, the ambitious Lady Macbeth, with the damn blood spots visible on her hands. Ill-fated Banquo. McDuff, born of no woman, but brought into the light by caesarian birth. There were others, but I didn't remember the play well enough to know who they were.

They moved toward us creepy-mouse style, but the wee-wee-inducer was that tulpa. You could taste it in the air; it tasted like the smoke from a funeral pyre.

Dana read the words, and upon completion we were engulfed in a yellow ball of gel. When the Macbeth crowd and the tulpa came up against it, it moved the barrier a little, but the magic gel held.

"Now," Dana said, "let Drake out of the jar. Then I have to let down the barrier to allow Drake outside of the protection."

"Do we have to do that?"

"We do. This barrier will only hold so long anyway."

I fumbled with the jar lid. "It's really on there," I said.

"Hurry. Break the jar."

I slammed it to the floor. Shattered glass clattered around our feet. The withered doll pulled its gristly legs beneath it and wobbled to a standing position.

It moved toward the gel and with every step grew larger in size. The doll extended its hands, touched the barrier. Dana recited a verse, and then the gel was gone.

All those things, now dripping like melting ice-cream, came for us.

Drake, stiff-legged, began to vibrate, and come apart and bleed red smoke that swirled to the floor. This was followed by an explosion that rivaled the Big Bang. It knocked us off the stage, away from the creatures, and into the gap between it and the first row of seats. The Book of Solomon sailed through the air and hit me in the head, and for a moment I blacked out.

I awoke an instant later, lying on my back with a view of my shoes. My head throbbed.

Dana was struggling to her feet.

The witches and most everything that had been there was gone. Most everything. But there was a strange green light, and Macbeth was crawling across the stage toward us. He had been knocked down and his shape was mostly a pulse of will and shadow, but there was a lot of will, it seemed.

Then he changed. He wasn't Macbeth at all. He was Percy, nude as the day of her birth, if on the day of her birth she was an old woman with eyes the color of volcanic fire.

She came to the edge of the stage, became slurpy liquid, dripped over the rim and onto the floor.

By this time, both Dana and I were on our feet. I pulled the amulet from around my neck, held it toward Percy, like they hold a crucifix in vampire movies to ward off the undead.

If it was working, it was a slow burn.

The liquid that was Percy gathered itself and rose. Dana was fumbling with the Book of Solomon, but she had lost her light, and I doubted she would be able to read it.

Percy lunged toward me, jerked the amulet from my hand, crushed it as if it were made of cellophane. She grinned at me. But almost immediately her face changed, and she collapsed to the floor, crumbled into a shimmering dust, and then she was gone.

The lights flickered as I caught my breath. "The amulet did that?" I asked.

"No," Dana said. "You can bet Percy just died, along with every-thing she stirred up, and I hate to say it, but none too soon."

We packed up, slipped out of the theater, went back to the hotel to lick our wounds. Dana was probably licking her ego. It wasn't her that had saved us. It was Drake and the natural death of Percy. When Percy died, she took her evil, her powers with her.

"Why did that thing, Drake, help us?" I asked.

I had a damp towel pushed against my forehead, which was bleeding slightly from having been struck by the Book of Solomon.

"Once he was out of that jar, which must have had a contain-ment spell on it, he was able to use his abilities. He wasn't so much helping us, as gaining vengeance on Percy for trapping him in that body, in that jar. Thing was, he merely put a crimp in her style. It was her dying that ended it all."

"Do we know for sure she died?"

"I'm sure, but it's easy to check."

Dana called the hospital, and while she was listening to the answer to her question, she nodded at me.

Ding-dong, the witch was dead.

Millicent Browning stood at the front of her car, waiting for us to arrive. She didn't appear to have been waiting long since her skin seemed dry and her makeup was still intact. We walked up the concrete steps together and made our way into the theater, just as we had before. Today though, Millicent had a pep in her step.

Once inside in the cool air, we huddled at a cocktail table as she reached into her purse, rummaging around for something we couldn't see. She pulled out a wad of cash wrapped tight with a rubber band. With it, some pens and chapsticks, a pair of glasses, and a piece of paper and some paper tickets overflowed onto the floor.

I reached down to gather the items as Millicent continued counting the money for Dana, picked them up, and slid them over to Millicent.

"It's all there," Millicent said, as she thumbed through, "and then some."

"I'm sure," Dana said.

"You're sure in a good mood," I said.

"Wouldn't you be? All intruders, spectral or otherwise, are gone. I might buy this theater now, fix it up, make something of it. Maybe even help bring folks back to the town square. Mercy, Oklahoma has a shot now."

Before I could respond, I heard a muffled voice echo out from behind the double doors.

As calling home our exiled friends abroad
That fled the snares of watchful tyranny,
Producing forth the cruel ministers
Of this dead butcher and his fiend-like queen…

"Rehearsals, already?" Dana said.

"Absolutely, we have some television producers on their way here. Want to see the theater exorcised by the great Dana Roberts."

I cleared my throat.

"Of course," Millicent said, "you were there, too, honey. Here, I have something for you both."

She held out the paper tickets, gave them to us, said, "Front-row seats. You two want to stick around? Maybe talk to the cameras a little?"

Dana and I exchanged glances. I handed her back the extra set of keys to the theater she had given us, said, "Flight to catch. Thanks, though. Mind if I grab a snack from concession, you know, for the road?"

"Help yourself."

Once around the concession booth, I squatted down behind the counter to study the snacks, using this opportunity to peek at the paper I had lifted when Millicent's purse had erupted onto the floor.

It was as I had thought, and as I now suspected Dana knew. There, at the top of the paper read:

"Certificate of Death, Persephone Browning."

That blank check Dana had left for Percy's medical expenses had been cashed all right.

Ding dong, the witch was dead. But which old witch?

I helped myself to some sour gummy worms—two boxes, seeing as how there were no bears—stood up, and walked back over to where Millicent Browning stood.

"Shall we?" Dana said.

"Think about it, could be good press for everyone," Millicent said.

I handed the certificate of death over to Millicent and nodded. Her eyes grew wide, her face flushed a deep crimson.

Back in the car, I looked out the window, said, "You going to do anything about it?"

"No. I will consider it an expensive lesson in humility."

With the tickets still gripped in my hand, I turned to face Dana behind the wheel.

"Let's never come back to Mercy, Oklahoma, okay? No gummy bears."

A Note From Your Secret Admirer

Lucy A. Snyder

For lo these last ten years
I've watched your comet soar.
Despite your parents' stodgy fears
You were born to tread the boards.
Your deft debut as young dead Edward
Caught the theatre critics' eyes.
Even bitter, jaded old Howard
Declared you worthy of a prize.
But oh, your turn as murdered Banquo
Drives your rivals into green-eyed rage.
Your silent, bloody glares do chill us so!
You're the finest phantom on the stage.
      This paper is poison, courtesy that envious fraternity.
      So, alas! Soon you'll play the ghost for all eternity.

(inspired by community theatre)

Contributor Bios

Linda D. Addison, five-time recipient of the HWA Bram Stoker Award®, including *The Place of Broken Things* written with Alessandro Manzetti, & *How To Recognize A Demon Has Become Your Friend,* recipient of HWA Lifetime Achievement Award, HWA Mentor of the Year and SFPA Grand Master. Her site: www.LindaAddisonWriter.com.

Megan Kiekel Anderson (she/her) is a queer neurodivergent dark fiction writer. Her work can be found in such places as *Flame Tree Press, The Arcanist*, and *Dark Recesses Press*. She lives in Kansas City with her chaotic family. Find her at her website www.megankiekelanderson.com.

James Aquilone is the Bram Stoker Award nominated editor of *Classic Monsters Unleashed, Shakespeare Unleashed*, and the *Kolchak: The Night Stalker – 50th Anniversary* graphic novel. He also writes the *Dead Jack: Zombie Detective* series. For more info, visit JamesAquilone.com.

Mary Berman is a Philadelphia, PA, USA-based writer of science fiction, fantasy, and horror. She earned her MFA in fiction from the University of Mississippi, and her work has been published in *Fireside, PseudoPod, Weird Horror*, and elsewhere. Find her online at www.mtgberman.com.

Simon Bestwick has been four times shortlisted for the British Fantasy Award. His short fiction has appeared in *Classic Monsters Unleashed* and *ParSec,* and been reprinted in *The Best Horror of The Year.* His latest novels are *Black Mountain*, from Independent Legions Publishing, and *The Hollows*, as by 'Daniel Church,' from Angry Robot.

Kenneth W. Cain is an author of horror and dark fiction, and an award nominated freelance editor. He has published over one hundred short stories and thirteen novels/novellas, as well as a handful each of nonfiction pieces, books for children, and poems. He has also edited eight anthologies, with two more coming in 2023. kennethwcain.com.

James Chambers is the Bram Stoker Award®-winning author of the story collections *On the Night Border, On the Hierophant Road*, and *The Engines of Sacrifice*, the Corpse Fauna series, and is the editor of the Bram Stoker Award-nominated anthology *Under Twin Suns: Alternate Histories of the Yellow Sign*. His website is www.jameschambersonline.com

Dan Coxon is an award-winning editor and writer based in London. He has been nominated for a Shirley Jackson Award and five British Fantasy Awards, and in 2022 his non-fiction anthology *Writing the Uncanny* (co-edited with Richard V. Hirst) won the British Fantasy Award for Best Non-Fiction.

Rebecca Cuthbert writes speculative, slipstream, and dark fiction and poetry. Her debut dark poetry collection, *In Memory of Exoskeletons*, will be out soon from Alien Buddha Press. For publications and more, visit rebeccacuthbert.com.

An emergency dispatcher by day, **Amanda Dier** has been previously published by *The Magazine of Fantasy and Science Fiction*, *Abyss & Apex*, and other markets. She lives in Florida with her partner and dog in a carefully curated forest.

Ian Doescher is the *New York Times* bestselling author of the *William Shakespeare Star Wars* series, the *Pop Shakespeare* series, the children's book *I Wish I Had a Wookiee*, and other books. He lives in Portland, Oregon with his family. Find Ian online at iandoescher.com.

Ahlissa Eichhorn is a freelance media writer and copywriter. She's a documentaries judge for Nightmares Film Festival and a regular columnist for Fangoria magazine. She's what you think any horror fan would be like, except way more into Meat Loaf than any one woman should be. You can follow her on Instagram at @hauntedbydeadlines.

Stephanie Ellis is a published writer of dark fiction and poetry. Her books include *Paused, Bottled, The Five Turns of the Wheel* and *Reborn*. Her new novel, *The Woodcutter*, is due 2023. She is an active member of the HWA and can be found at stephanieellis.org and Twitter at @el_stevie.

A resident of NY's haunted Hudson Valley, multi award-nominated writer **JG Faherty** grew up enthralled with classic horror books and movies. The author of 19 books and more than 85 short stories, he's proud to be a distant relative of Mary Shelley. You can follow him in social media as @jgfaherty.

Epiphany Ferrell lives on the edge of the Shawnee National Forest in southern Illinois. Her stories appear in more than 60 journals and anthologies, including *Pulp Literature*, *Unnerving Magazine*, and *Ghost Parachute*. Connect on social media and at epiphanyferrell.com. Member: Horror Writers Association.

Formerly a film critic, journalist, screenwriter and teacher, **Gemma Files** has been an award-winning horror author since 1999. She has published four collections of short work, three collections of speculative poetry, a Weird Western trilogy, a story-cycle and a stand-alone novel (*Experimental Film*, which won the 2015 Shirley Jackson Award for Best Novel and the 2016 Sunburst Award for Best Adult Novel). She has a story collection just out from Grimscribe Press (*In This Endlessness, Our End*, which won the 2021 Bram Stoker Award for Superior Achievement in a Fiction Collection), another just out from Trepidatio (*Dark is Better*), and another upcoming.

Geneve Flynn is a two-time Bram Stoker Award®- and Shirley Jackson Award-winning editor, author, and poet. Her works have been nominated and shortlisted for the British Fantasy, Ditmar, Aurealis, Australian Shadows, Elgin, and Rhysling Awards, and the Pushcart Prize. She is a recipient of the 2022 Queensland Writers Fellowship. Read more at www.geneveflynn.com.au.

Philip Fracassi is the Stoker-nominated author of the novels *A Child Alone with Strangers*, *Gothic*, and *Boys in the Valley*, as well as the award-winning story collections *Behold the Void* and *Beneath a Pale Sky*. His stories have been published in numerous magazines and anthologies, including *Best Horror of the Year*, *Nightmare Magazine*, *Black Static*, *Southwest Review*, and *Interzone*. For more information visit his website: *pfracassi.com*.

Maxwell I. Gold is a multiple award nominated prose poet who writes weird fiction. His work has appeared in publications including Weird Tales Magazine, Strange Horizons, Spectral Realms and more. He's authored *Oblivion in Flux: A Collection of Cyber Prose* from Crystal Lake Publishing and co-authored *Mobius Lyrics* with Angela Yuriko Smith from Independent Legions.

Jo Kaplan is the author of *It Will Just Be Us* and *When the Night Bells Ring*. Her short stories have appeared in Fireside Quarterly, Black Static, Nightmare Magazine, Vastarien, Nightscript, Horror Library, and various anthologies (sometimes as Joanna Parypinski). Find more at Jo-Kaplan.com.

Gwendolyn Kiste is the three-time Bram Stoker Award-winning author of *The Rust Maidens*, *Reluctant Immortals*, and *Pretty Marys All in a Row*, among others. Originally from Ohio, she now resides on an abandoned horse farm with her husband, their cat, and not nearly enough ghosts. Find her online at gwendolynkiste.com

Joe R. Lansdale (*Savage Season*, *The Donut Legion*) is the internationally-bestselling author of over fifty novels, including the popular, long-running Hap and Leonard novels. Many of his works have been adapted for television and film, most famously the films *Bubba Ho-Tep* and *Cold in July*, and the Hap and Leonard series on Sundance TV and Netflix. Lansdale has written numerous screenplays and teleplays, including the iconic *Batman: The Animated Series*. He has won an Edgar Award for *The Bottoms* and ten Bram Stoker Awards, and he has been designated a World Horror Grandmaster. Lansdale, like many of his characters, lives in East Texas, with his wife, Karen, and their pitbull Rudy, sometimes known as Roo-roo.

Kasey Lansdale has been in the fiction world since birth as a writer, editor, audio book narrator, and creative professional. Based in Los Angeles, Lansdale is an active voting member of the HWA, and currently serves as executive editor at Pandi Press. As an author and editor, she has released numerous short stories and anthologies from publications such as Harper Collins, Titan Books, and more. Lansdale has had her fiction adapted for television, as well as comic books, and her first scripted audio drama is in production. She lives in LA with her boyfriend, and some type of poodle doodle.

Vince A. Liaguno is an award-winning writer, anthologist, editor, and an occasional poet. He is the Bram Stoker Award-winning editor of *Unspeakable Horror: From the Shadows of the Closet* and the acclaimed *Other Terrors: An Inclusive Anthology*. Healthcare administrator by day, pop culture enthusiast by night, his jam: books, slasher films, and Jamie Lee Curtis. www.VinceLiaguno.com

Jonathan Maberry is a NY Times bestseller, Audible #1 bestseller, and 5-time winner of the Bram Stoker Award. He writes in multiple genres, edits numerous anthologies, edits Weird Tales Magazine, and writes comics for Marvel, IDW, and Dark Horse. He is also a popular writing teacher and speaker.

Alessandro Manzetti (Rome, Italy) is a three-time Bram Stoker Award-winning writer, editor, scriptwriter and essayist of horror fiction and dark poetry. His work has been published extensively (more than 40 books) in Italian and English, including novels, short and long fiction, poetry, essays, graphic novels and collections. Website: www.battiago.com

Seanan McGuire is a native Californian, which has resulted in her being exceedingly laid-back about venomous wildlife, and terrified of weather. When not writing urban fantasy (as herself) and science fiction thrillers (as Mira Grant), she likes to watch way too many horror movies, wander around in swamps, record albums of original music, and harass her cats. Seanan is the author of the October Daye, InCryptid, and Indexing series of urban fantasies; the Newsflesh series; the Parasitology trilogy; the Wayward Children books; and assorted other titles.

Jessica McHugh is an award-nominated poet, novelist, & internationally-produced playwright with twenty-nine books published in fourteen years, including her blackout poetry collection, "A Complex Accident of Life," her sci-fi romp, "The Green Kangaroos," and her horror series, "The Gardening Guidebooks Trilogy." Explore the growing worlds of Jessica McHugh at McHughniverse.com.

Lisa Morton is a screenwriter and author whose work was described by the American Library Association's *Readers' Advisory Guide to Horror* as "consistently dark, unsettling, and frightening." She is a six-time winner of the Bram Stoker Award® and the author of four novels and over 150 short stories.

Donna J. W. Munro teaches high schoolers the slippery truths of government and history by day. She lives with five cats, a fur-covered husband, and an encyclopedia son. Her daughter is off saving the world. Head to www.donnajwmunro.com to find more of Donna's strange little stories.

Lee Murray is a multi-award-winning author-editor, essayist, screen-writer, and poet from Aotearoa-New Zealand. A *USA Today* bestselling author, Shirley Jackson and four-time Bram Stoker Awards® winner, she is an NZSA Honorary Literary Fellow, and a Grimshaw Sargeson Fellow. Read more at www.leemurray.info

Michael Nethercott has authored two suspense novels, *The Séance Society* and *The Haunting Ballad*. His western novel *The Ballad of Black Powder* appears this spring. His short stories have appeared in numerous periodicals, including *Alfred Hitchcock Mystery Magazine, Abyss & Apex* and *Best Crime and Mystery Stories of the Year*.

Weston Ochse is the author of more than forty books. The American Library Association calls him "one of the major horror authors of the 21st Century." He could not have accomplished any of this without the ghosts in Hamlet, the witches in Macbeth, and Caliban in the Tempest. They were his first horrors.

Cindy O'Quinn is a Rhysling and Dwarf Star nominated poet, and four-time Bram Stoker nominated writer. She lives on an old home-stead in the woods of northern Maine.

John Palisano's nonfiction, short fiction, poetry, and novels have appeared in countless literary anthologies and magazines such as Cemetery Dance, Fangoria, Weird Tales, Space & Time, McFarland Press, and many more. He's been quoted in publications such as Vanity Fair, the Los Angeles Times, and The Writer. He's won the Bram Stoker Award© for excellence in short fiction and was recently President of the Horror Writers Association.

Marisca Pichette adds to her collections every eve. Find more of her work in *Strange Horizons, Vastarien, Fusion Fragment, Fantasy Magazine, Flash Fiction Online,* and *PseudoPod,* among others. Her speculative poetry collection, *Rivers in Your Skin, Sirens in Your Hair,* was published by Android Press in April 2023.

Hailey Piper is the Bram Stoker Award-winning author of *Queen of Teeth*, *No Gods for Drowning*, and other books of dark fiction. She is an active HWA member with dozens of short stories in publication, and she lives with her wife in Maryland. Find Hailey at www.haileypiper.com.

Zach Rosenberg is a horror and SFF writer living in Florida. By night, he crafts horrifying and fantastic stories. By day, he practices law, which is even scarier. A devotee of the Bard since he was young, his work has appeared or is forthcoming in Dark Matter Magazine, the Deadlands, and Seize the Press. His first books will be released by Brigids Gate and Off Limits Press.

Lindy Ryan is an award-winning author-editor. She is the founder of Black Spot Books, a small press with a mission to amplify the voices of women-in-horror, and a contributor to Rue Morgue, Booktrib, and LitReactor. She is an active member of HWA, ITW, and the Brothers Grimm Society of North America, and one of Publishers Weekly's 2020 Star Watch Honorees. www.LindyRyanWrites.com

Lucy A. Snyder is the author of the poetry collections *Exposed Nerves* and *Chimeric Machines*. Over 100 of her poems have appeared in publications such as *Chiral Mad 5*, *Weirdbook*, *Vastarien*, and *Nightmare Magazine*. She lives near Columbus, Ohio. Learn more at www.lucysnyder.com.

Sara Tantlinger is the author of the Bram Stoker Award-winning *The Devil's Dreamland: Poetry Inspired by H.H. Holmes*, and the Stoker-nominated works *To Be Devoured* and *Cradleland of Parasites*. She has also edited *Not All Monsters* and *Chromophobia*. She can be found on Twitter @SaraTantlinger, and at saratantlinger.com

Steve Rasnic Tem is a past winner of the Bram Stoker, World Fantasy, and British Fantasy Awards. He has published over 500 short stories in his 40+ year career. Some of his best are collected in *Thanatrauma* and *Figures Unseen* from Valancourt, and in *The Night Doctor* from Macabre Ink.

Tim Waggoner has published over fifty novels and seven collections of dark fiction. He's a three-time winner of the Bram Stoker Award, and he teaches creative writing at Sinclair College in Dayton, Ohio.

L. Marie Wood is an award-winning dark fiction author, screenwriter, and poet with novels in the psychological horror, mystery, and dark romance genres. Wood is also the founder of the Speculative Fiction Academy, an English and Creative Writing professor, and a horror scholar. Learn more at www.lmariewood.com.

J.K. Woodward is a life-long comic book fan who started his professional comics career in 2003. He is best known for his work on IDW's Star Trek comics like "Mirror Broken" and Harlan Ellison's "The City on the Edge of Forever." He has also worked with other comic producers, including Marvel, DC, Dark Horse, BOOM! and Image Comics, as well as other companies and individuals for specialized commissions.

Stephanie M. Wytovich is an award-winning poet, novelist, and essayist. Follow her at stephaniewytovich.blogspot.com and on Twitter and Instagram @SWytovich and @thehauntedbookshelf. You can also find her essays, nonfiction, and class offerings on LitReactor.

And thanks to our slush readers—**Leverett Butts, Jodi Shatz, Solomon Forse, Paula Limbaugh, Amy Drees, Maxwell I. Gold**, and **Cody Lumpkin**.

Kickstarter Backers

A huge thanks to everyone who backed
the *Shakespeare Unleashed* Kickstarter campaign!

A.R. Farina • Aaron Jamieson • Aaron M. Stultz • Abby Braunsdorf
Adelai M • Aiden Pearce • Allie Seale • Amanda Giarratano
Amanda L Parks • Amanda Q (truelight8) • AmyJean
Anas Abusalih • Andrew Hatchell • Andrew Hauptman
Andrew Martinez • Andrew R. Harris • Andrew Sanders
Angel R Kain • Angela Viveen • Animal Teachers • Anne Betz
Anonymous Reader • Anthony R. Cardno • António Matos
April "2B or not 2B" Ledebur • April A. Taylor • Arthur Castro
B Cohen • B Hill • Barbara Cottrell • Barry R. Hunter
Beatrice Hall • Beck Donovan • Benjamin Hausman • Bex Futrell
Bill Ginger • Bill LaMonaca • Bjorn Smars • Bob Covey • Bob Wiley
BOBBY ZAMARRON • Bonnie Warford • Boris Veytsman
Brandon Patrick Wong • Brandy Eckman • Brandy Pastore
Bret Smith • Brian Amaro-Jeppesen • Brian L. Black • Brian Saville
Allard • Brian Winger • Brick Rockbeef • Brody Gogatz
Bruce Karlquist • C.B. Cullen • Candace Nola • Carmen L Romero
Carol Gyzander • Carol Mammano • Caroline Couture
Carroll Best • Cathy Green • Charles Pavlack
Charles W. McCurdy II • Charles Wilkins • Charlie Cameron
Chris ~cliff~ Reichard • Chris DeFilipp • Chris Hill
Chris McLaren • Christine Buoy • Christinia Crippes
Christopher Bowers • Christopher Calloway • Christopher Murray
Chuck Black • Clare Janke • Claytemple Media
Craig Poliner & Niamh Tobin • Craken MacCraic • Cris Morris

Cubby and Roo • D Lanier • Dakota Reinhart • Dan Charleston
Dan Dalal • Dan McCoy • Daniel R. Hanson-Brown
Danielle Mckinney • Darc Rose • Darin Hlavaz • Darrell Z. Grizzle
Daryl A. Maxwell • David "Batman" Rivas • David Brooke
David Dilkes • David E. Ray • David Greenberg
David Lars Chamberlain • David Myers • David Swisher
Dawnie Waters • Dayna Abel • Deanna Destito • DeeDee Brustad
Deena B. Jarrett • Della B • Demopotus • Dennis Clarke
Dennis J. Clarke • Derek McCaw • Devin R. • Dixie May Hepworth
DJ • Dodie Sullivan • Donald Gibson • Donnie Morrell
Douglas Lanier • Douglas Menke • Dr Stephen Curtis
Dr. James Dougherty • Dylan W. Wyatt • ebarriusa • Ed Gosney
Ed Walters • Eddie • Edward A Maher III • Eggo Revolver
Eileen Ryan • Elfego Baca • Elise "Warriorjudge" Simon
Elizabeth "Biz" Hengel • Epiphany Ferrell • Eric Martin Strauss
Eric Peterson • Ericka L. Shepherd • Erik L. Smith • Erin deWard
Erin LF Jeffrey • Eugene Ramos • Eve Conte Seligman
EventHorizon • F Scott Valeri • Fr. Gerry Grossman+
Francesco Tignini • Frank Lewis • Fred W Johnson
Gabe Zuehlsdorf • Gabriel Casillas • Garrick A. Dietze
Gary Phillips • Gary Wrenn • Genevieve Cogman • Geoff G Turner
GeoffM • George Allen • George Hanna • Giusy Rippa
Glenn Dallas • GMarkC • Graham Pates • GRAMPZ OLDMAN
Grayson Sheldon • Greg "The Samoan" Frank • Greg Frank
Greg Gardner • H Casper • Hailie Gold • Haley Roady
Hals • Haywud • Heather Trindle • Hector Nuno • Heidi Lambert
Henry Herz • Henry Lopez • HexEnby • Hiram G Wells
Hollie Buchanan • Hoot Gibson • Howard Blakeslee
Hugh H. Davis • HV Patterson • Ingrid Emilsson • It's Terrific
J. Rocky Colavito • J. Shamberg • J.R.E. Toland • James Barron
James Boyer • James Waldrop • James Zieff • Janelle Janson
Jas. Phillips • Jason Bush • Jason Grund • Jason Miller • Jason R Frei
JBoyle • JD Reid • Jeff Bzdick • Jenny Robinson-Nagy
Jessica Enfante • Jim & Paula Kirk • Jim & Rhonda Lancaster

Jim Andrew Clark • Jim Jurasek • Jim Ryan • JK Sturgeon • JNovel
Jodie Harth • Joe Gold • Joe Kontor • John "AcesofDeath7" Mullens
John Averette Jr. • John Christopher • John Harlacher
John M Creagar • John M. Lancaster
John Maness - Bellona's Bridegroom • John P Hanna • John Peck
John Schutt • Jonathan Gensler • Jonathan Torres • Jordan Redmon
Joshua A. Shaw • Jp • Juan J Saldana II • Juan Morales Jr • Justin
Lewis • K.L. Sorgenfrie • Kal Powell • Kari J. Wolfe • Karla Berg
Karla Hyde • Kate Paisley • Kath6 Evans • Katherine S
Kathryn McLeer • Kathy Evans • KC Marie Pandell
Keith A Bowden • Keith and Cheri Martin • Keith E. Duval
Keith Murfee-DeConcini • Keith Ort • Kelly Marie • Kelsea Yu
Kenneth Dodd • Kenneth Lee Holliday, Jr. • Kevin Moreau
Kevin Wadlow • Kia Boone • Kimberly Williams
Kirsten Kowalewski • Kit Kindred • Kristen and Lawrence
Kristian Rodriguez • Kristina Meschi • Kristy Kearney
Larry Gelfand • Larry L Ostertag • Laura Goostree
Lauren 'The Upstart Raven' S. G. • Lawrence Person • Lena Hoff
Linda D. Addison • Linda Lorenzen • Linda Niehoff • Linda Wilcox
Lindsay Moore • Lisa Lindsay • Lisa Lyons • Lisa Segorski
Lisa Stewart • Lisa Westenbarger • Littlesuncat
Lord Joseph Blankenship • Louis Farber • Luke Luoh
Lyra Róisín Hopkins • Marcello Nicolella
Mark Boom Boom Bloom • Mark Boszko • Mark Newman
Mark Phillippi • Mark Slater • Mark Squire • Marla Hectic
Marty Lloyd • Martyn Lesbirel • Marvin • Matt Boyer
Matt Giles • Matt Lazorwitz • Matt Morgan • Matt Olsen
Matt Stepan • Matthew Dumbauld • Matthew Johnson
Matthew Siddall • Maximus • Melanie Tull • Meli(ssa) Hooker
Melissa Allen • Michael Ball • Michael Bradley • Michael Cieslak
Michael G. O'Connell • Michael Haynes • Michael Little
Michael Morse • Michael S. Manley • Michael Steadman
Michele Brittany • Mike Claytor • Miriam Perrin • Misha Dainiak
Molly Celaschi • Moose of My Heart • Morena Ruiz

Morning Glory • Mr.Fitz • Ms. Peesha Avocado
Nancy McCullough • Natalie Rosen • Natalie Tenner
Natasha R Chisdes • Neal Ross • Nicholas A. Battaglia
Nicholas A. Emmanuele • Nicholas Candelori • Nicholas King
Nicholas Stephenson • Nicole Reid • Noarvara • Nolyn Johnson
Pandemonium Books & Games • Patrick Barb • Patti Beghtol
Patty Karapinar • Paul Alan Smith • Paul Burger • Paul Lindars
Paul Popernack • Paul Popiel • Paul Rose Jr. • Paul Saunders
Paula Limbaugh • Pavlos Chatz • Penny Brown • Pete Tass
Philip Florian • Pocket the Fool • Preston Loomer
PunkARTchick *Ruthenia* • Query • R. Sterrett Beury
R. Warren Smith • Rachel Caudel • RAN RACHNITS
Randall Beaton • Randall D. Larson • Reb Craven • Rebecca Jacques
Regina Knorr • Rene Guzman • Rich Laux • Richard Leis
Richard Parker • Richard Shirley • Richard W. Gombert
Rick Hutchins • Robert Hood, horror writer • Robert I. Tkacz
Robert J • Robert James Orrbrun • Robert M. Hood
Robert Reynolds • Roberts family • Rod "Not to Be" Cressey
Rod Barnett • Rodney Barnett • Rodnock Sticklefink
Roger Venable • Roni Stinger • Ross ONeill • Rowan Stone
Russell J. Handelman • Russell Murray • Ryan Raney • Ryan Strown
S.D. Vassallo • Samantha Bryant • Samuel A. Henley
Sarah Ferguson • Scary Stuff Podcast • Scott Berger • Scott Casey
Scott Chisholm • Scott Culpepper • Scott D Hamilton
Scott Dennis • Scott Gray • Scott MacFarlane • Scott O'Neil
Scott Schiffmacher • Scott Sharritt • Sean Gatcomb
Sergeant "Aurelius" Esteves • Seth Alexander • SevinLD
Shane William Kegler • Sharon Stogner • Shaun Cobble
Shawn Hunt • Simon Elias • Sir Bobo Boberson • Sonnet Ireland
Sophie Turinsky • Stacey Hallock • Staci Lee York • Stephanie Carey
Stephen Ballentine • Stephen Henderson • Stephen Novacek
Steve Pattee • Steven J Sabatke • Steven Jasiczek • Steven Purcell
Steven Sautter • Su'ad Shoukri "Allyenna" • Susanne Stohr
Syndee Barwick • Tammy H. Glover • Tarhan Kayihan

Teresia Albertsson • Terry Austin • The Derby Kift's • The Jeff Word
Thea JN • Theresa A Robertson • Thomas Finnegan • Thomas P.
Vitale • Thomas Peak • Tiffany Armstrong • Tim Janes
Timothy Bedwell • Tina M Noe Good • Titus Belgard
Todd Dawson • Tom Finnegan • Tom Zurkan • Tony Anuci
Traci "Andronicus" Belanger • Travis Hines
Trevor 'Ratenef' Chapman • Trevor M. Moeller • Trevor Parkinson
TrevorRay51 • Trico J Lutkins • Trip Space-Parasite
Tristan Valentine • Tucker Christine
Tyler Will Davidson • Uriah Blatherwick • Vaughan Grey
Wayne L Budgen • Wesley Gift • Will Lorenzo • Wim Hoornaert
Xach Fromson • xIx Rav3n xIx • Yannick Ducret
Yarien Justo Suarez • Zachariah M. Long • Zack Fissel • Zandor
Zoe Kaplan

OTHER BOOKS FROM JAMES AQUILONE

Shakespeare Unleashed One-Shot Comic (editor, writer)
Classic Monsters Unleashed (editor)
Kolchak: The Night Stalker – 50th Anniversary (editor, writer)

Dead Jack and the Pandemonium Device (writer)
Dead Jack and the Soul Catcher (writer)
Dead Jack and the Old Gods (writer)